ANDRIY KOKOTIUKHA

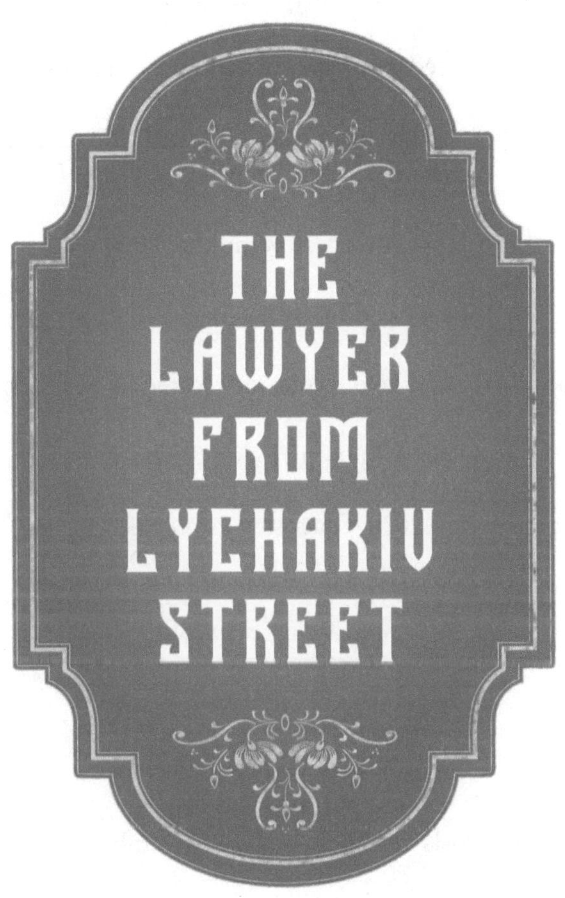

THE LAWYER FROM LYCHAKIV STREET

THE LAWYER FROM LYCHAKIV STREET

by Andriy Kokotiukha

Translated from the Ukrainian by Yuri Tkacz

This book has been published with the support
of the Translate Ukraine Translation Grant Program

© Andriy Kokotiukha, 2020

Proofreading by Michael Wharton

Book cover and layout interior created by Max Mendor

Publishers Maxim Hodak & Max Mendor

© 2020, Glagoslav Publications

www.glagoslav.com

ISBN: 978-1-912894-96-3

First published in English
by Glagoslav Publications on November 16, 2020

ANDRIY KOKOTIUKHA

TRANSLATED FROM THE UKRAINIAN BY YURI TKACZ

GLAGOSLAV PUBLICATIONS

CONTENTS

THE
LAWYER
FROM
LYCHAKIV
STREET

1908, LVIV, LYCHAKIV STREET

When it began to grow dark, he could hold back no longer, and asked the guest to leave.

Actually, he wasn't quite a guest. For the young man with long blond hair and darting eyes, who had simply become ensconced in the neighboring room, had not arrived on a business or private visit. He wasn't personally acquainted with the snub-nosed fellow. They had never met before. The owner of the apartment had nothing against the fellow personally: anyone else might have been sitting there in place of this Russian lad. Someone who was black-haired, blond, red-haired, or even bald.

It didn't upset him that the snub-nosed fellow was smoking cheap roll-your-owns, rather than fairly decent factory-made cigarettes produced in Vynnyky[1]. The tobacco industry in the provinces had lately come a long way, the newspapers were even heralding that they were planning to produce their own cigars soon. No worse than those from Cuba, but much cheaper. Although, the urban aristocracy would still rather pay more for the original, rather than for a locally produced product equal in quality...

To hell with them, those cigarettes: people like this young man in the adjoining room were far from being snobbish. They were quite indifferent to what the market had to offer and its quality. Having grown used to smoking cheap tobacco, they would continue to do so until the day they died. Even if the world went topsy-turvy.

And by the way, it was coming to that.

At the turn of this new twentieth century everything everywhere seemed suddenly to have gone mad, rushing forward, as if trying at all costs to win

....

[1]   Vynnyky – referring to the state-owned Vynnyky Tobacco Factory, founded in the late 19th century in the town of Vynnyky, now a suburb of Lviv. The factory became the main industrial enterprise in the city, providing jobs and contributing to the development of Vynnyky.

some undeclared race. And to win some enormous indescribable grand prize. But young people with an outlook on life similar to that of this snub-nosed fan of strong, foul-smelling, cheap tobacco were lucky, for they failed to sense the rapid changes taking place around them. And they surely didn't understand the times they were living in, or the processes they were playing a part in. And in general, what they were getting themselves into.

For such people, walking down the street with a gun in their pocket was already an adventure. Which they were happy to revisit again and again, day after day. And if the loaded weapon was used as intended, they would boldly declare: life's great, what more does one need, if one's meant to die – so be it.

The important thing was that death would come in battle.

Preferably in front of an audience, with a large crowd of people present.

The young snub-nosed Russian was assigned to him as a bodyguard, until he handed over what was being kept in his apartment on Lower Lychakiv[2]. They brought the travel bag in the morning – there were two of them. This blond fellow accompanied the main courier. Of course, that fellow was the more senior of the two, and not only in age. He was a real roly-poly of a fellow, everything about him was round: his mug, his belly, and he walked with a waddle, as if he was rolling along.

However, it was immediately evident: the long-haired fellow obeyed the round one. He never contradicted him, never said a word out of place. And he didn't say a thing when his boss ordered him to remain with the lawyer until morning, until someone appeared to pick up the travel bag. He nodded wordlessly, and from then on proved not to be very garrulous. He set himself up in the room that served as a bedroom. Made himself comfortable in an armchair and rested his feet, shod in well-worn dusty shoes, on the lawyer's chair. He pulled his cloth bourgeois peaked cap over his eyes and stopped moving, his arms folded across his chest.

The bodyguard's behavior was similar to that of a boa constrictor. Obviously, he hadn't seen one in the flesh. However he had read articles in various popular travel magazines, where the authors had described their

....

[2]   Lower Lychakiv – part of Lychakiv Street (originally named Hlynianska), which from 1789 became the main arterial road in the suburb of Lychakiv. In 1894 an electric streetcar line was laid along it. The Catholic church of Saint Antoniy nominally divided Lower Lychakiv from Upper Lychakiv.

impressions of what they had seen in the wilder parts of the world. The boa constrictor, it was said, mostly either slept or hunted. Having captured its prey, the snake consumed it slowly, and then just as unhurriedly digested it. All this time it lay quietly, it might seem that the enormous reptile was asleep, and that one needn't be scared of it. However, in this state the large fat snake was even more frightening. Because woe betide the person who intentionally, or accidentally, disturbed the boa constrictor while it was resting. They said that it didn't attack people needlessly. But such cases were dangerous because the snake was merely defending itself, instinctively sensing danger. If this was not the case, just try to explain that to this dimwit...

Because of his deceptive placidness, the bodyguard in the bedroom very much reminded him of the huge reptile. He seemed to be continually asleep. Alright, let him nap. But it was enough for the lawyer to get up from his desk, to walk across the room, or to simply shift his chair to make himself more comfortable, and the snub-nosed fellow would momentarily appear. He materialized like a specter in the doorway, his gun held firmly in his strong right hand, which was accustomed to holding weapons. The lawyer even took it for granted that this character had held a spoon or fork in his hand less often, and less deftly, than the handle of a Colt. In such instances, he placated his unexpected lodger with a gesture of his hand. The fellow nodded, slipped his 'piece' back into the pocket of his baggy pants, returning to his post and lit up. After once more filling the apartment with the stench of his cheap tobacco, he would turn to stone. It was as though, for him, the smoking of a cigarette was the same as swallowing another rabbit for the boa constrictor.

This went on all day long.

He had to write and post a notice on the door: 'Apologies, gentlemen, there will be no appointments today, I have taken ill, please come back in two days.' At first he had written the date of the following day, 6th of July, but then he extended it by a day. They had been expecting the travel bag for some time now, and he himself had no intention of keeping the package at his place for very long. But he took notice of one important nuance: tomorrow, coincidentally, the fellow for whom the travel bag had been left behind, was required to present himself to the investigator at the Central District Police Department. God only knew how long they would grill him there. And it was possible that he would be arrested there and then in the office. Not very likely, maybe only one or two percent, but the possibility was still there.

In either case, it would be risky to get in touch with the addressee tomorrow. It was better to allow for an extra day, to make sure that everything was going according to plan, and only then to deliver the package in person. Moreover, he needed to meet with the addressee on neutral territory. He had no desire to be visited by someone who was probably being followed by plainclothes police spies. Meanwhile, there were plenty of rather public places in Lviv, where people could bump into each other by chance.

The bodyguard had made him throw all his plans out the window.

There was no obvious threat. The lawyer turned out to be exactly the right choice, someone who was not directly linked to the group meant to receive the contents of the black leather travel bag. Contacts could be tracked down only if one knew where to look and who to look for. In the meantime, he was proud that he was considered to be a neutral person. When they proposed that he become one of the links between St. Petersburg and Lviv, he did not refuse.

The percentage promised, for the simple services he offered, could somewhat improve his situation.

Because lately he'd been through a rough patch.

Which was why the armed bodyguard breathing down his neck unnerved him somewhat.

The lawyer did not like it when uninvited strangers violated his personal space, and nothing could be done about it. He was annoyed at first, later he even began to be frightened by the blond fellow's habit of reacting quickly and silently to every sudden movement, loud exhalation, or unrestrained sneeze. Imagining that he had to put up with this throughout the night as well, the lawyer shuddered. No, he repeated to himself, he had nothing personal against the snub-nosed fellow. He was ready to accept the acrid stench of cheap tobacco, and the gun which was displayed from time to time. But the very situation he found himself in made him tense and irascible, and the longer this dragged on, the worse he felt, since this was not of his own doing.

He had been living in the small apartment in Lower Lychakiv for three years now. It was cozy and comfortable here. Maybe he didn't quite consider it to be his real home, but it was his fortress. And suddenly, the place had become transformed into a prison cell. This was how he felt: an overseer there in his bedroom, the hall like a large solitary cell, his every step being controlled, every action had to be coordinated with the armed man.

Toward evening his negative feelings became so intense, that he decisively opened the door to the bedroom. The unbidden visitor heard the movement and was already on his feet, his hand with the weapon stretched out before him. In a categorical tone he requested that the bodyguard leave the apartment.

He did not order him.

He simply said that in his opinion it would be better this way.

He could sense no danger. And in the event of anything, he knew how to look after himself. The presence of the bodyguard was superfluous. It was simply evidence of distrust. And this offended him rather a lot. The gentlemen from Saint Petersburg ought to understand that.

The snub-nosed fellow did not argue. He shrugged his shoulders, put the gun away, adjusted his cap and asked the respected lawyer to write a handwritten note addressed to the fellow who had left him behind here to guard the *package*.

It needed to state the following: so and so, surname and name, accepts all further responsibility. He understands the possible consequences of his actions. The necessary protection of the cargo by so and so, prior to it being handed over to the addressee, being so and so, has been properly provided for by the Russian side. That was that, after this the snub-nosed fellow would gladly heave a sigh of relief and wash his hands of everything.

He readily agreed to this – just a note, nothing more. He sat at his desk, grabbed a sheet of paper, and even for some reason refreshed the contents of the inkwell, which resembled a small barrel. He began to write in calligraphic handwriting, which had long since made him famous in his professional circle. But the blond fellow, who initially showed no interest, came up and glanced over his shoulder, which annoyed him – the lawyer couldn't stand this type of behavior. But there was no time to voice his resentment: the bodyguard had made a pertinent remark.

Out of habit the lawyer had begun to write in Polish, but realized his mistake only after finishing the note. The blond fellow was right, he needed to rewrite it. Those for whom the note was intended, the people from St. Petersburg, knew no Polish. Better to write it in Russian. He had to strain a little, and knit his brows in order to recall the language. Although it didn't seem completely foreign, after the time he had spent in Lviv he had forgotten quite a bit of it. There was no need to use it in his everyday practice here: people in the city were fluent in German, Polish, Ukrainian, and understood Yiddish. Russian was used, although in rather limited circles.

Scrunching up the spoiled sheet of paper, the lawyer pulled a small stack of blank paper from a drawer. He began to write, slowly recalling the grammar. Several times he used the wrong words, crossed them out, and started again. He could have handed over the note the way it was, but his education, his upbringing, and in general his outlook on life wouldn't allow him to leave it in a slovenly state, with corrections, no matter that it was a simple document, which didn't leave him duty bound to anything. Otherwise, he would have had no respect for himself afterward.

He tossed the scrunched-up sheet of paper under the desk, into a waste bin.

And grabbed a fresh sheet of paper.

The bodyguard waited patiently. When the lawyer finally finished at the third attempt, he wordlessly took the sheet of paper from him, folded it in four, and slipped it into the inner pocket of his jacket. He nodded, turned around and left without uttering a single word. It appeared that he too wasn't too keen on sitting here twiddling his thumbs. And luckily he had been given an excuse to leave his post. How the blond guy would explain everything to his roly-poly senior associate didn't concern the lawyer in the least. The fellow had left – thank God.

It was scorching hot during the day, although in summer the heat here was not as bad as in Kyiv. However, it wasn't the weather which had influenced his choice to move here. Obviously, he had emigrated for political reasons. But he had exchanged his Russian passport for an Austrian one not because of ideological considerations.

It simply made it easier this way to carry out the tasks Petersburg set him.

Nothing special was required. He simply had to do everything in his power to legally protect the interests of a local community of people who were close to the respected lawyer.

This community in the main city of a great Austrian province, the Kingdom of Galicia and Lodomeria[3], was being unfairly pushed to the margins

....

[3]   The Kingdom of Galicia and Volodymyria (Lodomeria) – crown land of the Habsburg

of society. The Austrian authorities could have paid more attention to the opinion of those who, until recently, had held much greater standing in society. It was no secret that they had influenced the development of, if not the whole province, then certainly at least the city of Lviv.

Closing one's eyes and burying one's head in the sand no longer worked. That slab of rock which had been shifted from its place far beyond the eastern border, fell so loudly that its thunderclap echoed all the way here, to this quiet and hitherto calm and prosperous Galicia.

He sincerely believed that violent upheavals were changing the world around him.

For several years now the world in which he lived, and which was not only limited to his apartment on Lychakiv Street, near the very center of Lviv, was being shaken. He saw these processes as painful and regrettable, however necessary. So, he was ready to facilitate them even in this simple way: to receive a travel bag from one set of hands and to pass it on to another.

Locking the door from the inside, the lawyer ahemmed with satisfaction, for some reason yanking at the door handle, as if checking it for strength. He threw the bedroom window wide open, and did the same in the hall, thus creating a draft.

The heat of the July day was dissipating, it would soon start to rain. He stretched his hand out of the window and at the same time looked down from his first floor apartment into the courtyard, where his windows faced. There was no one and nothing, it was usually very quiet here. Except for the odd beggar playing his hurdy-gurdy during the day. And some batiars[4] from Upper Lychakiv might wander in through the gate to cook up some cunning deal, away from prying eyes.

....

Monarchy, the Austrian Empire and Austro-Hungary in 1772-1918. United Ukrainian ethnic lands (historical Galicia), which began to be called Eastern Galicia, and the lands of Lesser Poland (Western Galicia).

[4]   Batiar – Galician slang for louts. Representatives of the Lviv urban subculture that existed from the mid 19th to the mid 20th century. The name batiar probably originated from the Hungarian *betyar*, which refers to a person with strange views who acts unpredictably, a rogue and a carouser. Appeared in Lychakiv and Pohulianka, in Pohulianka Park. They gathered in the beer gardens of local breweries. At first the batiars were hooligans, carousers and pickpockets. Eventually, they stopped stealing and brawling, and instead began to ridicule the 'old quack' of the Austro-Hungarian Empire.

He stood there a while, inhaling the cool, slightly damp air. He had stayed indoors all day long, and that was no joke. It occurred to him to step out for a walk, to drop into one of the downtown cafés. Although it was too late for coffee, he could down a few beers or something stronger. He might bump into some friends in the 'Viennese'[5], which in any case was always a part of such walks. But he immediately discarded the idea. While the bag was here, it would not do to leave the apartment. After all, he had assumed responsibility for the package. He could paint the town red once he had gotten rid of it. Because he would then have the means to do so.

Something wet struck his open palm.

It really seemed like it was about to rain. A light shower, which would soon stop. He waved his arm about, as if it was possible to hurry nature along. A few more drops fell, but no proper rain followed. Standing at the window a while longer, leaning against the wide sill, he caught himself thinking that it had been a long time since he had lounged about like this, eyeing the gray walls of the buildings opposite – no other vista was visible from his windows. He wondered why the sunset was making the peeling rear walls of the building look more mysterious than usual.

My, the thoughts that were creeping into his head...

Clearing his throat one more time, he moved away from the window, leaving it open. This past day he hadn't managed to do very much. He had not put his papers in order, although he had planned to do this. And he had no desire to embark on any serious work this evening, as it would mean staying up late into the night.

A carafe filled with liqueur had found a home for itself in one of the cupboards. It was strong and sweet, made from sour cherries steeped in pure alcohol. As he was taking it out, he suddenly recalled the stench of the blond Russian's cheap tobacco.

Well... it seemed they had something in common.

The young fellow did not smoke factory-made cigarettes, while he did not like the taste of alcoholic beverages produced by the Baczewskis[6], even

5   Viennese Café – one of the oldest cafes in Lviv, founded by Karl Hartmann. In the early 20th century it was the favored place for representatives of the city's business circles to meet, including the black-market dealers.

6   The J.A. Baczewski factory was founded in 1782 near Lviv and is considered Poland's oldest liqueur and vodka distillery. Alcoholic products made according to their technology were much

if they were sold in multicolored bottles. People drank them and praised them, but he was more drawn to such home-made products.

The cheap tobacco smelled awful. His cherry liqueur had a pleasant smell.

But, to hell with it, the lawyer, just like his unwelcome guest, wanted more independence from things that were mass-produced, factory made, industrial... *bourgeois*. Both valued an original approach, and thus their own individuality.

The liqueur was specially bought from a woman in the suburbs. Ukrainian peasants were gradually, confidently and assertively settling down around Lviv. So the recipe was their own, from the earth. He wanted to believe that it had been passed down through the generations, even though he didn't identify himself with their peasant traditions. To hell with it, the cherry liqueur was delicious. It was smooth drinking, spread out pleasantly inside, its effect wasn't immediate, but gradual, as if covering one with a weightless blanket. Just as his dear mother had done when he was a child, after finishing singing her lullaby, tucking in the edges of the blanket. When he was small he was never afraid of being left alone in dark rooms, and for some reason, felt more secure than when the lights were turned on.

So he didn't turn on the lights. Before the sun had set for good, he fetched the liqueur again, poured a little into a small silver shot glass, not too full. He made himself comfortable at his desk, swallowed and savored it.

He sat like this for a while. Then got to his feet, fetched some biscuits from the same cupboard, grabbing a candle along the way. Lighting it, he sat staring at the flame for a while, thinking his own thoughts: he had enough on his plate. Once more he poured himself some cherry liqueur, this time the shot glass was a little fuller. He threw off his slippers, neatly hung his striped jacket on the back of the chair. Dressed only in his vest, he moved across to the wide armchair – he could slip his feet onto it. Making himself comfortable, he closed his eyes.

Now he was surrounded by utter silence, if one discounted the ticking of the clock in the bedroom. He didn't mind. Just as the sounds of the

<hr>

more subtle and refined than most other brands. This brought great popularity for the company not only in Lviv, but also in other parts of the Austrian Empire. The company received the right from the imperial court to carry the prestigious "Imperial Eagle" label. Eventually the imperial court also granted the company the right to use the title "k.u.k. Hoflieferant", which translates into English as "Purveyor to the Imperial and Royal Court".

ANDRIY KOKOTIUKHA

hurdy-gurdy never annoyed him, which he probably heard every second day, when the local beggar ventured into the courtyard, so that the residents would once again send him on his way with their small change. The rattle and ringing of the streetcars in the street did not upset the silence here – yet another advantage of having windows facing the courtyard. He had heard the ladies and gentlemen from neighboring apartments and buildings complain about the people who had got it into their heads to build a streetcar line along Lychakiv Street. The result was lots of ringing, buzzing, rattling, and shaking. In the past they had lived peacefully and comfortably, but now they felt like they were living on a railway line. Although rail public transport had been a part of the Lviv landscape for some time now[7], not everyone had grown used to it.

Here was yet another example of why it was necessary to change this current stability, which had become impossibly stifling.

To pump fresh blood into the Galician – and in general the Austrian imperial – arteries. Of course, not in the literal sense, this was simply an expression people used.

Blood.

He opened his eyes. He found it hard to properly explain why such sentiments had taken hold of him this evening. As far back as he could remember, he had been energetic, business-like, active, but now he was relaxed, excessively relaxed. It seemed like nothing special. A person with a gun had entered his place and stayed awhile – but he could not let go of the thought.

Something was being hatched.

Something was approaching.

Not right now and not tomorrow.

Something great. Unrestrained. Destructive.

Lawyer Yevhen Pavlovych Soyka, thirty-five years old, born in the Kharkiv Gubernia, for five years now a subject of the Austro-Hungarian Empire, having a permanent residence permit and a law practice in Lviv, poured himself another liqueur.

He drank it, bit into a biscuit.

....

7   Electrical streetcars on rails began to run in Lviv on 31 May 1894. This was the second city in Ukraine and the fourth in the Austro-Hungarian Empire to have electrical streetcars.

And made himself more comfortable in the armchair.

He ran his gaze across the room, illuminated by a single candle flame.

His eyes rested on the chandelier. Cheap, utilitarian, it had a single globe. Round, it was made to resemble a traditional Chinese lantern. Only the lampshade was not red, but rather pale pink, and did not irritate the eyes. It was fixed to a strong hook in the ceiling.

He should probably get up and turn on the light...

There was a light tinkle of glass. The small droplets had probably transformed into a proper rain, it was coming down harder.

Another rattle of glass. The shutters in the bedroom creaked.

Boom-m-m.

From the bedroom. The clock struck ten p.m.

It was already quite dark. He felt sleepy, although usually at this time lawyer Soyka's active lifestyle only just began. Lviv's business circles gathered for parties, where there were always plenty of useful contacts to be made. Anyone who wanted to have his finger on the pulse of the city's affairs, simply had to attend them. There was a premiere scheduled at the opera for today, it had already begun, the finale would be coming soon, and then...

It was alright.

Assume that lawyer Soyka was taking a day off.

He'd earned it. It was his right.

Once more there was a soft tinkle of glass in the bedroom. There seemed to be movement. Footsteps.

Who could be walking there – this was the first story.

The draft was strong.

The apartment had been aired out. He needed to get up and close the window. Then he could sit a little longer and go to bed.

The clock ticked away.

There was movement in the bedroom.

But not because of the draft.

CHAPTER ONE
THE EMIGRANT FROM
THE SECOND-CLASS CARRIAGE

On this July morning a young man stepped onto the platform of the Lviv Railway Station dressed in a bespoke suit, blue with pale gray stripes.

His pants had become crumpled during the journey, bringing to naught the efforts of their owner to iron in some pleats, as dictated by city fashion. The cut did not look very contemporary. And in general, it appeared as if the fellow had not ordered the suit specially from a tailor, as was the custom, but had purchased a ready-made one, because it was cheaper. After this the tailor would have fitted and hemmed the clothes, taken his money, and would have even provided a discount. And both would have been left satisfied. The young man – because he had ended up with a cheap suit which at the same time looked quite decent. And the tailor – because he had finally gotten rid of goods which had been lying around, for which a former customer had not paid. That fellow had complained that he didn't like it, that the stripes were wrong, while in reality he had lost all his money playing cards, and was sitting in cheap accommodation somewhere in Yamska Street[8], waiting for his compassionate parents to respond and send him a little money. In his situation, he obviously was more concerned with finding a bite to eat than thinking about suits...

And that was in fact what had happened.

....

[8]   Yamska – a street in Kyiv which runs past Baykove Cemetery, which back then was on the outskirts of the city. During the period described here it was known as the 'red light district'. Described in A. Kuprin's novel *Yama* (The Pit).

Obviously, the young man, as he bargained with the Podil tailor, had no idea about the story behind the suit. He himself was not in the best of financial positions either, and this was not his only misfortune. The clothes in which he had been released from prison were blood-stained and dirty. The landlord, from whom the young man had rented an apartment in the Podil district of Kyiv, had unceremoniously taken his various odds and ends to cover outstanding rent. Adding at the same time the biting phrase 'to my detriment', but this was better than nothing at all. He didn't want to ask his father for money. He managed to borrow some from an acquaintance, one of the few left who were not afraid to greet him and stop for a chat. He had promised to return the money as soon as he had found his feet in the new place. He had enough for a suit, a shirt, a tie, a round straw boater hat and a one-way ticket on the Kyiv-Lviv train.

The man's name was Klymentiy Nazarovych Koshovy. He always introduced himself as Klym, and he also asked others to call him by this simple name. As he himself said, he didn't like all those upper-class types, although his profession required him to rub shoulders with them in the state's institutions[9].

He was a lawyer.

He had recently turned thirty.

And the police might already be looking for him no less than throughout the entire Kyiv Gubernia.

Although there seemed to be no obstacles to his traveling abroad, but who knows what could enter some official's head. To declare someone as a state criminal and issue orders for their arrest was as easy as pie. True, on the scale of the police and gendarmerie of the vast Russian Empire, the persona of Koshovy seemed far too insignificant, for him to be sought after across the entire country. At least Klym himself wanted very much for this to be the case.

The Kyiv lawyer was traveling second class, having paid twelve rubles and fifty copecks for a ticket in a yellow carriage[10]. In his situation this was a

---

[9]   State institutions in the Russian Empire, which included not only the offices of bureaucrats, but also reception rooms, chanceries and so on.

[10]   Passenger trains in the Russian Empire had carriages of three classes, which differed in color. Blue corresponded to first class, yellow – second class, and green – third class. The mail car was brown.

crazy amount of money. He had even wanted to skimp, to travel third class for eight sixty. But at the last minute he had changed his mind. While he was hesitating, most of the seats were purchased by an Orthodox Jewish family. Klym was afraid they might create a commotion that would make his head buzz the following morning. But the opposite was the case. The children, two boys with long sidelocks aged several years apart, and a younger girl sat quietly, and when the train left Fastiv behind, the mother began to put them to bed. The men, the older and the younger one, judging by everything – the father-in-law and son-in-law, spoke softly in the passage.

Straining his ears out of curiosity, Koshovy sighed with disappointment: they were speaking in Yiddish, which he did not understand. He was itching to know why the family was traveling. It was quite possible that the older man had been settling business matters in Kyiv. However, Klym immediately rejected this assumption – in that case the men wouldn't have encumbered themselves with a woman and three children. More than likely the family was moving to the West, because things in Kyiv were becoming progressively worse for them. The passengers had little luggage with them, which indirectly confirmed this: they had probably sold off their real estate, and the rest of their treasures had been shipped separately.

From time to time the Jews gave him suspicious looks. It was unlikely they saw him as a source of danger. They probably just didn't feel too comfortable in his presence.

Deciding to leave them alone, at least for a while, Koshovy got to his feet and made his way to the restaurant carriage.

He found no peace here either.

For he had no desire or money to splurge on dinner. And he had no intention of simply sitting there, as it wasn't the done thing. But his indecisiveness was misjudged by a group of his peers, who invited him to join their party.

It looked like they had been here a while. The whole car swayed from side to side because of the ruckus they had raised – or at least it seemed that way to Klym. Apart from them, there was an intelligent-looking gentleman with a small beard, wearing a pince-nez and an engineer's everyday jacket, sitting at a table in the corner. Placing his cap on the table beside him and resting his elbows on the tablecloth, he was trying to convince a lady half his age of something in a passionate whisper. Although she was dressed like a Kyiv townswoman, she seemed to be a person of a higher class. She did not speak with the engineer, mostly listening to him, occasionally throwing a few phrases in reply, which did not calm or please her interlocutor at all. Casting glances at the young men, he became more and more worked up, lowering his voice, and drawing his head into his shoulders.

Apart from these people, there was another patron sitting in the restaurant. A rather fat balding fellow, somewhat resembling a university lecturer, he was sipping tea, munching on some dried bagels and reading newspapers. One of these, which he had either read or was about to read, he placed under his left elbow, pressing it against the tabletop. Koshovy glanced at him and, spying part of the title, understood that it was *Russkoe slovo*[11]. Klym equally recognized the other newspaper in which the 'lecturer' was engrossed – *Kievskie gubernskie vedomosti*[12]. The loud threesome were obviously distracting him, for the fellow would throw them glances from time to time over the top of the newspaper, knitting his bushy eyebrows. Then he would wordlessly sip some tea, bite off a piece of bagel and become engrossed in his reading again. The local waiter was probably accustomed to this behavior – for as soon as the fellow finished a glass of tea, he was brought another, and the empty glass was removed.

At first Klym decided not to hang around. But then one of the young men called him over. He had decided that Klym could find nowhere to sit. With a welcoming gesture they invited him to join them, placed a glass before him and loudly, in unison, ordered another carafe of vodka. Koshovy downed the glass and helped it down with some fried bacon, even though he had eaten before leaving home. But he had decided that from now on and furthermore he would stop acting the timid invited guest: the train was taking him into an uncertain future, and who knew when he would have the opportunity to eat again.

His new friends made his acquaintance, introducing themselves, but Klym did not remember a single name. He knew that these young budding

---

[11]   'Russkoe slovo' (Russian Word) – the cheapest daily newspaper in the Russian Empire, published from 1895 to 1918.

[12]   'Kievskie gubernskie vedomosti' (Kyiv Provincial Gazette) – official Russian-language government newspaper, published from 1837 to 1917 in Kyiv. Published three times a week: on Tuesdays, Thursdays and Saturdays.

                                                      ANDRIY KOKOTIUKHA

merchants were definitely not in his league. Not because of disdain, on the contrary – most of his clients were mid-level landowners and industrialists. Literally, the purpose of their journey was different. Koshovy was a reluctant emigrant, in effect a fugitive from his home town, which he obviously did not mention to them, saying only that he was traveling 'on business'. The young men were off to the spas. First to Truskavets[13], for they had heard plenty about this new European resort, and the passions of their lives were already awaiting them there, having been dispatched earlier. From there they were heading to Baden-Baden for comparison. One of the lads turned out to be the son of some 'liquor baron' from outside Poltava, his friends from Kyiv had dragged him along with them. From time to time they called him a dumpling. Even though he may have been offended, the fellow strenuously pretended to like this.

When the threesome began to inquire, on what kind of business their new acquaintance was venturing to Lviv and whether he might be ready to turn his back on everything and come with them, so as to see a bit of the world and meet a nice gal, if he was lucky, Klym realized it was time to leave. He excused himself, had a drink for the road, said that he had a headache, and quickly made tracks. He didn't care what the budding merchants thought about him, or whether they would think about him at all.

Apart from him, none of the others present left the restaurant car.

Early in the morning, when the train stopped at the border in Volochysk and the passengers began to show their passports, Koshovy tried his utmost to stay calm and confident. He even forced himself to smile to the border officer. The fellow looked at him, shrugged his shoulders, took the passport, leafed through it, and returned it. Suddenly, noticing something out of the corner of his eye, he turned sharply to look out the window, still holding the document in his hands. Looking outside, Klym saw that a senior border guard and two junior gendarmes in uniform had surrounded the engineer he had seen the night before. The fellow was without his cap, disheveled, waving his arms about, and was zealously trying to prove something to them.

....

[13]   The construction of a balneological resort in Truskavets, a town lying 100 km from Lviv, began in 1836. From 1895 the resort was actively expanded, modernized, and became popular and fashionable.

At this moment, a gendarme officer appeared in their field of view, the scene looking as if a magazine picture had come to life, while behind him pattered the rotund 'lecturer', with a cane and a round hat. He was carrying a plywood suitcase bound in fake leather and dropped his burden right at the feet of the engineer. The suitcase popped open, and booklets tied together with twine came tumbling out of it. Before Klym managed to have a good look, the group of men on the platform crowded around, hiding the suspicious baggage from view. The rotund fellow pointed somewhere to the left; the officer made a sign. One of the junior gendarmes made off in that direction, the 'lecturer' hurried after him. The gendarme began to castigate the engineer.

Noticing that Koshovy was showing an interest in what was taking place, the officer shrugged his shoulders and grunted:

"Propagandists. Third lot this week that we've taken off the train."

Klym decided not to engage in dangerous conversation. And the official showed no interest in continuing to speak. He said nothing more, except for the usual traditional wish of a safe journey. And even this was uttered grudgingly: the subjects of His Imperial Majesty, the Tsar's servants, were never known for their excessive politeness or friendliness.

Klym, who had never crossed the western border before, concluded that they were given special instructions to maintain a sour demeanor. Their limited vocabulary was probably determined at the highest levels. The list of permitted words was probably written in some official document bearing a wax seal. When they greeted people, they said 'please', thanked everyone and wished them some blasé phrase, because there was some corresponding instruction regarding this. When the train finally left and crawled across the Zbruch River, Koshovy became so fascinated by his assumptions, that he began to believe that it all must be true.

He waited until the other, *Austrian* side of the river, sailed past his window, and then could not restrain himself from looking back, sensing a strange need to look back one last time at the country he was leaving. Involuntarily he recalled Lermontov's semi-forbidden phrase, popular in certain circles: *farewell to you, my unwashed Russia*[14]. Although Klym immediately

---

[14] "Farewell to you, my unwashed Russia, a land of slaves, a land of lords" – a poem by Russian poet Mikhail Lermontov (1814-1841), written 1840 or 1841. Written during his second and, as it

disassociated himself from these lines, even shaking his head in exasperation. He was not sure, if he was really bidding farewell. He was only going for a while, to sit out the storm, although he hadn't the slightest idea how soon it would die down.

And another thing – he wasn't bidding farewell to Russia.

He did not consider his native Kyiv Gubernia to be that country, from which more than half a century earlier the Russian poet had traveled into exile.

He knew that back there, from where this railway line ran, the present Russian province was called Greater Ukraine.

The customs officers on the Austrian side were not any more friendly, but all the same they were different.

The swarthy Hungarian-looking officer looked more refined than his Russian counterpart – an older fellow, sweaty and with a paunch. He saluted, took the passport, checked the photo, and Koshovy was not at all surprised at his reaction when their eyes met. However, where Klym might have encountered misunderstanding or rudeness from the Tsar's servant, the emperor's subject merely raised his eyebrows. Obviously, he was not sure of the correct way to react to what he had seen. Then he made the only right decision for himself: he ignored the passenger's grimace, returned the documents, saluted once more, and moved on.

Koshovy, resorting to a recently acquired habit, pressed his fingertip against the edge of his right eye, as if this might calm him down. He remembered again for the nth time how this had greatly angered the gendarme who was present at his release from prison. The fellow had decided that the former prisoner was acting very insolently. Grimacing, making fun of authority, wanting to go back inside. The fellow swore a mother oath at him and was about to land a fist between Klym's eyes, but an agent in civvies managed to stop him in time. He had enough authority to be able to curb the gendarme's righteous anger, even without his uniform. But he couldn't resist a laugh himself. He said that Klym had made the work of the police easier. Why? Because before they had written in his card – no distinctive features. But now there was one.

....

turned out, last exile in the Caucasus. Unofficially banned from publication.

And would be for a long time.

If not for life.

Lost in his thoughts, Koshovy did not notice the train finally pull out of Pidvolochysk railway station. And sometime later he stepped out onto the platform, clutching firmly onto a small travel bag – his entire wealth for the moment. It contained a small framed photo of his parents under glass carefully wrapped in a spare shirt, there was a vest, a stylish tie, a set of underwear, thin-rimmed glasses which he sometimes wore when he needed to read and write a lot, taking pity on his eyes, a pocket toiletry bag, in which he kept manicure scissors, a mustache brush and other necessary trifles. And right at the bottom there were several adventure novels, both French and English. The books were not very thick, convenient for travelers. Klym had been attracted to them from childhood, had not stopped reading them in his teenage years, and still had them. He kept his wallet and passport on his person. The document was well hidden inside an inner pocket, the money – in his trouser pocket. It was impossible not to feel someone trying to get at it.

There was something to watch out for: he had a 'Catherine', a one hundred tsarist ruble note, which was now Klym Koshovy's sole capital.

Standing there a moment and looking about, the young man transferred his travel bag from his right hand to his left, then confidently proceeded to the exit and onto the square in front of the railway station. There he stopped on the cobblestones and surveyed the majestic, elegant, and pompous railway station building before him. He immediately recalled the old wooden structure he had left behind in Kyiv, which was under orders from the governor-general to be demolished. The contrast was indeed great, and for the first time Klym imagined himself being not just in another city or another state – he felt more like he was in another world.

He could have spent forever staring at the building. Realizing this, Koshovy turned around decisively and stepped forward, diagonally crossing the square. Having traversed quite some distance, he glanced to the left, and spied a structure partly covered in scaffolding. Squinting, to see more clearly, Klym realized they were building a Catholic church here, and the construction had started a long time ago.

The appearance of the church reminded him that people here predominantly professed the Catholic faith. Koshovy himself had neutral feelings toward religion. Obviously, his parents attended church, he too adhered to Orthodox traditions, but he did not have that feeling in his heart which must have surely determined a true believer. He had heard and read, that Catholics had a different attitude toward the church and faith than Orthodox believers. But at the same time, he also knew and felt that in the outlying provinces of the Russian Empire people likewise had a different attitude to faith than in Greater Russia itself.

At any rate, the Jewish pogroms were carried out by activists of the Kyiv branch of the 'Union of Michael the Archangel', calling themselves fighters for the rule of the true faith. Meanwhile, Ukrainian believers were not seen taking part in similar actions. So that the Orthodox faith, professed by the Russians, allowed them to destroy Jewish streets and neighborhoods in order to affirm their religion, while the God to whom Ukrainians, or as they were more often referred to, *Little Russians*, prayed in their churches had no need of such dubious feats to shore up the people's religion.

Thinking such thoughts, not so much because of an intention to change not only his place of residence but also his religious denomination, but more simply to occupy his head with something, Klym reached the streetcar stop. It was signposted with a pole, on which he saw two letters – 'D' and 'H'[15]. While he tried to understand what they meant, and whether the streetcar would get him to where he needed to go, the streetcar itself arrived. But no sooner had it stopped, and the doors opened, than Koshovy suddenly changed his mind. He stepped back, waited for the carriage to turn around on the rails and set off from where it had come, ringing its bell.

Seeing the streetcar off and having reached, as it seemed to him, an important decision, the new arrival made his way to the opposite side of the square, where the coachmen and their horse-drawn carriages were assembled.

<hr>

[15]   The routes of Lviv's streetcars were designated by two Latin letters which corresponded to the first letters of the names of the final stops in Polish. D – was the main railway station (Dworzec główny), H – (Hetmanska).

CHAPTER TWO
ANOTHER WORLD

"Shall we go, sir?" asked[16] the fellow closest to him.

"Let's. Why are you standing here then?"

The coachman turned right around to face Koshovy, and nearly slid off his box in the process. Klym was able to get a better look at his first acquaintance in Lviv. Short, strong, with a narrow face, and a mustache neatly twirled up. He was dressed differently to his counterparts in Kyiv: a light-colored shirt, a vest, the buttons of which did not fit well over his rounded belly, black stovepipe pants, and dusty pointed shoes. His index finger pushed up his black hat, with its upturned rounded narrow brim, which resembled a small bowl.

"From Greater Ukraine, I can tell by your accent," he said confidently, and immediately asked, with a jerk of his sharp chin covered in the previous day's bristles: "What's the problem, sir?"

Klym pretended not to understand, once more pressing his fingertip to his eye, and asked:

"What do you mean?"

"This," the curious coachman repeated what Koshovy had done.

"None of your business," Klym answered somewhat rudely, not at all afraid to look uncouth in the coachman's eyes. "So, are we setting off or are we going to keep grimacing?"

The coachman cleared his throat, and with a courteous gesture invited the passenger into his carriage. After his passenger had settled in, he asked, without being in a hurry to turn his back:

---

[16]   Attention! Here and throughout the novel the characters communicate equally freely in Polish, German, and Ukrainian, as well as employing Russian and Yiddish. The occasional use of other languages will be translated separately.

"Where would sir like to go?" And once more could not refrain from asking: "You're off the Kyiv train, right?"

"You guessed right," Klym replied dryly.

"I'm no Gypsy woman, sir, to be guessing things."

Bold notes now sounded in the coachman's voice, which led Klym to conclude that coachmen in Lviv differed little from those in Kyiv. They also paid little attention to rank. Although he himself was not of such high rank in Kyiv, for the city's 'vankas'[17] to kowtow to him. He decided to hold his tongue, not prepared to start an argument with the first person he had come across.

But his new acquaintance would not relent:

"You know how long Zakhar Hnatyshyn has worked here, respected sir? For sure, well before the electric streetcars appeared, may lightning strike them dead! Back then people were only thinking about such beauty," he unceremoniously pointed in the direction of the station building. "It was built right before my eyes!"

"So you're Zakhar Hnatyshyn, as I understand?"

"At your service!" the coachman flippantly raised his 'bowl'. "Respected sir, I've been working this place for longer than most people care to live. Don't I know when, from where and which trains arrive in Lviv each day? I learned German because of all this, so I could pitch for passengers. What d'you think? A person arrives, let's say, from Vienna. They hear a familiar language. Obviously they'll come to me. There's no other way, sir. So where would you bid me go? Are you here on business? Then you'll need a hotel. I highly recommend the 'Georges'[18]. I can get you there on a breeze. We can be there in the blink of an eye."

"Are you making fun of me again? What if I were to get into another carriage?"

"You won't be going anywhere," Zakhar dismissed him. "It's my turn now. That's the rule here. We've agreed not to cadge passengers off one another. This was not the case with our lot before. But once they brought in the electric streetcars, we had to band together."

"Why?"

....

[17] 'Vanka' – an everyday term for street coachmen in the Russian Empire.

[18] Hotel in Lviv, a striking example of fashionable hotel architecture of the 19th – early 20th century. One of the oldest hotels in the city, which has been reconstructed on several occasions.

"Competition, heard of such a word? Older people, especially women, hated those streetcars from the very start. There was an incident, they even wrote about it in the newspapers, when one respectable lady turned her back on it and bared that part of her anatomy, that you wouldn't even mention in the company of batiars. And since the local batiars don't watch their words, then you should know! But those who are younger say it's progress!" Zakhar meaningfully raised his finger into the air. "So, the electric streetcars take away our passengers. We need to negotiate – and not squabble, as was the case before, so as not to frighten off clients. You need to stand politely and wait your turn."

"So I can't get into another carriage?"

The coachman shook his head.

"No one will leave before I do. So then, are we going to the 'Georges'? Or maybe some other hotel, of the same class, because the 'Georges' is not really good to stay in now. They're renovating it."

Koshovy's stomach growled treacherously.

"I can see you know everything here," he began indirectly approaching his subject. "Actually, right now I've no need of a hotel. I've come to visit an old friend. He lives on Lychakiv Street. Is that far from here?"

"Not too far. I'm thinking sir, that you need Lower Lychakiv."

"Is there a difference?"

"A big one. Lower Lychakiv is where respectable people live, there are lots of apartment buildings there for the well-to-do. Upper Lychakiv is something quite particular. Batiar on top of batiar and driven by batiar. Just imagine, the Lord sending such neighbors to those respectable ladies and gentlemen."

"You've mentioned these batiars several times already. Who are they? Thieves, bandits, burglars?"

"Hell, no! If you come across a batiar – don't ever call him that. Otherwise he'll become an enemy for life. They're brawlers, adventurers, that's what we say here. Well, the greatest crime they're capable of is to snatch a gawker's wallet. Or a gold watch. Or nice leather gloves. The Lychakiv batiars are no friends of real thieves and scary cutthroats, of which there are plenty enough in Klepariv[19]. Although that doesn't make things any easier

....

[19]   Klepariv – a district in Lviv, at this time it was a workers' suburb. Became a part of the city

for the respectable people. A batiar... what can I say, a batiar is a batiar. You'll see for yourself. So you need to get to Lychakiv Street? D'you know the number?"

"Nine." Koshovy had learned the address mentioned in the letter by heart. "There's just one thing I need to do before that, *Mister* Hnatyshyn."

"Oh! When passengers start addressing me like that – it must be something important. Speak up. Nothing criminal, I hope?"

"No," Klym assured him. "In any case, I think not. The problem is, I have no money."

The coachman let out a whistle, and once more pushed his hat up.

"Phew! Then why are you getting into coaches, if you have no money? You can go on foot, if you don't mind my saying so! It's a nice fine day."

"You don't quite understand," Koshovy cleared his throat. "I have the means to pay. You won't be left offended. I meant to say that I have no kroner. But I do have a hundred rubles, a 'Catherine', here."

For clarity, as a confirmation of his words, Klym retrieved his extremely thin wallet from his pocket, and fished out his wealth, showing it to the coachman – a banknote with a portrait of Empress Catherine the Second, being admired by a warrior from Antiquity with a saber in his right hand, and his left pressed loyally to his heart.

"They're not legal tender here."

"I know. I couldn't get any kroner or kreutzers before leaving. I need to change my money. Maybe you can take me to the nearest bank? And I can pay you there."

The coachman scratched the back of his neck.

"If that's the case... We could go to the bank. If you like. However, in my opinion you'd do better to go to Nyzhni Valy[20]."

"Where's that? Is it far?"

"In Lviv everything is close. Money changers assemble on the boulevard there. It's a 'black market', you know."

"Do I need to be careful there?"

....
in 1931. It was famed for being lined with trees of duke cherries – hybrids of sour cherries and sweet cherries.

[20]   Nyzhni Valy (Lower Ramparts) – central street in Lviv, also called Hetmanski Valy; currently – Prospekt Svobody (Freedom Avenue).

"Not at all! On the contrary, it's easier to come to an agreement with the fellows there. You don't need to show them any documents. And they'll give you the best rate. Much better than the banks can offer."

"They won't swindle me, will they?"

"What? Heck no, not when I'm with you. Although, in general, such things do occur here. There are enough batiars there on the boulevard. You can expect all sorts of things from them. But I often bring people to the money changers, I even know some of them. Even better – I'll introduce you to Juzio," after which he added for some reason: "Mr. Juzef."

"Whether he's Juzef or Juzio – makes no difference. As long as he can exchange my money. After that we can go to Lychakiv Street, to number nine. Does that suit?"

"Let's go! Hop in!"

Koshovy obediently settled into the passenger seat.

Turning around on the coach-box, Zakhar grabbed the reins, smacked his lips, and lightly struck the horse on its well-fed and thoroughly brushed flanks.

The horseshoes clattered over the cobblestones.

They set off.

Everything around him really gave Klym Koshovy the impression that he was in another world.

The droshky moved at a relaxed pace. The coachman was in no hurry because the passenger had not requested this. At first, they traveled alongside the streetcar line, and Zakhar, without turning around, spoke loudly, explaining that until recently the streetcar carriages had also been drawn by horses. It was only in the past year that they started to convert them to electrical ones, because the city authorities wanted things to be just as they were in Vienna. Some of the streetcars were still horse-drawn, but with time more and more horses were being replaced. The new lines, which now ran into the wealthy districts, were fed by electrical current from the very beginning. And it seemed this plague would not stop.

"Why plague?" Klym asked, leaning forward, so that the coachman could hear him better, and raised his voice.

"There's no need to shout!" Zakhar dismissed him, continuing to look ahead, and to a bystander it might have appeared that he was talking to himself, or conversing with the wide and rounded horse's backside. "There's no need to bay so that the entire royal city can hear you! I'm not deaf."

"Tell me, why do you hate streetcars so much? It's progress," and having decided that the simple Lviv coachman was totally aware of the changes and challenges of the times, he added: "I, for example, support progress. Electricity..."

"What has electricity to do with anything here?" the fellow dismissed his words again. "I have a kerosene lamp at home. I can't say that my wife and children suffer too much because of that. The streets need to be well lit, yes, that's true. Streetlamps – they're alright, in the evenings and at night it's much better to transport people on well-lit streets. But at least the streetlamps don't make a loud clatter."

"I still don't understand."

Zakhar sighed.

"Look, sir. When horses used to pull streetcar carriages, they traveled more slowly. But they were quiet. As soon as they electrified the lines, the speed increased. But the clatter they make on the cobblestones – Mother of God!" He crossed himself with his free hand, all the more since they were passing another church. "And at times sparks fly from under the wheels! Horses are living creatures. In the early days they would take fright, and bolt. My kumpel[21], well his mare took off, with passengers in the carriage."

"Who?"

"My buddy," the coachman readily explained. "It's a term the batiars use here – kumpel. Since you're off to Lychakiv Street, you'll hear the word used a quite a lot. And as for the incident with my kumpel, the newspaper *Kurjer Lwowski*[22] later wrote: a respected engineer from Lodz, his wife, and their two children, girls aged eight and six, were seated in the droshky. They barely managed to rescue them, and they got away with just a fright, albeit an awfully bad one. The respected engineer would have forgiven him, and the wife's experiences were bearable. But the children were half scared to death, the younger girl even fainted. In short, my kumpel would have paid

....

[21]   Kumpel – meaning buddy or mate, borrowed from the German and originally meaning 'coal miner'.

[22]   *Kurjer Lwowski* (Lviv Courier) – Polish-language daily newspaper published in Lviv from 1883 till 1935. The Ukrainian writer Ivan Franko (1856-1916) worked there for a long time.

a hefty fine. He said later that he had already begun thinking how much he would be able to raise from the sale of his horse and harness, because he had nowhere else to get money from. Thank God, Mr. Genyk came along and extricated him from that mess."

"Who?"

"The lawyer."

"My-my!" Klym became interested. "The lawyer, you say?"

"No great wonder! There's too many of their ilk in our Lviv as it is. They can't get along with one another. The shrewder they are – the more money they have. They simply rip off ordinary people. Is it the same where you're from?"

"Depends. How did all this end? I take it your… what's his name… kumpel, wasn't well off?"

"On the other hand our council makes good money from those street-cars!" Having declared this, Zakhar Hnatyshyn straightened his back, spread his shoulders, pushed his chest forward, and was now sitting on the coach-box looking very much the victor. "You may well ask, sir, what the council has to do with it? I'll tell you! That lawyer, who knocked on the door of my friend's place, turned up of his own accord. With a copy of the newspaper in which they had written up this unfortunate incident. And they had added a cartoon, in which my friend was depicted with a contorted muzzle. Funny, but it weren't for him to roll around laughing. So, the lawyer located him and says: your mare, sir, took up and raced off, because it was frightened by the clatter of the electric streetcar. And it had also seen a sheaf of sparks shoot out from under the wheels. So, what d'you say, is it the mare's fault? Or, God forbid, the fault of its owner, a coachman with many years of experience, whom every one of his colleagues knows as being competent? Not at all! The streetcar is to blame! And not the fellow driving it, he's not at fault here, he's just a hired hand. The council paid damages to the engineer. On the very same day that they had begun proceedings in the imperial Ministry of Transport, to allow them to get rid of the horses and convert all the streetcars in Lviv to electrical power! There! You need to demand money from the city's mayor for losses suffered by the people!"

"And was he successful?"

"Why wouldn't he be? When my kumpel told me about it, I grew angry."

"At whom?"

"Myself! Such a thing would never have entered my head! Because to shake down the mayor of the city is a sacred thing, is it not? In short, a while later that Mr. Genyk brings my colleague a fresh issue of that same newspaper, *Kurjer Lwowski*. He opens it up and shows him. There's an article there about him again, but this time without the cartoon. Citizen so-and-so managed to get a finding that the council was guilty in the case of the family of a respected engineer from Lodz who suffered regrettable moments and sustained losses. Because a streetcar had frightened his mare, harnessed into a droshky, in which they were traveling on personal business, on their way to celebrate a relative's name day. And compensation was also ordered to be paid to the owner of the mare and droshky. Because he sustained equivalent damages. Know what I'll also tell you? Before this, the *Kurjer* editor himself had visited my friend at home. He brought him one hundred kroner, so that the fellow would not listen to his lawyer and take the newspaper to court because of the insulting illustration. My friend could have won much more. By the way, the lawyer was extremely angry when he found out. It turns out he really had intended to take the editor to court as well. Because things had gone so well, he decided to keep going."

At this point the talkative Zakhar Hnatyshyn drew up to a carriage traveling along the same street, but in the opposite direction and, digressing, greeted the coachman with a loud: 'Servus!', raising his hat as well. In reply he heard: 'Salut!', and the friends bowed to one another from their coach-boxes.

During the short exchange of courtesies, Klym went through everything he had heard.

Based on his own, albeit not so long-established lawyer's practice, he could not recall a single instance when it was possible to win a lawsuit against the city authorities, or to take Kyiv's governor-general to court. Even more – he could not recall anything similar happening in the cases launched by his more senior colleagues. It seemed no Kyiv lawyer would have taken on such an obviously hopeless case. What's more – even in Kharkiv, Moscow, or Saint Petersburg itself, such processes were hardly possible. Otherwise the newspapers would have long ago written about similar legal precedents.

It appeared that here in Lviv everything was indeed different. It would not be easy to practice here. Although Koshovy never expected things would go smoothly here, the final realization struck him only now: no matter how much time he intended to spend in this city, he needed to get used to the new rules. He was hoping he wouldn't have to study again. Otherwise, he would be forced to sweep the streets. Or at the very least to become a coachman. Being Ukrainian, Zakhar could become his mentor.

Meanwhile the fellow continued, obviously now on his high horse:

"So, respected sir, we have enough such cases here."

"Against the council?"

"Frightened horses! And if it were only horses! Until they began to lay rails everywhere, the city slept peacefully. The outer suburbs don't complain even today. But where the wealthy live, there's no peace anymore. Streetcars start running early, rattling and clanging. In winter one can close one's windows more tightly, but even that doesn't always help. But come summer, when it's scorching hot, which is not a common occurrence in Lviv, because it usually rains here at this time of year… In short, streetcars disturb people's sleep. Our nobility here is the same as yours, and everywhere else – they love to loll about in bed. They begin their mornings late. And here you have all this clatter outside your windows each day, as if goods wagons are being loaded at the railway station! Who would like that? Not many. Especially builders and owners of rental properties."

"Why?"

"Because of late there have been fewer people willing to live on the streets along which streetcars run. No matter that it's the center of the city and the places are prestigious. Of course, you can sell your place. And it's also not a problem to rent out apartments. But no longer for the same price one could get before the introduction of the streetcars. Prices have dropped to almost half of what they had been. What do you say to that?"

Klym could find nothing to say in reply. He had no intention of judging the way of life of a city in which he had spent only a little more than two hours. Since locals always saw things more clearly, he would have lost even the smallest argument.

Instead he leaned back against the slightly worn leather of the seat and began looking where he was going.

The first impression received from viewing the station building, was now only intensified and consolidated.

All around him everything appeared majestic, mighty, built to last. A spirit of conservatism pervaded the place. Being a young man, Klym unwittingly picked this up. At first there was a feeling as if he had found himself in some crypt, surrounded by cold gray stone. But that only lasted for a short while, and soon passed.

Afterward it was practically supplanted by another feeling – the city's grandeur merely seemed impenetrable and inviolable. In fact, the droshky was transporting him between modern buildings, none of them resembling one another, and which only at first glance seemed gloomy and sullen. That, which had at first seemed antiquated to Koshovy, even reminding him of places he had read about in history books about the Middle Ages, had in reality been well planned, well ordered and almost perfectly organized.

The streets here were winding, coming together, diverging, and then again converging in quite unexpected places. Residential neighborhoods resembled ancient labyrinths. The city's brick buildings seemed to be straight out of Klym's favorite novels about knights – the place only lacked perhaps warriors in frightening armor and beautiful ladies with bouquets, standing on the sidewalks and in the windows of the buildings. But all this was somehow strangely very much alive. On one hand, it existed according to provincial customs Koshovy was familiar with, but on the other hand in fact it had its own special rhythm, incomprehensible to strangers. The not-so-wide streets only proved how close the locals could be to one another.

But they were by no means relatives. On the contrary, it was hardly possible that in Lviv, where there were almost two hundred thousand residents, the city dwellers knew each other, something Klym was used to in Kyiv. There he could walk from Bessarabian Square along Khreshchatyk and up Prorizna Street to Saint Sophia, and from there across to Andriyivsky Descent – and down to the Podil, and during his walk he would be able to greet a heap of friends. A good half of them would ask him to pass on their regards to his father. Others would ask how things were going, and it was not just a show of good manners. People knew what each of their friends were up to. Meanwhile Lviv, at least it seemed so to Klym, by the way it was set out, emphasized a completely different level of relationships, even between strangers. Even if they lived in the same place, they lived in different parts of it.

This old city was the main one on the eastern outskirts of a great empire. It was officially considered the center of the province.

But at the same time, it did not appear peripheral as such – at least to the extent which Koshovy was accustomed to perceiving provincial cities in the Russian Empire.

Which meant that the local city dwellers must be removed from total fraternization and kinship, which was characteristic of truly provincial places. And it was easier to stir up Kyiv than a city which had become suspended in its own self-respect and greatness. For, even having arrived in Lviv for the first time, Koshovy sensed how everything around him was not only changing, but was ready for change and growth.

The coachman Zakhar's complaints directed at the streetcars were living confirmation of the fact that changes were evident.

So that one became used to them in the end, after complaining one's fill.

Whereas the surroundings, remaining stock-still, tried hard to resist any external or internal influences. For this would bring with it at least some inconvenience.

A closed world was very easy to destroy from within. And it was easy to befuddle its inhabitants for a long time, if not forever.

Klym had the misfortune to personally experience this. And he had tried to escape this very thing when he had boarded the train the day before at the railway station in Kyiv.

Immersed in such thoughts, Koshovy stopped looking about from side to side. Government departments, shops, salons, offices, cafes, and residential buildings continued to float past him at a leisurely pace. Had he hopped off the droshky and continued walking on his own, he would certainly have become lost. And the further they went, the less he imagined where this Lviv coachman was taking him.

So, it came as a complete surprise when Zakhar pulled on the reins, stopped the horse, and barked:

"We've arrived, sir! Thank you!"

"Where?"

"Nyzhni Valy, I said! Out you get!"

CHAPTER THREE
WELCOME TO LVIV!

Koshovy grabbed his travel bag and stepped onto the ground, looking questioningly at his unexpected guide.

Zakhar got down off his coach-box as well. He gestured for his passenger to stay where he was, and slowly proceeded down the boulevard in the direction of what Klym ascertained to be the bank building. Before he reached it, he took a few steps to one side, singling out among the pedestrians a tall man in an elegant costume, a round wide-brimmed hat and a light cane in his left hand.

He gave the impression of a man with nothing to do, with more free time than his inspiration could handle. He strolled along the boulevard, playing with his cane, which he held more for the looks, like some element of clothing – he did not limp at all and the tip of his cane never touched the pavement. It seemed as if he was playing with the cane, imitating the deft moves of a circus artiste. At first glance the people around him and what they were up to didn't seem to interest the tall fellow one bit, he seemed to be out for a stroll, ostensibly for no particular reason. It didn't even appear as if he had come here to meet someone – time had no meaning for the tall man.

But on closer inspection, Klym realized that the man's idleness was deceptive.

In actual fact he gazed intently from under his hat, quickly and thoroughly checking out everyone who appeared in the small square. Koshovy also noticed that the appearance of the coachman had caught the attention of the man with the cane. And he deliberately turned away from him to greet some friend who was walking past, exchanging a few words. He only allowed himself to notice Zakhar once the coachman was an arm's length away.

There was a brief exchange, after which Zakhar looked over his shoulder, and with a nod of his head called Klym over. He stepped up and the coachman retreated to one side:

"Please, this is Mr. Juzio."

Now, when the newly acquainted men stood facing one another, Koshovy noticed how well-ironed Juzio's suit was, but despite this the collar of his shirt had two buttons undone, and there was no tie around his neck. This was meant to make him look, and probably did create that impression, like a businesslike person, and at the same time – very democratic. You can deal with me without ceremony, straight up, I'm all ears: that was what his unbuttoned starched collar seemed to intimate.

Hnatyshyn wanted to continue talking with the money changer. But, guessing the coachman's intentions, Juzio moved his hand sharply before him, as if he were closing a curtain.

"Are you dealing with me?"

The coachman shook his head, and again opened his mouth, but the money changer interrupted him: "Then you'd better shut up. See this chatterbox?" He was now addressing Klym. "His mouth is never shut, I know his type well. There was once a fine idea proposed to forbid coachmen to talk to their passengers. They get so carried away, and keep looking over their shoulder. Taking no notice of the road ahead and knocking over living people. Maybe we can talk alone?"

He looked at Zakhar again. The fellow was probably used to the money changer's manner: he closed his trap, took a few steps back, leaving the two men alone. Juzio got down to business.

"Sir has a problem?" he asked quickly. "Hopefully everything is lawful?"

Koshovy had no time to reply. Because an expression of amazement suddenly appeared on Juzio's elongated face, and then he behaved rather unexpectedly.

He moved forward a little.

Then craned his neck and winked at Klym with his right eye, shutting his eye forcefully on purpose. Then, after a short pause, he winked hard with his left eye. And then, to top it off, he blinked briefly with both eyes.

"No need to feel embarrassed, sir. Everything will be fine. We're all friends here, we need to trust one another."

Klym sighed, habitually touching his right eye, and said:

"They say one can exchange money here."

"It's not a bank. But one can," Juzio nodded. "Only the rate will be different. Is that alright with you?"

"How much different?" inquired Koshovy.

The money changer looked at the coachman, and the fellow shrugged his shoulders.

"I haven't seen it today."

"What do you need to see?" Klym failed to understand.

"I'll explain, so that you know for next time," Juzio said. "There's a system of symbols, not invented here, but it works very well. The rate of exchange of the krone to other currencies is set there in Vienna," he gestured with his head up into the air, as if this took place in some heavenly chancellery. "The rates are quite flexible. Therefore, the information can be transmitted by telegraph, as banking institutions are wont to do. See over there, those people assembling outside the Savings Bank? They're all Jews, waiting for telegrams. But there's another way to notify the exchange rate – by rail. The method is practiced by other business people."

"How does it work?"

"Yesterday in Vienna, on a train carriage headed for Lviv, someone chalked some figures. The system was prearranged. It only requires for someone to meet the train here on time. Thus we here in Nyzhni Valy know the actual exchange rate of the krone, rather than the official bank rate."

"And they differ?"

"Not by much," Juzio conceded. "But if sir operates in large sums, the difference may be significant. In your favor."

"Sir has one hundred tsarist rubles at his disposal."

Taking out his wallet, Klym took out the 'Catherine' and showed it to the money changer.

"May I?"

Juzio's thin fingers deftly snatched the banknote. He did some fast manipulations with it, difficult for any bystander to understand, scrunching it up and lifting it to the light, at the same time maintaining his grip on his cane. Finally, he folded it in two, twisted it up, as if he were holding a piece of paper, and could not resist winking once more.

"For some it's a paltry sum. While for others it's their sole capital. Depends how much value sir places on himself," he explained ambiguously.

"I can offer you an exchange rate, which I know was in use the day before yesterday. For one tsarist ruble they were asking two kroner and thirty kreutzers. Right now it could be a little higher, or a little lower…"

"I'm not about to niggle over a few kreutzers," Klym interrupted him, even though this didn't sound too polite. "Besides, I'm in a hurry. Another time I will be pleased to discuss financial matters with you. True, I know little about such things, but if it makes for a pleasant acquaintance…"

"To make the pleasant acquaintance of others you can chat up the ladies in Market Square[23]," the money changer also decided to avoid unnecessary chit-chat. "We have a business deal going here. So, two hundred and thirty kroner then. Here."

Juzio slid the banknote deep into his jacket pocket. Hanging the cane off his arm, from another pocket he pulled out a rather plump purse, tightly packed with banknotes of various denominations. On one side was a pile of Austrian kroner, on the other – banknotes of various other currencies grouped together. Pulling out two one hundred kroner notes, he offered them to Klym.

"Hold these while I get the rest."

Koshovy shook his head.

"Is anything wrong?"

"Everything's fine, Mr. Juzio. It's just that I prefer smaller denominations, if you don't mind."

Shrugging, the money changer neatly slipped the large denomination notes back in their place. He spat on his fingertips and pulled out some notes of smaller denominations. He repeated the amount out loud, and Klym assiduously counted the money, also wetting his fingers with spittle. He nodded – everything was correct, and placed the money in his wallet. He could not resist victoriously slapping it against his open palm.

Quite close by there was a cry, like the crack of a whip:

"Thief! Thief! Catch him!"

Koshovy shuddered.

The shouts had been rather sudden. It appeared, his new acquaintances also never expected such a thing.

---

[23]   Market Square (Ploshcha Rynok), the central square in Lviv, located in the historical old city.

But a moment later the fugitive raced lightning fast between him and Juzio.

Before Klym had a chance to look at him, someone's shoulder struck him on the run. He reeled, crying out, and almost lost his balance. Another push, this time in the back, was more forceful. Now the lawyer was falling onto his knees and stretched his arms before him so as not to hit the ground headfirst. As his right hand opened involuntarily, his wallet fell onto the cobblestones, and landed no further than half an arm's length away. Having landed on all fours, and trying to ignore the sudden commotion, Klym lunged after his wallet, but suddenly someone stepped heavily on his hand.

Koshovy shrieked not so much from the pain, as from the suddenness of everything that had transpired. He couldn't help himself and swore. In reply he also heard swearing, but it wasn't him they were swearing at: the curses were directed at the fugitive who had created the disturbance. A moment later Klym was being helped back onto his feet. Someone was carefully dusting his jacket, another person was handing him back the dropped wallet.

"Here, take it, it's yours, sir!"

Grabbing hold of the well-worn leather, the lawyer said a loud thank-you, not sure whom he was thanking.

He put the wallet into his pocket.

And heaved a sigh of relief.

It seemed like a minor incident, nothing major. All the same a little bit much for someone who had just arrived in a strange city. While he rearranged his clothes and slapped the besmirched knees of his trousers, everything around them settled down as quickly as it had begun. The Nyzhni Valy were returning to their usual rhythm of existence, and Juzio again approached Koshovy. He was no longer blinking, hamming it up, but looked concerned, grabbing him by the shoulder and asking:

"Is sir alright?"

"Phew... What was all that about?"

"Just the batiars playing their little games, by God," the money changer threatened with his cane in the direction that the thief had run off, whom they had tried to catch. "These fellows won't knife you, they're not real criminals. It might not have even been a real chase after a thief."

"Meaning?"

"Just that!" Juzio spread his arms apart. "The lads have an urge to kick up some dust and they rile people up. I can't say that it's always just larking about. Sometimes the police come to pick one of them up."

Koshovy suddenly realized what was missing.

"Really, the police!" he exclaimed. "No one is calling the police! They should be catching the thief!"

"Oh!" Juzio seized on his words. "Sir has also noticed this! Listen here, if this was a real chase, and not just loutish games, the police would have already caught the thief. See, the square's small. There are not too many ways out of here. It's easy to catch someone running away, especially since there's no dearth of policemen in this part of the city."

Someone cleared their throat nearby – it was the coachman.

"So, are we going on our way, sir?"

"Is it far still?"

"Nope, almost there."

Bidding farewell, Juzio pressed two fingers to the brim of his hat and saluted.

Klym returned the gesture. When the money changer couldn't help himself and blinked again, he wasn't surprised.

The rest of the journey was without incident.

Zakhar stopped the horse near the sidewalk opposite a massive gate, pointed out the number on the building, and announced:

"If you please, we have arrived, sir. Lower Lychakiv."

The required building had three stories, with an elegant well-tended façade. A little further on there was a streetlamp adorned with a frivolous green wreath on top of a tall post, which noticeably added to the majestic atmosphere. Having decided to take a walk down the street later that day, and especially toward evening, in the lamplight, which would probably make everything here seem more mysterious, Koshovy stepped onto the sidewalk.

"How much?"

Without waiting for an answer, he fetched his wallet, once more he slapped it against his outstretched palm and, demonstratively spitting onto his fingers, opened it.

There was no money inside.

None at all.

At first Klym thought – it couldn't be. That he had put it in the wrong place, not where he always placed it, and that the notes were now lying in a different compartment. He checked with his fingers – it was empty. Except for a small piece of paper deep in the wallet, folded several times. Klym knew what it was, but all the same he pulled it out. A note with the address in Lviv. The one he had learned by heart.

Confused, he looked up, and met with Zakhar Hnatyshyn's gaze.

"You saw yourself… I put it in here…"

"Gone," said the coachman. "True, the money was there. Now it's gone."

"Where… The notes must have fallen out. I'm a butterfingers, I must have misplaced them," Koshovy began to fuss about. "Let's go back there, quick. Someone was bound to have picked the notes up. You know a few fellows there. Even that Juzio… Mr. Juzio…"

"We could try Mr. Juzef," Zakhar reminded him.

"Even that Juzef – he wouldn't have simply pocketed the notes! He's a friend of yours!"

"He has no need of your money," ahemmed the coachman. "That's the black market, on Wekslarski Square. But Mr. Juzio is no dark soul. He's an honest dealer. His eyes don't miss a thing. Had he seen the notes, he would have picked them up straight away and returned them to you."

"Where then…"

"Forget about it."

"Meaning?"

"Just that. Simply forget about it. It seems they were indeed thieves. There's all types among those batiars."

There was no need to explain any more to Klym. He began to recall the recent unfortunate incident. He had taken the money from the money changer, placed it in his wallet. But before he was able to put it away – someone had already been watching him. They came running up behind him, the nimble thief ran between him and Juzio on purpose, although he could have avoided them. The push, and the shove, actions which were well practiced ages ago. The wallet falls, more precisely – it is knocked out of his hand. For a short instant they obstruct his view. Then before he realizes what is happening, the wallet is returned to him. All made to look as if it has been kindly picked up, so that no one will be tempted to steal it.

Koshovy had friends in the criminal police in Kyiv and he was friends with journalists, for without press contacts a lawyer could not operate. He had heard a thing or two in his time. So the local pickpockets did not surprise him at all. In such cases there were usually three players. One played the thief, knocking the prey. The second covered, while a third fellow cleaned out the wallet and returned it to its owner. And one could never get a good look at any of them. One moment, and they dissolved into thin air, like ripples disappearing on water.

But having understood the ploy made it no easier.

"And what now?" Klym asked.

"I'd like to know that myself," the coachman replied in the same tone of voice.

The decision was not delayed. It was obvious, for they had…

"We've arrived. This is where I need to go," Koshovy said.

"And what good is that to me? You got a free ride. I understand everything, of course, and I sincerely apologize, but I've wasted several hours on you, sir. I could have made some money, meanwhile, and instead, I have to commiserate with someone on their misfortune. I warn you – I don't take any notes."

"Notes?"

"Promissory notes. It happens that gentlemen have a big night out on the town, they party long and hard, I deliver them home fairly drunk, and outside their gate they grab at their heart: they've got no money. They tear out a sheet of paper from their notepad and write these promissory notes. Then you have to waste even more time to get back the money they owe."

"Lord Almighty, I'm not asking you for credit? My friend must surely be at home! I received a letter from him, he wrote back – he should be waiting. I'll just go up to his apartment, or better still – we can go together! Mr. Soyka will settle the account; I'll explain everything to him."

A new expression suddenly appeared on the coachman's face. Klym had noticed this expression on his face just recently, when Zakhar had pointed out the dandy money changer, Mr. Juzio.

"You said – Mr. Soyka? Am I right in asking that here in this building lives the lawyer Yevhen Soyka?"

"Why, do you know him?"

"Not personally. Although he doesn't avoid our lot. He's the one we call Mr. Genyk! Pulled my kumpel out of a spot of bother, helped him sue the council for damages!"

"That sounds very much like Yevhen Pavlovych," announced Klym.

Although he wasn't sure whether Soyka got up to such things. For he hadn't seen him for a long time, not since the fellow had left Kyiv for good.

"If that's the case, all the more reason not to worry," continued Koshovy. "Do you trust Mr. Soyka?"

"After he saved my kumpel's skin – I would trust only him."

"Then let's go!"

Slapping the coachman on the shoulder, Koshovy grabbed his travel bag and hurried to the gate.

The janitor was already hurrying toward them, sooner sensing the appearance of the visitors, rather than seeing them from his post. Fat, with a generous mustache, the red potato of his nose did not look as if it was part of his face, but as if some wag had played a bad joke, fitting it any old how in the middle of his mug while the fellow was asleep.

"We've come to see Mr. Soyka!" Klym called out, then came to his senses, and greeted the fellow: "A good day to you!"

"Mr. Soyka never said anything about visitors," came the respectable reply.

The janitor assumed a businesslike pose, standing with his arms akimbo, as if intending right there and then to send the uninvited guests packing. He was standing his ground, acting as if they were trying to enter his private territory.

"Meaning, he is at home?" Koshovy asked again, grabbing hold of the gate.

"It makes no difference."

"Listen, countryman, I'm from Kyiv. An old friend of Mr. Soyka! He's expecting me!"

The janitor shrugged his shoulders. It didn't appear that he was about to exchange his anger for mercy.

"Mr. Soyka is a well-known man. Our landlord respects him. So his word is law for me too. Meanwhile Mr. Genyk never gave any specific instructions regarding you."

"My God! Is he at home, or not?!" exclaimed Klym, feeling another surge of despair, and answered the question himself: "He's at home! Where else could he be!"

"How do you know?" the janitor inquired with suspicion.

"One needn't have any inside knowledge here. If your Mr. Genyk wasn't at home, you wouldn't be standing here, my dear fellow, like some Cerberus. Step inside, respected guests, you'd be saying, go kiss his lock, if you're so keen. As it is, you don't know what to do. Because, it seems, Mr. Soyka told you to say that he was not in, and who to say this to. Or looking at it differently: he's in, but not for everyone, and you were given clear instructions, who to let in, and who not to. Although it's unlikely that you have the right to not let in visitors to see the tenants in broad daylight. So, what's the conclusion, d'you know?"

The janitor, clearly not expecting such a rapid-fire tirade, silently shook his big shaggy head.

"Mr. Soyka paid you to do this. As our Gypsies say, he gilded your palm. That's alright, don't worry. I'll tell Mr. Genyk that you acted correctly, honestly and conscientiously. Maybe he'll slip you a few more kreutzers."

The last deduction sounded so convincing, that the janitor no longer carped at them and opened the gate, letting the guests into the reception area. With his peripheral vision Koshovy caught sight of the janitor's outstretched right hand and eloquently slapped his pockets. The coachman, who was following, stopped for a moment, pulled out a coin from his pocket and placed it into the outstretched hand. As they set off, he grumbled behind Klym's back:

"You'll be owing me that too. I won't be paying for you everywhere."

"We'll sort it out!" Koshovy fobbed him off, for his mood had improved markedly.

The Kyiv lawyer found the location of the stairs here disconcerting.

Walking through the main entrance and then passing around it, they ascended the stairs onto a wide veranda with railings, which led straight to the required door. There was a view into an inner courtyard. Imagining what it would be like to return home drunk in the middle of the night, so easy to break one's neck, Klym finally reached his goal.

He exhaled.

And banged on the door.

When no one inside answered, he began to pound harder. The noise would have woken the most inveterate sleeper. Yevhen Soyka had never been known to lounge about in bed for long, but then habits were prone to change…

Phew, how long could a person stay in bed. This was too much even for the biggest lazybones. And Mr. Genyk, judging from all accounts, did not twiddle his thumbs in Lviv.

A fresh portion of knocks again produced no result. There was no movement inside.

It seemed there wasn't a living soul there.

But if Koshovy had been mistaken, and Soyka had left in the morning on business, why then was the janitor with the bulbous nose giving them a hard time… Because he was mean and wanted to show who was in charge here…

"Why the hell bang on the door! You can be heard from the street!"

No, it didn't look like it. The janitor had already joined them, standing on the veranda and catching his breath.

"You said that Mr. Genyk was at home!" Koshovy chastised him.

"That he is! Never walked past me, by God! Nobody can get past me here!" the bulbous fellow said angrily. "He warned me yesterday, you guessed right, sir! That today he would be working from home, and I was not to let anyone in. I was to let him know about anyone who came around, but only if they began to shout – like you here! Step aside!"

Now the janitor hammered at the door. Klym admitted that the fellow's fists were far more effective than his own. The racket, he surmised, would have even woken up Sleeping Beauty from that old fairy tale…

The knocking stopped.

"Something's not right," mumbled the janitor, as he scratched his round nose. "Something's not right."

He seemed to have read Klym's thoughts.

"Can the door be opened some way without the tenant?"

"Everything's possible. The owner, Mr. Singer, just needs to be notified. But should we…"

"Listen, Mr. Soyka didn't go anywhere! You yourself swear to that! He's not old, just five years my senior! Who knows, he might have taken ill! I've read in the papers that heart attacks can affect men who are not that old…"

"Ah, you and your papers!" the janitor grimaced. "Forget the papers. Mr. Genyk once mentioned something like that to me. I asked him not so long ago: like, how are things, Mr. Genyk? Before he would always say he was fine, but this time he complained about a pain in his chest. I even sympathized with him, as one does…"

Koshovy's patience ran out. He no longer took any notice of the coachman, who stood there without uttering a word, sullenly watching the unfolding events, and ordered:

"Run and fetch the owner!"

"What for?"

"Phew! Because we can't break down the door without him being present! And we need a doctor, just in case."

"Why a doctor?"

"Oh, Lord! If he had a pain in his chest, anything could have happened."

The bulbous fellow no longer argued and pattered off to carry out the order. Zakhar Hnatyshyn pressed his backside against the railing and froze in anticipation of receiving his payment. He had a dour expression on his face, the look of which made Klym feel sick.

The building owner, a big-bellied Jew with a face abundantly covered with droplets of sweat and sparse bushes of hair on his elongated skull, came running soon after. He kept blabbering that he didn't meddle in the private life of his tenants, and so did not keep spare keys to their apartments on principle, so that there would be no temptation to come and check on people when they weren't at home. And he began to say, that other landlords, who were not so conscientious, at times did the opposite. Koshovy completely abandoned courtesy, stamped his foot and slammed his shoe against the closed door. No more explanations were necessary: the fat man ordered they fetch an axe.

They had to potter about with the door for quite a while. It proved to be rather strong, and the janitor, having thoroughly examined it, suggested it was better to take the door off its hinges, so as not to have to chop out the lock. The bald fellow gave the nod, the coachman now came to their aid, curiosity having gotten the better of him. Together, levering the door up where necessary with the axe, the men removed the hinges and moved the door to one side. The building's owner didn't simply enter, he jumped in first.

Klym was behind him, when he heard a hysterical scream, which was at the same time filled with despair and fear.

Preparing himself for the worst, he raced in and pushed past the bald fellow.

The first thing he saw was a man lying face down on the floor.

There was a dark stain around his head.

His right hand was clutching a gun.

And only then he noticed the drawn curtains and locked windows.

"Call the police," he blurted out.

And immediately added:

"Everyone to remain here and wait. Don't come inside. I'll stay here and guard the place."

And only then he barked, stamping his foot:

"Out of here! Get out! Go, I said!"

CHAPTER FOUR
MAKING SOMEONE'S ACQUAINTANCE BEHIND BARS

When the key clicked, as it was turning in the lock, something clicked in Klym's head as well.

The whole time, while he was being escorted to the police station, Koshovy did not even stop to think what a dangerous situation he had gotten himself into. He didn't even try to put his thoughts in order, formulating at least an approximate plan of action for the near future.

He couldn't recall the name of the state he was in now. He tried to recall so hard, that his head ached.

Father was sometimes visited by a professor, whom the Koshovys called an old friend of the family. Considered an authority on the treatment of mental illness, he had last visited them quite recently, just after Klym's release from prison. In conversation that time he had used a new medical term, which described a phenomenon that his colleagues in Europe were just beginning to explore. Professional magazines were already writing that patients, especially epileptics, often had obsessive thoughts, when they had the feeling of having previously experienced a situation they found themselves in. Either in a past life, or in their dreams, or in general in another body. The phenomenon was of particular interest because some of these stories turned out to be quite true. This was when scientists recalled all those described cases from the times when epileptics were considered to be almost holy people. It was believed that they experienced visions during the fits. Which was why the feeble-minded were thought to be endowed with prophetic abilities. People were also prepared to pay a lot of money to be present when such a person entered into a trance.

Now, with the advent of this new, perhaps the most enlightened century in the history of mankind, there were ways to carefully investigate such phenomena.

Of course, the professor complained about the backwardness of the Russian Empire, still sticking to its roots, the archaic ard plow. Airplanes were already soaring in the skies, electrical lights were appearing in cities, automobiles were driving along pot-holed roads – meanwhile most people seemed to be lurking, hoping to be left unnoticed. They sat quietly, snorted angrily, waiting for a signal, after which they could, without undue hesitation, burn the heretics and sorcerers at the stake. All the same, albeit with great effort and reluctance, everything new from Europe was already beginning to reach the imperial outskirts. In actual fact, it made its way into the provincial cities even faster – for in St. Petersburg or Moscow it might get lost, slip past the far too suspicious attention of the authorities, while somewhere in Kyiv or Odesa it would find fertile ground. Speaking this way in his favorite rebellious manner, the professor had declared: European doctors have already come up with a separate name for this phenomenon. Right now, discussions have begun on the subject in scientific circles. Only faint echoes of which reach such cities as Kyiv, of course. But even that is enough for the moment.

Klym was suffering, as he convulsively tried to remember what he was dealing with here. Only after he heard the clicking in the lock, did the word finally surface: *déjà vu* – that's what it was called!

Only, unlike the weak-minded, Koshovy knew for sure that he was not experiencing a *déjà vu*. He hadn't dreamed of the prison cell. On the contrary, he was returning to one after not more than two weeks. And he had left for Lviv, or to be frank, he had escaped, if one were to call a spade a spade, to avoid prison and other similar unpleasantries served up by Russian laws to people like himself.

A heavy door swung open. Without waiting for a special invitation, Klym crossed the threshold of the cooler. His eyes had grown accustomed to the dim light, and he noticed that, apart from himself, there was only one other person in the cell. Koshovy was about to greet him, but the stranger, whom he did not yet have time to properly make out, deftly scrambled to his feet off a wooden bunk, and rushed to the door, yelling:

"Mr. Zaremba! Mr. Zaremba! Is it time yet for me to leave?"

The man had trouble pronouncing the letter 'r'. His speech impediment wasn't that prominent, but it wasn't that unnoticeable either, sounding like the tinkle of a small bell. He simply couldn't pronounce the letter. Mother nature had not endowed him with such an ability from birth. So that the surname of the warden sounded like 'Zayemba', leading Klym to conclude that his cellmate at the police station was no first-timer. Only an experienced criminal could know a jailer's name.

"What's the hurry, Mr. Shatsky?" the warden replied indifferently. "Your case won't be dealt with for some time yet. It's a serious charge, you're aware of that."

"And you, Mr. Zaremba – don't you know Jozef Shatsky!" the fellow called out, and his voice contained undisguised notes of despair. "Half of Lviv knows Shatsky…"

"…and the rest Shatsky knows himself," the policeman finished the sentence, and it became apparent to Klym that he was equally familiar with this phrase and it was grating on him. "Only what can I do? In our midst there are people, about whom you sometimes learn things that make your hair stand on end. Do you know how many such people have passed through this cell, for instance?"

"But that's not the case with Shatsky!" the fellow was getting worked up and in the heat of the moment pushed Klym aside, as if he were a chair or some other piece of furniture. "I've never lived a double life and it will be that way until the day I die! I love the life I have! It's a very comfortable life! From time to time my Mrs. Shatska says: life is so boring with you, Jozef, may you live a healthy life! You don't know how to give me surprise gifts! I always know, what you will give me for my name day, where you'll buy it, from whom, for how much and how long you bargained to get it! Do I resemble someone who harbors bad intentions, Mr. Zaremba?"

"Quieten down there, Mr. Shatsky!" thundered the warden. "I know you very well! And my older sister's oral cavity knows you even better! She's been trying to convince me for more than a year that you are a swindler, rather than a dentist."

"God forbid, Mr. Zaremba! If I were a swindler, would your older sister have remained my constant and favorite patient for so many years?"

By now the policeman had stepped inside the cell. Klym had the impression that he was in the middle of a domestic tiff, and that he was in their way. He felt like asking, as if in passing: 'Gentlemen, might I be on my way?'

Meanwhile the warden was already towering over him, vis-à-vis.

"If our family were better off financially, Mr. Shatsky, my sister, as well as my wife and my children, would have long since forgotten the path to your practice! But at present, of all the dentists in Lviv, you are the only one we can afford."

"Why are you unhappy, Mr. Zaremba? Have you come up with a new complaint?"

"No, the same old complaint!" the policeman was noticeably getting worked up. "No sooner does my sister get one tooth fixed, than a month later she has to go to get another one done! We try to limit the number of visits to no more than four a year. But then later we must pay again for teeth that you've already fixed! You do that on purpose, Mr. Shatsky! You are a very, very cunning man!" Zaremba stretched out his hand, wagging his finger in front of the prisoner. "You have the knowledge and experience to put my sister's mouth in order! Not to mention my wife's! But no! You do everything in your power to make our family remain your patients till the end of time! And we can't afford to go to another dentist! Because they charge much more for the same work! So, there's no need to tell me anything more, Mr. Shatsky! I won't be surprised if everything you're being accused of turns out to be true."

Shatsky wanted to say something in reply but the warden was no longer listening – he ominously blinked in parting and closed the door, leaving the new cellmates alone.

While the key was still turning on the outside, locking the door, Jozef was already tugging at Koshovy's sleeve:

"There, did you hear that? Respected sir, have you ever seen such an ignorant neanderthal as this respected policeman? I'd love to learn the name of that wise guy, who enlightened him that teeth can be cured once and for all! Even His Royal Majesty the Emperor doesn't have access to such things, let alone the Pope! Although our family attends a synagogue instead of a church. When it comes down to that, rabbis also have problems with their teeth, and they need to have them fixed from time to time. No one has ever managed to get all their teeth fixed once and for all! Every person has thirty-two of them. So, it's no surprise when a hole is sealed in one, and another starts hurting a while later, in quite the opposite corner. Because of which I became a dentist, rather than a surgeon."

So here was an experienced criminal…

"Because of what?" Klym asked, just to keep up the conversation, for Shatsky was speaking to him now and probably expected to hear something in reply.

"Teeth, my dear sir, teeth! If I were to remove a patient's inflamed appendix, they no longer have an appendix. They recover and never return with the illness. Meanwhile people have thirty-two teeth. Lots of work. By the way, want me to reveal a secret to you?"

"Which one?"

"Nothing frightening. You'll understand why this Franek Zaremba is picking on me. It's all because of his sister."

"I heard. He seems to think you're diddling her. That you don't fix her teeth properly, so that she has to come back to see you."

Shatsky took a step back, now taking a closer look at Koshovy, puckered his lips and smacked them, while moving his head from side to side, and then said:

"What word did you use? Diddle? Interesting, few people use that word here. You're not a local, right? You've come to Lviv, so that you could be arrested and thrown behind bars into a damp jail cell. And with Shatsky to boot. Right?"

"Not quite," Klym could not hold back a smile. "I had no intention at all of ending up at the police station, nor for that matter, in prison. By the way, it's not that damp in here. I've seen real jail cells, believe me."

"They say Austrian jails aren't among the worst," Jozef readily agreed. "Although… When it comes to places where people are held captive, I don't know if it would be correct to talk about the quality of accommodation behind bars. In France, in the times of Louis XIII, from memory, and not only under this Louis, nobles could pay for themselves when they ended up in the Bastille. If you had the money, an appropriate cell could be found for you."

Koshovy nodded in the direction of the barred window:

"Out there – it's the start of the twentieth century, and not the middle of the sixteenth. And this isn't France."

"Great. And so?"

"Today, to find an aristocrat behind bars is a rarity."

"You are certainly not a subject of His Majesty Franz Joseph!" exclaimed Shatsky.

"In general, you're right. But why have you arrived at this conclusion?"

"It's evident, sir. Shatsky sees and hears! Our courts do not discriminate, whether the person before them is of noble birth or of lowly origins. Everything depends on which of the defendants has the best lawyer. But if you can't wrangle your way out, the prosecutor won't skimp on meting out punishment. I suspect that where you've come from, the institutions of justice work a little differently, am I right?"

Koshovy once again brought his finger to his eye, and replied:

"Unfortunately. Only, if you trust the local laws, what have you to fear? You haven't been tried yet, as I understand. I have some idea about the procedures here. Both you and I have been detained for the moment. Until the matter is determined, so to speak. If you aren't guilty of anything, they'll get to the bottom of it and let you out."

"As for that, dear sir, I haven't the slightest doubt!" said Shatsky. "I am offended at the very suspicion, because of which I find myself here! I never explained why Franek Zaremba has it out for me. When his sister complained yet again, and you heard the gist of her claims against me as a dentist, I was careless enough to recommend that the lady have every single one of her teeth extracted. For good. And to have a denture installed. False teeth. Also for good. The conversation took place in the presence of her brother! Do you think people forgive such things?"

"Not always, I guess," Klym could not hold back a smile once again.

"So then, after that, Zaremba, where necessary, is ready to believe that Jozef Shatsky secretly salts human meat at night!"

"That's what you've been accused of?"

"It is possible that something similar is awaiting me," Shatsky nodded. "Until now it's not as bad as that. I've been accused of performing backyard abortions. Can you imagine? Me! I've been fixing teeth for twenty years! I have an unsullied reputation! To state that Shatsky practices the illegal termination of the fruits of a woman's frivolity is the same as…" he tried to find the necessary comparison, failed to do so, and instead continued out loud: "This is worse than… than…"

"Than if you had been detained beside a body, which you yourself found, and even summoned the police," Koshovy burst out. "How does that suit?"

His cellmate grew quiet. He looked at Klym for a while, as if what he had just heard was something impossible to comprehend. And then he blurted out, as if the question were the most important thing on his mind:

"I heartily apologize, sir, but why do you keep winking at me all the time with your right eye, like some streetwalker from Akademichna Street? My sincerest apologies once more…"

Koshovy had no intention of recounting his entire his gloomy odyssey.

He was not about to confess to his new friend Jozef Shatsky, the Lviv dentist, or to anyone else. To the criminal police – even less so, let alone the political department, who would most certainly have become interested in the story of a suspect lawyer from Kyiv. He had intended to relate the whole thing to Yevhen Soyka, because one couldn't write everything in a letter. Interception of mail and censorship were not yet abolished in the Russian Empire, despite the famous tsarist Manifesto, issued in the tumultuous October of 1905[24]. A year ago, after its abolition, everything returned to the way it had been before, and things even became much worse. It was no big secret, to be accused of being an accomplice of a banned anti-government organization, to be under investigation and to spend three whole weeks in the jail cells of 'Kosy Kaponir', the political jail in Kyiv. He was released, but only thanks to the incredible efforts of his father's friends. And they had allowed him to leave the country. Klym did not stop to think then whether he was emigrating or just going abroad until the dust settled. He was released, his case closed, and his documents were amended without delay – but all this did not make Koshovy a dangerous criminal and a potential violator of Austrian laws.

All the same, he had decided not to be too open about his recent past. If only because he had not been able to fully take it all in himself. How should he have acted: sat quietly and watched as a case was being manufactured against his university friends, with a clear hint of a sentence involving capital punishment – or to become one of them, to leave the

....

[24]   The Supreme Manifesto of October 17th 1905, signed by Russian Tsar Nicholas II following a wave of revolutionary protests. It expanded the rights and freedoms of citizens of the Russian Empire. It was de facto abolished on July 3rd 1907, when Nicholas II announced the early dissolution of the State Duma and the introduction of changes to the electoral system.

                                            ANDRIY KOKOTIUKHA

practice he had just started and to follow the example of others and live outside the law. It was only at first glance, and a very fleeting glance at that, that it seemed all so very romantic – with passwords, secret meetings, changes of clothing, disguises, and makeup – something akin to the practices of Arsène Lupin, the hero of the new sensational French novels by a Monsieur Leblanc[25], which Klym had recently read with enthusiasm.

In fact, Koshovy had no intention of jumping at the sight of his own shadow and gradually degrading, becoming a typical exile. It was easier to accept a handout from your investigator, a gendarme captain with a constantly red face, to break all established ties with a few swift desperate movements – and to set off into the unknown, heading west, boarding a train for Lviv…

Koshovy decided not to tell Jozef Shatsky the story behind his appearance in this city, even in an abridged form. He limited himself to the explanation that he had been imprisoned because of a series of coincidences. Where during questioning the gendarme investigator had decided to refresh the prisoner's memory, and summoned two of his dogs into the office, and these bone-breakers became so caught up in their task that they bashed the victim's head several times against a stone wall. He was revived with cold water and they wanted to continue to pummel the obstinate fellow. But then a captain arrived, blasted all present, and ordered that a doctor be summoned, after which they stopped interrogating him for two days. But after recuperating, Klym found that his right eye had begun to twitch.

They explained to him that it was a nervous tic.

These things happened.

When you struck your skull against something hard.

The doctor promised him that it would pass. But he did not say when, or what had to be done for this to happen. And throughout the whole time that he had now been living with this tic, becoming accustomed to it only with great difficulty, Koshovy noticed only one peculiarity. His right eye began to twitch, making it look as if he was winking, the moment Klym felt even a bit nervous.

....

[25]   Arsène Lupin, a fictional gentleman thief and master of disguise in novels written by French author and journalist Maurice Leblanc (1864-1941), famous for his crime novels.

"That's clear, it's all because of your nerves!" Shatsky agreed wholeheartedly, as if no one had been able to explain the reason to date. "You, young man, must think seriously about your health. And you need to start now, otherwise with time your tic will become incurable."

"Is it still possible to cure it?"

"If you are lowered deep underground and left on your own for a long time. Leading the life of a reclusive monk because you won't be guaranteed peace and quiet anywhere else. But sadly, even after such cave therapy, I can't promise you a full recovery. Our times are not conducive for this, trust an old Jew."

"I know," Klym nodded, immediately adding: "By the way, you're not that old, you know, Mr. Shatsky. How old are you then?"

His comrade in misfortune again habitually smacked his lips.

"Does it matter if I don't look my age? As my wife says, it's better for you, Jozef, if everyone who sees you, thinks of you as an old and wise Jew. Ask me why."

"Why?" Koshovy asked obediently.

"Because of the three assumptions, only one will be correct."

"Which one?"

"That Jozef Shatsky is a Jew," his new acquaintance nodded clownishly. "Not as old as he looks. Not as wise as one would wish. These are the words of my wife, yes. But I have no intention or desire of arguing with Esther Shatska, the daughter of Isaac Boyarsky, a wise merchant, well-respected far beyond the district of Krakidaly[26]. If we go back to this thing of yours," he touched his own eyelid, "the best approach is to control yourself. Banish foolish thoughts. And you'll see for yourself, Mr. Koshovy, it will pass. You'll be reminded of your annoying eye only perhaps in extreme cases. And you did the right thing."

"What do you mean?"

"You've come to the right place. You thought there'd be peace here? Hah! We have certain upheavals of our own here in Lviv. If the world is slowly but surely rearing up, then why should our beautiful progressive city fall by the wayside of these tumultuous processes? But still, it's far

---

[26]   Krakidaly – a district of Lviv, at that time one of its suburbs, which began at the Krakivsky Market. One of the poorest districts in the city, compactly settled by Jews.

more peaceful here, than in your parts. Once you regain your senses, you'll recall my words."

The whole time they were talking, Klym sat on his wooden bunk bed, while Shatsky paced about the cell from the door to the wall and it seemed that some of his words were addressed to the walls or the barred window. When he spoke, he didn't always look at his interlocutor, as was required by the rules of etiquette, which Koshovy had once heard about somewhere. Despite this fact, that his new acquaintance was continually moving about, he was still before him. So that Klym managed to get a good look at his cellmate.

Jozef could have just as easily been aged either forty or fifty years old. He wasn't fat, but then he wasn't thin. Even in the dim light of the cell his jacket, with its long hems, looked somewhat dirty, and hung loosely on its owner. This created a false impression. It made Shatsky appear rakish. However, in the course of the conversation, once he became carried away, he tugged at his unbuttoned jacket from time to time, revealing that underneath he was wearing a light-colored shirt with a high collar, buttoned all the way to the top, almost up to his throat. So that Koshovy realized: the jacket was simply too big for the dentist. More than likely, he deliberately wore such a jacket, to appear more staid.

Given his height, lower than average, the intention was quite clear. When they stood facing one another, Klym noticed that the difference in their heights was more than half a head, not in his cellmate's favor. His disheveled, seemingly untidy hair was streaked with the first signs of gray, but the locks were still quite painstakingly cut. The beard looked more well-groomed, but it too had a touch of silver through it and was not too bushy. It appeared that a hairdresser's scissors laid into it more often, than into his hair. His elongated face was adorned with fleshy, slightly protruding ears and a straight, rather broad nose, with a small hump.

In other words, nothing about his external appearance suggested how many years dentist Jozef Shatsky had existed in this world.

Although he was older than Klym, there was no doubt about that.

On top of everything Koshovy was at first quite taken aback when his new acquaintance referred to himself as a *zhyd*[27] without flinching or stumbling for a moment.

....

[27]   *Zhyd* – the accepted term for Jews in Western Ukraine under the influence of the Polish

It was categorically unacceptable to use this word in the home into which Klym was born and where he grew up. And not only because among father's good friends there were quite a few famous Kyiv Jews. Considering himself an ardent liberal, it generally raised his hackles when he heard the word '*zhyd*' used, albeit involuntarily, without bad intentions, simply out of habit. But if it was uttered in his presence on purpose and the person who was speaking understood what they were saying and why, then a scandal was not long in ensuing. His father did not mince his words and could even demand that the transgressor leave the premises, and then promised to make every effort to never shake the hands of such black-hundredists[28] in decent society.

One of those, whom Nazar Hryhorovych Koshovy publicly sent packing, turned out to be a gendarme officer. He had arrived in civvies, but everyone present, including his father, knew about his office in the building on Bulvarno-Kudriavska Street[29] and his uniform in the closet. Eventually it was because of his efforts that Klym hadn't gotten away with a mere fright, although he could easily have, and instead found himself in the jail cells of Kyiv's equivalent of Schlisselburg prison[30]. And it was before this fellow that Nazar Hryhorovych had to humiliate himself when he began to seek the release of his son…

When Koshovy, feeling awkward and carefully choosing his words, decided to satisfy his own curiosity, Shatsky reacted calmly. He explained, that after the emperor had pardoned the unfortunate Leopold Hilsner[31]

<hr>

word *żyd*, meaning Jew. In Russian *zhid* is equivalent to the English 'yid'. Was in common use in Eastern Ukraine until the 1930s when the Soviet regime forbade its use and replaced it with the Russian word for Jew – *yevrey*.

[28]   An ultra-nationalist movement in the Russian Empire in the early 20th century. Noted for their extremism and incitement to conduct Jewish pogroms and promote anti-Ukrainian sentiment.

[29]   A street in Kyiv, renamed in 1937 in honor of Vaclav Vorovsky, a Bolshevik activist. The original name was restored in 2014. The headquarters of the Kyiv Security Department, the political police of the Russian Empire, was located in this street until 1917.

[30]   A notorious political prison in tsarist times in northern Russia.

[31]   Referring to the case against Leopold Hilsner, a Jew accused of committing ritual murders. In March 1899 in Bohemia (now the Czech Republic) a Czech Catholic girl, Anežka Hrůzová, was killed. A 23 year old vagrant Jew was arrested on suspicion of the murder. He did not admit to the crime during the inquest. Instead, facts emerged that allowed Hilsner to be charged with another murder perpetrated a year earlier. The trial lasted from 1899-1900, accompanied by

                                    ANDRIY KOKOTIUKHA

eight years earlier, no one had heard anything about pogroms across the entire territory of the empire. That is, maybe they had occurred somewhere, and they probably had – for that was the fate of his chosen people. But usually they were a result of private misunderstandings between Poles and Jews, rather than as actions approved almost at an official level and intentionally kept under wraps.

Young Hilsner was accused of the ritual murder of a young Christian girl. The pogroms flared up far from here, in Bohemia. And even then, as Shatsky hastened to explain, for a very short time. Up until that incident, the good Lord had protected the Jews, in particular those in Lviv, from such shameful acts.

So that Jozef placated Klym: in a city, where *judaeus* comprised more than one third of the population, Jewish pogroms would only be organized by someone bent on suicide. Thus, one needn't fear negatively perceived words, the public use of which by subjects of His Imperial Majesty Emperor Nicholas II was always a verbal warm-up before a brutal, shameful, often bloody orgy.

At that, they decided to stop talking about self-determination by mutual consent.

And they did not manage to start on another topic.

Although there were enough of them to discuss. For example, Shatsky was quite eager to know what Koshovy's thoughts were on the suicide of his friend. For Jozef had known the lawyer well, although mostly through hearsay. He was already intending to recount many interesting stories about him.

But a key turned in the lock on the outside.

The detained Klym Koshovy was asked to step out.

....

Jewish pogroms in Bohemia. Hilsner was found guilty. The death penalty was replaced with life imprisonment, but in 1918 he was pardoned.

CHAPTER FIVE
WOMAN FROM A SECRET ROOM

"What's with your eye?"

"It's a tic," he explained for the second time that day, deciding not to go into too much detail with the investigator, limiting himself to a brief explanation: "Nerves."

"Such a young man – and nerves already."

The criminal police investigator, a tall lean Pole, looking somewhat like a cricket, belonged to that group of people that were hard to imagine without glasses.

On seeing him, Klym thought: this Mr. Olshansky must even sleep with them on. For the formidable official, his elongated face adorned with a stiff brush of a mustache beneath a sharp nose, looked defenseless as soon as they were removed. It was as if the investigator was standing completely naked in a crowd, and everyone around him didn't care less about his position in the police department.

The bridge of his nose was so narrow that his glasses would not remain sitting on it, continually slipping down, and Olshansky had to regularly push them up with his index finger. Once the glasses slipped down, the investigator had to look over the top of his glasses, which made his gaze look suspect.

At least it appeared that way to Koshovy.

He made an intense effort not to let something slip involuntarily off his tongue which might be to his detriment.

"So, you say you knew the lawyer Mr. Soyka well?"

"He had a practice in Kyiv. He is older… *was* older than me. Not by much, just five years, but all the same he had more experience. And had already made a name for himself, he was known in the right circles. I had just finished university at the time, and Yevhen Pavlovych took me on as an assistant."

"*Yevhen Pavlovych*," repeated the investigator. "Here we don't use the patronymic when we refer to people," the investigator explained. "Ruthenians occasionally might use this form of address. Or Russophiles."

"Who?"

"We have such a community. You'll get to know them yet… or maybe not. In general, it's not common practice here to use a person's patronymic. I'm explaining this to you in case you decide to act conspiratorially, so take that into account."

"Why would I act conspiratorially?" Koshovy shrugged his shoulders. "I'm past the age when lads play at being spies."

"But you read books about them," Mr. Olshansky nodded in the direction of Klym's travel bag, which stood on a wide bench in the corner, opened and disemboweled. "Your mention of spies was appropriate, by the way. Here in Lviv, such talk is no longer idle chatter, unfortunately."

"You think I'm a spy? A Russian spy?"

"If that were so, Mr. Koshovy, you would be in the hands of counterintelligence. You should be aware that anyone who crosses the Zbruch River, can be," the investigator raised his long thin manicured finger, "I repeat, can be a Russian spy. Given the present international situation… You must realize this, if you read the press. Besides, of late various subversive elements have moved here from the Russian Empire."

"Why have you mentioned this to me?"

"Because you, if you'll pardon me, were found in the apartment of Mr. Genyk Soyka."

"Wait," Koshovy leaned forward a little. "No one found me anywhere. On the contrary, it was I who found my friend Mr. Soyka dead inside his locked apartment. There are two witnesses to this, plus the owner of the place makes three. Instead of questioning me on the spot, as is standard procedure, or taking a statement from me at the police station, I've been thrown into a cell. As if I'm a suspect in the murder."

The investigator looked at Klym over his glasses.

Then with a habitual gesture he pushed them up his nose and relaxed into his high-back chair.

Saying nothing for a few moments, he rose to his feet, walked around the table, and stood facing Koshovy, his arms folded across his chest.

Now he was looking at his interlocutor from above, which made Klym feel uncomfortable, so he too stood up to be on an equal footing with Mr. Olshansky.

"There was a reason I mentioned spies, Mr. Koshovy. You were detained not because you were the first person to see the body of lawyer Soyka. You came to him from abroad. You are a subject of the Russian Tsar unless you simply decide to change your citizenship. Of course, you had no way of knowing that an order went out recently, that all Russian subjects that Mr. Soyka comes into contact with be put onto a watch list. The instruction was sent to everyone in the police department."

"I don't understand a thing," Klym admitted honestly.

"Lately the deceased maintained some rather suspicious connections. To check and verify their bona fides is not within our competency," explained Olshansky. "That is, if we are to be absolutely correct in our definition, the political police determined that their local informers were in touch with Mr. Soyka. He was not being specifically monitored. But he came to the attention of the police because of his lack of discrimination in whom he dealt with. Which had been one of his faults for quite some time. You knew him in Kyiv. Tell me, did he have a dubious clientele there as well?"

"You and I are legal people," Koshovy replied, and noticed how the investigator's eyebrows shot up in surprise, so he quickly explained: "I'm a lawyer, you're an investigator, we both work in the legal system. We studied law at different times, in different places, but the law is the law."

"Excuse me sir, why are you telling me this now?"

"The criminal police mostly have to deal with not quite the best representatives of our society. Maybe you'd prefer your official duties to include listening to poetry or visiting the opera each evening," Klym felt he was warming to his topic, and his eye twitched more strongly. "However, into this office they bring those who have committed a crime, or know something about a crime that has been committed. So, whichever way you look at it, they are people of dubious character, agreed?"

The investigator rubbed the bridge of his nose and pushed up his glasses.

"An interesting approach. An original interpretation. Strange, but you're right. Only what are you trying to prove, except that you are right?"

"Lawyers too, Mr. Olshansky, for the most part, are unable to choose the people they have professional dealings with. Prosecutors accuse. Lawyers defend. For both of us a person is either a criminal, or he simply has a dubious reputation. Until, of course, the defense has done its best to prove otherwise. Thus, from the point of view of the police, the client base of any lawyer is always questionable. Isn't that right?"

"Very clever," the fellow nodded. "On the other hand, what you have just said is nothing more than a typical example of demagogy. Lawyers are masters of the art of professionally pulling the wool over people's eyes. To call black white is your hobby-horse."

"*Mine?*"

"Of lawyers. All of you."

"In that case, forgive me, but the hobby-horse of police investigators and prosecutors is to call white black. We extol people, while you try to vilify them. Like me, for example."

"Why do I want to vilify you?"

"You suspect me of God knows what, only because of my acquaintance with the victim. Who has managed to earn, as I've understood, not the best of reputations. Meanwhile, my arrival here is not at all suspicious. If Mr. Soyka hasn't destroyed my letters to him, you can find them among his papers. And read there about my interest in coming to Lviv and requesting him to give me a helping hand at the start. Why I left Kyiv is a separate conversation. And it has nothing to do with what has transpired here."

"You think logically, Mr. Koshovy," the investigator agreed once more. "However, I have similarly explained the reason you have been detained. Of course, no one suspects you of involvement in Mr. Genyk's suicide."

"Suicide?"

"That is the preliminary finding."

Olshansky returned to his desk, which allowed Klym to sit down again and make himself more comfortable. The investigator moved a large cardboard folder toward himself, opened it, adjusted his glasses, pulled out a sheet of paper covered in handwriting from underneath, and cleared his throat.

"So, there were no signs of violence on the body. A shot to the temple, at close range. Alcohol was consumed prior to this, there was a carafe of liqueur on the table. Looks like he had arrived at his decision and had a drink

to give him courage. Given his questionable connections and the interest
the relevant authorities have shown in him, Mr. Soyka decided that to end
his life was the best way out. Now it only remains to learn what prompted
him to shoot himself in the head. The case will be closed and the matter
handed over to the political investigation group. It seems to me that finding
the reasons for such things is their specialty."

His eye twitched strongly.

"Quite possibly so," agreed Koshovy. "I'm new here, I arrived in the city
only this morning, and have never been here before. You probably know
more than me. And the investigation may reveal more than is evident now.
Only this isn't a case of suicide."

The bridge of the glasses once more slipped down the investigator's nose.
The next question sounded very naive:

"So, what happened then, according to you?"

"Not according to me. This is no assumption, Mr. Olshansky. Murder,
a typical murder inside a locked room. Like in books, where they often
dream up such things."

"You're dreaming now too, after reading too many books."

"I'm not dreaming anything up. The lawyer Yevhen Soyka was killed.
And you'll be investigating a murder."

"So it's like that!" he suddenly heard behind him.

The words were unexpected, and Klym sat up with a jolt, as if someone
had fired a gun next to his ear.

The voice behind him continued:

"Murder, you say? It would be interesting to hear how you arrived at
such a conclusion."

The woman had walked through the wall.

At least that is what it seemed like to Koshovy the moment he turned
to face the voice and saw that the woman was not behind his back, but to
his left. There was yet another factor: the door to the office creaked. It was
a nasty sound and Klym had thought earlier – why don't they call someone
in to oil the hinge. So, he would have surely heard, if someone had opened
the door on entering. But the woman had appeared as if out of thin air.

Of course, that was impossible. Just as she couldn't have walked through
the wall, for she was no ghost or specter, but a real live flesh and blood

                                   ANDRIY KOKOTIUKHA

person. And besides, she was enveloped in an invisible, although an easily perceptible cloud of an extremely delicate, refined aroma. The stranger had particularly good taste, and this was manifested not only by the fragrance she wore.

She was dressed immaculately.

And Klym, who had never considered himself a great connoisseur of fashion, nevertheless noticed that the lady had herself provided instructions to her tailor. While striving to follow the latest trends in fashion, she nevertheless retained the right to individual convenience. The Moderne style, which was lately popular among ladies, some of them advanced in age, demanded the narrowness of the waist to be emphasized. Her dress was black, but did not look austere, and did not make its owner look gloomy or sinister. On the contrary, even the color black could give off a soft velvety tone. And the wide gray belt seemed to divide her torso in two exactly in the middle, and only made her clothes look more stylish, strangely emphasizing the stranger's contradictory nature.

The upper part had quite a large neckline to emphasize the roundness of her white shoulders and did not disguise the breasts too much – yet despite this the cut was not too revealing, thus did not give free rein to impudent and shameless male eyes. The woman left men unlimited room for imagination. The lower part of the dress, on the other hand, went somewhat against accepted fashion. The skirt, contrary to its requirements, was designed and sewn so as not to restrain, but to allow her free movement.

Looking closer, Klym noticed a pattern – a thin vine curled from the edges of the dress up around the waist, disappearing under the belt and emerging again to chastely, while at the same time boldly, wrap around the bodice.

The path of the vine was outlined by tiny beads. The woman's hands were hidden inside thin black semi-transparent gloves, and there was a massive rhinestone bracelet around her left wrist. Her right hand played with a folded fan, which she lightly slapped against her left palm. Her chestnut brown hair was hidden under an elegant hat with a brim that was not too wide, which, as Klym involuntarily noted, often restricted women to some extent, making them not that graceful.

This woman always wants to feel comfortable and achieves her goal, concluded Klym.

Seeing how Olshansky jumped to his feet upon her appearance, almost tipping over his chair in the process, Klym realized that this woman had not entered by chance. And her appearance, as well as her very persona, had a huge, hitherto unexplained significance for the investigator. Rising to his feet as well, Klym waited until the policeman had bowed and kiss her obligingly offered hand, and in this short period of time, understood that she had not appeared out of thin air or through a wall. Like all people, she had entered through a door. Its rectangle could be made out in the wall, well disguised, and merged with the paint.

It meant there was a secret room fashioned here. People sitting there could hear conversations taking place in this room. That part was understandable, except for one thing: who was this woman, who was allowed to overhear what was said during interrogations? And it appeared the criminal police investigator also accepted it as an honor. If that was the case, then the chief of police must also know about this practice, for without his knowledge hardly anything would happen in the department.

Hurriedly piecing the facts together, Koshovy arrived at the only possible conclusion: the woman, who had intervened in the interrogation, for some strange reason had a significant influence among the police. And unprecedented rights and opportunities, which was unusual for a woman. Quite a mystery, if one took her age into account – she looked like she was Koshovy's age or perhaps a little younger.

There were no more chairs in the office. Klym grabbed the back of his chair, wanting to offer the lady a seat, but she waved her fan and shook her head, coming up to the bench on which stood his disemboweled travel bag, effortlessly shifted his rags to one side, and settled down, elegantly crossing one leg over the other.

"Please sit, gentlemen," the voice turned out to be throaty, ever so slightly hoarse, and, when the men returned to their places, she repeated, this time addressing Koshovy: "You say Genyk Soyka was murdered. Why?"

"I have no idea," Klym blurted out. "It's for the police to find out the circumstances. To find a motive, likely suspects…"

"The police know their job," the woman interrupted him curtly. "They will do everything that needs to be done. Explain to me, why you discount suicide. Because I too," now the gray eyes looked at Olshansky, "am of the same opinion."

"Mrs. Bohdanovych, but what about the facts!" the investigator grew restless. "That is… There are no facts! The door was locked from the inside! The first floor windows were also closed! The liqueur on the table, the gun in his hand, the bullet in his head! No signs of a struggle, Mrs. Magda! It's all cut and dried!"

"Mr. Olshansky, my late husband always warned against seeking simple answers to complex questions," the woman said. "I have discounted suicide, because I was personally acquainted with lawyer Soyka. A rooster would have laid an egg, before Mr. Genyk would have done himself in. However, my female intuition and experience of associating with the deceased are not enough for the police. Who, if not me, knows this?"

"Exactly," Olshansky picked up on her tone of voice. "Who, but you, Mrs. Magda."

"You probably have an explanation, Mr. Koshovy," the mysterious lady again transferred her gaze to Klym. "Don't be surprised, I saw your passport. You've hardly used it. It's brand new, recently issued, as I understand."

"It's my first trip abroad," he muttered, then blurted out completely inappropriately: "I haven't even been to Paris, and all my acquaintances travel there, as if on a pilgrimage…"

"What has Paris and pilgrimages to do with it?" Magda's thin painted eyebrows shot up. "I've been to Paris. But I see nothing special about going there. We subjects of His Imperial Majesty can travel freely throughout Europe. I've been thinking of going to the New World, so as not to…" at this point she grew silent, and waved her fan, as if driving away any unnecessary chatter. "So, I beg you, dispel my doubts. If you can declare so confidently that the lawyer from Lychakiv Street was murdered, it means you know more than the police. We are all ears."

Now two expectant pairs of eyes were looking at Klym.

He cleared his throat into his fist, immediately sensing his own importance.

"Well, if that's the case… It's been a while since I've seen Yevhen… Mr. Soyka. We've only corresponded. However, as you heard, I used to work for him as an assistant. I got to know some of his habits. And I don't think that he changed them during the years that he spent here in Europe, in Lviv."

"What do you mean by that?"

"I had more time than the police to examine the apartment," explained Koshovy. "While the police were being fetched, I remained in the apartment to guard it, to stop anyone else from coming in. I myself didn't believe it was suicide. However, like I said, I hadn't been in close contact with Mr. Soyka for quite some time. Something might have changed. But if you, Mrs. ... Bohdanovych, right?"

"Correct. Continue."

"Aha, so then, if you, Mrs. Bohdanovych, knew him well enough to also reject the assumption of a bullet to the head, he must have really remained unchanged in his attitude to life. Of course, bare suppositions are not enough. So, I took the liberty of examining the apartment before the police arrived. Mr. Olshansky, there's no need to look at me like that – I was about to share my thoughts with you and outline my conclusions."

"We're all ears," Magda spurred him on.

"First of all – someone had been in the apartment," said Klym. "One person at least, a grown man. Not a close friend, but some significant person. Perhaps an important client, or a business associate."

"What do you base this on?"

For clarity, Koshovy inhaled through his nose.

"Smells, Mrs. Bohdanovych," he explained, finally realizing he was reporting to her, since for unknown reasons the investigator was limiting himself to the passive function of a listener. "In the room adjacent to his office, which Soyka used as a bedroom, as I understand, someone had been smoking for a while. The tobacco was quite strong, the smell was pervasive, sharp, if you'll pardon me, madam, foul. Mr. Soyka did not smoke such cigarettes, he preferred aromatic tobacco, something much more refined. Only the visitor could have smoked such cigarettes, but why was the smell so pervasive, that it lasted until morning? You were right, Mr. Olshansky, because the bedroom window was closed, and rather tightly at that. And one more conclusion – the visitor spent quite a bit of time in the lawyer's apartment since it smelled so strongly of tobacco smoke. The window didn't help, which Mr. Soyka must have opened. I heard that it was quite unusually stifling weather for Lviv yesterday. The place couldn't be aired out properly, there was no draft, I mean where could it have appeared from.

"Judging by his behavior, Mr. Genyk, as he is called here, had secrets. Let's say he didn't want that Cerberus at the entrance to see his guest. Besides, I saw with my own eyes – there were no signs of a struggle. Soyka allowed his killer to approach him. So, he was not startled that this fellow had come in through the window, rather than the door. They might have even agreed to meet this way… Having carried out his deed, the killer left, and I came. Only he did everything to make it look as if the victim's apartment was closed everywhere from the inside. Murder inside a locked room, I'm telling you. A classic of the genre."

"This is just an assumption," grunted Olshansky.

"Correct. And to continue the investigation, to check the facts and establish the truth is the work of the police. Granted, it might seem that I have the gumption to be telling you how to do your work in your city and in your country…"

"It's obvious that you are a lawyer," the investigator interrupted him. "You're just as slick with your tongue, as the late Mr. Soyka. Like the rest of your lively ilk…"

"Mr. Olshansky," said Magda, again lightly tapping her fan against her left palm, "the lawyer Koshovy is a witness, not a suspect. As you know, I don't know much about police work. However, my late husband would have taken notice of the words of this man. Agreed?"

"No one knew the respected Mr. Gustav better than you, Mrs. Magda," Klym heard notes of obeisance and surrender in the investigator's voice. "Honestly, it's even better this way."

"Which way?" Magda pierced him with her glare.

"Murder."

"Better that Soyka was murdered?" Koshovy blurted out.

Olshansky blushed, for a moment or so lost control, but then quickly reigned in his feelings and explained:

"Suicide is a great sin, sir. Those who settle accounts with life voluntarily, throw down a challenge to the Creator Himself. This way Mr. Yevhen Soyka is the victim of a horrible crime. He will be buried with dignity, there will be no problems, as is the case with suicides. The police will search for the perpetrator. All the same… Your suppositions alone, sir, are hardly enough."

Koshovy shrugged his shoulders.

"Then accept some more gifts, I'm not ungenerous," he looked at Magda as he spoke, again as if reporting to her: "People who commit suicide leave behind notes. Or blame the whole world for their death, or they say their farewells, without pointing the finger at anyone. No epistle was found near the body. The rubbish bin was empty."

"Could be one of those instances where he was unable to write a parting message," Olshansky noted.

"Could be," Klym was quick to agree. "But there's also the matter of the gun."

"The deceased was holding it in his hand."

Koshovy shook his head.

"He wasn't. When a person shoots themselves in the head, they don't fall to the ground the way Soyka was lying on the floor. With arms spread out like wings. Pointing in different directions and spread quite wide apart. The gun could have dropped to the ground. Or it could have remained in his right hand. But in either case the hand would inevitably have been pressed against the body. Either the left hand, or the right one," Klym spoke, choosing his words carefully, so that what he said sounded as accurate as possible and he would not be misunderstood: "I carefully inspected the body while I was waiting for the police. The gun was *placed* under the right hand. Strange, that the police didn't pick this up…"

CHAPTER SIX
TWENTY KRONER AND JEWISH LUCK

Klym stepped out of the police station into the street feeling as if he had been acquitted and released.

But his mood had deteriorated, compared to the way he had felt that morning. The novelty effect had already worn off. The euphoria he had experienced upon arriving, not only in a new city or a new place, but having arrived in a completely different world, had already disappeared. Right now he felt defeated. He imagined himself inside a cramped prison cell, from which there was no way out. What had been unfamiliar, but interesting, over the past few hours had become foreign and hostile. The city had defeated him, immersing him in its customs and linguistic diversity, proposing different, but no less strict laws of existence.

After all, it was not just about Yevhen Soyka's sudden death, the only person whom Klym knew here and whose advice he had expected to rely on initially. In his letter the lawyer had written that upon arrival his younger colleague could stay with him, until he found his feet. He promised to help him. He hinted that he needed an assistant in Lviv. Koshovy could grow used to this new place and this new country, and eventually maybe even be able to set up his own practice, as he had anticipated.

However, acquaintances and experiences were things which were acquired. Soyka's murder was a tragic coincidence, and as a result Klym was left without a roof over his head. And, most importantly, without any money, and therefore without the means to rent a room.

There could be no question of returning to Kyiv. He might not be arrested straight away. But he would continue to have problems, and not him alone. He had been blacklisted, so at best he would have to find work as a janitor or laborer, and at worst – travel far into the depths of Siberia and live in exile under police supervision. For some reason it seemed to Koshovy that he would be sent into the cold backwoods: that was one way for the authorities to be able to proudly report on the successful fight with unreliable elements.

No, he would not return, that was out of the question. At least in the ensuing years.

Besides, he had no money, not even for a cheap ticket. And pawning off his things was also not a way out, for his travel bag was probably the only valuable thing he had. For this reason, Klym was in no hurry to leave the police station, and loitered about on the paved sidewalk, swinging his repacked travel bag about. He simply had nowhere to go. And he had no thoughts regarding what he might do.

"Young man!" he heard behind him.

It was Shatsky. Unlike Klym, the fellow exuded satisfaction and at the same time looked anxious, focused, and full of energy. As he drew closer, Koshovy noticed something which had eluded him in the badly lit cell: small unruly patches of hair protruded from Jozef's ears and nostrils. Together with his bushy eyebrows, it made him look like some fairy-tale forest creature, which had just shaken off leaves and moss, and donned a shabby city suit and hat.

"You've been released, Mr. Shatsky?"

"Even better, Mr. Koshovy – I've been acquitted!"

"But, as far as I could understand, you were never officially accused of anything, for these charges to be dropped."

"They apologized to Shatsky!" he declared solemnly, straightening his shoulders and pressing his skinny chest forward. "I demanded they write on watermarked paper, that there was no evidence that I conducted illegal abortions! I'll show it to my Esther. Because she already knows why the police detained me in front of everyone in Krakidaly! Right now this is big news back there, and I'll give them something more to talk about for another day."

"How's that?"

"It's like this! Right now the Jews of Krakidaly, if not every Jew in Lviv, are discussing the vileness of your faithful servant. The women are heaping pity on my Esther and our children, who, it appears, have such an unscrupulous father. But now these very same Jews will begin to think out loud, who could have slandered Shatsky, dragging his honest name through the filthiest dirt in town! I'm telling you, their boredom will disappear in a flash!"

"And they gave you the document?"

"They wouldn't dare not to!" Jozef wanted to retrieve the piece of paper from his pocket and to show it off, but changed his mind at the last moment, and only slapped his hand against the spot in his jacket where he had an inner pocket. "Excuse me, but I know my rights! You can congratulate me!"

Klym offered his hand to Shatsky, which the fellow grabbed tightly, squeezing it and shaking it vigorously. He was about to add something – and suddenly froze, without letting go of Klym's right hand. Catching his gaze, Koshovy saw Magda Bohdanovych.

A stout mustached fellow in uniform had personally opened the door for the young lady. Of high rank, no less. A policeman at the entrance stood at attention, saluted, and Magda waved her fan in his direction, making it clear that she had noticed and appreciated his gesture. At this point a covered phaeton arrived. While Mrs. Bohdanovych leaned on the kindly outstretched arm of the man accompanying her and got into the carriage, the investigator Olshansky came out of the building, for some reason showing the policeman standing outside a clenched fist. Magda was already in the carriage, the mustached fellow pressed his lips against her gloved wrist, Olshansky bowed, even clicking his heels, which was done quite elegantly. The coachman tugged at the reins, the phaeton set off, and its female passenger nodded in farewell to the police officials.

Waiting until the female guest had disappeared around the nearest corner, the fat fellow, who seemed more senior than Olshansky, glanced in Koshovy's direction. From where he stood Klym noticed that his look was not affable. The young lawyer could not understand what the senior police chief had against him personally. Meanwhile, the mustached fellow grunted something to the investigator and returned inside the building, no longer taking any notice of Klym.

"Mr. Poniatowski," Shatsky announced.

"Who is he?"

"Tomasz Poniatowski, head of the Criminal Police Department," Jozef explained eagerly. "But if at this moment some other police official had been present, dear sir, Mrs. Magda would have been seen off just as ceremoniously. The city's mayor himself greets her. And the police reckon with her, no matter what department they are from. Forget the police, Mr. Koshovy! More than half the deputies in the sejm kiss Mrs. Bohdanovych's hand!"

"Does she have an influential husband?"

Before Shatsky had a chance to answer, the investigator made his way toward them, loosening his tie as he approached. Jozef brought his index and middle fingers together, touching the brim of his hat, and enacted a slight bow.

"Kindly accept my regards, Mr. Olshansky! How is your second lower molar?"

"Leave us for a moment, Mr. Shatsky," the fellow said through gritted teeth, ignoring the remark.

After the dentist had obediently moved away, he stood before Klym, having slipped the bent thumbs of both hands into the side pockets of his vest. This made him look even more like a large cricket. Looking straight into Koshovy's eyes through the round lenses of his glasses, he spoke in a tone that did not foreshadow a conversation. This was how mandatory instructions were read out.

"You are a very attentive and observant person, Mr. Koshovy. Just don't expect that the criminal police will thank you nicely for this. Or even take you on as a consultant. Mrs. Bohdanovych considers your conclusions worthy of attention. Because of this the police will be searching for Soyka's killers… if no evidence surfaces during the investigation to show that he did in fact commit suicide. But he will be given a proper burial. At least here you've saved the reputation of your older colleague. Therefore, I advise you, and not only on behalf of myself, but on behalf of the management of the department not to meddle in police matters anymore. Your reward for this assistance – your identity will not be checked as scrupulously as Mr. Genyk's close acquaintances deserve. Even though you have not seen one another for many years. For us, this fact means nothing and does not excuse you."

His eye twitched strongly.

"Excuse me? I'm guilty just because I knew the lawyer Soyka in the past and worked with him?"

"Allow me to explain nothing more to you, Mr. Koshovy," the investigator declared. "Otherwise you will once more want to meddle in matters which are of no concern to you. And here," his right hand fished out a banknote folded several times from his vest pocket: "There's twenty kroner here. You were robbed, but you assisted the police. Consider this a small reward from the department. To be left without money in Lviv, and with no friends or roof over your head is dangerous, not only from the point of view of morality, but also from the point of view of the law. You might suddenly have the urge to obtain a penny or two by illegal means."

Freeing his left hand, Olshansky took Klym by the right wrist, placed the banknote into his palm, pressed his fingers on top, and let go. Only then did he take a step back and wave his hand.

"I wish you success, Mr. Koshovy. And hope that we never meet again under such sad circumstances. It is probably better for us to meet such smart people less frequently."

With these words the investigator turned around and unhurriedly returned to the police department building. Before he had disappeared inside, Shatsky was already standing beside Klym, tugging at his elbow:

"What's wrong? What did he say?"

"It seems, the lawyer Soyka was not well respected in the police department," Koshovy said pensively, unclenching his fist. "And it seems, the civil servant slipped me a handout, so that I clear out of here as quickly as possible. Have policemen ever given you bribes, Mr. Shatsky?"

"I'm not sure what you would call the money, which they pay Shatsky to bring order in their mouths," sighed Jozef. "Too little for the work done, as my Esther says. Although she is convinced, that I generally don't value myself highly enough. Otherwise I would have long ago been in possession of all the gold in the world. But they pay me enough, to maintain my clientele. Chickens peck one grain at a time, young man, and you see before you just one such chicken… Why are we standing here?"

"Off you go," sighed Klym, continuing to squeeze the bill in his hand. "Don't let me hold you up."

"I'll be off," agreed Shatsky. "And where will you be headed? Recalling your unhappy incident, these twenty crowns can be considered a gift from heaven. Although it's not enough to survive on for long."

"An astute observation," Koshovy agreed. "Do you have any suggestions, Mr. Shatsky?"

"I invite you to come visit me, since you have no other plans," Jozef made an inviting gesture with an aristocratic flourish of his wrist. "You'll be able to see where I live. And we'll try to persuade my Esther to feed you. Because I could hear the growling in your stomach when we were still in the cell together. And then, you'll probably want to find out why the bigwigs of this city tremble so much before Mrs. Magda Bohdanovych."

"It intrigues me," Klym smiled, slipping the money into his pocket. "I'm probably not so interested in the persona of Mrs. Magda, as the prospect of sinking my teeth into something. I have no choice. After you, Mr. Shatsky."

The dentist smacked his lips.

"You know, you and I have experienced a lot of injustice in a very short time. We were imprisoned, which is completely unacceptable for an innocent person. Therefore, it appears to me, that a closer relationship needs to be established between us. More trusting."

"Maybe," Koshovy announced carefully. "But… why are you saying this now…"

"Because, young man: I suggest from now on we stop addressing each other *formally*. Simply call me Shatsky. Or, even better, Jozef. I appreciate your Ruthenian aristocratic values, but I detest formality. Agreed?"

Klym wordlessly shook his proffered hand.

They went on foot.

At first Koshovy wanted to continue talking, for he had too many questions for his unexpected guide and savior. He already understood: this Jewish man was not the simple fellow he tried to make himself out to be. He knew quite a few things, and the source of his knowledge, Klym sensed, would long remain a riddle to him. Something told him that until he had resolved what he would be doing in the near future, he would need to stay close to Shatsky, whether he wanted to or not. Jozef himself was obviously rejoicing at his mission, and this made Klym arrive at a strange conclusion: for a dentist who praised himself to everyone, the last thing he wanted to do was fix teeth. At any rate, poking about in other people's mouths every day was not exactly what Shatsky wanted to dedicate his entire active life to, or at least the better part of it.

But soon after they left, all desire to talk had disappeared. From early that morning Klym had experienced so many adventures in this unfamiliar, completely foreign city, that he already involuntarily considered himself an integral part of it – up until the moment Jozef began to lead him along the city's narrow winding streets. Koshovy felt lost once more, although he had a guide: he realized that left to his own devices, he would never be able to find his way out of this place, which he had already christened an enormous stone maze. The feeling of helplessness was highlighted by the fact that the old part of the city was alive. People calmly made their way along such streets. Some were rushing off on business, some were just out walking, but all the passers-by felt free, as if they were at home.

Actually, they all were at home. Klym's head was spinning from the knowledge that he was the only such person here for many blocks around, if not in the whole of Lviv. An adult, with a higher education, literate – and yet all the same he felt like a child thrown into the deep end of a pond. If you want to make your way out – learn to swim. For God's sake, he had no strength left to swim, only a desire to sink. The locals were full of self-respect, self-confidence, and they were somewhat arrogant.

At least this was Klym's first impression.

If it wasn't for the fear of becoming hopelessly lost among these gray stone walls and the humiliation of needing to ask for help, Koshovy would not have been filled with despair. Even in the jail cells of Kosy Kaponir he had felt a lot more at ease: the authorities knew about the prisoner, his fate would be decided one way or another, so just sit back and wait patiently, if you have no desire to escape. But now, being at large, Klym did not feel completely at ease.

This was why he had grown silent, moving in Shatsky's wake, afraid to lose his guide and meanwhile trying to recall the name of every street, every turn, to memorize the entire route. Focusing his attention on this, completely immersed in his familiarization of the city, Koshovy decided not to distract himself with talk that was necessary, useful, and interesting, but at this moment – superfluous.

For his part, Jozef also did not try to keep the conversation going. The apparent security he felt had disappeared for a short time and he was thinking his own thoughts, which did not stop him from perfectly navigating the streets, lanes, and alleys along which he now led his guest. Only after they had emerged, after one last turn, onto the avenue, did Koshovy realize that in fact they had not been walking for as long as he had thought. On the contrary, Shatsky had brought his companion to the central part of Lviv along a shorter route. A streetcar clanged past them on the rails, and after it had passed, Jozef indicated the broad boulevard, which opened before Klym's eyes.

"Please be acquainted, we are in the heart of Lviv. Hetmanski Valy, that is what people call this place here. I still remember the time when the Poltva River flowed where the boulevard is now."

"River?"

"Once vessels navigated along it," nodded Shatsky. "But for twenty years now it's been underground, like the Styx. Except perhaps that it does not lead to the realm of the dead, although who knows, I can't vouch for that. The city's residents complained: there were flies, insects, and after a flood – mud and silt in which carriages became stuck and young ladies sullied their dresses. Which was why they hid it," he tapped himself lightly on the chest. "I saw it all happen with my own eyes. While today my elder son cannot even imagine that at one time these here streets were two banks of a river. We need to go this way, we're almost there. Just a little longer."

Shatsky's hand pointed toward a grand, not so much festive, as more a majestic building, which Klym unmistakably guessed was the theater.

"The opera house," Jozef seemed to have read his thoughts. "It hides the districts behind it. Evil tongues say the opera house was deliberately built this way, so that the beauty of it caught one's eye, and hid what was behind it."

"Is it really that bad?" Koshovy tried to joke, not quite understanding what the joke was about.

"Beyond it is a district inhabited mainly by Jewish rabble, although the largest and cheapest local markets are there," explained Shatsky without a shadow of a smile. "It should be inhabited by more wealthy people. Because they engage in business, buying everything and selling everything. You'd expect them to have money. Only for some reason they don't have too many kroner, but plenty of kreutzers. Maybe that's what Jewish good fortune looks like in Krakidaly. Although there are places, where that fortune appears different," having said this, Jozef immediately stretched his large hands in front of him, palms forward, as if defending himself, and quickly chattered: "Only God forbid, lest someone should complain! We have the destiny we deserve. We rejoice that the Lord sends us what we have, and that it's enough to feed the family."

Suddenly ending the topic, which he must not have found very pleasant, Shatsky set off in the direction of the Opera House. Klym had no choice but to follow him.

Walking around the theater building and coming to the back of it, they almost immediately found themselves in a place where life did not look as calm and prudent as it had in front of its facade. Seeing before him a boisterous, noisy human anthill, Koshovy stopped for a moment.

His fear of becoming lost in the maze of the city's streets was replaced by an even greater fear of becoming lost in this crowd. For it seemed that here everyone was selling everything, and that now this swirling mass of humanity would engulf him, utterly confusing him. For the most part they were Jews, for the most part men, young and not so young, with sidelocks and beards, not always smartly dressed, but every one of them nimble, vehemently urging customers to buy their wares. The trading activity did not resemble an Eastern bazaar – Klym had visited Turkestan – for the commotion here was an order of magnitude less. But all the same, for someone unused to such a spectacle, it resembled a single living organism. Which, it appeared, would never rest.

The wild mix of languages astonished him: Polish was heard just as often as Yiddish. Klym had visited places were Jews had settled, hearing how they talked among themselves, and after that at least no longer referred to their language as *Jewish*, as it was defined in the Russian Empire. Praising their wares, bargaining desperately, arguing, and finally slapping hands, having agreed on a price, people in this large market understood each other perfectly. Even German was added to the bouquet of languages, recognizable by its clipped phrases, and on the rare occasion one heard Ukrainian.

When the initial fear of becoming lost in this noisy crowd passed, Klym sensed a new feeling slowly begin to take hold of him. He suddenly had the urge to become lost, to dissolve into the crowd: the very reason why he had hastily left Kyiv, or if one were to call a spade a spade, why he had fled. Meanwhile Shatsky became noticeably livelier, obviously finding himself in a familiar environment, feeling safe now among his own people. Although Klym couldn't understand what exactly might have threatened the middle-aged dentist.

Ordering Koshovy to stay at his side, he dived into the tumultuous crowd, greeting practically every third person as he moved along, managing to ask some about business matters, others about the health of their children, and still others how their teeth were going, and if they had toothache, he urged them not to delay and to come and see him straight away. Weaving among the traders and buyers with the agility of a river pilot, capable of helping ships navigate the most difficult and treacherous fairways, Jozef crossed a square and turned into the nearest street. Now Klym was unable to keep up with him in the crowd and had to call out for his guide to stop. The fellow waited patiently, and when Koshovy caught up, slightly out of breath, he explained, indicating the direction they needed to move in with a nod of his head:

"Please sir, look and remember. It's hard to get lost. Here, if you please, is the synagogue. Next to it is the mikvah, the Jewish baths. If you are on your own and looking for my place, simply ask for Lazneva Street[32], anyone here can direct you there. Beyond it is Lamana Street. And it totally reflects its name[33]. Let's go then."

It was not so noisy beyond the market square, although there were shops with traders here too. Although the number of shops was far greater than Koshovy had observed in the central, more *respectable* part of Lviv, and was roughly the same as he had seen in the Podil district of Kyiv, which in recent times was becoming an important and integral extension of the city. Marching down Lazneva Street, Shatsky continued to greet people to the right and left, at times barely raising his hat, and at times merely bringing his fingers to its brim. His mood had already noticeably improved.

Turning into his Lamana Street, he suddenly stopped dead in his tracks. Not expecting the change of pace, Klym, who was hurrying behind him, ran into him, bumping his guide in the back. Recovering quickly, he immediately apologized. But Jozef had suddenly lost all interest in his guest, at least for a short while. Koshovy first heard the voice:

"Aha, Shatsky, so you've finally come home?" and only after this did he see the woman to whom the voice belonged.

She stood before them in the middle of the street, on the cobblestone pavement, setting her strong feet apart, wearing clodhopper shoes with blunt toes. It appeared as if she was digging her heels into the cobblestones,

32   Literally 'Bathhouse Street'.
33   Literally 'Broken Street'.

preparing to stop an enemy attack, and intending to remain standing afterward. She was of average height, practically the same height as the startled Shatsky, only his hat probably made him look slightly taller. The only difference was that this no longer young woman had filled out a little, which together with her arms pressing into her sides gave her a militant look. The lower part of her no-longer-new white blouse, which was nevertheless spotlessly clean and buttoned up to her neck, disappeared into a broad tartan skirt. Her neck was adorned with a simple necklace, her hair, the color of thick resin, was twisted into a knot on her head and resembled a large lump.

Knowing what was about to come and attempting to forestall the verbal waterfall, Jozef stretched his arms out toward her, as if defending himself with his outstretched hands:

"Esther! Don't say anything, Esther! I was acquitted and released! Do you really think that the police set people free if they're guilty of something? Don't you know what imperial justice is?"

"And what is it?" Esther Shatska asked menacingly.

"It is propriety! Law and order! And anyway, you know yourself –there are enough of those in Lviv now who need to be put behind bars! Schlimazels with bombs and guns who are completely devoid of all shame! Should Shatsky occupy someone else's place in the clink!"

Only now did Klym notice that the meeting of the Shatskys was being watched with interest if not by the entire street, then at the very least by the residents of the nearby houses. Sensing that some of the attention of the local Jews was being directed at himself, he became embarrassed once more, shrugged, and grabbed firmer hold of the handles of his travel bag – as if this might have helped in some way or saved him from something.

Meanwhile Esther began to advance toward Jozef.

"Maybe I don't have the slightest idea of what this imperial justice is about," she said sternly. "But in that case, Shatsky, you have disappointed me even more! Because I can see, you don't know your wife very well, with whom you've lived for twelve years with God's help! How am I supposed to react to that?"

"Esther, don't tell me I don't know you! Shatsky knows half of Lviv…"

"…and the rest know Shatsky himself!" Esther completed the saying he had already heard earlier that day. "But your wife is an exception! You know everyone except for your own wife, Shatsky!"

"The Lord protect you, Esther! How on earth did such a thing even enter your head!"

"If you knew me, Shatsky, the way I know you, you'd understand that no sooner did they let you out, than rumors of your release already reached me. Mazel tov! If you had been released, it means you didn't do what you were accused of doing by that slandering Lapidus!"

"So it was Lapidus!"

"You could have guessed! Ever since he opened his own practice in the district, he's been trying hard to get rid of a competitor like you. He wags that sticky tongue of his about, may it fall off, in front of all and sundry, wherever and whatever comes to mind! The schlimazel doesn't know that the only person who is capable of destroying Shatsky is Jozef himself!"

"There you go again, Esther! And in front of everyone!"

"Do you think people know nothing about you? For the past twelve years, ever since our first child was born, I have been trying to find where you've buried your talents. And I can't for the life of me work out why you don't want to unearth them! And weren't you able to guess, that your Esther would learn about your innocence? How poorly you think of your wife, Shatsky! That's why you didn't hurry home as soon as they let you out! Didn't the police feed you? Or do they feed people better in prison now, than at home? Then I heartily apologize, my dear, go back there, let them feed you!"

"What made you think that I wasn't in a hurry to return home, Esther? On the contrary, I was very much in a hurry, so that I could comfort you and the whole street with the good news: Shatsky does not perform back-yard abortions! And I still need to have a serious conversation with that rascal Lapidus…"

Esther clapped her hands, calling on the neighbors to be her witness:

"Look at him, fellow Jews! Listen to him! Think I don't know where they held you? Don't I know, how long it takes to walk home from the police department? You should have returned two hours ago, Shatsky! Where have you been? Were you afraid to come home? Ah, not sure of yourself? So Lapidus was onto something, and you've got a guilty conscience, hah?"

This time Jozef turned around to Koshovy, seeking his support.

"Esther, I know you very well! As always, at first you're suspicious and you mete out blame, and only later do you listen calmly to how things really were. While their daddy was away, the children must have gotten on your nerves, my feigale[34]! I'll explain: I waited until they released this schikets[35]! He needs help. He was robbed by those mishigas[36], the batiars. He has nowhere to go, and he's probably hungry as well. Because, unlike me, he had no breakfast, and was taken to the police station directly from the railway station."

Esther Shatska's righteous anger immediately changed to mercy, as if with the wave of a magic wand. Her face, so stern only a moment ago, spread into a broad smile, and Klym saw that she was younger than she appeared.

"Is he hungry? Vey, Jozef, why did you not say that straight away? So you hung around there so you could invite this young man home? You're a bigger schlimazel[37] than that Lapidus, that's what I'll tell you! You should have warned me that we would be having guests."

"How could I have, my feigale..."

"Quiet, Shatsky. You spoke, I heard. Does our guest have a name? Or will you keep calling him a schikets?"

Jozef cleared his throat for authority.

"Please be acquainted. Esther – the best thing that I have in my home. Apart from the children, of course. The young man's name is Klym. He..."

"Stop pestering people, Shatsky. Invite the young man in, because no matter who he is – he has no right to remain hungry, once he finds himself in Krakidaly."

34   Feigale (Yiddish) – little bird.

35   Schikets (Yiddish) – young man, youth.

36   Mishigas (Yiddish) – abnormal, insane.

37   Schlimazel (Yiddish) – a consistently unlucky or accident-prone person.

CHAPTER SEVEN
HERRINGS ON APPLE

Koshovy didn't expect to find any luxuries in the dentist's home.

So, he wasn't at all surprised, coming into the ground-floor apartment of a rather neglected apartment building. It would have been quite spacious here, for the rooms were much larger than was usually the case in buildings in the poor quarters of the city. Obviously the good dentist Shatsky must have had a decent practice, to be able to choose the better from among the worse dwellings, because the owner had also installed a water closet here. However, the space was terribly cluttered.

The only place Shatsky kept more or less in order was his office, which was probably the smallest room here, and into which Klym managed to peek from the corner of his eye, since the door was slightly ajar. Jozef gently pushed his guest along, and Klym decided that although Shatsky was not in a hurry to invite him to the table, he had no desire for an outsider to poke his nose into his holy of holies.

The guest room, which Klym entered, was dominated by a heavy table with straight legs which narrowed toward the bottom. Oval and quite wide, it was meant for lots of guests, which clearly pointed to the host's hospitable nature. At first a girl's curious face appeared from behind a door leading to an adjoining room, and then the girl herself appeared. She was aged about ten and looked very much like Esther Shatska, especially her round dark eyes. Involuntarily Klym caught himself thinking that if one could become lost in those eyes of hers now, what would happen in eight years or so when they would really drive young men insane. The black hair was formed into two plaits, thin and tight, and each was finished off with a simple white ribbon. Blinking her eyes, the little girl nodded silently, welcoming the guest.

"Riva," the host introduced his daughter, making a gesture with his hand, which he himself probably considered to be elegant and theatrical, but which viewed from the side did not look too graceful. "She is my pride and joy, my princess. God can't be everywhere at once, Mr. Koshovy. Which is why he created my Esther."

"Your Esther?"

"Together with other wives who become mothers," there were indulgent notes in Shatsky's tone of voice. "One day someone will say the same about my Riva."

He smacked his lips, as if searching for more words. Meanwhile the daughter modestly lowered her eyes. And suddenly another girl's head popped out from behind the same door – an even smaller copy of Esther now stood beside Riva. Her little sister was about six years old, her hair cascaded freely onto her shoulders.

"Ida. The oldest Jewish name in the world," Jozef announced proudly, immediately asking with feigned sternness: "Girls, are you helping your mother?"

"Mum never told us what to do," squeaked Ida, as she grabbed Riva by the hand.

"Now she is more like her mother!" the father's index finger was now aimed at the little girl. "How often do I need to remind you: men would achieve far more, if women spoke less."

"Even if I say nothing in this house out loud, you will never do any more than you want to!" Riva shook her pigtails defiantly.

Now Shatsky aimed his finger at her.

"Please take note, Mr. Koshovy! I myself often get confused which of these two are more like their mother, God grant her health! They aren't yet thinking where their father will find their dowries! But already they keep repeating everything Esther is wont to say!"

"Since there's a ruckus in the house, dad must home."

This was declared by a lad of twelve, thin, hook-nosed, his hair cut short, and looking like Jozef. He emerged from another door, with a thick battered book under his arm. His face betrayed his real age, but the vest worn over a gray linen shirt made him look a little older than he was.

"Shmuel, you're sitting in your parents' bedroom again?" now Shatsky's indignation was real. "I begged you, I implored you, I took you to Rabbi

Yakob for him to instruct you that boys of your age should not sit on their parents' bed!"

"I was sitting on the floor!" Shmuel parried, from which Klym understood that father and son had been snapping at each other like this for quite some time. "Where can I go to read a book, when these two gerutene[38] have created bedlam in our room? I have nowhere else to study in peace!"

"Putz!" the girls sang out in unison.

"How am I meant to live in this home?" Shatsky drew a ritual circle over the children's heads. "Shmuel, you didn't read on the floor! You took the book and lay on your parents' bed! I've never seen anyone as lazy as you in all my life! Will you be telling me that it's not true?"

A child's crying was heard from behind one of the doors. The girls turned around, as Shmuel puffed out his chest with a victorious look on his face, imitating his father, and Esther appeared in the hallway. Taking no notice of her son, she aimed the arrows of her righteous wrath at the daughters:

"Is this how you look after your baby brother? Is this how you look after Daniel, while I'm waiting on your father?"

"She doesn't want to!" Ida pointed her finger at her sister, after letting go of her hand.

Taking half a step back, Riva lightly slapped her younger sister's right hand.

"It's her that doesn't want to! She says Danny cries all the time!"

"You cried all the time too!" Esther hissed sternly, and with a wave of her hand let it be known that the conversation was ended. Sizing up the situation, she said: "Riva, go back to Danny, you're older. Ida, I need you in the kitchen. All the same I can't leave you and Ida together in the one room now. Shmuel, if you want to read and you don't know where, go into your father's office. As I can see, he won't have any need of it anytime soon. Shatsky, my late father used to say about you: you'll become a great person if you have the urge to work at least out of curiosity, and merely show an interest in what does not apply to human teeth. Invite the gentleman to the table."

After putting everyone and everything in their places and being incredibly pleased with herself, Esther disappeared once more into what Klym

....

[38]   Gerutene (Yiddish) – blunderer, dunderhead.

understood was the kitchen. Her head bowed, Ida followed her mother. Frowning, Riva returned to be with her little brother, and Shmuel, looking as if he had just won an important victory, made his way into his father's office. As he was walking the child's crying stopped.

Now the men were left alone in the guest room.

Jozef heaved a sigh of relief.

And Koshovy realized why Shatsky needed a table of such proportions.

They sat down facing one another.

The dentist stretched out his long arms and folded them in front of him, interlacing his fingers. As Klym settled into his chair, he heard it treacherously creak under him. Not too loudly, there was no danger of it being ready to fall apart. All the same, the furniture had fallen into disrepair and unless the host intervened soon, it would not last very much longer. At least that was the conclusion Koshovy had arrived at. On the other hand, the table stood rock solid, and it seemed it would stand forever.

"So, we were chatting about something," Jozef reminded him.

"We were going to have a bite to eat," Klym was really hungry now, and didn't feel like engaging in unnecessary chit-chat.

"Well, we've sat down at the table," Shatsky said, as if this very fact was enough to appease their hunger.

Ready to accept such a game, Klym shrugged his shoulders, demonstrating composure, and cleared his throat:

"Well, I'm also interested in Magda Bohdanovych."

"If only you knew, young man, how many gentlemen of various ages and of a far higher social status than yours or mine are also interested in her person."

"My interest is not that way directed," Klym hastened to explain, for it occurred to him that Shatsky might be thinking, God forbid, about passion, or perhaps even love at first sight. "The beautiful and no doubt aristocratic young lady treats policemen like her domestics. Just like a Tsarina with her courtiers, if not servants."

"A Królewna," Jozef said, deliciously smacking his lips. "Yes, a Queen, you guessed right there."

"Queen or Tsarina, it makes no difference! It amazes me that policemen of high rank prostrate themselves before her!"

"And not only policemen!" Shatsky freed his fingers, lightly drummed them on the surface of the table, and then called out: "Esther! We've been sitting here with our guest an indecently long time!"

Riva appeared in the guestroom in answer to his words, carrying a round plate piled high with yellowish-gray small flatbreads. Koshovy was expecting he would be offered matzoh in this Jewish house and, to be honest, was ready to dine merely on this. Castigating himself for his intemperance, Klym grabbed a hard rectangular piece as soon as the girl had placed the plate on the table. He greedily took a bite and crunched away on the unleavened bread devoid of taste and smell. Shatsky looked at him without a trace of condemnation, and merely said:

"It will taste much better with what Esther is preparing now."

Munching away, Klym nodded wordlessly. Meanwhile the hostess entered, carrying a wide oblong platter, resembling a boat. The dish smelt sharply of herring and something else, not quite familiar for such a composition. When Esther placed the dish before them, Klym lost all sense of proportion and pulled the plate toward himself for a better look.

It was in fact shredded spicy herring topped with onion. The gray substance, into which the skilful hands of the hostess had turned the salted fish, was evenly and neatly laid out on top of something greenish, not unlike grated vegetables. There were competing strong smells. While Klym was trying to guess what it was, Esther explained:

"It's herring on a bed of apple."

"Fish with apple? Koshovy asked, although he'd understood everything.

"We don't eat this every day," Shatsky added. "This is something that can be put together rather quickly. A snack, so that you don't have to wait too long. Have you never tried this? I highly recommend it."

"Hm… Where can you find apples now? It's July, a long way off from harvest time…"

"The women from the surrounding villages store certain varieties in cellars," explained Esther. "There's not too many apples, but enough to be able to bring them here to the Krakivsky Market. It's no longer possible to use the apples whole, however they can be finely grated, black pepper added, mixed well, and laid out so that the base layer doesn't look too thin. You can also add grated carrot to make it look nicer."

"And herring on top?"

"And herring on top," Esther nodded, getting obvious pleasure from such explanations. "There's no need to stir it. Help yourself, bon appetit."

"And you…" Klym gestured in the direction of an empty chair.

The hostess shook her head.

"I still need to work out what to feed the children for supper. Because several patients, who were able to pay for their appointments, have canceled thanks to the efforts of Mr. Lapidus," and as she was leaving, she said, looking back: "Although our Shatsky doesn't always need Lapidus to help with such things. He was sent by God Himself."

"Why?" Koshovy failed to understand.

"Who else would give him an excuse to while away the time," her words reached him from the kitchen.

Jozef eloquently spread his arms apart.

"We've been at one with each other for more than twelve years. Shmuel is our second. The first child died on the third day, before we could give it a name. After that Esther was afraid to conceive, she cried a lot. We had to visit the rabbi on more than one occasion. Happily, more children followed, but it's left a mark on her. Sometimes she lets her nerves get the better of her."

"I don't like to discuss other people's marriages. Especially in their homes," Klym replied with restraint, not quite sure how he was expected to react.

"I'm in a better position. Because I have the right to discuss my wife in my own home. Help yourself, Mr. Koshovy. Here, let me show you how it's done."

Grabbing a fork, Shatsky picked up some herring with the apple mixture, placed it on the matzoh, bit off a good-sized chunk, and munched away. Following his example, Klym tucked in as well. The pepper added piquancy to the sourness of the apple, together with the spices in the herring marinade.

For a while the men allayed their initial hunger.

Jozef was the first to speak, after wiping his lips with a napkin:

"Yes, about Mrs. Magda. How did it end? I want to tell you, young man, that she is a very secretive person. Or, in other words, when you see her for the first time, you immediately have a desire to unravel the romantic mystery surrounding her. But you would be mistaken."

"Me? Why me?"

"Alright, not you. Not only you, Mr. Koshovy. I mean, anyone who sees Mrs. Magda for the first time and is unaware of what stops many residents of Lviv from sleeping peacefully. Oh, so many of them! Even the city's mayor."

"Magda is that dangerous?"

"Not for everyone. And then, Mrs. Bohdanovych herself does not pose the threat. She's a young widow. The influential citizens of our city, those who defer to Magda and do not object when she says something or wants something, are afraid of the legacy left behind by her late husband. Which, if you please, is something of an unexploded bomb. One only needs to light the fuse. Everyone trembles at the thought, that the young widow might one day set it alight."

"Who do you mean by 'everyone'?"

"The list of people is enormous. More than two hundred, beginning with the city's respected mayor, whom I mentioned earlier."

Klym's eye twitched sharply.

"Listen, Mr. Shatsky…"

"We agreed to avoid formalities."

"Alright. Listen, Shatsky, I arrived in the morning, but it seems as if I've spent half my life here already. Too many impressions for the first day in an unfamiliar place. And all these impressions have already become jumbled. I'm completely exhausted."

"I believe you."

"Therefore, I beg you – don't beat about the bush. Tell me straight why Magda Bohdanovych has the right to speak with policemen with such authority. And to influence their thoughts and decisions."

"Not only policemen…"

"Lord Almighty, Shatsky!"

His patience ran out – Koshovy slammed his fist down on the table.

The plate shuddered. Jozef shook his head and clicked his tongue. Esther peered into the room from the kitchen.

"Shatsky, you're showing your true colors! It's not only me that you drive insane with your chatter! Don't forget, that the person is not sitting in your room with his mouth wide open, unable to say a thing in reply! This young man has a sharp tongue and a strong character!"

"Darling!" Jozef lay his hand on the left side of his chest, over his heart. "Please, my dear – be off! Leave, and stop getting on my nerves! We'll work things out ourselves!"

Esther raised her head proudly and again left the men to their own devices. In this short time Koshovy had become ashamed and began to back-peddle. His eye twitched even more strongly.

"My apologies. I had no right…"

"Forget it," Shatsky generously forgave him. "These are new times, life in the fast lane. Nerves. You want the short version? I'll explain as briefly, as I can. The dental chair, which my Esther mentioned, is sometimes occupied by people who want to talk their fill. But they don't know whom they can speak to. So that a humble dentist is often a bit like their father-confessor. Esther is not right. If need be, Shatsky knows how to listen, and not only talk. And so my ears hear things, which the ears of a poor humble Jew should never hear…"

"On your bandwagon again."

"On the contrary, I'm racing ahead of your curiosity. Because you'll want to know how I found out about all this and even more."

"I understand. Stop dragging this out, though."

Shatsky again interlaced his fingers.

"Magda was married to the chief of criminal police, Mr. Gustav Bohdanovych. Gustav Bohdanovych was thirty years her senior. When he married a second time, a year after having become a widower, various rumors circulated about the city. Not so much explaining Bohdanovych's actions, as examining Magda's intentions. But the head of the criminal police did not live long enough to see his resignation, he died of an apoplectic fit. The widow shed sincere tears of sorrow. No one dared talk about any part she may have played in his death. Besides, Bohdanovych did not leave behind a huge fortune. He lived in an apartment owned by the state. They couldn't let the widow stay there. But she has patrons, so she settled quite luxuriously into rooms on the third floor of the Georges Hotel and still resides there. True, construction works have just started, and the lady has found temporary accommodation elsewhere. However, the rooms in the hotel remain hers. As soon as everything is completed, the widow will return there."

"More to the point, Mr. Shatsky."

"My apologies, all this is important here. Alright, let us return to the sad date. So, soon after the funeral," there was a dramatic pause, and then he repeated, "soon after, Mr. Koshovy, rumors were confirmed about Mr. Bohdanovych's index cards."

"Index cards?"

"He collected compromising information on practically everyone. From the city's mayor, members of parliament, bankers, and industrialists, to prosecutors and judges. He was unable to do this on his own. Bohdanovych had a network of agents, who collected the indelicate information on his personal orders and were paid extra for this. It was these people, by the way, who blabbed about it."

"And no one tried to find the cards?"

"At first no one believed the agents. People thought they were trying to elevate themselves in the eyes of their new chief. But some six months after her husband's death Magda let it be known that she had everything. Mr. Gustav had commanded that she keep the cards. Where he had hidden all those folders, what was in them – no one knew. More correctly, all those who were in the dossiers knew. As if anyone would not know about their own sins! As you saw, she's young, healthy and beautiful. She'll live a long time, thank God. So, she'll keep all the influential people in this city in her little fist."

Koshovy scratched the back of his neck.

"So that's what it is… What does she get out of it?"

"Anyone Magda speaks to is ready to fulfill all her whims," Jozef again spread his arms apart. "Is this not the cherished dream of every woman? Is this not the very essence of a woman's happiness? Ask my Esther, she'll confirm it. And meanwhile, Mrs. Bohdanovych need not worry about her own life, for she is protected by the entire police department. No one is interested in her demise, especially a sudden one."

"Why?"

"Because everyone will then suspect everyone else. How can you live after that in the same city? No, while Magda Bohdanovych lives a good and happy life, everyone around her will be calm. She doesn't abuse her position. Although occasionally she may express an opinion in the city council. To influence the deputies. And she likes to take a special interest in police matters," Jozef leaned forward and lowered his voice: "There are rumors, Mr. Koshovy, that back in the day she even gave advice to the chief of criminal police. Most of which was valuable and helped solve crimes," he sat up straight again. "So, as you can see, the woman is quite unique. If you are entertaining an interest in her, listen to the advice of a wise Jew, sir: keep your distance. Here, have some more herring. It's delicious, yes?"

CHAPTER EIGHT
CHANGE OF PLACE — CHANGE OF LUCK

That first day Klym had to experience one more small adventure.

Against the background of all the difficult and unhappy things which had transpired that day, the incident did not merit much attention. However, for Koshovy and his immediate future, it was crucial and practically life-changing.

After all, the purpose of the negotiations, which Shatsky actively promoted, was to find a roof over Klym's head.

The twenty kroner note, allocated to him on behalf of the police department, ensured one or two nights in the cheapest hotel. After that he had to either find a means of returning to Kyiv, or needed to write a letter to his father with a request to send some money, or else go begging or finding work unloading goods wagons at the railway station.

Klym decided to leave until the very last the option of telegraphing his father and asking for financial help, after all other means had been exhausted. To hire himself out as a laborer was, in his situation, a more acceptable way out for a young man. His father was not keen on his son running away from his problems to Europe, having hinted at other possibilities. For example, to leave Kyiv for a while and to open a notarial office somewhere deep in the backwoods. Having been branded as being unreliable, Klym had little hope of a future in the provincial capital, whereas if he moved to some small district town hardly anyone would take any notice of him.

All the more since through his contacts Nazar Hryhorovych Koshovy was able to learn that if Klymentiy, who, as agreed by the parties to the conflict, had made some foolish mistakes because of his inexperience and propensity for adventure, were to move to some rural area this would even be welcomed. It would be enough for him to settle in some dusty district town, in voluntary exile, and all his 'exploits' would be forgotten in time. Five years of such exile – and he could safely return to his native Kyiv.

Of course, Koshovy-junior categorically refused to take such a step. Thinking not only tactically, but also strategically, Klym calculated what his prospects would be like five years hence. And he reached a disconsolate conclusion. Namely, that after being bogged down in provincial mud, it would be impossible to quickly adapt to life in Kyiv once more.

Yes, the twentieth century, which was only in its eighth year, was proceeding at a rapid pace. Even if belatedly, Russian gubernial cities were still developing much faster than district towns, where the peasant way of life and thinking could not be breached even with a cannonball fired at point-blank range. In the larger cities everything was moving forward. Together with education and technical practices. Having served his time in some provincial backwater, ensnared in eternal agrarian cobwebs, Klym would find it oh so difficult to return to an active life. In the large scheme of things, he would be viewed as a hick, who was trying hard to make a name for himself in the city. Even though he had been born in the city, had grown up here, received his professional education here and because of it had come to grief.

In having to choose between the backwaters of Central Ukraine and the eastern outskirts of Europe, he quite logically selected the latter. How would it look now, when on the second day after arriving, he would be sending his father telegrams permeated with veiled despair: I've been robbed, I have nowhere to live, the person I was counting on has been murdered, I feel like hanging myself, so please send your prodigal son some cash, dad. No, he would rather sweep the streets or lug sacks at the railway station, than stoop to this.

It was interesting that Shatsky seemed to have read Klym's dejected thoughts, literally extracting these confessions from him.

He did not have to try too hard. Koshovy needed to speak his fill, and Jozef merely encouraged him. And after hearing him out, from time to time shaking his head and habitually smacking his lips, he rose decisively, and ordered his guest to follow. He left the house without really explaining anything to his Esther, except for asking her not to refuse any patients who wanted to come the following day. To which his wife replied: his regular customers were already taking their teeth to Lapidus. But she would do everything in her power to convince people of the underhandedness of his main competitor. Reminding her husband that it was possible win back his clientele only if the dentist was at home, waiting patiently in his room for everyone who needed his help. But if this schlimazel is never home, then people such as Lapidus have no need of spreading evil gossip to lure patients over to their practice.

Klym was surprised when Shatsky brought him to the already familiar place on Lychakiv Street. He saw no reason to return here. The menacing janitor blocked the entrance to both uninvited guests, and eyed Klym malevolently. For that morning this nobody had shouted at him. And he, the respectable keeper of this gate, whom not every gentleman would dare to contradict, instead slipping him a krone or two, had succumbed and run off to carry out this fellow's bidding. Standing there immobile, the bulbous fellow intended to have his revenge for the humiliation he had suffered that morning – at least that was how Klym understood his behavior. Knowing only too well the psychology of Kyiv's janitors, he did not entertain any illusions that those in Lviv would be any different. Especially if they were Ukrainian.

But the antagonism of this Cerberus failed to stop Shatsky. He began to create a scene and waved his long arms before the janitor's turned-up snout, finally convincing the fellow to fetch Mr. Veslav Singer.

Koshovy wasn't at all surprised that a dentist from the poor district of Krakidaly knew not only the name and surname of a local landlord, but that he knew the man personally. The surprise came when the fellow stepped out to see them, just as nervous and sweaty as he had been that morning, except that now his bald patch was covered by a skullcap. He demonstratively took a gilded pocket watch out of his brand-new vest, clicked open the cover and showed the unbidden visitors the clockface – as if to say that he didn't have much time for them. Klym still couldn't understand what his guide wanted from Singer. But at that moment Shatsky took no notice at all of Koshovy, immediately grabbing the bull by the horns:

"I have a serious and advantageous offer for you, Mr. Singer. Let's take a walk over to your apartment."

"I won't be walking with you anywhere, Mr. Shatsky," the landlord stood his ground, and even tried to push Jozef away with his belly. "Serious and advantageous offers can be made in the street. I can hear just as well out here, as at home."

The whole time the janitor stood brazenly beside them, moving away only some three steps from the small group, and did not conceal his great interest in the conversation.

"We can stay out here then," Shatsky was quick to agree. "But all the same, it would be better to talk there, Mr. Singer."

"And why's that, if I may ask?"

"Behind closed doors there are no prying ears. Do you really want your janitor to be present while we conduct our business?"

Understanding what was meant, Veslav Singer gestured for the curious bulbous fellow to leave. Throwing a hostile glance at Shatsky, the janitor disappeared into the depths of the yard.

"I'm all ears, Mr. Shatsky, but not for long."

"I'll be very brief, Mr. Singer," the dentist rubbed his broad palms together in a business-like fashion. "Have you already decided what you'll do with the apartment, where the horrible misfortune occurred earlier today?"

"The police have examined it. Poor Mr. Genyk's things are still inside. If no one lays claim to them, the law allows me, after a certain amount of time, to take them for myself or to sell them off, but in any case I can have them," the landlord explained enthusiastically. "There are also various police procedures which need to take place. But I think that's a secondary, if not a tertiary consideration."

"Who can lay claim to the property of the deceased, Mr. Singer?" in this rather innocent question Klym sensed a hint of intrigue.

"As far as I know – no one," the fellow replied calmly. "The lawyer has been renting from me for the past three years. I've heard nothing about any family or anyone who might be direct heirs. You know, the unfortunate fellow didn't have too many valuable things. He dressed well, frequented the best tailors, observed the latest fashion. Being a public figure, he needed to have a decent respectable appearance. And apart from his clothing and several pairs of shoes, I don't know what else he owned. A typewriter, perhaps… I also saw that he had a beautiful gold watch, a real Swiss 'Breguet'. Earlier he had boasted having an 'Adriatica', also a good Swiss workshop. But less than a year ago Mr. Genyk changed his watch. And, excuse me, gentlemen, he had the real thing! A pity it disappeared…"

Klym's heart skipped a beat:

"A gold watch disappeared? From the apartment, you say?"

"Why are you so agitated by this, sir?" the landlord squinted suspiciously.

"Mr. Soyka appreciated expensive and accurate watches," explained Koshovy. "I'm sure he didn't change his habits during the time that I haven't seen him. But while everyone ran off to fetch the police, I had a look around the apartment. I was also present during the police search, and you were there too, Mr. Singer. The watch, which you mention, was not found either in the deceased's pocket, or in any drawer, or on his bedside table."

"The lawyer was killed and robbed. The police have already notified me. And I'll be donating money in the near future to 'Levi Israel', thank God the synagogue is on our street. I don't want to have the dubious reputation of a landlord, whose tenants do themselves in, committing the sin of suicide."

"Now you've touched on the heart of the matter!" Shatsky rubbed his hands together once more. "Forget about the 'Breguet', it's no longer there anyway. The suits and other trifles, along with the suitcases – you'll certainly be able to flog them all off to your advantage. Mr. Veslav, we've known each other a long time: you don't do anything which is not to your advantage, and that is very wise, otherwise it would go against God's commandments. Our Lord commanded us Jews to look out for ourselves first and foremost. Only in that way will everyone around us live well, not upsetting our peace and quiet. If we have benefits, we can share them generously. While this is the case, no intelligent person will give our people a hard time, for we are strangers in this world, we are guests everywhere, Mr. Veslav..."

"Enough of your clucking, Mr. Shatsky!" the landlord began to show signs of irritation, and Klym understood him perfectly: only a few hours earlier he himself had exploded after Jozef's chatter began to grate on his nerves. "What an approach you have, never coming to the point straight away! You hinted at a favorable proposal, so out with it, I'm listening!"

Shatsky stretched his arms out, spreading his fingers apart:

"Now there, Mr. Veslav! I'm only helping you reach the right decision! You are justified in being happy that Mr. Soyka died a violent death. Under other circumstances, you could not have adequately rented the apartment in the near future, which has become vacant because of these unfortunate circumstances. Who would have wanted to live in a place where someone had committed suicide? Am I right, Mr. Singer?"

"Absolutely right, Mr. Shatsky. One would think that all your life you've been looking after rental properties."

"But who will want to live in an apartment where someone was murdered?" Jozef blurted out, throwing a sly glance at the landlord. The people who settle here, are seeking status, and Mr. Genyk had some weight there. This violent incident will negatively impact on the rental price of the apartment, Mr. Singer, am I not right? At the same time, it will impact on the reputation of your building as a whole. You will need to lower the rent to encourage tenants. Your respected colleagues will not be pleased with this. If you start knocking down the price, they will immediately remind you, Mr. Veslav, that you are competitors. Right? You lower the rent – and they think that you are beating down the price! Through your actions you will create a house of cards effect, you must realize this."

As Shatsky spoke, Singer grew more and more sullen with each word. By the time the dentist had triumphantly finished his small speech, the landlord's face had turned completely gray. And the droplets of sweat, which he mopped from time to time, had become plentiful. Koshovy sensed that the climax was approaching.

"What do you want from me, Mr. Shatsky?" the landlord's voice sounded hollow.

"I am trying to save your profitable business and reputation," Jozef said modestly. Stepping a little to one side and nodding in Klym's direction, he continued: "I've brought you a worthy person, someone who can help balance out the situation, so to speak."

"In what way?"

"Let Mr. Koshovy move into Mr. Soyka's former apartment. And while he's settling in here and finding his feet, you will treat with understanding any delays in rent payment. And in general, given the circumstances we've discussed, you might be able to lower the rent for Mr. Koshovy. Obviously not for good, just for a pre-determined period. Do you agree, Mr. Singer? No one will be able to make you a better offer for this apartment today."

The landlord said nothing, his breath was labored. He no longer mopped the sweat with his handkerchief, using the sleeve of his shirt instead. He glanced at his watch for some reason. Finally, he grunted:

"You and I are not at the Krakivsky Market, Mr. Shatsky. There's no need to haggle."

"Am I haggling, Mr. Veslav?" Jozef expressed utter surprise. "If I knew how to conduct business, would I be pulling out people's teeth?"

"You're poking your nose into other people's business," Singer said through gritted teeth.

"That's true. I won't profit at all from your arrangement with your new tenant, Mr. Koshovy. You know that Shatsky gives valuable, pertinent and free advice. For which he sometimes gets an earful from his dear Esther. So then? Shake on it? Come on, agree with me, Mr. Singer…"

They grumbled for a while longer, but this was more for show. The result was that Klym received a key to the first-floor apartment from the landlord, which had been occupied that morning by Yevhen Soyka. On the condition that he touch none of the deceased's belongings. And if suddenly the gold 'Breguet' with engraving inside the cover or any other valuables should be found somewhere, then he was to hand them over to Singer as compensation for his losses. It was decided to draw up all the formalities which legitimized Koshovy's residence in the apartment of the murdered lawyer Soyka at a later time.

The landlord even kindly agreed to take care of this himself. Klym was not a local, it would be hard for him to understand the local customs at first attempt. And Shatsky practically forced Mr. Singer to thank them both nicely for helping him to resolve this rather involved problem. Klym's new situation was explained to him succinctly and pithily in a single sentence:

"Meshane mokim, meshane mazl," which was immediately translated: "Here we say: change of place – change of luck. Isn't that right, Mr. Singer…?"

…And so now, as Koshovy slowly began to settle into his new place, Jozef took it upon himself to drop by in the evening, the day before Soyka's funeral, to notify the time and the place.

That was, of course, if Klym intended to see his friend off on his final journey. Even if Koshovy had had other matters to attend to, he assured Shatsky that he still would have gone to the funeral.

Although, if the truth be known, he didn't like cemeteries – they made him feel miserable.

CHAPTER NINE

FRANKNESS AFTER A FUNERAL

One could reach the district where the Lychakiv Cemetery was located by streetcar.

But Klym decided to go there on foot. Especially since he had already studied the route and knew how to reach St. Peter's Street, where the majestic arch with the sharp Gothic spires marked the entrance to the necropolis. In the couple of days he had been in Lviv, Koshovy became convinced that his new friend Jozef Shatsky was omnipresent. So, he was not at all surprised, when the fellow appeared in Soyka's former apartment, to personally inform him where and when the lawyer would be interred.

As Klym expected, not that many people turned up to see the lawyer off on his final journey.

But it was not even this which had astonished him. He would never have thought that he would one day need to consider the religion of his recently departed colleague and the church where the service would be held. He was used to the fact that in Kyiv, and other Little Russian gubernias, the service for the deceased was conducted in an Orthodox church. The exception were the Jews, who were limited by the pale of settlement – they were buried according to Jewish traditions. As for converts to the faith, Koshovy considered them being no different to Orthodox people like himself.

But Soyka's service was being conducted in a Catholic church.

Which led Klym to reach the only correct conclusion: the former Kyiv lawyer had converted to the Catholic faith. Otherwise Soyka would not have been farewelled in the church of Sts. Peter and Paul, which belonged, as Jozef explained, to the Roman Catholic denomination. As it was, he was buried in a prestigious section of the cemetery. However, as Koshovy later learned, it could not have been otherwise. Favorable final resting places were the privilege of all who resided in Lower Lychakiv.

The farewell procedure itself was not drawn out. On the contrary, keeping his distance and trying not to engage with anyone, Koshovy suspected that Soyka was interred a little faster than might have been expected in such cases. When he approached the man whom he had missed out on meeting, to see him off on his final journey, Klym caught several curious looks in his peripheral vision. He pretended not to notice, tossed a clod of earth into the grave, laid down a bunch of flowers and proceeded to the exit with a sense of having carried out his duty. But Magda Bohdanovych, all dressed in black, her face covered with a wispy mournful veil, had left this place of grieving before him. Before this, she had managed to exchange a few words with some gentlemen who were also farewelling Soyka, lightly touching the arm of one of them.

On a foreign chessboard among unknown Kings, Queens, rooks, and knights, Koshovy was left with nothing else to do but to play mental gymnastics and to make various assumptions. He understood that the lawyer Soyka was well known in Lviv, and that his reputation here was equivocal. But then Yevhen Pavlovych's Kyiv period was not strewn with roses either, it had its own thorny patches and impenetrable thickets.

Even more, Klym was disturbed and alarmed at the small number of those who had found the time to come to the funeral. Another contradictory circumstance was in play here: the criminal police persistently tried to present Soyka's death as suicide, the implications being, among other things, that a funeral service for the sinner could not be conducted in church and, as a result he could not be buried in the distant fields of Lychakiv or any other cemetery. Klym did not forget that it was his testimony which had prompted the mysterious and influential Magda Bohdanovych to force the investigator to continue further with the case. Therefore, this young woman had a personal interest in the proper running of the investigation.

Had there been something between them? Before he had become more closely acquainted with Shatsky this might have occurred to him. Although, when Klym had worked as an assistant for Soyka, he noticed that the lawyer was not especially attracted to women. Of course, the opposite sex interested him. Koshovy knew about Yevhen Pavlovych's regular visits to the cheap bordellos on Yamska Street, as well as the private salons, where ladies of higher class accepted regular clients individually. However, there was no one with whom the lawyer maintained a close, personal, genuinely *loving* relationship. He even avoided them – at least these were the conclusions reached by his young assistant. There was no reason to believe that six years after moving to Europe, Mr. Soyka would have radically changed his habits, passions and attitudes.

Except for the fact that he had changed his religion – but even here things were not all that clear. For when Klym recalled the years he had spent alongside Yevhen Pavlovych, he was unable to place his hand on his heart and sincerely declare that Soyka was a true believer. On the contrary, religion meant very little to him, and he did not celebrate church festivals, but looked on them as a ponderous, unnecessary, uninteresting, and obligatory duty which needed to be performed. So that if Soyka – a subject of His Majesty Nicholas II – didn't care which God he prayed to, or whether he should pray at all, then having changed one emperor for another, his indifference to the church would not have changed.

Thinking such thoughts, Koshovy slowly passed under the archway into the street. Shatsky was standing across the way, patiently waiting for him to appear. Magda too was in no hurry to leave. Her carriage was standing a little down the street, and the young woman was pacing the sidewalk, waiting for someone. Stopping, Klym raised his hat, and gave her a slight bow. It was ridiculous to pretend that they were not acquainted. In reply Magda moved her familiar fan from side to side, showing no more interest. No, Koshovy, decided, there had been no love here, not even any sinful secret passion. This aristocratic woman, who had almost every influential person in Lviv in her small claws, could be nothing like *that* to a man who perceived all women as prostitutes, be they high-class or streetwalkers. Mrs. Bohdanovych hardly needed to sell herself, not even for big money. The widow was not in dire financial straits and could have anything she laid her eyes upon. Although, it seemed she didn't abuse her position too often.

However…

Soyka, with all due respect, was far too insignificant for her grandeur, her needs and did not measure up to her.

Of course, there had obviously been some kind of relationship between them. Definitely nothing intimate, but maybe business? The widow of the head of the criminal police department must have required the services of the best lawyers in Lviv. The likes of those with whom it is better not to deal with, to whom one quickly concedes defeat, because they will have you over a barrel sooner or later. The lawyer Soyka, despite the respect Klym had for him, hardly belonged to the same circle of people as Magda.

All the same, the young widow had taken it upon herself to organize Mr. Genyk's funeral…

The weather was not at all mournful on this day. The heat, which had marked the previous few days, had eased. There was a gentle sun, a light breeze – July was in full swing. Not knowing how to occupy his time now and seeing no reason to remain standing there, Klym waited for a carriage to drive past, adjusted his hat, and stepped onto the pavement, intending to cross the street and join Shatsky.

"Mr. Koshovy!"

The voice was not all that loud, but it was loud enough so that Klym would hear and turn around. Behind him, near the cemetery gate, stood a small group of men. He had already noticed these three in the cemetery, for they had kept to themselves near the open grave. Klym was being addressed by a stately gentleman dressed in a dark suit and wearing a round hat with a slightly upturned brim, with an elegantly trimmed beard and a strip of a mustache. On his sleeve he had a black ribbon, but the look of the man was not at all of someone in mourning.

"Did you mean me?" Klym asked, just in case, even though he understood how absurd this sounded.

"Don't be surprised, we know your surname and who you are."

The stranger moved away from the group and came up to Koshovy, offering his hand, which he shook mechanically, sensing that the fellow's right hand was like stone.

"Adam Wiszniewski, engineer," the fellow touched the edge of his hat. "Allow me to invite you to the funeral feast. We knew the departed. And you are an old friend of his as well. So let's remember him according to the Christian custom."

"But I…"

His eye twitched treacherously again.

"Don't worry," a smile played on Wiszniewski's thin lips. "There's no need to worry. You were recommended to us by Mrs. Bohdanovych, which means a lot to me and my colleagues. We have some matters to discuss, and Mrs. Magda's advice is always valuable."

"And what matters, if I may ask, do you gentlemen wish to discuss with me?"

On the far side of the street Shatsky was making completely incomprehensible signs, even though he was attracting attention to himself.

"First, let's get to know one another better," Wiszniewski stopped smiling. "In general, we have things we want to discuss. Or more precisely, we have some things to tell *you*. And you should hear us out, if you want to remain here in Lviv and start conducting business. Anyway, it is high time we had some lunch, don't you think?"

Meanwhile one of Wiszniewski's friends was already helping Magda get into a carriage – the young woman was leaning on his arm. With his other hand he summoned an open phaeton, which had already been standing for a while some distance away.

"We'll go in this one. Mrs. Bohdanovych will follow us. Please, Mr. Koshovy. Klymentiy, if I'm not mistaken. Did I get the name right?"

"I prefer Klym, it's shorter."

"In that case – please, please get in, *Klymentiy*."

He failed to retain in his memory the name of the small restaurant in Virmenska Street.

It wasn't important now. Given Koshovy's current financial standing, he wasn't about to start visiting restaurants anytime soon. Neither this one, nor any other one. It was evident that his new acquaintances came here frequently – the head waiter came out to personally greet them. He was respectful, without being obsequious, as was often the case in similar establishments not only in Kyiv, but all over the Russian Empire. They were immediately escorted to a private room, where a table was already set. Though modest in appearance, it was none the less decent. Mechanically having counted the number of settings, Klym found there were five, and came to the logical conclusion that the lunch had been booked earlier for exactly five people. Therefore, they had already agreed among themselves from the very start who would attend.

It was not likely that someone else was meant to come, and because they were unable to attend, they had conveniently decided to invite Koshovy, who had been in Lviv only three days now.

This could mean only one thing: Klym's modest persona had interested these solid and, without a doubt, influential citizens. And certainly it had not been without the recommendation of Magda Bohdanovych: for, apart from her, no one was yet acquainted with the Kyiv lawyer. It was left for him to work out whether he should be thankful to the young, stern and mysterious lady for this honor, or was she, on the contrary, now creating even more problems for him than he had up until now.

She was the last to arrive. With a deft movement she raised her veil, then removed her hat, resting it on a special shelf. The men had waited for her to arrive, and only after Magda had made what seemed like an innocent (although in fact it was significant) gesture with her fan, did everyone begin to take their seats. Engineer Wiszniewski, who was the closest to her, prudently moved a chair with a low curved back so that the woman could sit down, and positioned himself beside her. The empty place remaining for Klym, whether accidentally, or – more likely – by prior agreement, allowed him to sit ostensibly at the head of the table, but at the same time Koshovy found himself in the sights of four pairs of attentive eyes.

"Will the respected gentlemen allow me to start?" Magda asked in a level voice, and having received their silent agreement, continued: "Dear Mr. Adam, please see to our company."

Wiszniewski rose to his feet, grabbed the carafe of cognac, and filled the shot glasses. Not everyone was fond of it: the young widow and the rotund bald gentleman with the turned-up waxed mustache were drinking rowan liqueur. Apart from the drinks, there were two platters on the table containing canapes with smoked pork brisket and liver pate, finely grated stewed beetroot with a hint of horseradish, and potato pikelets. Delicious, though not at all appropriate to this sad moment, was the fresh, still steaming blood sausage, cut into neat slices. Koshovy was already acquainted with such dishes, having spent the previous evening roaming Lviv and perusing various menus, as he sought somewhere to eat on the cheap.

"According to Christian tradition, let's remember the one who has come before the Almighty," Adam announced.

Everyone rose to their feet and drank – Klym did not fail to notice that Magda completely emptied her glass, instead of merely wetting her lips. After that they said nothing for a while, then sat down and devoted their attention to the dishes for some time. Wiszniewski looked after Magda, assuming the rights of a man sitting on her right. Koshovy finally had an opportunity to placate his hunger, for these past few days he had not eaten much, although he tried to make an effort so that the others would not notice this. None of those present seemed at all interested in his healthy appetite. The clatter of knives and forks stopped fairly soon, Adam patted his lips dry with a napkin and cleared his throat:

"Respected guests, now that we are in a quiet setting and more intimate company, I have the honor to present to you Klymentiy Koshovy, our guest from Central Ukraine. He knew the departed… hm… *deceased* before us and accidentally became witness to the tragic event."

"A participant, Mr. Wiszniewski," the rotund fellow noted.

"Thank you, Mr. Popeliak," the engineer nodded. "So, you already know me, Mr. Koshovy, and Mrs. Magda as well. Mr. Janusz Popeliak is the editor of our municipal newspaper. One can boldly state that he is the voice of our city's mayor. And our respected mayor, in turn, listens to the opinions of Mr. Popeliak. Because the publication which he has the honor to head, nevertheless collects and presents to the city authorities the opinions of those same people who have elected them. Finally, Mr. Kazimierz Morawski, a councilor on the city council and, you can take my word for it, by no means the lowliest person making important decisions here in Lviv. All of us, in one way or another, knew not only your colleague Mr. Soyka. The activities in which he participated of late are also known to us."

"Which is why we invited you!" blurted out Mr. Morawski, a tall man with dark brown hair and round glasses who stuttered slightly. "You need to know everything! You need to understand, sir, with whom you almost became associated here!"

Magda lightly tapped a knife against the side of her shot glass.

"Mr. Kazik, I implore you. We invited Mr. Koshovy here to remember Mr. Genyk. Not to hold a show trial of the deceased. And your harsh tone, Mr. Morawski, in light of everything that is taking place, appears inadmissible."

"My apologies, Mrs. Magda," the councilor readily agreed with a nod. "However, I wished to warn our guest against continuing to be involved in the business which Soyka was quite firmly entrenched in. Which, by the way, may have cost him his life."

"That it may have," agreed Wiszniewski. "But the police are conducting an investigation. As far as I know, Olshansky is an investigator with experience. The case is under the personal supervision of Commissar Novak. Therefore, there is hope that the truth will be established soon. By the way, gentlemen, Mr. Morawski is correct when he assumes that in the end lawyer Soyka's demise was due to the business he was involved in."

This time Klym was forced to clear his throat to have his say.

"Excuse me, but you are talking here among yourselves. At least it seems that way to me." No one interrupted him, four pairs of eyes looked on with interest, and he continued, gaining confidence with every word. "Judging by what I've heard, none of you were well disposed toward Yevhen Soyka. Nonetheless, you have attended his funeral. Seen him off on his last journey. You've assembled here to remember him and invited along a complete stranger to join your respectable company. I don't expect that our meeting here under such circumstances is merely a formality."

"You're right," agreed the engineer. "Thanks to you, Mr. Genyk's death is not be written off as a suicide. Which, by the way, would have also suited the criminal police, and the readers of Mr. Popeliak's newspaper. Do you want clarity and openness? Please, it's a free country here, you have the right. Are you agreed that your quick release was due to the intervention of Mrs. Magda, who is respected by all of us?"

Klym caught her eye. Her initial curiosity was replaced by a slight air of excitement, the gleam of her eyes giving her away.

"I'm still not well versed in local laws, Mr. Wiszniewski. However, I *know* the law. Obviously, I have played no part in the death of the lawyer Soyka. So I would have been released sooner or later, it was just a matter of time."

"Not only," Morawski interrupted once more. "The criminal police could have handed you over to their colleagues from the secret police. After that, even military counterintelligence might have taken an interest in you. After all, you're a foreigner who has arrived from Russia to visit Soyka with some unknown purpose…"

"I'm from Ukraine," Koshovy reminded them. "Or, if you are more comfortable, you can use the term 'Little Russia', which is officially accepted in my homeland. The city of Kyiv was never a part of Russia."

"Enough of that," Morawski dismissed his words. "We're not talking about geopolitics, to hell with it! Your province is part of the Russian Empire. So that you, having appeared at the wrong place and the wrong time, could be considered by our counterintelligence colleagues to be a Russian spy. Who has arrived to establish secret contacts with someone who is suspected of cooperation with Russian agents. Mrs. Magda's intercession has saved you from such an unfortunate adventure. Have I made myself clear? Or do you need me to elaborate?"

Klym caught his breath.

Suddenly he felt not just unarmed in the face of an enemy attack, but humiliatingly naked, completely defenseless. He felt like covering his shameful places, curling up into a ball, turning around and awkwardly dashing off somewhere far from here. Let them consider him the biggest coward, but Koshovy was not prepared for such a tirade.

The lawyer Yevhen Soyka was a Russian agent.

Not knowing how he should react to this or whether a reaction was indeed necessary, Klym grew quiet, no longer having any desire to talk about anything. This did not go unnoticed by those assembled. They looked at one another. Magda waved her fan in the direction of editor Popeliak, meanwhile engineer Wiszniewski filled the shot glasses, but did not invite anyone to drink, and merely wet his lips. The councilor followed his example, the others did not even touch their glasses. After wetting his lips, the engineer cleared his throat:

"Mr. Koshovy. Everyone present knows and understands the things, which are unlikely to interest coachmen, janitors, waiters, shopkeepers, shoemakers, tailors, or barbers. Just as the batiar from Lychakiv, the thief from Klepariv or the trader from the Krakivsky Market also hardly have the time to worry about such things. Maybe all these, and even other citizens not mentioned by me, right down to the last tramp, can pick up certain moods in society. However, they do not fully realize the danger, which is no longer merely smoldering, is not in its infancy, and which needs to be taken quite seriously. Mr. Morawski has quite a few close friends among the deputies in the Galician Sejm. So, he knows full well the forces which are gathering there now and confidently raising their heads after the Russian revolution. And Mr. Popeliak writes a column in almost every issue of his newspaper, where he sounds the alarm. However, something shields people's vision and blocks their ears. Understood, maybe they can't hear Mr. Janusz's desperate calls, but then they don't hear the shots either!"

"Shots?" Klym asked.

But not because he had not understood. Just so as not to remain silent, for he continued to feel naked, helpless, vulnerable and more foreign than ever. His eye twitched more strongly than usual.

"Exactly that!" Popeliak intervened, pressing forward. "Shots are being fired in Lviv! Today is exactly a week since the Sichynsky verdict was announced – he was sentenced to death. The lawyer filed an appeal, and something tells me they'll manage to weasel their way out. By the way, according to some rumors, your colleague Soyka was meant to defend the killer…"

"Stop!" Koshovy interrupted him, no matter how rude it may have seemed. "Wait. Who are we talking about? I really don't know who you are talking about here. And in what dubious cases Soyka was involved. Can you explain, maybe then I'll be able to better understand everything. Who is this Sichynsky?"

"Correct, gentlemen," Magda's words sounded like an observation. "We invited our guest here for a chat, so that he would better understand what is happening here, what he needs to stay away from and how he should behave. Therefore, please, start from the very beginning, Mr. Popeliak."

"No one is intimidating you," Wiszniewski hastily interjected. "Honestly, please don't take offense, but your persona as such does not interest any of us too much. It is only thanks to the goodwill of Mrs. Magda, who took a liking to you after a short meeting at the police station, that we have all been brought together here. To save you from a greater mess, if possible, than the one you've already found yourself in."

"What are you referring to?"

"You are in a foreign city. The only person whom you knew here has been killed under suspicious circumstances. He did not have the best of reputations, because he defended bombers, terrorists, and criminals. People who pass off their crimes as a struggle for the idea of equality and fraternity, and act in the name of uniting the Russian people. In recent years Mr. Genyk has acted as a lawyer mostly on behalf of the so-called Russophiles. I, as someone not indifferent to politics, personally consider their current representation in the Galician Sejm to be quite critical."

"And not only you," Morawski noted from his seat. "Mr. Koshovy, I know nothing about you personally. But believe me, I'm pretty well versed in the situation there in the Russian provinces. Do not take offense, but the Kyiv Gubernia, in the possessions of Tsar Nicholas the Second, is equivalent to our Kingdom of Galicia and Lodomeria on the eastern outskirts of the possessions of Emperor Franz Joseph. The Austrian authorities, that is – Vienna, have long hoped that the national unrest taking place here would spread closer to Kyiv. Much better that the Ruthenians[39] seethe away under the nose of Tsar Nicholas. I am well acquainted with the views of this community. Kyiv, as they write, needs to become the center of gravity of the Ukrainian national movement. Let me remind you, this is a quote, Mr. Koshovy. So, it would be better if they struggled for their rights somewhere else, for example, in that self-same Kyiv. That is no longer a quote, but uniquely my view. So that you know," the councilor leaned forward and lowered his voice, as if revealing some terrible secret, "this very political movement in your Greater Ukraine is supported financially by various organizations from here."

"Which ones?"

"Austrian ones. And even Polish. Not being too vocal about it, of course. Apparently, Mr. Stolypin's government began to tighten the screws of various national movements and associations not so long ago, and the Ukrainian ones have suffered quite a bit, right?"

Not wishing to go into explanations, especially since it might inadvertently reveal some of his own secrets, which was undesirable given the present company, Klym confined himself to a nod of the head. All the same he could not refrain from adding:

"Forgive me, gentlemen, I still don't understand what you are on about. Forgive me once more, but you keep jumping about all over the place."

"Yes, gentlemen," Magda intervened once more. "You are confusing our guest even more. Mr. Morawski, you are far more lucid at meetings in the Town Hall."

"What I wanted to say, Mr. Koshovy, is that the Russian government openly, but more often tacitly, supports very similar processes here in Lviv, and in general across a large part of Galicia. The Austrian authorities, the Galician Sejm and the Lviv City Council find it convenient for the activities of the mindful Ruthenian community to spread throughout your territory.

....

[39]   Ruthenians – the ethnic Ukrainian population of Bukovyna, Galicia and Transcarpathian Ukraine. In the late 19th – early 20th century the term Ruteni (Lat. Rutheni) – a Latinized form of the name for Ukrainians and Belarusians, as well as the ethnic groups of Ukrainians in the Austro-Hungarian Empire. Used in the Austro-Hungarian Empire as an ethnonym for Ukrainians and their sub-groups or closely related peoples.

The Russian government is stirring up utter Muscovite sentiments here. Do you know their motto, which is not new, but very much to the point? Better to drown in a Russian sea than in a Polish puddle!"

"Even so, aren't these ideas freely expressed?"

"It's a free country!" Morawski theatrically spread his arms apart. "They have their own newspapers, clubs and parties. They congregate around the Orthodox church, and it is against the law to forbid their activities. Mr. Soyka was not buried in the Orthodox cemetery, because he converted to Roman Catholicism. Word has it, shortly after he moved here. However, I want to tell you, for him and those like him, the church played an unimportant role in their lives. It appears he simply intended to assimilate here in Lviv, as much as humanly possible. The fact that he belonged to a different parish, than his Russophile friends, formally highlighted the distance between Mr. Genyk and the adherents of the Russian liberator-tsar."

"And emphasized the independence and impartiality of the lawyer," Wiszniewski added. "That is, he had nothing to do with their parties and movements, which were involved with Russian Orthodoxy."

"In actual fact these gentlemen with their leaders in the Russian Council have in recent years become noticeably quieter," Morawski noted. "But they have not curtailed their activities. They have continued to assert that Russians, Ukrainians and Galician Ruthenians are part of the same single brotherly people. That there is no difference between them, and that the *Tsar-father* will unite them all," the councilor said in broken Russian, which sounded to Klym rather strange and comical. "Everything would have been fine, Mr. Koshovy, had the Russophiles[40] not started more often than necessary to talk about Galicia as a land which is historically part of Russia."

"Why?"

"Allow me, gentlemen, I'll explain, because I write about this a lot myself."

Now Popeliak seized the initiative. No one objected, and so he continued:

....

[40] Russophiles – linguistic, literary and socio-political movement among the Ukrainian population of Galicia, Bukovyna and Transcarpathia in 1819-1930s. Defended the national-cultural, and later – state-political unity with the Russian people and Russia.

"You've already heard, Mr. Koshovy, that the Russophiles talk of Russian seas and Polish puddles. If everyone who espouses these ideas are to be considered, as they insist, as being *Russian*," the editor also resorted to broken Russian, "then their critical mass will one day mean that they are living on their land. It's not so important, that only some of them are actually Russians, while others are Galician Ruthenians. They will consider it their right to demand help from the Russian Tsar, and not only financial help. They will want to be liberated from under the rule of Franz Joseph. This is possible only by taking these territories by force!"

Popeliak made a theatrical pause, and then continued:

"Mr. Koshovy! It has long been no secret to mindful citizens, that the Russophiles want our country to go to war with Russia! So that they can surrender immediately, handing the liberators the keys to Lviv and all of Galicia! When we make mention of Mr. Soyka, may he rest in peace, this is what we are referring to."

Having said this, the editor emptied his shot glass and bit into a sandwich. Then he rose to his feet, unbuttoned his jacket, slipped his fingers under the edges of his vest, and began to move about, walking around the table because of a lack of space. The others remained silent. Koshovy rubbed the bridge of his nose and smacked his lips, as he gathered his thoughts.

"Please, let me summarize," he said cautiously, as if stepping through mud, afraid of sinking too deeply. "Yevhen Soyka, as a lawyer, offered his services to local citizens, who thought of themselves as so-called Russophiles. People's attitudes toward them, to put it mildly, are not very good. They are tolerated, but not loved. You're right: in Kyiv, Poltava or Kharkiv those who create national movements, in particular Ruthenian ones, are not tolerated by the authorities. For their activities they are persecuted, fined, arrested and tried. That's not the case here, and it's probably for the better. Why then was Soyka a Russian agent?"

Morawski clicked his fingers.

"Forgive me, no one has directly called him an agent. However, I have enough contacts to know that for some time the political police have had their eye on Mr. Genyk. They had all the grounds for that."

"For example? Why I'm asking," Klym explained, "is that you intimated, that because of my one-time close association with Soyka I could be accused of being a spy. I would very much not like that. I need to know, what I possibly might be dealing with here."

"That's right," nodded the councilor adjusting his glasses. "Mr. Genyk defended not only those individuals, connected in one way or another with the Russophiles. However, he, and you are probably aware of this, was in general quite skilled as a lawyer. He was able to seek acquittals for defendants who seemed unable to escape their justified punishment. If you like, Mr. Wiszniewski will tell you one day."

"To hell with that," grunted Adam. "It's nothing to do with me."

"Of course," Morawski readily agreed. "In general, we are talking about Mr. Genyk's incredible agility as a lawyer. He was notorious, without exaggeration, throughout the city and even beyond it. And this ability of his to take on any dubious case and get an acquittal for his client or at the very least a significant reduction in punishment, attracted the Russophiles to him. Because behind them stood the bombers and other nihilists, whom the police were catching, the courts were trying, and whom Soyka brilliantly and successfully defended. All that rabble drifted here, escaping the persecution of the tsarist regime. This became especially apparent some two years ago, after the revolution erupted in Russia. It is significant that the Austrian authorities preferred to support them or for the most part ignore them. For it was considered that the bombers were revolutionaries, whose activities undermined Russian power. So, they needed to be given shelter here. But, Mr. Koshovy, the Russian secret service understands this as well! So, under the guise of fighters against the tsarist regime, they send secret agents here. You have written about this, Mr. Popeliak, right?"

"Their actions weaken the monarchy from within," grunted the editor, who had grown tired of circling the table and settled into his chair. "Besides, one need not mix with the Russophiles to become radicalized, obtain weapons and begin shooting at senior officials in broad daylight. Which is why I mentioned the student Sichynsky. In April not only all Lviv – the whole of Galicia was shaken by the news of how brazenly he had shot Count Potocki in his own office. And the killer did not belong to the Russophiles and had nothing to do with their activities. On the contrary, he was shooting at the governor in protest at the oppression of the *Ukrainian* population. This plague has come to us from Russia, Mr. Koshovy, you must agree."

"I don't intend to argue. You say this student has already been convicted?"

"Unanimously, every one of the twelve jurors declared: 'Guilty.' He had his own lawyers, and Soyka somehow became involved in the case. At first he took the matter seriously, but then withdrew his services. Why – God only knows. And my friends at the trial told me that supposedly before this Mr. Genyk had persuaded his colleagues to appeal the verdict, demanding a statement of mental incapacity. When they first caught Sichynsky, even back then, they tried to persuade him to act as if he had a few screws loose. He refused, but after the verdict he supposedly agreed."

"You are truly well informed."

"That's what editors are for. So, let's bring everything together then, Mr. Koshovy. The assassination of the governor was only a small part of this. In my opinion, although a prominent person was shot, one thing is significant: radical terror has become a big problem. If they were able to get the governor, then everyone else is fair game."

Morawski again adjusted his glasses and sighed:

"And the danger lies in the fact, Mr. Koshovy, that the Russophiles enjoy far greater support than that enjoyed by a Ruthenian student. The Russophiles, as previously mentioned here, are reviving their activities once more – in the form of more radical movements. The difference between their prior and present actions goes unnoticed by those who are not in the know. But we, those citizens who are not indifferent and who are aware of the real situation, understand one thing. Ten years ago the Russophiles, apologists for the Russian Tsar, had no army. Today their secret army is those same bombers. The ones who spy for the Russian state. But judging by the existing mood, which few of the average city dwellers feel, they are actively preparing for something. However, to identify suspects is the immediate duty of counterintelligence. Your Mr. Soyka hardly realized whom he was dealing with and whom he was defending so adroitly. So, he was placed on a watch list. And suddenly he is visited by a guest, a subject of the Russian Tsar and from a state which is, in essence, our enemy. Who can guarantee, Mr. Koshovy, that you are not an agent?"

Klym pressed his right eyelid.

"Gentlemen, I am no agent," the words sounded quite naive, like a teenager's justification. "Everything you've told me now is news to me and sounds bizarre. I came here seeking peace and quiet. And find myself in a stormy sea. But there's nothing I can do about that."

"So keep living peacefully, Klymentiy," Morawski said. "Assume that from today you have colleagues here in Lviv. Who wish you only well. Which is why they've invited you here to make your acquaintance, and to explain everything that can be explained," the councilor grew quiet, but only for a moment. "And stay away from this incident, from everything which is in any way associated with Yevhen Soyka – as far away as possible. Actually, that is all we wanted to say."

He had expressed himself delicately and beautifully.

He could have fooled someone else.

But not Klym Koshovy, whose head a policeman had recently battered fiercely against a prison wall.

Now he was being warned not to poke his nose into things which weren't his business.

He came out into the street last.

The wake, if this gathering could be called that, had continued for almost another hour. After the engineer's words those assembled at the table quite quickly lost interest in the foreigner, and set about discussing common issues, common acquaintances and, without colluding, forgot not only about the dead lawyer Soyka, but also about his living friend Koshovy. Also, a lawyer, but for the moment a person without anything to occupy himself with, without a residence permit, and, more importantly, practically penniless. Klym understood that these influential city residents were well aware of his present circumstances. However, he never even expected anything more substantial from them than an invitation to dine. He did not consider it advisable to get up and leave with his head held high. So he behaved as was most appropriate in the given situation: he remained quietly seated, listened to the conversation, which had nothing at all to do with him, and ate heartily, to last him until the end of the day. Having a modest amount of capital in his wallet, he tried to spend the twenty charitable kroner very economically, only on coffee and food.

So that when Morawski, taking it upon himself, finally got up, thanked those present and began to prepare to leave, Klym decided to wait until the private room was vacated by the others. He found an excuse – standing near the door, he shook hands with everyone as they left. He wanted to kiss Magda's hand, but the woman, anticipating his intentions, nodded dryly, lowered her veil, and allowed Wiszniewski to easily, without any hint of intimacy, take her by the elbow. Finally left on his own, Koshovy – either the consumed alcohol had played a part, or his own pride had unfurled a white flag – called over the waiter and requested, nodding in the direction of the leftovers on the table, that he wrap them up and let him have them. He was expecting to be subjected to rudeness or ridicule, for restaurant employees were sometimes known to behave haughtily. However, the fellow showed no surprise at all, didn't even raise an eyebrow, and after a short while Klym was handed a neatly-packed parcel. Slipping it under his arm and to display at least some sense of decorum, he fished out every last kreutzer he could find in his pockets, handing them to the waiter, and left.

Magda Bohdanovych's carriage was standing a little further up Virmenska Street.

The horse was marking time on the cobblestones. The coachman played with his whip, decorated with a brightly-colored ribbon. The young widow was seated so that she could see the entrance to the restaurant, and so that whoever stepped outside would notice her straight away. Klym felt his eye twitch strongly, and his face flush red – he must have looked quite a sight in his hat, badly-ironed suit and the packed leftovers of their lunch. To put it mildly. And at the same time, it dawned on him: Magda was making it very clear that she was waiting for him. There was nothing left to do: slipping the package more conveniently under his left arm and with his right smoothing out the lower part of his jacket, he decisively walked up to the carriage. Mrs. Bohdanovych was looking at him through the netting of her veil.

"Headed for Lychakiv Street? I invite you to take advantage of my carriage. Let me give you a lift."

"Thank you, Mrs. Magda," his fingers touched the brim of his hat. "I'm in the habit of walking, exploring the city. Each time I take a different route, trying to remember the streets. It's so easy to get lost here, I'm trying to acquaint myself with the streets."

"You've plenty of time for your walks. Please."

Magda moved over and Klym sat down beside her, no longer acting capriciously.

The horse set off.

"People don't refuse me."

In the way this was said, Koshovy once again became convinced that the widow of the former criminal police chief was truly accustomed to special and reverent treatment. Even if she was talking to a person who was clearly beneath her status in Lviv.

"I'm sorry, but quite the contrary."

"What do you mean by 'quite the contrary'?"

"No refusals. Quite the contrary, your invitation is an honor for me to accept. It's just that I didn't want to, did not feel I had the right to impose on your time…"

"Holy Mother of God! Can't at least you stop twittering!" Magda did not hide her irritation this time. "It seemed to me, that you were simpler, than those who surround me."

"Simpler?"

"Different. That would be more accurate. On the contrary, not as simple, as you would like to pass yourself off to be. Maybe you are already aware that I am the widow of an experienced policeman. So it's hard to fool me. Especially after you explained everything in detail to that fool Olshansky."

"Why is he a fool?"

"I know what I'm saying," the phrase sounded sharp, like a slap. "When I call you simpler than the others, I mean that you're not like those people who adhere to unnecessary convention and so-called decencies when it is inappropriate and unnecessary. Mr. Koshovy, you are hardly a big fan of subordination, social distancing and other conventions, both secular and official. You are not an easy person to tame, so there's no need now to argue with a woman."

"I don't intend to. You would know better," Klym said and lowered his head, feigning complete obedience. "And thank you, for warning me of your intention to tame me. So, I take it to mean that you see a wild animal in me."

"Why an animal?"

"Well who else needs to be tamed?"

"Let's not play word games, Mr. Koshovy."

"God forbid! Several hours ago, your engineer friend clearly showed me my place. The others silently agreed. Now you have asked me to join you in your carriage like some trained puppy. You could have also added 'alley-oop.'"

He was becoming riled up and realized this. He was sick and tired of controlling himself – he'd had enough of the accusations of espionage. Magda had noticed that he had teeth. Well, he needed to show them at least a little bit, so as not to disappoint the woman.

But she remained silent. For a while they listened to the hubbub of the city's streets and the clatter of the horse's hooves on the cobblestones. Magda adjusted her veil, waved the fan about with her right hand covered in a thin glove, and sighed.

"You didn't quite make proper sense of everything which took place today. But I have no intention of convincing you of your erroneous conclusions. None the least because I hardly intend keeping in touch with you in the future. As for Adas…" she paused, and corrected herself, "the engineer Mr. Wiszniewski, he is a much more imposing person than you can imagine. Industrialists hold him in high regard, which means he can allow himself to knock at the doors of some especially important people. Doors are opened, he is gladly invited, and people take note of his views. He is also a sportsman and inspires other citizens by his example. Mr. Popeliak has described his sporting prowess in his newspaper on many an occasion."

"Why are you telling me all this? I've already understood that Mr. Adam Wiszniewski is by far not the lowliest of people in Lviv."

"I'm mentioning this, Mr. Koshovy, so that in the end you reach the correct conclusions. A man of such status as Wiszniewski would never belittle himself to show you where your place is, to use your words. Of course, there have been occasions when the engineer put people in their place, who behaved not quite correctly in his company, in the company of ladies or in other circumstances, where it is worth controlling oneself. However, he has taken an ungrateful task upon himself today, having invited you along and offering to summarize the dissenting opinions of his colleagues."

"Hence, how am I to react to his warning to keep well away from everything associated with Soyka's murder? Mrs. Magda, you are taking me to Lychakiv Street – not only to the building in which Soyka lived, but even to his apartment. I have moved in there, as you are probably aware. So, there's no way I can stay well away from all this."

Once more she waved her fan about.

"Mr. Koshovy, all the same you have misinterpreted the substance of the conversation. But let us leave it at that. The important thing is that you have learned things about your old friend which, I hope, will help you avoid unnecessary acquaintances and dealings. Anyone could have moved into an apartment, which had been vacated in such tragic circumstances. I am guessing the landlord is only too happy, for under different circumstances he would have been forced to suffer losses, as I doubt that anyone decent and worthy would have moved in there in the near future."

"I thank you for your high opinion of me."

"Stop acting the fool. I know it's a defensive reaction. If you need to defend yourself, it need not be from me. On the contrary, I am very grateful to you for the way you showed up Olshansky. For he, as I've already mentioned, is an *idiot*. He seriously intended to pass off Mr. Genyk's death as a banal suicide, so that he could quickly close the case, forget about Soyka, and wash his hands of the case. Now, after your explanation, everything is different. A criminal case has been opened, the police are working, the killer is being sought. Whether they find him is another question."

"That is, it was important for you personally that the investigation into Yevhen Soyka's death not be thwarted?"

"Exactly, Mr. Koshovy."

"Why? Were you fond of him?"

"Are you making fun of me? On the contrary, you heard what the respected gentlemen thought about him, the company he kept and his activities. Having begun the investigation, the police will formulate various possibilities. One of these you heard accidentally – suspicious associations with groups focused on *Moscow*, the Russian Tsar. One way or another, as they dig in that direction, the police will have every reason to ruffle the feathers of the Russophiles. Although it could have been simply a banal burglary."

"You think like a policeman, Mrs. Magda."

"It was my departed husband who thought like a policeman. He loved to think out loud. At some point, he began not only to think out loud in my presence, seeking my support, but even to ask me for advice. You see, everything is quite simple. No sensations, no conspiracy theories. So you, Mr. Koshovy, are blessed."

"Really?"

"Thanks to you, the case is now moving in the necessary direction. For which I am personally incredibly grateful to you. I have my own reasons for this. Please allow me not to voice them. And," she barely leaned forward, "I think we have arrived. Your place on Lychakiv Street."

As he was getting out of the carriage, Koshovy almost dropped his package.

CHAPTER TEN
THE FIRST BIG LVIV STREET RACE

Even Klym was highly skeptical of his chances of finding at least one of the fellows who had stolen his money.

The only way that he could justify his actions, was the fact that he had nothing else to do in the foreseeable future. And even in the long term Koshovy could hardly see himself catching the bird of good fortune here in Lviv. It would have been enough just to catch a glimpse of it, to grab it by the tail and pull out a few feathers – a ready-made good luck charm.

However, Klym had no intention of sitting around and doing nothing.

He had tried that, and it was not to his liking.

But he had had a burning desire for revenge from that very first day. It had not appeared at once, but all the same it came to him.

…As soon as he had moved into the apartment vacated by Soyka under such tragic circumstances, Klym had unexpectedly enjoyed a good night's sleep. He had thought that he wouldn't be able to sleep normally and tried to drive away childish thoughts about the ghost of an innocent murder victim which returns to the apartment and makes its presence felt all night long.

Koshovy was thinking these things merely for want of something better to do, to occupy his tired brain, for he personally did not feel threatened by the ghost of Yevhen Pavlovych. When the fellow was alive, they were not enemies, so on the contrary, the deceased lawyer would also more than likely be protecting his younger student and friend, from the other side. In the frightening and at the same time romantic stories that Klym like to read, the ghost occasionally revealed the mystery behind its death. Just like the father of Prince Hamlet…

Jokes aside, but such thoughts, strangely enough, pacified Koshovy. Drawing on every single thought he could muster about things he had once read, he logically and rationally reached the only conclusion possible under such *unreal* circumstances. Who, if not Klym, had convinced the police investigator, that Soyka had not committed suicide? Otherwise he would have been buried as a sinner, outside the cemetery grounds, and then his soul would have roamed accursed between the two worlds, having not been properly blessed in church. This way he had been buried according to the Christian tradition. His soul was in repose, so there was no reason for it to trouble those who were still living – even if they lived among his things in the apartment where he had died a sudden death.

Who knows, maybe it was this strange conclusion that had decisively reassured Koshovy on that first night. In order to consolidate the feeling, he found the carafe of liqueur in the cupboard, drank to Soyka's memory once, then yet again, and finally a third time, and only then bedded down on the couch in the lounge room: all the same he had refrained from going to bed in the bedroom, which still bore vestiges of his predecessor's warmth.

The city woke early and equally went to bed early. The landlord was already on his feet, so Klym asked him to send someone around to clean up the apartment, change the bedlinen and to generally arrange the place so that it appeared as if the previous tenant had simply moved out. Mr. Singer grumbled but did not particularly object.

Koshovy himself went out for a walk on his first morning in Lviv.

The day before Shatsky had explained in detail, where it was better to dine for those who were experiencing temporary financial difficulties. One had to get up early to visit the breakfast rooms – these were places in many of the respectable hotels which offered city folk meals. The closest turned out to be that same Hotel Georges, mentioned many times the previous day, and where Mrs. Magda supposedly resided. Despite the building works, it continued to accept guests, and Klym also managed to have breakfast there.

Apart from bacon and eggs, and sandwiches with butter, they suggested a shot of Baczewski vodka. He did not refuse, although he was unaccustomed to drinking in the morning. He rationalized that he wouldn't have enough money if he were to drink during the day. Washing his breakfast down with coffee, he paid less than a krone for everything. And made the decision to hold out until five in the afternoon, if possible, once more taking Shatsky's advice, to grab some buns in one of the Jewish bakeries. By late afternoon the baked goods were no longer that fresh, and so the bakers lowered their prices toward the end of the day.

When he returned, the dexterous landlord was already overseeing the clearing out of the apartment under the watchful eyes of his thin as a rake long-nosed wife, with the things left behind almost as a kind of inheritance being packed away. Klym already knew there was no material evidence here, useful to the police investigation. And if in the near future no one laid claim to the suits, books and suitcases, the landlord would wholeheartedly take everything for himself. Mr. Singer must have countless friends, capable of quickly and painlessly preparing the necessary documents for him. So, despite the arrangement which Jozef Shatsky had almost forcibly convinced him to agree to, the fellow wouldn't be suffering too much when it came to finances.

Koshovy needed a little time to settle in. After thinking a while, he placed the small photo of his parents on the desk at which Soyka had worked, moving to one side a small pile of writing paper while he was at it. His parents would look better under the desk lamp. On the bookshelf, which, loomed nearby, he set out his small literary treasures, making a mental note: now the purchase of his favorite adventure novels would have to be postponed until better times – there was no money for books now. He would also need special, professional literature. Deciding not to worry too much about this now, Klym slipped a clean, although unironed shirt, vest, and tie onto a coat hanger, and hung it in the closet. The toiletry bag with his things he placed near the handbasin.

He settled into the chair, suddenly realizing that this was it, there was nothing more to occupy himself with.

He lay around for a few hours, studying the ceiling and trying to put a swarm of thoughts in order. And only then he decided to venture into town again.

He was hungry, and lunchtime was drawing near. In Lviv this meant closer to five in the afternoon. Guided by Shatsky's instructions, Klym tried some żurek[41], then wandered off to get some buns. Afterward his feet took

....

[41] Żurek – a traditional Polish dish, a sour thick soup with added flour and eggs; many differing versions exist. Also called 'yesterday's soup' and considered a good hangover remedy.

him to the Nyzhni Valy. At first Koshovy did not attach any significance to this, as it was one of the not too many places where he had already been and which he was familiar with. He sat down on a bench and summed up his situation. Expenses – a little over a krone, at this rate he could last two weeks or so. But he immediately sat up with a start: there was no point giving in to fate, admitting defeat and waiting until he gradually became destitute. At this point he caught himself involuntarily surveying the crowd, searching for, at the very least, yesterday's money changer Juzef.

Because there would probably be scammers nearby.

This idle wandering became transformed into a steadfast desire to find one of the batiars who had duped him, no matter the cost.

The police handout – it was the only way Koshovy perceived the graciously donated money – only delayed his inevitable financial ruin. The need to get a job as a loader at the railway station or a sales assistant in a shop, or at the very least as a porter, of which there were plenty near every market, was beginning to look fairly plausible. The need to reach such a decision drew inevitably closer by the day, and this realization surprisingly added to Klym's anger. He, a man who had quite recently defended revolutionaries from the death sentence, and in the process almost lost his own freedom, and, to his own amazement, had suffered not the best of his days in a prison cell, would now be forced to leave here. He had to reconcile himself to the fact that some wretches had robbed him out of the blue in broad daylight.

This gave rise to his first goal…

Which was why, for the third day after Soyka's funeral, Koshovy assiduously preened himself each morning, as if he were going to work, and left home, each time politely greeting the janitor. He tried not to return before evening, because each time this Cerberus in an apron knitted his brows and gave the new lodger a murderous look. His whole demeanor was meant to remind Klym that he needed to slip the fellow some small change for the kindness he was showing by opening the gate. To refuse to hand over such a paltry amount meant that he would make himself an enemy under his nose, which Koshovy could not allow himself, as he already felt in a precarious enough position. So, the only solution was to appear before the janitor as little as possible. Inasmuch as one couldn't enter or leave without walking past him, Klym solved this problem very simply: he tried to leave in the morning and skulk about Lviv, until he no longer had any strength left and saw circles before his eyes.

The surname of this Cerberus from Lychakiv Street was quite consistent with his appearance, and especially reflected his distinct bulbous nose. The janitor was called Hnat Bulbash. He was Ukrainian, and for some unknown reason stubbornly refused to recognize Koshovy as his countryman. In general, he would have given the impression of being an unfriendly man, if this hostility of his had extended to the other residents. But Bulbash was surprisingly nice toward them, and Klym, after suffering for a while, decided that it was simply the effect his presence had on the *proletariat*. Because Kyiv janitors also disliked him, even after seeing him for the first and the last time.

Recalling that there were people, at whom normally placid dogs began to bark for no reason at all, Koshovy resigned himself to the janitor's hostility. Which gave him an extra reason to part with his small change every time Bulbash opened the gate for him, so as not to tease the geese even more.

Thank heavens, you don't want to be paid when I need to leave here, thought Klym, as he walked past the janitor one morning and greeted him, even saluting with two fingers. In reply the fellow turned his back on him, pretending to be busy with some urgent job. Taking advantage of the fact that Bulbash was not looking in his direction, Koshovy could hold back no longer and spat on the ground. My, the times we live in: even janitors had no regard for him. What could he expect then from people like Adam Wiszniewski or Magda Bohdanovych…?

Stepping out into the street and seeing that at least today the weather was not overcast, Klym adjusted his hat and set off on his usual, already familiar route, which he had been taking these past few days.

Not to the boulevard, but to Wekslarski Square.

There is a saying: your tongue will get you to Kyiv.

And even in Lviv the Kyiv lawyer's tenacity and well-hung tongue did not let him down. He did not come across the money changer at the Nyzhni Valy. After a few correctly posed questions he was informed that it was better to look for Juzio in Wekslarski Square. They gladly explained to him how to get there. It did not take long to reach the place, but when he did, his first thought was that he had been duped, that they had taken advantage of his complete lack of knowledge of the city.

Koshovy had seen various squares in his life, from large open ones, to small cozy piazzas. He had also managed to cross several of Lviv's squares, the names of which had slipped his mind. But the place where had Klym arrived at first glance had nothing in common with its name.

For a real square the Wekslarski appeared far too small. At least it seemed that way to Klym. It sooner resembled a small cozy courtyard, a quiet nook for meetings and business transactions in the central, lively part of the city. The lawyer found himself in an enclosed space, where the gray, unwelcoming walls of the brick buildings seemed to be pressing in from all directions. This impression was intensified by the July sun, more precisely the lack of it. The sun's rays added life to the city streets, making their grandeur and aloofness seem more subdued, and instead highlighted the elegance, order, and thoughtful planning of the urban environment. But for some strange reason the sun seemed to avoid this small square. A whiff of dampness reached Klym from somewhere, distantly reminding him of the jail cell where he had been imprisoned.

Trying to forget his unpleasant memories, the lawyer shrugged his shoulders. Really, what was this… So, he had reached a place where the usual city bustle died away. There was no need to worry. Moreover, his first impression was misleading. The small square had its own life, and the city's residents did not come here for walks, for there was nowhere to wander here. If someone turned into this square, then they had important matters to attend to.

In a few days people began to recognize Koshovy here.

Klym still couldn't forgive himself the naivete with which he had come here that first time. Of course, as he realized now, all this might have become only a mere annoying misadventure, had Soyka been alive. They would probably be recalling it as no more than a waggish local anecdote. As if to say: see, this was how this royal city greeted subjects of the Russian emperor. So, the attempt to find Mr. Juzio and to ask him personally for help was justified by the despair and hopelessness of the situation he now found himself in.

However, Mr. Juzio, like every habitué of Wekslarski Square, was indifferent to the problems of some blockhead. Even more: at first the money changer pretended not to recognize Klym, and when he did decide to remember him, he abandoned his feigned courtesy of a street wheeler and dealer, and asked Klym to stop bothering him with his nonsense. But Koshovy did not relent, and then with a nod of his head Juzio asked him to step to one side, whereupon he explained, waving his cane about each time Klym tried to get a word in sideways:

"Hear me out carefully, sir. I don't know every batiar in Lviv. I know other people, who also don't have connections in Upper Lychakiv. If you think that because of your own carelessness you were a victim of thieves – then please! Look for the offenders among the criminals. Take a walk along Upper Lychakiv on foot. Maybe you'll come across someone who might help you. Although personally I have great doubts in that regard. You'd do better to say goodbye to your stolen money for good, mister scatterbrain. Rather than pester decent people here and annoy everyone with your silly questions. Lastly, you have the right to go to the police. They will receive you there and hear you out, that's their job. However, I'm ready to bet your hat that the police will tell you the same thing."

"Do you have need of my hat?"

"I have need of peace and quiet, sir."

Having uttered these words, the money changer, as on the day of their first acquaintance, leaned forward and winked. Then, with the agility of a juggler, he tossed his cane from one hand to the other and left Klym, returning to his business.

Since that time Juzio hadn't spoken to him again. For his part, Koshovy no longer approached the money changer. But he continued to come to Wekslarski Square, arriving there as if coming to work, simply attempting to keep a respectable distance from the unfriendly local. After his failed conversation with Juzio, Klym decided not to question any of the others whether the batiars got up to their antics very often here, and if any of the eyewitnesses could recognize at least one such trickster. Quite reasonably fearing he would get the same, if not a worse reply.

So, he adopted a tactic which, given his regretful experience, he considered not ideal, but the best given the circumstances.

He was counting on the following.

That what had happened to him at the Valy, wasn't the first and only time that this had occurred, nor would it be the last. The hooligans and petty thieves had taken a liking to this place for their hunting because it really was quite an advantageous spot. Having appeared here once and deftly robbed a victim, they would definitely return to the square with the same purpose in mind. Although it might not be tomorrow, or the day after tomorrow, for some time needed to elapse. But something told Koshovy that if he was patient, and did not attract too much attention to himself, he could make Wekslarski Square a place of ambush, and the wild game would soon show itself to the hunter. The main thing here was not to be caught napping, not to lose one's head, but to act as circumstances dictated.

The stubborn succeed.

Later Klym could not remember whose words these had been. They probably belonged to some eminent person. But if no one had hitherto thought of such an aphorism, apart from himself, then let the deduction be his own. Because as it turned out, it was simple and correct.

After three days of silent stubborn patience the heavens finally rewarded him.

At first his attention was drawn to a fellow who was far too fidgety to be one of the 'black market' regulars.

Although he himself did not stand out from others because of his clothes, having been born and bred in the city, Klym immediately recognized the fellow as someone from the provinces, who had suddenly come into a heap of money. It wasn't due to any miracle – the fellow had earned his first capital through hard work. But it was all too evident that he felt uncomfortable wearing a suit. And neither the cut, the style, or the color suited him. Everything looked awfully expensive and very tasteless. But the man was obviously trying extremely hard to look like the rest of the city's residents, even pretending to be an aristocrat – otherwise Koshovy could not explain all this expensive lack of taste. The clothes sooner reminded him of a carnival outfit than everyday garb.

The fellow moved with a quick waddle, making him look very much like a bear. He mopped his sweaty forehead with a handkerchief as he walked, and when he stopped before one of the money changers, he blew his nose and then ran the handkerchief across his forehead. What the fidgety fellow discussed, Klym could not hear from where he was standing, but he saw the money changer point the strange client in the direction of Mr. Juzio. Juzef had also taken note of the provincial but was in no hurry to join in the game: according to unwritten rules, no one could steal a client from their colleague. But as soon as he saw that the man was hurrying toward him, he grabbed his cane with an artistic flourish and made his way toward him.

They approached one another.

A brief business-like conversation ensued.

Either because of all the long waiting, or perhaps his attention had become so well honed that he sensed something – in his peripheral vision Klym had caught sight of two young fellows, whom he had taken no notice of only minutes earlier. More than likely, they had simply not been here before. Otherwise, they would have caught his eye. One of them, who was slightly older, had trousers supported on wide suspenders, a striped shirt with rolled-up sleeves, a checkered cap cocked to one side. The other fellow, who was younger, wore a white shirt with an unbuttoned collar tucked into plaid pants; over the shirt he had a vest, the same tone as his pants. The lad had pushed his light-colored monotone cap to the back of his head. From under the peak protruded a defiant blond quiff. A cigarette sat in the corner of his mouth, as if it had always been there.

Koshovy already knew how batiars looked. For he had even taken Juzio's advice and been for a walk through Upper Lychakiv, but he had not ventured far, losing all interest in such idle wandering. Of course, one couldn't walk down the street, bugging everyone with the stupidest question in the world: 'Excuse me, respected sir, would you know who might have nicked my two hundred and thirty kroner?' It was better to lie in wait here, even if he looked like a complete gook.

His eye twitched.

His gaze jumped once more from the couple to the fidgety fellow. The fellow had just taken a bulging wallet from his pocket. Wetting his fingers with spit, he counted off notes to give to Juzio.

The batiars no longer took any notice of anyone or anything, concentrating on the ritual actions of the money changer and his client.

His eye twitched again.

In anticipation of something about to happen, for the sake of which he had been wiling away all these days, Klym for some reason clenched his fists and took several steps forward.

Checkers had a quick word to Quiff and began to move in the direction of Juzio and his conspicuous fidgety client almost in unison with Koshovy.

Meanwhile Quiff spat his cigarette onto the ground, landing it right in the gutter, turned up the peak of his cap even more, at the same time pulling it snugly onto his head. He was *already* preparing for something. Was it only Klym's imagination, or had he really bent his legs at the knees.

Taking the pile of kroner from the money changer, with a preoccupied and at the same time clearly satisfied look, the man began to place his treasure into his wallet with a sense of accomplishment.

Meanwhile Juzio had lost all interest in the man.

He turned around to disappear into the shadows of the gray building.

He looked Koshovy straight in the eye, as he was already moving to intercept him. Who knows what he was thinking at that moment? Because Checkers had already come up behind the provincial, stretched his arms forward and hit him hard in the back.

"Thief! Stop the thief!" shouts filled the air.

The man was already falling, very badly at that, not like Klym in his time: he hit the ground like a sack of flour, awkwardly kicking up his foot. He dropped his wallet onto the ground, as was to be expected. The checkered fellow, having carried out his job, was already running for his life across the square, while Quiff, continuing to holler at the top of his lungs, hurried after him, making more noise than was necessary. He swept up the wallet before the owner got to it – but Koshovy no longer waited for his deft fingers to empty it and was standing beside him in two leaps.

"Stop!" he barked, leaving Quiff confused. "Thief! Here's the thief! Grab hold of him!"

It was a waste of time – now the people in the square looked about, not sure how many thieves there were here, where they were, who needed to be apprehended, who to run after or whether there was any need at all to do so. Realizing that his cover had been blown, the batiar tossed the hot wallet straight at Klym, yelling:

"Here! Catch!"

Koshovy took the bait, but only for a split second – he deftly jumped aside, and dashed forward, trying in a last desperate bid to shorten the distance between himself and Quiff. The fellow though – who would have doubted it! – turned out to be more agile. He spun about on his heels and ran off in the opposite direction to Checkers.

Klym was not about to chase two birds.

He then acted as he would not have done under other circumstances.

He rushed up to Juzio, who was standing motionlessly quite close by and, before the fellow had enough time to recover, he abruptly snatched the cane from his right hand. Having taken control of it, he transformed it into a makeshift weapon.

Taking aim, he lunged forward and tossed the stick, so that it twirled through the air.

They had done this as teenagers on the outskirts of Kyiv. He had done the same with his village coevals, when during his childhood and early teens his parents had moved in the summer to their dacha.

Although he hadn't done this for a long time, the skill was not forgotten.

The spinning cane hit its mark – Quiff stumbled.

He clearly did not expect such an attack. Although he lurched forward, he did not lose his balance and managed to stay on his feet, but all the same it slowed him down.

Not for long.

But long enough for Klym to once more reduce the distance between them.

All the same the Lviv batiar turned out to be more nimble. It seemed that any moment now Koshovy would be able to stretch out his hand and nab the fellow, but instead he only managed to grab at the July air. Quiff bounded ahead even faster, at first weaving among the passers-by, who had not yet understood what was happening – and then began to push them, in an attempt to make them get in his pursuer's way. Klym was also forced to push people aside, which was why the air filled with a weighty assortment of Polish, Jewish and German swear words.

"Help! Help! They're trying to kill me!"

It was Quiff hollering as he ran, pointing his finger behind him, and suddenly Klym realized that the fellow was pointing at him. With his luck the passers-by might band together and try to catch him, and then hand him over to the police, where it would take too long to explain everything. But the main thing was that he would not have another chance like this for a quite some time to hunt down the thieves. If at all.

All this flashed through Klym's head. As if to confirm his thoughts, a red-faced mustached gorilla was already dashing toward him, his long arms stretching forward. Koshovy had little desire right now, under these circumstances, to recall his boxing experience from his high-school days and his attempts at mastering the skills of French wrestling. Klym had been no sportsman, and was not that good at either of them. But nothing learned is forgotten.

He surprised himself when he stopped the unwanted adversary with a direct blow to the jaw.

The gorilla did not fall but he stopped, rubbing his bruised face. While he decided whether he should chase after his attacker, Koshovy, pressing on, again significantly shortened the distance between himself and Quiff. Knowing the city like the back of his hand, the fellow dived into courtyards, wove about streets, taking Klym along various byways. Under different circumstances Koshovy probably would have given up. However, he was spurred on by persistence, perseverance and understanding – he had to make use of this sole chance.

Finally they ran out onto the Promenade.

There was probably no other way to go. Later Klym understood that if the bushy-haired batiar had wanted to shake him off, if he saw a *real* threat in this unexpected adventure, instead of treating it as a light-hearted game – he would have tried to lose him much earlier. Taking a different route, diving more deeply into the jungle of Lviv's streets. Instead, having fun and not worrying about the consequences, Quiff bounded over the streetcar tracks practically in front of the streetcar, to cut himself off from his pursuer.

And then, with an agile and, most likely, well-rehearsed flourish, he grabbed hold of an external handrail at the back of the streetcar, and jumped up onto the footboard.

While he held on with his right hand, with his left he removed his cap and waved it at the breathless Klym. Finally, to completely consolidate his victory, he turned his hat back into place, pulled it on more snugly by the peak, slipped two fingers into his mouth, and let out a defiant whistle. But even that didn't seem enough to him, and so he twisted around and shook his backside about.

Koshovy thought he heard a gawking passer-by begin to clap.

There was no time to think. Only move forward.

He was guided by instinct. Not fully understanding what he was doing and how it all might end, Klym jumped into the nearest horse and carriage and hollered:

"GO!!!"

And only after the coachman tugged at the reins, sending the horse off at a gallop, did he notice that Zakhar Hnatyshyn was sitting on the coach-box.

"After him! Fast as you can!" the words were at once a request and an order.

"Does sir wish to catch up to the streetcar?"

"To the fellow hanging off it!"

"What's your business with that batiar?"

"We'll discuss that later, Zakhar! Hurry, we need to catch up!" Hnatyshyn yelled at the horse.

The springs creaked. The horseshoes clattered over the cobblestones. The streetcar rumbled and clanged, turning from Akademichna Street in the direction of Lychakiv.

Quiff made no effort to jump off. Equally he had no intention of moving inside. He knew that the streetcar driver and the passengers could see his maneuvers. But until there was a stop, no one would be braking. This was not foreseen in the regulations, and the batiar must have sensed his advantage. For this had not been his first ride like this.

But he had not taken one thing into account – the coachman Hnatyshyn had an enormous chip on his shoulder when it came to municipal electric transport. So he spurred his horse on, which it appeared, was liking this race with a machine, which had more than one horsepower. Though at first lagging significantly behind the streetcar, the carriage gradually made up the distance. Klym was already preparing to catch up to the fugitive.

"He's looking to reach Upper Lychakiv!" Hnatyshyn called out, without turning around. "He'll hop off there and become lost in the crowd!"

"What can we do?" Koshovy yelled over the rumble of the streetcar.

"Remain seated for the moment! Hold on tight!"

The carriage bumped about on the cobblestones more violently. Lurching from side to side, Klym clung hard to the handrails.

A spurt ahead.

Applying all the energy it could muster, Zakhar's horse drew up alongside the streetcar. And even began to slowly overtake it. Now Koshovy was threatening Quiff with his fist. Taking no notice of the fact that their race was at the center of everyone's attention. People in the streets were bolting in all directions, pressing against the walls of the buildings even where neither the carriage, nor the streetcar could have injured them.

Suddenly to the general commotion there was added the coordinated clatter of several more horseshoes. Three horsemen dressed in police uniforms suddenly galloped out of an adjoining street which ran into Lychakiv. They stayed together, then the more senior horseman moved a little ahead, maybe by half a head. Reaching into a holster fitted to his right side, he pulled out a gun and yelled something unintelligible.

Then he raised his hand.

And fired.

An utter commotion of sounds took hold of Lychakiv Street. Which together played out in a great urban symphony – a symphony of fright.

One of the police horsemen dug his spurs into his horse's sides, directing it across the tracks onto the opposite side of the street. The pursuer was thus able to overtake the streetcar on the opposite side. He gestured to Hnatyshyn to rein in his horse, to let the servant of the law pass, or even to stop altogether, to stop this mad pursuit.

Klym knew that Zakhar understood the order – but he refused to obey, continuing to keep his carriage alongside the streetcar.

Now he and the horsemen had the streetcar surrounded.

There was a clank. The brakes squealed.

The driver slowed down, spying his designated stop up ahead. He did this quite abruptly. Whether he meant to or not, the streetcar gave a sudden jerk, shaking the batiar off the sideboard, like some pear. Quiff could no longer stay on his feet, and began to roll across the cobblestones, like the little round bun in the fairy tale. Zakhar pulled on the reins as well, and Klym jumped out almost on the run, catching himself thinking a completely unnecessary thought: just as well that his hat had not come off, otherwise it would have taken quite some effort to find it later… With wide leaps he rushed toward the batiar, catching up to him and knocking the fellow off his feet.

His feet gave way under him and he crouched beside Quiff on the warm cobblestones. He was breathing heavily, like an exhausted hunting dog. The fellow tried to break free one last time, and Koshovy grabbed his foot and pulled on it, as if trying to move him toward himself. For certainty he pressed down on top of him, not caring in the least how his suit would look.

He felt something in the lad's right pocket. The fellow grabbed at it; even having lost he was prepared to guard his treasure.

The next moment they were surrounded by the horsemen. The senior officer dismounted, and boomed in a thick deep voice:

"What the hell are you up to here! What games are you playing at, kitty whiskers!"

"They're trying to kill me!" whined the hunted-down batiar.

"Pull the other one!" the policeman snapped back, turning his gaze to Klym.

Now Koshovy needed to say something. Unable to come up with anything suitable, still short of breath and not fully understanding how he had managed to catch the fugitive, he breathed out, so as not to remain silent:

"Take a look at what he's got in his pocket there!"

The policeman towered over Quiff like a mountain.

"Empty them!"

"I haven't done nothing!"

"Hurry up, empty your pockets, you sonofabitch!"

He had no choice. And acquiesced.

"What can one read here, mister commissar? Your handwriting is like a pharmacist's, haven't I said that before?"

Tomasz Poniatowski once again ran his eyes over the handwriting on the sheet of paper, lightly tugged at his right mustache gleaming with brilliantine, and glanced at the person who had brought the document.

A man approaching forty years of age was standing before the desk of the director of Lviv's criminal police department. Criminal Commissar Marek Wichura stood out not because of his threatening height, but primarily because of the color of his face. It seemed to be glowing, an unhealthy red hue, and made the detective look sinister, enabling him to threaten murderers and rapists. The color of the commissar's face made him look like all men without exception, who are either continually drunk, or at best continually live in a state of terrible inebriation. And it was better not to cross paths with drunk men in times of trouble. This was exactly the case with Marek Wichura. It was better not to cross his path, and was dangerous to get in his way.

There was only one reservation.

Among most of his service colleagues the criminal commissar was well-known for his almost total indifference to alcohol.

He might allow himself a glass or two of champagne at some solemn reception in the department, sometimes during informal social gatherings he might slowly drink a mug of light beer, helping it down with fried German sausages. At the same time, everyone who needed to, knew: Commissar Wichura's family doctor had forbidden him to drink alcohol, whose advice the scourge of Lviv's criminals had taken. The red color of the man's face was a congenital thing, something had happened to the blood vessels, and blood constantly flowed to his face. When others turned pale, Wichura simply became pink. At such moments he appeared far healthier.

His red face and illegible handwriting, which more resembled some ancient encrypted message, were the very traits which distinguished Commissar Wichura from among the other policemen in the Lviv department.

"Why couldn't you let the gentleman write an explanation in his own hand?" Poniatowski grumbled.

"I need to draw up the identification report myself, mister director. Mr. Veslav Singer only confirmed with his signature that it was all correct. The gold Breguet found in the pocket of that batiar really did belong to the murdered lawyer Yevhen Soyka."

The air of Poniatowski's spacious office was stirred by a faint rustle. Magda Bohdanovych had settled into a chair in the corner, folded her fan and lightly tapped it against her open hand. The young widow did not utter a single sound the whole time that the commissar had reported to his superior. She sat there unnoticed, as if detached from these events. Nevertheless, the presence of Klym Koshovy in the holy of holies raised several questions, and even irritated the police officers more than Magda's presence.

"Get the clerk to rewrite it," ordered Poniatowski, returning the document to the commissar. "After which you can summon the witness Singer to come in and sign it again. At the same time, find at least three more people who can attest to the same thing."

"It will be done, mister director," Wichura nodded with restraint. "But you… *we* can see and understand everything for ourselves: Zdenek Novotny, that same batiar, who was pursued in full sight of practically all of Lviv, is involved in the sudden death of the lawyer from Lychakiv. From the very start we were under the impression that he was killed during a burglary…"

Magda once more raised her fan, this time attracting the attention of the men.

"I'll remind you, mister commissar, that from the *very* start everyone here had agreed that Soyka had committed suicide. If the police hadn't detained Mr. Koshovy, who happened to be here by chance, you would have had a different picture of events."

"Mrs. Magda, we've always valued your concern and persistence," Poniatowski's tone reflected restrained anger battling with cold respect. "At the present time I personally, just as Mr. Wichura here, am interested why your unexpected protégé, Mr. Koshovy, has been getting in the way of the police from the very beginning. Even Mr. Bohdanovych in his time would not have called this a coincidence, you must agree."

Klym stepped from foot to foot, and cleared his throat. When three pairs of eyes looked at him, he said, diligently imitating the local manner of speaking:

"Forgive me, respected gentlemen. You can regard my humble persona as you wish. But since I am already here, albeit by chance, to use the words of Mrs. Magda, I implore you not to discuss me in my presence as if I am not here. Over my head, as they say. And then," he briefly nodded in Magda's direction, "I am grateful to you for your attempts at trying to defend me. Except that I myself am a lawyer, dare I remind you."

"Thank you for reminding us," Poniatowski again twirled his mustache, this time the left side. "Since you know the laws and are well acquainted with them, you will be quite able to understand me. You are a subject of another state. Tsarist and imperial laws likely differ. However, all the laws in this world, yes-yes, this world, I'm not afraid to use this word, concur that outsiders are not allowed to interfere in the work of the police, investigative bodies and the courts. What you have done today in broad daylight, all these chases are simply intolerable, Mr. Koshovy! And quite unacceptable! Such actions violate public order! I can already imagine the headlines in the city's newspapers today! The first great street race in Lviv or words to that effect, loud and nonsensical – like everything that most of the newspapers write! You became the hero of the day, Mr. Koshovy! You have brought a completely unnecessary sensation upon our quiet and comfortable city!"

Koshovy glanced at Magda.

"I wouldn't call the city that quiet… Judging by certain recent events. For example, a fellow was tried for the murder of the governor quite…"

"Until the unrest in the Russian Empire began, together with their bloody revolution, things were much quieter here!" Poniatowski raised his voice. "Nowadays, various troublemakers emigrate here! I've no time now to engage in empty discussions with you, Mr. Koshovy! Your perseverance has helped the police get on the trail of Soyka's killer or killers. And just as well that it was batiars who were involved, and there were no political implications! From now on the case will be taken over by the person whose job this is – Commissar Wichura. And during this time, Mr. Koshovy, I will personally petition that you be put under house arrest!"

Arrested once more.

How many times had this happened since the start of summer?

No matter, it was like some kind of curse. The evil eye, as Klym's departed grandmother used to say.

"Can I appeal this?"

"No. Mrs. Magda is also unlikely to defend you in such a situation. Maybe, you will be unpleasantly surprised by what you have heard. But we have already managed to discuss a similar prospect with her. We have agreed, everything must be done in the proper fashion."

Now Klym looked at Magda with reproach. The young widow held his gaze, understood, and added:

"You can argue, Mr. Koshovy. But believe me, it is better this way. Especially for you. Mr. Wichura has experience, my late husband valued him highly. Mr. Marek became the commissar on his recommendation. What I mean is that now that he knows where to start and how to proceed, the investigation will take just a few days. Then the house arrest will be safely lifted, I myself shall petition on your behalf. And then we can calmly discuss everything, which is troubling you about the near future."

So, the arrest was for his benefit.

That happens too.

Well-well.

CHAPTER ELEVEN
THINGS TO DO WHILE UNDER HOUSE ARREST

The ban on leaving the apartment had its unexpected advantages.

The first thing Koshovy did that evening, after he was returned home in accordance with the police order, was to promptly finish the liqueur left by his late predecessor. Klym was pleased with himself, and allowed himself the honor of celebrating his small victory in this new place.

He did not want to consider whether his insane chase after a streetcar, unprecedented in Lviv, gave him any advantage in the near future or held any long-term prospects. Something else pleased him: having set himself a goal, and stubbornly making his way toward it, he had flawlessly calculated both his own steps, as well as the behavior of the batiars, and had hunted down the offender even sooner than he had anticipated.

He refused to speculate about tomorrow and the following days. He had caught the thief, although it had resolved nothing, and the stolen money had not been returned. Which meant that in the morning he would be left with nothing to do. If that was the case, then the best course of action was to relax and loll about in bed for as long as he wanted.

The liqueur hastened his sleep, made it deeper, and after he opened his eyes, he didn't feel at all like getting up.

Of course, the call of nature forced him to get out of bed, and from the toilet, Klym returned to his bed, as if that was what all people did. His head was not hurting. On the contrary, it was surprisingly clear. The opened window looked out into the courtyard, from which came the sounds of a hurdy-gurdy. The bedroom was not sunny, but now Koshovy had no need of bright light. On the contrary, it was more cozy this way. Making it easier to think.

It was this window which provoked his thoughts.

Zdenek Novotny had climbed through it late at night. Whether on his own or with someone else made no difference. No one had revealed the details of the investigation to him, of course, but the thief was searched right there in the middle of the street at his, Koshovy's, behest. He recognized the Breguet, previously described by Mr. Singer, straight away. Having discarded for some reason the thought that in real life there could very easily be two identical gold watches on chains.

His last doubts evaporated when to his exclamation: 'Where d'you get it?!', the batiar had cried: 'It's not mine!'

If the fellow had been as experienced as he looked, having stolen the Breguet or obtained it in an equally criminal fashion, however in no way connected to murder, the first thing he would have declared was that he had bought it. Or that it had been a present. And on the spot, to clear himself, he would have declared from whom, when and for what he had received such a generous gift.

At least the young lawyer Koshovy had had the opportunity to observe such behavior among Kyiv's petty thieves.

Realizing that local batiars had a slightly different make-up to ordinary criminals, Klym still did not see too much of a difference between the ways of people who stole. After being caught, they tried to lay the blame as quickly as possible onto someone else. Criminal solidarity did not apply in such instances.

But Zdenek Novotny was picked up in the street quite by accident.

He had not even contemplated the likelihood. Otherwise he would not have been carrying the expensive watch with such confidence. Batiars, as Klym already understood, did not care what those around them thought. On the contrary, the greater their exploits in public, the more prestige they enjoyed in their company. Of course, you had to explain, when others inquired, how you came by such a toy. And understandably the reply would be different each time, progressively becoming embellished with fresh details, each time bringing the boastful story closer to the nocturnal tales of the legendary Scheherazade. Everything was forgiven.

But when the defiant batiar was surrounded by mounted police, and the man who had chased him so obstinately poked the watch straight in his snout and barked: 'Where d'you get this?', Zdenek immediately remembered *where*, and hastened to renounce ownership of his treasure. Out of sheer fright. And in doing so he had brought even more grief onto himself. Because when Klym explained the course of his thoughts to the commissar at an opportune moment, the experienced Wichura immediately drew the necessary conclusions. The strong vice of the police investigation, the bulldog-like grip of people such as such Olshansky would soon squeeze out of the batiar how he had come by the Breguet belonging to the lawyer Soyka, who had been shot dead in his apartment.

They crawled in through the window. Wanted to rob the place. Miscalculated, a brief struggle – and the tenant was shot dead. After that, they quickly arranged everything to look vaguely like a suicide, grabbed what they had come for, and left the same way they had come. Managing to close the window behind them, employing a cunning device used by thieves.

With this train of thought, Klym got to his feet all the same.

He rested his hands on the windowsill and glanced out into the yard. He could not see a thing. The fellow with the hurdy-gurdy had left. There was only the gloomy wall opposite on this late July morning. He remembered that he had once toyed with smoking, and from Soyka he had inherited not only the liqueur, but also some expensive cigars. Although he had had no longing for tobacco after leaving the jail cells of Kosy Kaponir, the urge reappeared now. Dressed as he was in his long johns, he walked through the apartment and found the box, after some searching. He was about to bite off the end of the cigar when he spied the special knife in the nick of time. He made the cut, lit the cigar. He waited for the coughing, the forgotten sensations. But nothing happened, his lungs quickly recalled what they had been denied for some time. He turned to face the window, squatting, blowing the smoke outside.

Something prevented him from accepting his own conclusions.

Something was missing.

Something wasn't right here.

After drawing on the cigar a fourth time, Koshovy understood. The batiar he had hunted down was the least likely person in the world to be a cold-blooded killer. Who knows, if he even knew how to hold a gun. Let's assume that first impressions were deceptive, and Quiff and the young lad really took people's lives as easily as they took their wallets. But then, Klym reasoned, in that case an experienced killer would not carry on his person something which he had acquired through murder. He would try not to attract any attention to himself. Moreover, he would not have engaged in primitive, albeit lucrative earnings in Wekslarski Square, and probably not only there.

It was obviously that Zdenek Novotny had entered the apartment through this very window from which Klym was now studying the courtyard.

Only he had not been alone.

The police could reach that conclusion. It was unlikely that Commissar Wichura didn't earn his keep.

It remained to be established, who had fired the cold-blooded shot: the captured batiar or his mate. Or, as they said here, his kumpel.

All the same, from the very start Koshovy sensed that this had nothing to do with ordinary burglary.

A *cold-blooded shot* had been fired.

Just that. The killer, whoever he might be, was aiming at the head. He had pressed the gun barrel to the victim's forehead. For this to happen Soyka had to not only be knocked off his feet. The lawyer never had an athletic stature, however he was not completely helpless either. He could look after himself, did not give up easily, so the killer must have had more physical strength than his victim. And – what was most important! – he must have known Mr. Genyk personally.

If need be, Koshovy could also explain his reasoning. And not only to himself. Everything was clear now, there was no need for additional arguments. And his internal dialogue would in fact produce no results. The criminal police were least of all interested in other's people's suppositions.

But no one could stop Klym from having such thoughts. Because every conclusion that he arrived at now was another step closer to the finale. Or, if one were to assume that the detained batiar had something to do with the murder, and sooner or later Zdenek would name him, then Koshovy would be able to explain the killer's motive.

Burglary.

Which very quickly turned into armed robbery.

And ended with a deadly shot.

And it was this which was the ultimate goal of those who had made their way at night through the open window into the apartment of the lawyer Soyka, who had an oh-so-dubious reputation, as it turned out.

Koshovy inhaled once more. He tried to let the smoke out in rings. It was a waste of time, and he abandoned this stupid occupation. It was good that there was a wall facing his window. There was nothing to distract him from his thoughts.

His eye twitched. This time lightly, almost imperceptibly, even very habitually.

Decisively picking up his backside off the windowsill, Koshovy sought and found the former tenant's old velvet dressing gown. He did not hesitate one bit as he put it on. Walking into the office, he merely wanted to put down his reasoning in writing, so as not to forget anything. Klym drew up the chair and settled down behind the desk.

Here, it seems, Soyka had spent the final hours of his life.

Pushing the massive inkwell closer, Koshovy cracked the knuckles of both hands.

He could have made himself a coffee. There was a little left in Mr. Genyk's apartment, and there was a kerosene burner nestled in one corner, and on it stood a small cezve slightly covered in soot. But he was not thwarted by his desire to hurry and jot down his thoughts in point form. It was just that until now Klym had rarely brewed coffee himself. At home this was usually done by his mother or father, or the woman who assisted in the kitchen. He merely did not want to mix the two processes. Firstly, he needed to sort through his thoughts and conclusions, as there was nothing more to do under house arrest. And only after, as a reward, he could get the hang of the cezve and the burner.

With his left hand he picked up the top sheet from a small pile of clean paper.

Placing the white rectangle before him, Klym took a pen, removed the lid from the inkwell, and dipped the pen into it. But after taking a closer look at the sheet of paper, he stopped.

On its surface he could barely make out the contours of some letters.

Koshovy lay the pen to one side. He lifted the sheet of paper to the light. Squinting, he looked attentively.

Hm, there were not only letters here – there was a whole note. It could be recreated if he worked diligently. Soyka had probably written something not too long before dying, placing the sheets of paper on top of one another, pressing quite heavily against the paper with the tip of his pen. Leaving an impression of the letter on the paper underneath.

Nothing with writing had been left on the desk. The same went for the drawers. The rubbish basket was empty, which Klym had managed to confirm for himself.

The note – or whatever the lawyer had written shortly before his death – had been taken out of the apartment.

His eye twitched more strongly.

Klym held his breath, as if one careless word or movement might destroy something very fragile, tender, brittle and especially important.

He placed the sheet of paper before him once more. As if it was the most valuable thing in his life. He opened a drawer and removed something he had noticed earlier – a large round magnifying glass, like the ones they drew on the covers of his favorite dime novels in the hands of brilliant detectives. Enlarged by the magnifying glass, the impressions could be made out more clearly now.

Carefully, letter by letter, Koshovy began to run his pen over the text, which had been written by Soyka. He recreated words where letters were missing, since the more he did, the more he could decipher the text, understanding both the content and the context of the note.

He was not even interested how long it would take to recreate the lawyer's note. He had no desire to eat, the sensation of hunger being replaced by excitement. Once he'd finished, he waved the piece of paper about in the air to dry the ink. Then carefully, for he had stumbled on a remarkably valuable find, he folded the paper in four. At first he slipped it into the pocket of the dressing gown. But then immediately changed his mind and transferred it into his wallet. He would keep everything on his person.

And, as if to top off this tedious but necessary task, there was a knock on the door.

At first moment Klym froze: this was how urchins felt, when they were caught in the act of doing something shameful, deserving of severe punishment, including repeating "The Lord's Prayer" many times over. But then the feeling passed and Koshovy opened the door with confidence.

The janitor Bulbash stood in the doorway. Beside him towered a corpulent policeman, sent by the directorate to guard the prisoner.

"How can I be of assistance?" Klym was now the epitome of civility.

"I must remind sir of the ban on visits while you are under house arrest," reported the policeman.

"Yes, I've been warned. Why have the pair of you turned up together? Have you decided that you can't move about the territory entrusted to the janitor without him being in attendance, mister sergeant?"

"It's hard to follow you, sir," Bulbash grunted.

"All the same, why are the two of you here? Do you want to step inside? There's no point standing in the doorway."

The sergeant and the janitor exchanged glances. Bulbash offered Klym a newspaper folded in two – a fresh issue of 'Dilo'[42].

"This is for you. I was asked to pass it on."

"Who by?"

"The man I saw you with before. His name is Mr. Shatsky. He wanted to see you personally…"

"…but visitors are forbidden," the policeman finished.

"So, the two of you graciously decided to bring me the newspaper from Mr. Shatsky?"

"There's an article there about you. With a picture," the janitor harrumphed, and shook his head: "So, you've became famous."

"Is that good or bad if the newspapers write about someone?" Klym inquired.

"The newspapers never print anything good," grunted the sergeant. "There's also a note there for you. It's in an envelope, and I am not disposed to open it without your permission. But I implore you to open it now. The police need to know about the correspondence of people kept under house arrest. The janitor is here to confirm that all these procedures are lawful and that I am conscientiously adhering to them. Otherwise competent gentlemen like you can write complaints…"

"Of course, if people weren't competent, then no one would be complaining to the police," Koshovy nodded. "All right, if these are the rules, be my guest."

Together with the newspaper there was a sealed postal envelope. Tossing the newspaper onto an armchair, Klym demonstratively tore open one

---

[42]   'Dilo' – the first and the oldest Ukrainian daily in Galicia (and for many years the only one). Published from 1880-1939.

corner. He shook out a quarter sheet of paper folded in two, cleared his throat, and read it out loud:

"Mr. Koshovy! The whole city is talking about your brave exploit. I wanted to talk with you. To learn the interesting details because my Esther cannot sleep. After all, such a well-known person has visited us for lunch. Here is hoping your troubles with the law will pass. In the meantime, do not break any laws. And stay where you are. Especially late at night. I raise my hat to you. Sincerely. Your devoted servant, Jozef Sh." He turned the note around, brought it up to the light, and spread his arms apart: "That's it. Nothing secret or forbidden. On the contrary, notice that the good fellow is warning me not to break any laws and to sit tight within these four walls."

"Wise people," the sergeant agreed. "Otherwise, Mr. Koshovy, you will be forced to sit in quite different lodgings."

With a casual gesture Klym slipped the note into the pocket of his dressing gown.

"Can someone be dispatched to fetch me breakfast? They can prepare it in some nearby restaurant and bring it here by courier."

"Your money, Mr. Koshovy, and everything will be tip-top!" the janitor grinned.

"In that case, I'm hungry."

The strange couple left. Klym heaved a loud sigh of relief. Then he pulled out Shatsky's note and ran his eyes over it once more.

That Shatsky, that sonofabitch! The cunning fellow knew that others would read the note.

One thing was made clear: Klym was being asked to wait until late in the evening and to be ready for something.

So, someone desperately needed to see him.

He could draw no other conclusion.

CHAPTER TWELVE
WINDOWS AND LABYRINTHS

Klym could barely wait until it became dark.

After lunch he had already changed. At first he had not wanted to, but afterward he even decided to put on a tie as well. In the mirror he saw a serious businesslike young man, encumbered with matters of paramount importance, whose cramped daily schedule started early in the morning and ran until late at night. He touched his cheeks, frowned, and diligently began to shave. But he was not distracted by this for too long, and the intense anticipation returned, together with anxious expectation of the unknown and, out of the blue, a feeling of emptiness.

In July the twilight encroached on everything without haste. At times it seemed to linger, to prolong the warm summer evenings and give people a little extra time for pleasant walks. The blanket of night slowly began to cover the city only after nine o'clock. From his open window Koshovy could not hear any sounds coming from the street. Except perhaps for the clang of a streetcar, and even then the sound was not that loud or sharp, as it was for those who were unlucky enough to have windows facing Lychakiv Street.

Another time such silence would have left Klym completely satisfied. The previous tenant must also have liked the location of this apartment. But now the silence made him tense and wary. It was even oppressive, there was something truly reminiscent of the silence of prison yards. Koshovy felt that after the days he had spent in the jail cell, he had forever lost the ability to enjoy peace and quiet. Street noise, evidence that life was raging and not thinking of stopping – these things were now much closer to his heart.

When the gray suffocating twilight finally flowed into night, unusually dark, so black you could cut it with a knife, Koshovy decidedly ran out of patience. He had no idea how Shatsky planned to reach him and how he would let his presence be known. But something told him to stay close to the window. He did not hesitate for long in deciding which one to wait beside. It did not matter. They all faced the courtyard. Only the bedroom was located further away, at the end of the block. Thus, the window, correspondingly, looked out into the depths of the deserted courtyard. A most convenient place for secret meetings. Small wonder the thieves had chosen it when they were looking for a way to break into the apartment.

Finishing smoking the cigar, Koshovy stood in the open window.

The figure and the flame were noticeable from afar. Anyone who knows where and what to look for will find them without fail.

He had waited for perhaps ten minutes. Maybe twenty. He had completely lost all track of time.

But it was not in vain.

Someone whistled from below.

At first softly, then louder, and then the person meowed like a cat. Trust Shatsky to act like this, it occurred to Klym. He didn't expect him to be into such games. The meowing especially appealed to him. He felt like hamming it up, and barking back in reply, although he understood, how badly it might turn out. Suddenly the signals ceased and instead shadows stirred in the yard.

Koshovy failed to understand what was happening. That is, if he'd had more time, he probably would have worked it out.

He wasn't allowed the luxury.

He heard a barely audible groan, followed by a soft knocking sound, then it seemed as if someone had scraped against the wall. Suddenly someone's strong hands appeared from the darkness and grabbed hold of the edge of the windowsill. They took firm hold, there was a push from below – and a moment later someone unknown to him and nimble hoisted themselves up, pressed their body forward, and cartwheeled their long legs inside with the deftness of a circus acrobat. Klym backed off, letting his nocturnal guest inside. He had no time to examine him, for instead of a greeting the fellow hastily ordered with a slight lisp:

"Quiet. Turn off the light."

There was a light in the office. Hurrying there and throwing the switch, Koshovy returned, smoothing his jacket as he moved. He was about to speak to his guest, but before he could open his mouth, the fellow gestured that he remain silent and pointed to the window.

"Kindly step outside, sir."

"Jump?"

"Climb. There's a friend of yours out there. I'll leave after you. Quiet, otherwise there'll be trouble."

Even without him, Klym understood that it was desirable to make no noise. He was more worried about something else: how to get out without injuring himself, with the distance here between floors being one and a half times a person's height. But his guest wasn't about to give him time for reflection, as he obviously had serious intentions in relation to him. Silently he shepherded him toward the open window, and Koshovy was left with nothing else but to sit on the windowsill and lower his feet outside. If someone had decided to organize his escape without his personal consent, this sooner reminded him of a kidnapping. Although no brute force was used, Klym nevertheless had no doubt that were he not to listen or if he tried to refuse to leave, he would simply be thrown out into the yard.

He crossed himself.

Turned over. Lay on his stomach and lowered his body, lower and lower.

His soles came across a foothold, not too wide, and quite adequate to allow him to step from one foot to the other, and to safely unclench his fingers, letting go of the edge of the windowsill. Next Koshovy squatted in one continuous motion, holding onto the wall with his hands, straightened his left leg, stretched it as far down as he was able, found his balance and pushed away. He slid down and struck solid ground. Klym managed not to stumble or make any noise. He might have lacked the agility of his nocturnal visitor, but he still had enough of his own, left over from his high-school years, which were brimming with various adventures, not all of which the parents of the future lawyer needed to know about.

He caught his breath, feeling almost like Edmond Dantès in the first minutes after escaping from the Château d'If. The darkness to his left filled with the soft voice of Jozef Shatsky:

"Everything alright, Mr. Koshovy? Don't be scared, we're all your friends here."

The stranger slid down from above. Now Klym finally saw the big wide plank placed against the wall at a slant. If anyone accustomed to such tricks stood on top of it, they could reach the window on the second level. Grabbing firm hold of the sill, they could hoist themselves up – and, hey presto, they would be inside.

The thieves and killers must have entered the residence roughly the same way.

The stranger who had come to fetch him was adept at doing such things. And Shatsky was accompanying him for some unknown reason.

"What the hell is going on here?" asked Klym in a whisper, but trying to sound stern.

"You're being invited for a conversation, Mr. Koshovy," explained Jozef. "We were seen together. Have you forgotten, that half of Lviv knows Shatsky, and Shatsky himself knows the rest? I was asked to pass on the note to you and to warn you of our nocturnal jaunt. My appearance here will not arouse any suspicion. Because Shatsky is probably the only person in the entire regal city, who never arouses suspicion in anyone."

"Couldn't we have talked back in the apartment?"

"No," the lisping stranger joined in the conversation. "The person who has an important matter to discuss with you can only enter through the door. He cannot wait until you've been released from house arrest. We need to act straight away. Tomorrow will be too late."

"Act?" Koshovy began to get upset. "Listen, I'm not too happy when people use me without my consent. Even if the go-between is the honorable Mr. Shatsky. Where are we going? Who are you? And who is looking for me? These are three questions to which I need an answer right away. Without this I won't take another step. And I'm still not saying anything about the main thing – the subject of the conversation."

"You will."

The lisping fellow came right up to him. As if he were about to embrace Klym.

Another instant and something sharp pressed against his side. Even piercing his jacket, it seemed. Shatsky let out a soft cry.

"We are not murderers, Mr. Koshovy," the stranger said calmly. "There's no need to fear for your life. My apologies, but I simply have no other way, no other words or desire to explain why you need to come along with me."

"But…"

"And you can keep your questions for the person who will be answering them. Mr. Shatsky, I'm very grateful to you. And I won't hold you up any longer."

A smacking of lips came from the darkness.

"No way, Mr. Tyma," Jozef answered. "Seeing as I am already here with you, I'll keep following. Don't worry, Shatsky knows how to keep other people's secrets."

Either the lisping Mr. Tyma really didn't mind, or he simply didn't have time to argue. He moved the sharp spike away from Klym's side and said:

"Watch out, Mr. Shatsky. You have children."

"Which is why I'll be careful," came back the serious reply.

"Then – off we go. Stay behind me, Mr. Koshovy. You won't get out of here on your own."

And the strange threesome dived into the night single file.

There were more straightforward ways out of the courtyard – one only needed to take a left and pass under the archway which led to the main entrance.

Which was the exit all the residents used. While standing at his bedroom window and aimlessly examining the not so picturesque grayness of the courtyard, Klym had already noticed this route. So, he automatically lurched that way to take the shortest route. But the fellow whose name was Tyma grabbed him by the elbow, stopping him.

"Not there."

"Why?" Koshovy burst out, and immediately asked: "Which way then?"

"That way we'll reach the gate," Shatsky explained hastily. "We would then be forced to walk past your janitor. And I'm telling you, that schlimazel with a potato nose will definitely catch sight of us."

Tyma didn't even bother to explain this. He set off in the opposite direction, into the depths of the courtyard. Following him, Klym and Shatsky passed through another archway. Either it only appeared so to Koshovy, or it really was a little narrower and darker. Bringing the small procession into the next, even more remotely situated courtyard, Tyma nodded at the still-lit windows, once more reminding everyone about the need for being cautious. Then he took a right, and their threesome continued on its way, hugging a blank brick wall. Soon it turned, and they dived into a narrow laneway.

Suddenly Tyma raised his right hand, stopping their progress. Following his example, Koshovy and Shatsky pressed against the wall and stopped breathing. Only now did Klym understand why they had stopped: in the darkness to their right a couple was making out. Enraptured with one another, the lovers had forgotten about everything in the world, as they kissed ardently. From where they stood, none of the trio could see them, but they could hear the characteristic sounds of passion.

Who knows how long this would have lasted? Taking two steps back, Tyma began to cough loudly. There was a shrill female cry, followed by the incomprehensible mumbling of a deep male voice, and the shadows began to move. One of them the smaller one, slipped into the depths of the small yard and disappeared into a building. The other, bigger one, stamped about and then turned around and headed straight for the trio. And then at the very last moment turned off and disappeared into a small labyrinth of passages.

The group continued on its way, skulking in the shadows. Klym stopped counting the number of times they had made a turn, how many arches they had passed under and how many courtyards they had slipped across like silent ghosts. He understood only one thing: on his own he would never have found his way along these Lviv walkways hidden from prying eyes, not even in broad daylight. At least for the moment, they remained unknown to him. He did not know whether in future he would need to learn all the ins and outs here. But in any case, he made a mental note to look into it.

They emerged from the urban labyrinth just as suddenly as they had entered it. It only seemed that they had traveled a long way. In fact, their journey behind the scenes of Lychakiv Street had taken no more than fifteen minutes. They came out into the street a little further on from where Koshovy lived. Three buildings further along the street a covered carriage was patiently waiting for them near the sidewalk. It felt as if Tyma had taken them along secret underground passages. As soon as they emerged from the nearest courtyard, the coachman on the coach-box stirred, came to life, and tugged on the reins. The horse snorted and lightly struck its hoof on the paved street. With a nod Tyma ordered Koshovy to get in first, and Klym hopped inside in one deft movement. Shatsky turned out to be not so graceful, and Tyma had to help the dentist inside, hopping in after him as the carriage was already moving.

The street was not too crowded. Streetlamps burned along the sidewalks. Koshovy knew where they were. So, he didn't need long to guess that they were headed in the direction of Upper Lychakiv.

Everyone was quiet the whole way. Only Jozef snuffled away, saying something very quietly under his breath. Klym was ready to wager that Shatsky was praying. Although Koshovy himself could not see any threats to either himself or his acquaintance in this nocturnal adventure. Having passed the Catholic church of Saint Antoniy, the coachman soon after turned the horse to the right. There was no lighting here, however the night sky was bright with stars and Koshovy saw a long row of luxurious, very cozy single-story houses, which were hiding in the trees growing on both sides of the street. At this time of night romantic couples no longer roamed the streets here, but there were sauntering groups of people which one wanted to avoid at all costs.

They were already in the inseparable dominion of the batiars. Although this was not designated in any municipal document.

They did not have long to travel after that. Stopping outside a very ordinary small building, the coachman let go of the reins, while Tyma gave Koshovy a slight nudge – they had arrived. Stepping outside, Klym looked around. His new acquaintance asked him to follow. But when Shatsky wanted to join them, he was stopped.

"What's wrong?" Jozef was startled. "Do you think I'd let Mr. Koshovy go unattended to join your Christmas play?"

"You wanted to come here with us, Mr. Shatsky," Tyma chirped through his teeth. "But we never agreed for you to listen in on our important conversations. You can take a walk in the fresh air here. If you're scared – hop back in the carriage and fall asleep. It'll take you home."

"To Lychakiv Street?"

"All the way to Krakidaly, if you like," Tyma slapped Klym lightly on the shoulder, losing all interest in Jozef. "Let's go. Welcome to 'Under the Louse.'"

Only now did Koshovy notice that before him stood no ordinary building, but rather a small restaurant. The light emanating from the windows, covered from the inside with curtains, obviously did not wink to every passing person. This was a place where not everyone could freely walk in at this time of night, Klym understood. Something akin to a batiar headquarters, no less.

The sign outside was not obvious. But as they walked past it, Koshovy managed to read the name.

It really was called 'Under the Louse'.

CHAPTER THIRTEEN
A SECRET MEETING AT 'UNDER THE LOUSE'

Coming through the doorway, Klym became immersed in a thick swirl of smells: beer, crackling, something fried too much, cabbage and tobacco smoke.

Inside, the restaurant proved to be not too big, but it wasn't tiny either. Round tables stood on either side, forming an irregular semicircle and leaving a clear path to the bar. On chairs at the bar sat respectable broad-shouldered and broad-arsed gentlemen, all to a man looking alike, resembling birds perched on a wire. Half the places to the left of the entrance were empty and except for two wenches sitting at the corner table, most probably local prostitutes. The appearance of the new visitors instantly caught their attention, and they swung their heads around together. Klym also rested his eyes on the whores, completely inappropriately recalling just how long he had been leading a monastic life. Did it only seem to him, or could the experienced girls have sensed at a distance that he had been celibate for quite some time? One of them swiveled about on her chair, made a barely noticeable gesture, and winked.

Although… he might have imagined it, given the thick bluish smoke in the air.

To hell with them. This frivolous life of his must have brought on sinful thoughts. But the wind in his wallet sobered him up. So Koshovy turned away and glanced to the right. This half of the hall was occupied by small groups of people, predominantly male, discussing things over mugs of beer. In the far corner, at several tables drawn together, sat a motley boisterous group of batiars, diluted by female company. When Koshovy and Tyma entered the establishment, they were in the process of grabbing their freshly poured beers, although carafes of vodka were also visible on the table. As they made their way across the hall to the opposite corner, where a solitary middle-aged man was already sitting on his own at a table and waiting for them, the group of batiars brought their beer mugs together and burst into song, though not too harmoniously:

Then a policeman came
And took the floor;
And I swung my fist:
Straight into his snout.[43]

Throwing a dissatisfied glance in their direction, Tyma shook his head. They made their way toward the table assigned for their meeting to the accompaniment of the defiant words:

But nothing happened to me,
'Cause I'm a carouser, as you can see!

A pot-bellied fellow with a mustache and a well-oiled parting in his hair was already hurrying toward them with a waddle. They knew Tyma here, but before the waiter could utter a word, he declared abruptly:

"Mr. Cezar, tell those crazies to quit hollering for the whole of Lychakiv to hear. They're acting like real jerks. Otherwise, they will be very politely asked to holler in another, not so pleasant place."

"I hear you, Mr. Tyma," nodded the mustached fellow, reminding him: "You're expected."

"I can see, Mr. Cezar. Warn that noisy rabble, and then bring us the usual."

Swinging about on his heels, the big-bellied fellow made his way to the group of batiars, grabbed the one sitting closest to him from behind by the shoulders and whispered something into his ear. When the fellow tried to turn around, Mr. Cezar gave him a light clip to the ear. After this, with a sense of having fulfilled his duty, he made his way back to the bar. Scratching the back of his neck, the batiar leaned over toward his friends, obviously relaying the request to them. Not everyone was pleased – two voices, one of them belonging to a girl, seemed to deliberately launch into the chorus once more:

....

[43]　An actual batiar street song. Source: Ihor Chornovol. Review of: Urszula Jakubowska, *Mit lwowskiego batiara* (Warszawa: Instytut Badań Literackich, 1998), *Ukrains'kyi humanitarnyi ohliad 7* (Kyiv 2002) 254-265.

But nothing happened to me,

'Cause I'm a carouser, as you can see!

The answer this time was a stronger slap to the back of the neck. It was meted out by the fellow sitting next to the impertinent lad who was taking no notice of the request. The lad tried to launch into song once more, but someone flicked the cap off his head and it was tossed across the table, again and again, stopping its owner from retrieving it. Finally, it was slipped back onto his head, this time back to front, and only after this did it become quiet in that corner.

"Come on over, Mr. Koshovy."

This was uttered by the man sitting at the table. A hand pointed to a place in the corner. Klym made his way there and sat down. Tyma sat to the right of him and the lawyer found himself as if in a vice. A large thick candle burned on the table, so Koshovy could see who was sitting opposite him. And at the same time make out the features of the fellow with the lisp.

Apart from his lisp, Tyma did not stand out at all. He was tall and sinewy, but there were many like him walking the streets. The older fellow sitting opposite him had no discerning features either, except perhaps for his bushy eyebrows, hair that was longer than required by the rules of decency, and a small wedge-shaped beard. Shaking the hand offered to him from across the table, Koshovy felt the force of the hand, and this relayed the power and position of the person who had sought to make his acquaintance in such an exotic way.

"They call me Gustav Silezsky," the man introduced himself. "I've read about you, but not in this morning's paper. I was provided information the moment you caught my stupid nephew, and he got nipped because of that damned klinger[44]," but seeing the utter incomprehension in Klym's eyes, he put it another way: "They arrested him because they found that pocket watch on him."

"Who's this?"

"Novotny, Zdenek," Silezsky repeated patiently. "My nephew. They allowed me to visit him in prison today. Before they transfer him to the Bridgettines[45], they're holding him in the clinker, the remand prison, the

----

[44]   Klinger (slang) – pocket watch.

[45]   Bridgettines (pol. Brygidki) – the oldest operating prison in Lviv. Located at 24 Horodotska

former city arsenal. Which was why I was able to organize our meeting. You don't need to know, Mr. Koshovy, who I am and what I do. It's enough for you to know that I wield a lot of influence in certain circles in Lviv. Under other circumstances you wouldn't have been able to find me so easily. Even if you had very much needed to see me and your life literally depended on it."

"Should I be proud of such an honor?"

"There's no need for irony here."

"I'm not being ironic at all. On the contrary, I want to understand the local customs. In case I suddenly have need of your help, Mr. Silezsky."

"If you ever have need of it – I won't envy you."

"Oh! Why's that?"

"Because people, and not only those like you, seek me out in cases, when things are worse than bad. But you have been lucky. I think, that when push comes to shove, you can sort out your difficulties in a far easier way."

"Meaning?"

"Well, Mrs. Magda has never given me a lift home in her carriage. Her late husband and I spoke informally several times on various important subjects. Although, I admit, the late Director Bohdanovych very much wanted to see me in the Bridgettines, and for a long term. Mrs. Magda has significant influence in those places, where I only cautiously seek it. She has more opportunities, Mr. Koshovy. But even she can't get my nephew out of the clinker."

"I understand, Mr. Silezsky, that you want to talk to me about the batiar who robbed me, and before that the lawyer Yevhen Soyka."

Cezar materialized beside them and the conversation broke off. The waiter placed a small four-faceted shot glass beside each of them. Then a bottle made of green glass materialized in the exact center of the table. Beside it appeared a large platter of sauerkraut and small fried sausages, which were still sizzling.

"Help yourself, Mr. Koshovy. I doubt that you've had dinner inside those four walls of yours," Silezsky invited him.

"Bon appetit," the waiter wished them and left.

....
St., in a building rebuilt from a former ancient Roman-Catholic monastery of the Bridgettine Order.

"The sausages here are excellent," nodded Tyma, spearing one with his fork, laying it on his plate and liberally smearing it with mustard.

"Have you forgotten?" Gustav frowned theatrically, feigning anger.

Slapping himself on the forehead, Tyma grabbed the green bottle. The vodka in it was white. As he poured it, smacking his lips, he urged them to drink, and after the men had emptied their glasses, he exhaled:

"Ah, a fine 'baczeruvka'!"

"Jerzy Tyma, my right arm," Gustav belatedly introduced his colleague. "If you like, consider him my secretary."

"For a secretary Mr. Tyma is very skilled at crawling through windows," Klym said, taking a sip of beer. "And he knows the local back streets very well."

"He grew up on the street," Silezsky explained. "And I picked him up off the streets. Otherwise Tyma would have been knifed one day in some secluded place like this, because he was an andrus, a street thief. He had no respect for other people's property. If he saw something – he nabbed it. Alright, if you don't like the term secretary, then let him be someone who performs special errands."

"So, sneaking me out through the window and secretly bringing me here, to 'Under the Louse' is considered a special errand? You flatter me, Mr. Silezsky," Koshovy bit off a piece of the sausage straight off his fork, even though there was a knife beside his plate, chewed and swallowed, and then added: "I am growing in my own eyes. I've been in Lviv less than a week, and already for many I've become a very important person."

Gustav grabbed a mug and looked through it at the candle flame. Holding it like this for a while, he took a sip, placed the mug on the table and folded his hands in front of him on the table.

"Enough jabbering, Mr. Koshovy. We've made each other's acquaintance. But believe me, no one and nothing is threatening you here. Furthermore, Zdenek, apart from the fact that he's a batiar and stole your money, has done nothing wrong. If you help me extract him from behind bars, you can always count on my benevolence."

"Agree, Mr. Koshovy," Jerzy Tyma interjected. "It's well worth the effort."

Klym sensed the taste of cigars in his mouth.

He had the urge to smoke.

For some reason he had no doubt that were he to ask for one – a cigar would be found, and of the highest quality, nothing cheap.

With his peripheral vision he noticed one of the prostitutes slowly get up, smooth her skirt, and slowly begin to make her way across the hall, heading straight toward them. One of the fatsos at the bar called out to her. But she ignored him completely, moving toward a clearly defined goal. Along the way she toyed with a cigarette, rolling it between the fingers of her left hand.

A left hander, what's more, it occurred to Klym.

Continuing not to rush with his reply, he had some more beer. He raised his fork vertically with the bitten-off sausage and held it there. Then placed it neatly onto his plate. Which he then smoothly pushed away, also resting his hands on the table, and leaned over to Gustav.

"I'm not in a position at present, Mr. Silezsky, to turn down someone's proffered hand."

The prostitute was already standing beside him, and only now did the others notice her. Silezsky frowned. Tyma grimaced with the corner of his mouth. The three men became immersed in the smell of cheap perfume. Its pungent odor did not upset the cabbage and tobacco smell at the table, and only gave it more piquancy, like some spice. But one which had been added by a not very skilful or clever hostess.

Not paying attention to anyone, apart from Klym, the prostitute stepped forward, pressing her breasts, which were too big for his taste, against his shoulder. The fingers of her left hand continued to play with the unlit cigarette.

"Hi, sugar-darling, can you give me a light."

Koshovy was forced to look at her over his shoulder. From close up he noticed the carefully powdered mesh of wrinkles under her eyes.

"You're a handsome cutie," her voice was low, throaty, and did not sound coarse at all.

Her thin, thickly covered lips looked even more vulgar, and were already pressing against the end of the cigarette. Realizing that he needed to say something, Klym, instead of answering, began to search for the non-existent box of matches in his pockets.

"Get lost! Skedaddle!" Tyma intervened.

The prostitute glanced at him, as if he were some insect.

"My God, no need to turn your nose up? Don't be so full of yourself! You don't know, what you're missing!"

"Exactly nothing, just another whore! Get lost, I said!"

Shrugging her shoulders, the prostitute stood up straight. She removed the cigarette from her mouth, ran her right hand across Klym's head, appearing to either stroke or ruffle his hair. Returning to the bar, she made a point of saying loudly, so that all present could hear:

"O-oh, who do I see! This handsome gentleman will give me a light. Sir has such a lovely anzug[46]! D'you work in the city council? Or for the railways[47]? Why are you sitting on your ownsome? I could entertain you."

As she was leaving, Klym could not help himself, and watched her go. But he quickly regained his composure and focused on the conversation at hand, clearing his throat:

"Well, I'm not in a position to ignore your offer of friendship. However, I want to understand one important thing for myself – how can someone like me, that is a random person without money or friends, except for Jozef Shatsky, help someone like you?"

Meanwhile the prostitute had sat down at the bar. Her right hand caressed the shorn back of the head of one of the fatsos.

"I'll repeat, since you did not hear," said Silezsky. "Zdenek Novotny is a batiar. Nothing good will come of him in the near future. Unless, of course, this unfortunate incident, which he's found himself in, makes him come to his senses. If it does, I will gladly help him out. His dear mother, who happens to be my sister, has already wept her eyes dry. See, she's a widow, her husband died of consumption, and her son, instead of helping her – is playing the batiar. Of course, he brings some money home, and occasionally even does a spot of work. Saws firewood here and there, but that doesn't happen too often. Hard work isn't for people like Zdenek. For the most part he sells stolen birds, puppies or cats."

"And he's also a pickpocket," Klym added.

"That too."

"And now – a murderer."

---

[46]   Anzug (German) – suit.

[47]   Working for the railways was considered prestigious not only in the Austro-Hungarian Empire.

Tyma slammed his half-empty mug far too loudly against the table.

"Zenyo never killed anyone!"

"He had the murdered lawyer's watch on him."

"But that doesn't mean my nephew shot Mr. Genyk!" Silezsky raised his voice somewhat, and immediately lowered it, continuing in a level tone, though he could barely control his agitation: "However, I know how the criminal police work. Commissar Wichura has an iron grip, and on top of that is not happy, if a case drags on for too long. You've handed him a trump card – the murdered man's watch."

"Excuse me!" Klym grew startled. "I never gave anyone the Breguet! You're intimating that I slipped the evidence to the batiar, so that…"

"Hear me out, please!" Gustav interrupted him, annoyed. "No one is accusing you of anything! Something happened by coincidence, which I hope will teach my nephew once and for all to keep away from apartment burglaries, Klepariv thieves and in general – explicit, undisguised crime."

"Zdenek was in the lawyer's apartment," said Tyma. "Together with that well-known burglar Liubko Tsipa. When these two lunatics climbed in there, they saw the body on the floor."

At the bar two fatsos had surrounded the prostitute. For the third time one of them was trying to light her cigarette. The second was pouring a drink from a carafe into a prudently held glass.

Koshovy sat bolt upright.

"What?"

"Someone had already killed your Soyka when Zdenek and Tsipa entered the place," Silezsky snapped back. "My frightened nephew told me this today, during our brief meeting. He's not saying anything to the police, because he's more scared of Tsipa, than of Commissar Wichura. Tsipa will definitely find out who snitched on him, and then I won't be able to save my nephew, despite all my connections. Such things are punished severely. And, frankly speaking, in other circumstances, I would welcome the punishment of a snitch. Once you're caught, you should hold your tongue. But I repeat, not this time."

"Why?"

"Even if I convince Zdenek to tell the police everything, and they pick up Tsipa, both will be tried for murder. Unless they make the burglar take the rap, and my nephew becomes only an accessory and a witness, who has withheld information about a crime. In addition, they robbed the deceased, that's true. Zdenek told me, they didn't need to rummage about for long. They found a travel bag stuffed full of cash in the bedroom under the bed. None of them stopped to think how Mr. Genyk came by such wealth. On the contrary, it was what they were expecting to find. Since your colleague's reputation wasn't one of the best. You must have heard about it." Koshovy nodded. "Lawyers, who successfully get villains off the hook, always have lots of cash. Or valuables. And they don't keep everything in the bank. That's what Tsipa explained to my Zdenek. And the fellow gladly agreed to the escapade."

His eyelid gave a mighty jerk. Koshovy pressed his fingertip against it and held it there for a short while.

"Didn't they know that Soyka was at home?"

"They were sure he wasn't."

"How could they have been?" Klym expressed surprise.

"Like this!" Gustav sat up straight, spread out his arms and glanced at Tyma, as if calling on him to bear witness. "Tsipa is an experienced thief. At first he decided to find out if the lawyer was at home. He pretended to be a client, but the janitor wouldn't let him in. A real Cerberus, that one. He declared that the lawyer was not in and told him to skedaddle. Said the lawyer was away and no one knew when he would be back. There was no light in the window. So our two heroes decided to wait an hour or so, before they scrambled in through the open window. The rest you know."

Now Klym stopped paying the slightest bit of attention to the babble of the drinkers at the other tables or the unrestrained cries of the batiars. Or even to the inflammatory laughter of the prostitute, who was already working over three habitués, while her friend for some reason remained sitting at the table with a bored look on her face.

What Mr. Silezsky had said very much sounded like the truth.

Koshovy was about to admit it out loud.

For Soyka had indeed given orders that no one be let in to see him. And he had even paid Bulbash to drive away random visitors. It appeared the thieves had bought the lie… They could easily have bought it.

"Did Zdenek mention when they entered the apartment?"

"When it became completely dark. Round about that time. If it was a little earlier or later, it wasn't by much, I guess. Does it matter?"

Klym decided to say nothing at this point.

"So, they found the travel bag with the money? And it appears Zdenek also grabbed a watch?"

"Exactly. He was tempted. Because Tsipa had no intention of divvying up the booty anytime soon. He'd decided to wait it out. He rightly assumed that someone would know about such a large stash. And would start looking for it. They would decide that whoever stole the money also murdered the lawyer. So Tsipa decided to cover their arses."

"How?"

"Zdenek said the fellow had come up with the idea to make it look like the lawyer had shot himself. Then he made sure that the window was closed from the inside. Liubko is good at such tricks."

His eyelid twitched again.

"You mean…"

"I'm just repeating my nephew's words, Mr. Koshovy."

The original crime scene is disturbed. The police are left confused. And all because of two petty criminals. But Klym dismissed any last doubts he might have had: the batiar was definitely not guilty of the murder. Neither was he the killer's accomplice.

"How can I be of assistance?" he asked, preparing for a business-like exchange.

"You know Mrs. Magda. Let her know what you heard from me."

"And about Liubko," Tyma added with a lisp.

"Correct. Instead of my nephew, it will be you who let the police know through Mrs. Bohdanovych where Tsipa is hiding. Let them mess around with him, since it was his idea. Frankly, I'm not really happy handing this loser over to them. Therefore, there's another way out: Tsipa returns the money in full, to the kreutzer. And hotfoots it out of Lviv, the further – the better. Let them search for him as the murderer, burglar or witness – it's all the same to me. Only all of this in exchange for Zdenek's release," the corner of Gustav's lips contorted into a smile. "He can just as easily be put under house arrest."

The prostitute was leading all three fatsos from the bar to the corner table where her demonstratively bored girlfriend was sitting.

One of the drinkers rested his head on the table. Another tugged at the shoulder of his fallen comrade.

Meanwhile the group of carousers in the opposite corner began to prepare to leave. There was a protracted loud argument going on about who would be paying and Klym was afraid it might turn into a brawl. The police would hurry over then, and here he was – a fugitive.

"How long do you need to think this over, Mr. Koshovy?" Silezsky hurried him along. "To allow you to think more clearly: how much money did you say that batiar grabbed from you?"

This time Klym could not hold back a smile.

"What's the matter?"

"I just remembered. Right now, though. Look, yesterday your nephew, together with a friend, suffered an adventure with a dead body in an apartment, from which he emerged with a gold watch, and with half the money crammed, to use his words, into a travel bag. And today, as if nothing had happened, he fraudulently steals a hundred kroner from a visitor to the city. Wouldn't you say that's crazy?"

"For batiars, Mr. Koshovy, the spoils of such games are meaningless," Tyma replied. "The game itself is the all-important thing."

While he was talking, Silezsky extricated an expensive leather wallet from an inner pocket, extracted several banknotes, and solemnly placed them on the table before Koshovy.

"All yours. There's four hundred there. I'm reimbursing your losses. Make sure that the unfortunate mother stops shedding tears on account of her stupid son."

It was better to forget about pride. Especially with his luck.

Trying to remain as dignified as the situation allowed, Koshovy took the money and without counting it, slipped it into his pocket. The deal was done.

"How do you think I can get to meet Mrs. Magda?"

"There's a policeman hanging about outside your building. Tell him you want to see the commissar. When he appears – demand the conversation take place in the presence of Mrs. Bohdanovych. Do I really need to teach you what to do?"

"I need to know how I came by the information about the thief Tsipa and the travel bag full of money," explained Klym and, without waiting for a reply, declared: "Your Zdenek will tell them himself. I'll join them later." None of those present knew anything about the sheet of paper which Koshovy had on his person, and he planned to play this trump card later, when the time was right. "I won't tell you now, what I've come up with. But you can rest assured that before lunch tomorrow Zdenek Novotny will be out of prison. You just need to see him again and find out where the stolen money is hidden. Once I know, it will be my turn to join in the play. Agreed?"

The men looked at one another.

"Agreed," Gustav slapped his palm on the table.

"Then Tsipa needs to be picked up now!" said Tyma. "Soon as he heard about Zdenek, he lay low. He's in Klepariv now, at his moll's place. They say she's gone to visit her parents in the village to drop something off. She's left him some food and Tsipa refuses to poke his nose outside. Trembling on the dosh."

"What's he waiting for?"

"God only knows, Mr. Silezsky."

"Well, we can ask him while we're at it."

Gustav rose to his feet. The new acquaintance turned out to be a head taller than Klym.

"Coming with us? Or can we drop you off by the same route?"

"After everything I've heard? Excuse me, gentlemen, there will always be time to stay under house arrest," Klym also stood up and, unable to stop himself, took another bite of the sausage. "Let's go. Let's bring this show to a close."

Where they needed to look for the killer and even who they should be looking for, Koshovy was not about to reveal to these two.

"Shatsky is still sulking out there," Jerzy Tyma reminded them, getting up too. "We had to drag him along with us. You know him, Mr. Silezsky…"

"It's because I know him that I allowed him to become involved in all this," Gustav sighed. "It can't get any worse. We'll go together…"

They reached Klepariv in half an hour or so.

Shatsky asked no questions. He curled up silently in a corner of the carriage, with Koshovy pressed against him, and was once again breathing evenly. The others were silent as well, each probably thinking their own thoughts. As for Klym, he really had something to rack his brains over. Enjoying albeit a small victory, but a victory all the same, he repeatedly kept recalling the text written by Soyka before his death and which he had recreated today. In the end, he could boast that he knew it by heart. Suddenly becoming the bearer of valuable information, Klym was proud of himself. And he considered what advantage he might gain out of this, to conclude the annoying start to his Lviv odyssey without suffering any more losses.

Avoiding a steep hill along the way, the carriage turned down a street and they found themselves in a fairly quiet neighborhood, which even in the dead of night looked picturesque. The air was filled with the scent of blossom, everything around them looked utterly peaceful. Sitting next to the coachman, Tyma showed him the way, and they finally stopped outside a building surrounded by a low fence. This time they did not even need to ask Shatsky to stay behind, and openly entered the yard in a group. At first Tyma knocked on a window, loudly and forcefully, until there was a tinkle of glass. Then, without waiting, he turned back, stepped onto the porch and began banging on the door.

It was enough to strike the door twice with his fist to realize by the third time that the door was unlocked.

Gesturing for everyone to step aside, the lisping Jerzy pulled a small gun from his pocket. The moon had appeared in the sky, and the cold steel glinted in the moonlight.

"Put that away," Silezsky blurted out.

Without listening to him, Tyma pulled the door toward himself.

The door opened.

He stepped inside, leaving the door ajar behind him.

And a short moment later he emerged. The hand with the weapon was dangling at his side. Even in the darkness he looked visibly shaken.

"What's wrong?" Klym and Gustav asked in unison.

They saw for themselves when they stepped inside.

On the lounge room floor a fellow by the name of Liubko Tsipa was lying face down in a pool of his own blood.

Everyone saw this – but Koshovy also sensed a familiar smell.

It was the same smell that had been present in lawyer Soyka's bedroom.

That same cheap tobacco.

The smell of it still filled the air. Someone had been smoking here quite recently.

CHAPTER FOURTEEN
FROM ANGER TO MERCY

"You're not only under our feet. You're breaking the law, and you'll be punished for this."

The color of Marek Wichura's face was entirely consistent with the state he was in. Under other circumstances, a chance observer would probably have said that the commissar's face was burning with indignation and anger. The color resembled a hotplate, or a glowing iron billet removed from a blacksmith's furnace.

But now, looking calmly at the angry policeman, Klym once again realized the advantage Wichura had. His red muzzle made him look angry even when the commissar was in a different, contrary state of mind. The commissar always, no matter what the circumstance, resembled an angry bull which no one was capable of reining in.

This time Wichura's indignation was real and, judging from his bloodshot eyes, the commissar was half a step away from exploding. True, there was a different explanation for Wichura's bloodshot eyes: lack of sleep. He had been woken in the middle of the night, and at a time when the policeman had finally resolved to have a good night's sleep. Koshovy knew only too well what that was like.

Since Soyka's killer had now been caught.

But the longer the batiar delayed his confession to the police, which he had admitted to his uncle one on one, the more opportunities it presented for the investigation to charge him. Zdenek should have told them everything straight away, however the lad had failed to do so for the reasons Klym was already aware of. As a professional lawyer he rejected them, but at the same time he understood. Were he to defend Novotny, his first serious problem would have been the lad's indecisiveness, which would later be quite difficult to remedy.

From now on, every hour that the batiar remained obstinately silent, he would be digging himself a deeper hole, if it were appropriate to say so. And he hastened the commissar's victory.

"You should get some sleep," Koshovy declared, looking Wichura straight in the eye.

It was not clear what riled up the commissar more – the murder, about which he was notified late at night, or Klym's bold escape from under house arrest, or this very natural absolute calm of his. Wichura clenched his fists.

"Are you making fun of me? You… you, you cheeky little pup!"

The policemen who were stamping about in the yard, grew wary on hearing these words, becoming like hunting dogs in expectation of an order from their owner.

Everything took place in the yard – a special team had been inside the house for over an hour now examining the dead body and the crime scene, having asked Wichura and everyone else to step outside. Looking at the policemen, gauging the danger they were exuding, and agreeing with himself that it would not make things any the worse, Koshovy again turned to face the commissar.

"No, sir. You need to sleep. In the state you are in, it's awfully hard to think clearly. And even more difficult to make the right decisions. You might do something you'll regret, so before this happens…"

"Decisions, you say. I've already decided everything! They'll put handcuffs on you, you bastard! And you'll go straight from here to the Bridgettines!"

"Why?"

"There are more than enough reasons, lad! Escape from custody. From now on you won't have such an opportunity. Next – having been in Lviv for less than a week, you have managed to find two bodies! Moreover, this second fellow, before he became a body, was sliced up with a knife! He was stabbed in the stomach like a pig! They cut a belt from his back. Stuffed a rag into his mouth, so no one would hear his moans!" the commissar became more and more worked up. "And both times you have the impudence to call the police!"

"So, I shouldn't have? I shouldn't have called the police?"

"Now he's playing the fool!" Wichura hollered, giving free reign to his anger. "You keep stumbling on homicides! And then you become practically the principal witness to the crime! We need to take a closer look at you, Koshovy! It is not clear who you are, not clear at all!" the commissar let out a sigh, having let off steam, and continued in a calmer tone. "As for your kumpel, Mr. Genyk Soyka, everything has been clear for a long time. Sooner or later he would have had steel bracelets clamped on him! But we still need to find out why you came here from Russia!"

"Kyiv is not Russia," Klym corrected him. "The Russian Empire, Mr. Wichura, likewise did not all once belong to the Russian tsarist dynasty."

"Stop that!" the commissar snapped back. "We're not talking about politics here! I have a suspicion that the royal imperial gendarmerie will take an interest in you! So, don't get too worked up, lad! As soon as you get behind bars, they'll find a hundred reasons to keep you there for a long time to come."

Koshovy sighed. He wanted to add, that he was well aware of this. But instead he said:

"Your mention of the security service was timely, mister commissar. And appropriately reminded me of your power over me, a transgressor of the law. Formally – the subject of a neighboring state. And still without residency rights on the territory of the Kingdom of Galicia and Lodomeria. I am ready to admit to all my mistakes. If the law deems my actions to be criminal – let it be so. I am used to obeying the law and complying with it. You know that I am a lawyer by profession. That is, a servant of the law. And I'll submit to the will of my master. But before you arrest me, let me explain everything."

"What do you mean by 'everything'? You'll explain to me, why you escaped from under house arrest and how you found yourself here in the middle of the night, in Klepariv, beside the well-known thief Liubko Tsipa, who was shot dead at close range, what's more? No one knows where Tsipa hides out! No one!" the commissar wagged his finger before Klym's face. "The police need to engage countless agents to find him whenever they need to talk to him! But this fellow Koshovy, who cannot remember the names of our streets, he arrives at night exactly at the place where this fellow's been shot! And by the way, it's probably a result of them settling personal accounts. Which is common practice among criminals."

"What makes you think that?"

"And why should I have to report to everyone?" Wichura exploded, and immediately explained: "Inside everything's been turned upside down. They were obviously looking for something. I'm of the opinion they found it. And my guess is, that it's highly probable that Tsipa took something from a person or persons who considered themselves untouchable. He broke the rules – he's been known to have done that in the past. So, they took back what was rightly theirs and punished Liubko. Punished him demonstratively, you can't get any more demonstrative."

"I completely agree with you, mister commissar," Klym was amazed at how easily he had managed to stay calm, despite everything. "Even more, I'm ready to make a deal."

"A deal? Already up to something, you slippery eel? Mrs. Bohdanovych, by the way, won't rescue you this time, have no illusions!"

"For quite some time now, mister commissar, I have relied only on myself. Mrs. Bohdanovych has nothing to do with anything here. There is no need to mention a respectable lady's name in vain. As for the deal – it's very simple. You allow me to walk free. You don't level any accusations against me. You cancel the house arrest. And in general, the police leave me in peace. Can you agree to this part of the deal?"

"You have a big appetite, lad. I haven't heard yet what you can offer me in return. What confessions? After all, that's what we're talking about here, right? You're admitting to something?"

His eye twitched violently, giving away the enormous effort Klym was making to stay calm.

"I have nothing to confess. I'll give you the name of the fellow who killed the thief Liubko Tsipa. And it's highly likely that this same man first killed the lawyer Yevhen Soyka," he pressed his finger against the edge of his right eye. "I'll hand you the name of the killer, mister commissar. Here and now."

He spoke loudly.

And unable to stop himself, he looked around at the policemen. They had heard him and drew closer, without any special order being issued.

The night was becoming more interesting.

…The decision came the moment Koshovy saw the thief's body.

He didn't explain anything to his new friends or Jozef Shatsky. Sensing that fragile moment when events can be reined in and he could take control of everything, Klym immediately began to act. The advantage lay in his wallet, folded in four. It was unwittingly handed to him by the late Yevhen Soyka.

And Koshovy had taken full advantage of the acquired knowledge.

Silezsky and Tyma were to leave the scene of the crime as soon as possible. Nothing was to be touched here. Shatsky, who was now scared to death and had completely stopped enjoying this nocturnal escapade, had to be quickly delivered home. And for his own good he needed to keep his trap shut. He needed to independently come up with a good explanation for his Esther, and the more improbable it sounded, the sooner she would believe him. Because, judging by everything, Shatsky found himself in similar situations all the time. Anything but the brothel, please gentlemen, Jozef had declared then, but no one took much notice of him – Klym was far more interested in how to notify the police about the murder and yet not reveal his source. The fact that he had become personally acquainted with Mr. Gustav Silezsky, Koshovy suspected, wouldn't augur well for him in the future.

I need to wait here on my own for the police to come, he told them, without launching into the details of his plan. Everything will fall into place from here, besides – you asked for help, and you'll have it. Silezsky decided not to argue, and did as he was bid.

And more than an hour later, Koshovy received his first great helping of anger from Commissar Marek Wichura…

Now came the time to strike. All the same Klym was finally asked the question:

"How did you come by this information?"

And he replied:

"Soyka himself wrote down the surname of his killer. I discovered this by accident, mister commissar. I was staying in the apartment, under house arrest. I had some ideas. I decided to jot them down, which I often do. I took some paper from Soyka's stocks. And noticed this."

With a flourish he pulled the wallet from his pocket, fished out the valuable sheet of paper. Taking it, Wichura for some reason sniffed at the paper. Then he unfolded it, and made a sign:

"Can I have some light!"

"No need, it'll be a waste of time."

"Why?"

"Do you know Russian?"

"Russian?"

"Soyka wrote a release note. He took great care as he wrote and pressed hard with his pen. He was known for that, being very assiduous with his handwriting. Words and letters were partly impressed onto the sheet of paper underneath. As I began to ink in these impressions, in an attempt to read the note, it became evident that it was written in Russian."

"What does this mean?"

"Soyka wrote his note in Russian," Klym was now speaking patiently with Wichura, as if he was talking to a small child. "It means it was meant for some Russian person. His name is Ignat Yartsev, and he was meant to be guarding the money in the amount of thirty thousand rubles. Soyka was meant to hand the money over to Simeon Danovich – who that is, I have no idea. But Yevhen Pavlovych, or Mr. Genyk, as people call him here, undertook in writing to assume full responsibility for the package. The note is addressed to Yuri Kniazev, who is also unknown to me. Mister commissar, as a result of all of this you and I reach the only correct conclusion: Soyka released Yartsev with this document, for the fellow, as I understand it, simply burdened the lawyer with his presence. Which is why Soyka behaved so strangely on the eve of his murder, refusing to see any visitors whatsoever. He had an armed thug sitting there in his apartment, who was also chain-smoking cheap smelly cigarettes. Ask Mr. Olshansky, the investigator will probably relay to you my conclusions about the smell which continued to linger in the residence of the deceased. Especially in the bedroom."

"I know," Wichura waved him away. "So who killed Soyka and Tsipa? You promised to name them."

"I already have. Ignatiy Yartsev, that same bodyguard who is a lover of strong cheap tobacco. He was here in the yard. I expect he was waiting for Tsipa to return from his carousing. He could have bumped into him here. But unfortunately, his moll, in whose bed he was hiding here, had set off for the village a few days ago. So that Tsipa, suddenly feeling free and having no idea what to do with himself, acted like most men would act in his shoes – and went off looking for a bit of skirt."

"And how do you know this?"

"Firstly, I am after all a man," Koshovy smiled. "Secondly, while I was waiting for the police, I couldn't help myself and examined the body. Tsipa was at first badly tortured for a while, you've already seen that for yourself. Then he was shot with a bullet to the head. The same way Soyka was killed.

But the smell of alcohol remained after death. It enveloped Liubchyk, which proves that the thief had returned home late and was drunk. Which means, he had been out drinking. He found an uninvited guest at home. Whether he managed to sober up or not – the Lord only knows. One way or the other, the strong smell of cheap Russian tobacco has remained because Ignatiy Yartsev was smoking as he patiently waited for his victim.”

“Why did that Yartsev of yours come to Klepariv in the middle of the night?”

Koshovy grew tense, squeezing an invisible tight spring inside him. This was the most responsible and most dangerous moment – the logical explanation for his presence here. Because this question was about to leave the commissar’s lips.

“Allow me to speak briefly, and in order, Mr. Wichura.”

“Be my guest.”

“Thank you. What did I realize, having read the note? That those who linked my older friend Yevhen Soyka to the subversive activities of the Russophile organizations aimed at undermining the Austro-Hungarian Empire had hit the nail on the head. Most likely, the thirty thousand rubles delivered by Kniazev and Yartsev, was money meant to finance some political or more likely terrorist organization. I am correlating this with the nationalist terrorism rampant in Lviv of late. I read the newspapers and have my ear to the ground. Let’s assume that Soyka knew that he was being secretly watched. And that he decided not to hand over the package straight away to Simeon Danovich. He keeps the money at his place for safekeeping, and at the same time has no intention of tolerating the likes of Ignatiy Yartsev hanging around. Very much like Mr. Soyka, I can tell you. Well, meanwhile Yartsev, having received the unexpected release note, decides to grab the money for himself. Whether he concurred with Kniazev, I can’t confirm for the moment.”

“Suppositions, Mr. Koshovy.”

“Exactly, Mr. Wichura. And if it weren’t for the body of the thief Tsipa with signs of torture, I wouldn’t be hurrying with my conclusions. But now everything falls into place.”

The dark night slowly began to turn gray.

An early July dawn approached. The covered body of the deceased was already being carried out of the house. The policemen, watching the stretcher being taken away, spoke softly among themselves, for some reason also throwing glances at Klym. He felt uncomfortable and shrugged his shoulders.

"So what do you see as having happened, Mr. Koshovy?"

It appeared the commissar's anger was beginning to transform into mercy.

"Ignatiy Yartsev leaves Soyka's place," explained Klym. "Waits, and then returns sometime later. This time secretly, through the open window. The lawyer does not expect such a turn of events. And puts up a fight. A brief struggle, Yartsev presses him to the floor, shoots, kills him. But the money remains in the apartment, and not as well hidden as one would imagine."

"How do you know this?"

"Because the money was found by the burglars who entered the apartment *after* Soyka had been killed. They were Liubko Tsipa and the batiar we both know – Zdenek Novotny. Finding the travel bag and grabbing the expensive pocket watch while they were at it, they left the apartment, very satisfied with themselves and frightened at the same time. And they were hoping that in the event of anything the burglary and the murder would be attributed to the same person, that is if anyone ever detected the theft. And none of them would come under suspicion."

"I didn't hear, why you consider this course of events to be what actually took place, Mr. Koshovy."

"The answer is there," Klym nodded in the direction of the yard. "If Tsipa hadn't snatched the money, which was not intended for him, Ignatiy Yartsev would have had nothing to do with him. But I learned only a few hours ago that Liubko and Zdenek cleaned out Mr. Genyk's apartment that night. Which is why I found myself here in Klepariv."

"I don't understand."

"I'll explain," now Koshovy was on thin ice. "After I had recreated and read the note, I realized that a hefty sum of money had been stashed away in Soyka's apartment, which was not found after his death. Because no one had been looking for it. The police weren't aware of its existence. That got me thinking," his eye twitched, but Klym took no notice, warming to his subject: "The burglars wouldn't have been satisfied with just taking the pocket watch, which was found on that defiant batiar. They had probably taken the money as well. Then I imagined Ignatiy Yartsev. I know a little, just a little bit, Mr. Wichura, about the customs of such people, having encountered them in Kyiv and having read about them in Russian newspapers. I realized that the bodyguard would not rest, he would turn over every cobblestone in Lviv until he found the thieves and punished them, retrieving the money. For him and Kniazev, it was a matter of honor."

"I'm baffled," the commissar again began to grow irritated. "Why didn't you summon the police straight away, why are you telling me about your find only now, in the moonlight next to the body?"

"Punish me," sighed Koshovy, his appearance showing boundless and deep repentance. "Pride got the better of me. I wanted to find out everything on my own. And present it all to you on a platter, as a present. I'm vain, yes, it's a sin, I know, but which of us is not without sin… Because of my pride I ended up in this mess."

"In greater detail, if you please, sir."

"You're aware that I was robbed by batiars. Every day I went out looking for them. I also asked around where they liked to congregate. That's how I found out about the 'Louse' in Upper Lychakiv."

"A popular place," it seemed the commissar was beginning to buy the story.

"I had been there a few times before. Understandably, no one had wanted to talk to me. But now I had something to go there with. Waiting until it was dark, I left by the window. I expected to return home the same way. In short, I chatted once more with local clientele there, the batiars. Explained to them, who and what might be threatening them. A judgment, mister commissar, naive and rather likely: that the thief or thieves, who are still free and hiding the money, would return it to the police. Dropping it off with a note indicating who in fact could have killed Soyka. Then I step in, boasting of my unexpected find, among other things, and present you this note. After which everything is simply a matter of police procedure."

Dissatisfied, Wichura snorted:

"Nonsense. Child's play."

"Maybe so," Klym readily agreed. "Even surely so, mister commissar. I got in too deep – it happens. Allow me not to name the persons who finally suggested, where I might find Liubko Tsipa. Agreed – I found his barely-cold corpse and could have avoided any unpleasantness. However, I decided to wait for the police to arrive. And equally, please don't force me to tell you, how

I came to find out about the murder in Klepariv. Word of honor – in light of what has transpired here, people who have obviously nothing to do with this crime need not interest you."

Marek Wichura crumpled the sheet of paper with the handwriting with his fingertips. Thinking hard, he slipped it into the pocket of his jacket. He rubbed his chin, then his whole face.

"You were right, Mr. Koshovy. I need to have a good night's sleep," and after a pause, he added: "It only remains to be ascertained, why Yartsev didn't take the money. Leaving it behind, so that Zdenek and Liubko could make off with it. Do you have anything to say on that account?"

He had carried it off. There had been a shadow of suspicion – and then it had all vanished.

"Only more assumptions," Klym said. "I'm guided, once again, by my knowledge of Soyka's character and habits. He could have, I emphasize – only could have begun to play a risky game with Yartsev. To win time, and not give away the treasure immediately. Who knows how long Yartsev had kept an eye on Soyka? Let's try to imagine that late at night Yartsev, like some apparition, comes climbing in through the window and begins to shake down the lawyer – let me have it now! And Mr. Genyk in reply says something like: quiet, I'm no fool. I took on the responsibility, and so I'm carrying it. The money's not in the apartment. It's hidden elsewhere. When d'you manage? None of your bloody business! Once again – this sort of behavior, such moves are quite in the style of Yevhen Pavlovych. In critical situations he was good at bluffing and would stop at nothing. Often, very often, it went his way."

"We know only too well," nodded Wichura, calling on the policemen as witnesses. "And now, Mr. Koshovy, I'll finish for you. The bluff worked only in part, a painfully common story. Yartsev decided that Soyka had named the correct place where the money was stashed out of fright. And decided to get rid of him there and then. Because he had already decided his fate and was not about to go back on his words. Meanwhile the money he dreamed of lay under his nose. The killer could not have thought such a thing possible. After he left, fate sent two thieves into the ominous apartment a short while later, one of them being a batiar. They easily located the unexpected treasure and took off. Meanwhile Novotny had never even expected to find such booty. Finally, after the burglars left, the killer returned to the apartment, only to luck out."

"I didn't notice any signs of a thorough search," Klym added. "Although Yartsev must have searched for the money."

"He only looked where a travel bag might have been hidden. Don't forget, the police had to be thrown off his trail. By ransacking the apartment, he might have led them to believe that this was no ordinary burglary, that people were after something. Besides the crime scene indeed resembled a suicide. Well, these are all suppositions. Although awfully close to the truth, if you ask me. The Russian emissaries had no right to write off the disappearance of such a substantial amount. And so there began a race."

"With who?"

"You, Mr. Koshovy. You were looking for the batiars, the Russians – for the thieves. It so happened that the dilettante and the professionals were moving in parallel. Then your adventure with the race the day before was written up in the newspapers. And they mentioned the pocket watch of the murdered lawyer. For the Russians, from that moment on, getting on the right trail became not only a matter of honor, but also finesse. Well, and now we won't be dragging our feet. How much longer are they going to be?" Wichura, standing on tip-toe, looked over Klym's shoulder into the yard, then waved his arm. "Anyway, there's work to do. Good, I need to go. Come with me!"

"Under arrest?" Klym wanted to make it sound like a joke.

"You deserve that, Mr. Koshovy. As a matter of law. You know, I like order and respect the law… But this time you've been lucky once more. You'll write down in detail what you've just recounted to me now. We'll add the note which you have as physical evidence. And you can return home. I'll make sure they lift the sanctions."

Klym stepped from one foot to the other.

"Mr. Wichura… Maybe…"

"Out with it! I don't have time for you!"

Intuitively he felt the rapid approach of the finale to this drama. His eye twitched only slightly, which was a good sign, he had already managed to understand this new self of his. He had stumbled across it at the very beginning, and now he very much wanted to stay until the end.

"I'll be needed, Mr. Wichura. At least as a witness in the investigation. If I go home, you'll need to send for me again. It would be better for all concerned if for the moment I stayed not too far from you. Close at hand, so to speak. You could even put me in one of the cells – you've probably never had a volunteer for that during your career."

The commissar rubbed his chin.

"Into a cell, you say? That's true, I've never seen anyone volunteer to go behind bars."

"But into solitary!" Koshovy added hastily. "So that I can at least catch up on my sleep."

"You think prison is like the Hotel Georges? Anyone who wants to can come and spend the night there?"

But Wichura grumbled more for show, than because he was outraged. For he had made up his mind. Though the night was barely beginning to turn into dawn, Klym understood from the expression on the man's face that everything had been decided.

CHAPTER FIFTEEN
CHEAP RUSSIAN TOBACCO, AMERICAN GUN

"Fine, gentlemen."

Koshovy was ready to wager anything that standing there at the head of the large, heavy oval table made of solid oak, the chief of the criminal police department looked very much like a military commander. And he had dubbed the meeting in his office a service meeting. Although he had summoned only three people, Klym was unable to understand, why he was also awarded the honor of being present. For the moment he stayed away from the others, for the most part remaining silent. Apart from him, Tomasz Poniatowski had invited Commissar Wichura and another lanky gentleman who very much resembled a rat, and didn't even bother to greet Koshovy, let alone to make his acquaintance. His gaze radiated a total, immense, universal suspicion.

Eventually Klym understood why this was so: the fellow turned out to be Karl Linda, head of the intelligence service, in charge of everyone who worked secretly for the police. The meeting opened with Linda's speech. Outside it was bright daylight, before noon, and the agents had not only already received their instructions, they had carried them out.

Simeon Danovich, the man mentioned in the note, had turned out to be a rather well-known person in the Russophile community in Lviv. He was a member of the Russian National Party[48], inside which disagreements had

....

[48]   Russian National Party – the first political party formed in 1900 by the Galician Russophiles on the initiative of the Russian Council. They enjoyed the support of the governor and the Polish parties, in particular during elections to parliament and the sejm, against the backdrop of a growing Ukrainian (Ruthenian) national movement. From its inception the party had two orientations: the old and the new course (the Old Ruthenians and the Russophiles), which in 1909 led to a final split of the party into two groups – one moderate, the other radical.

begun. At first he had allied with the radical wing. Then, having publicly quarreled with one of its leaders, Mr. Markov, for a short time he completely withdrew from party affairs. He was well known for being a publicist in the periodicals 'Russkoe slovo' and 'Russkaya beseda' and did not give the police any reasons to be seriously interested in him. But recently, less than a year ago, he had come under covert surveillance, after joining the leadership of a small radical group. He wasn't caught doing anything himself, although he didn't try to conceal his activities, continuing to remain a public opponent of Markov and another radical from his once 'native' party – Dudykiewicz[49]. He attacked them for not being radical enough. Coupled with his feckless rhetoric, it seemed comical. But then suddenly a year ago Danovich's name began to be bandied about in Lviv in connection with the bomber school.

Several 'students' of this school were released from the courtroom to the stormy applause of the Russophile community thanks to the efforts of the lawyer Yevhen Soyka.

Wichura had managed to explain all this earlier to Koshovy, when he treated the voluntary 'prisoner' to coffee and a slice of strudel which his wife had passed on. She always did this when the commissar remained at work after an all-night stint. The strudel was not to Klym's liking, being a little on the bland side. There was an explanation for this: Wichura couldn't eat too many sweet things, but he loved coffee and was generous with the milk. They discussed the situation over a light breakfast and now Klym understood without further need for explanation, how Linda's agents were able to establish so quickly where Ignatiy Yartsev was hiding.

This too was a science – it was enough to merely follow Danovich competently, ask the right people several, at first glance, innocuous questions, and that was that. The killer was sitting it out on the far side of the railway line, practically on the outskirts of Bohdanivka[50], and at present did not suspect any storm clouds gathering around him.

....

[49]   Włodzimierz Dudykiewicz (1861-1922), lawyer, Galician politician, Russophile ideologue, adherent of the radical group; Dimitry Markov (1864-1938) – public figure, publicist, one of the ideologues of Russophilism in Galicia, a supporter and ally of Dudykiewicz. After the start of WW1 he was accused of treason.

[50]   Bohdanivka – district in Lviv, at that time a suburb. Founded on the site of an estate of the Armenian Bohdanovych family. In 1861, when the first railway line was being laid in Ukraine from Lviv to Peremyshl (Przemyśl), a part of Bohdanivka was cleared to make way for the

                                    ANDRIY KOKOTIUKHA

There was only one problem…

"Good, gentlemen," Poniatowski repeated. "Although there's really nothing that good about the fact that our suspect is not sitting alone in that building. How many of them are there, Mr. Karol? Can you determine exactly?"

"The neighbors saw three," Linda's voice sounded like the rustle of autumn leaves. "We're not sure, if there are more. They might come, stay a while and leave. And someone else will turn up in their place. And the gendarmes are already skulking about there, my people came across one of their agents."

"They're working effectively," boomed Poniatowski. "But the criminal police are no worse, Mr. Wichura, you've done a fine job today. I have no complaints, and of course you'll be commended when all this is over. But, but, but… There is one problem, gentlemen. A big one."

Catching Koshovy's gaze and noticing his incomprehension, the commissar explained:

"If the secret police are watching them, it means they are launching an operation of their own, and Ignat Yartsev will end up in their department. Together with the others. Although the murder was uncovered by the criminal police, all the glory will go to the royal-imperial gendarmerie."

"Just because of the glory…"

"It's about fairness!" Poniatowski thundered once more. "We all work for the good of one state and are the subjects of our noblest emperor! And had the secret police found Yartsev first – as a murderer, rather than an agent of a foreign intelligence service who is smuggling in cash from the Russian Ministry of Internal Affairs and Finances to finance agents here! But where we might have played first fiddle, God willing, they may allow us to play only second. For the criminal police department, which I have the honor of heading, this is, I am deeply convinced, a terrible disgrace, gentlemen. Which is why, Mr. Koshovy," he turned around to face Klym, "I've invited you here. Although in relation to our matters you are just as much a subject of the Russian Tsar, as Ignatiy Yartsev and his comrade, what's his name…"

"Kniazev, Yuri," the commissar reminded him.

....

line. It was inhabited by railway workers, who were traditionally considered to be the richest representatives of Lviv's working classes.

"Yes, the two of them. And you too, are foreign nationals, with no connection to our local matters. But, gentlemen," Poniatowski paused for a short moment, "we are not gendarmes, we are investigators. We've never had anything to do with Russian terrorist groups. You, Mr. Koshovy, must know, what they are all about. Maybe you can suggest how best to get our hands on Yartsev, at the very least, before the secret police nab him."

"Ah, so it appears, I'm an adviser of sorts," ahemmed Klym.

This was not the time to admit that not too long ago he had associated with revolutionaries. True, they weren't like these ones – but would someone be able to tell the difference…?

"You may consider yourself as such, for the moment," Poniatowski allowed himself.

"Alright. Then you already have a plan," Koshovy replied.

"Meaning?"

"To get your hands on Yartsev. Simple and ingenious. Gentlemen," Klym ran his eyes over all three men, "*our* killer needs to be lured out of that building, where all of them are hiding. The secret police are not ready to grab them yet, otherwise they would have done so long ago. We have a little time, very little, to act before they do. To lure Ignat Yartsev from the building, lead him away some distance and then to grab him. Before the gendarmes realize what has happened, you'll have already pinned him down with Soyka's note, the main proof. And after this, let them try to wrench him from the clutches of *your* department!"

The policemen exchanged glances.

"Are you trying to say, Mr. Koshovy, that I came up with this plan?" Poniatowski muttered cautiously.

"Is there anything I can come up with here?" Klym appeared the epitome of modesty.

"Alright. How do we lure him out?"

"We need someone who knows Russian well. Who speaks without an accent, otherwise Yartsev won't believe them. What do you think, gentlemen, where can you find such a person quick smart?"

He asked, without hiding the cunning glint in his eye.

After two and a bit hours his blood had cooled noticeably. As he was knocking on the door, behind which the militant group was hiding.

Up until now Koshovy had never taken part in police operations. Even more since he could not imagine that he himself would volunteer to do such a thing. Or that he would even insist. After his time in Kosy Kaponir he had erected an invisible, but impenetrable wall between himself and the gendarmes. His attitude extended to the criminal police, and in general to anyone who faithfully served the state.

Something had changed that night.

That moment when, instead of running away from the tortured body and returning to his apartment unnoticed and continuing to remain under house arrest, Klym had suddenly decided to remain at the crime scene, waiting for the police to appear.

Later, while discussing the details of a hastily hatched plan to capture Yartsev, he was able to reach maybe not an exhaustive answer, but at least an explanation.

Encountering misadventure after misadventure from the very first hours of his arrival in Lviv, involuntarily coming to the notice of the police, he always managed to come out on top. The first time when he had to practically take the investigator by the hand to convince him that Soyka had not taken his own life. Then – quite unexpectedly having done the work of the police for them by capturing the batiar, who was maybe not directly, but still in some way involved in the murder. Finally, fate had left him the sheet of paper with the imprinted letters, the note written by Mr. Genyk, which the made the efforts of the police to solve the crime not only useless, but also comical.

The possibility, but principally the intention, to once more show up the police department, took precedence over a terrible desire to put this adventure behind him, excising it from his memory and beginning to find ways to settle into this new place. Behaving like this, realizing that the director and commissar, the investigator, as well as the ordinary detectives were listening to him, because they had to, Klym felt like the winner in this unexpected duel.

By venturing into the lair of the armed bombers, he was going to finally consolidate his own success. Even to feel a little above these dumb police-men. Because, having associated with them in their line of work, he realized that the authors of his sensational adventure novels were often right when they described the defenders of law and order as bumbling fools.

How useless the British police were in comparison to the one and only Mr. Holmes. Back in the time his father could not understand why Klym, who already seemed to be a grown man, and had a legal education, collected books in his personal library about the adventures of this London sleuth. Rather, Nazar Hryhorovych Koshovy had nothing against the literature itself, calling it dime novel trash, especially the writings of Mr. Conan Doyle and Monsieur Gaborio[51]. The father could not understand why his son was buying each new publication of the adventures of this famous detective, published by the Panteleyev brothers. Klym gave away the earlier books to fans of the genre, thus recruiting new readers. And the fresh ones he bought, he read again, as if they contained something totally new.

In general, Koshovy senior was utterly convinced: the incident because of which his son ended up in jail with all its sad consequences, was nothing more than a result of his son's fascination with such lowbrow books. He even quoted Mr. Chukovsky, whose critical opinion he deferred to, despite the fellow's fascination with revolutionary leftism. "Intellectuals are disappearing, understand that!" Nazar Hryhorovych yelled, waving a recent issue of some thick magazine before his son's downcast eyes. "All these holmeses, pinkertons and lecoqs[52] are an invasion of hottentots, Klymentiy! Korniy Ivanovych is right to call it a flood, a wildfire, complete degradation, utter, if you'll pardon the word, pornography! It is completely devoid of any ideals! Not only national ones – it is completely devoid of them! Mere hooliganism, without any program, or strategies of development – only hit and run!" Klym had no strength to argue with his father. Nazar Hryhorovych had chosen a bad time to put some sense into his son's head, for he had just been released from prison and was feeling depressed.

All the same, Klym Koshovy did not give up his favorite novels, even if they were considered to be trashy a hundred times over by various respectable people, meaning therefore that they were harmful.

And on this night for the first time he felt he was a character in one of those sensational novels.

....

[51]   Émile Gaboriau (1832-1873) – French writer, one of the pioneers of the detective genre. Influenced the work of Robert Louis Stevenson, Wilkie Collins, Arthur Conan Doyle, as well as Edgar Wallace, the 'father' of works about King Kong.

[52]   Lecoq (Monsieur Lecoq) – young police officer, a hero in several of Gaboriau's detective novels.

                                          ANDRIY KOKOTIUKHA

He understood that reality was always far harsher, and things never finished as well as the literary gentlemen liked to write in books, allowing themselves to be swept up in the adventure of the moment. At first there had been the furious pursuit along Lviv's streets, followed by secretive wanderings in the middle of the night through sullen courtyards and along walkways. Of course, Klym yearned for more. He sensed that he was part of something particularly important, intricate and, despite the very real danger, terribly interesting.

However, before knocking on the door of this single-story brick house with a mansard roof, he paused for a moment, his hand clenched into a fist.

Only now did he finally realize that inside there were no policemen, who acted level-headedly. There were no criminals with a desire to talk. Those hiding out here were extremely dangerous people armed with guns, and possibly home-made bombs. The killer was among them – it was hardly likely that Ignatiy Yartsev was alone. Even the body he had encountered could be considered at a pinch as an adventure of sorts, albeit unpleasant and creepy. A dead person was safe, they didn't threaten anyone or anything. They came to life only in horror stories.

Yartsev would shoot as soon as he sensed even a hint of danger.

Which was why Koshovy tightly clenched his fist and involuntarily took a step back. He realized that he had gone a little too far and wasn't quite prepared for such a turn of events. It was still possible to turn around and run away. He would be able to dream up some explanation, a justification, or even better – merely tell the truth. He had taken fright, overestimated his capabilities. You already know who the killer is and where he is. You can take over from here, gentlemen, thank you very much, I am no police agent…

Too late.

Out of the corner of his eye he spied a barely noticeable movement behind the curtain in the window.

They had noticed him.

Without a second thought, he stepped forward and knocked.

The door did not open at once, and not completely. A small sharp nose appeared in the narrow opening. It was a young freckle-faced girl with light-colored hair looking as if it had been hastily tucked under a kerchief. Her darting eyes looked the stranger up and down, checking out his linen pants and gray linen shirt with the buttoned vest on top, and a cap with a pointed visor. As far as Klym was concerned, these things didn't go together at all. But this was all they had managed to rustle up in the police wardrobe. Since he wasn't about to go in his own clothes.

"Who you after?" chirruped the girl.

Before answering, Koshovy cautiously glanced to the sides and said: "Call Ignat."

"Good day," the girl suddenly greeted him for whatever reason.

"How are you," nodded Klym, trying hard to imitate the mannerisms of the Podil ragamuffins and spoke through his teeth: "Can I come in or will he come out himself?"

"Who?"

"Don't give me a hard time, princess. Yartsev Ignat, he's here. Call him."

"There's no Yartsev here," the girl said. "You're mistaken, no one by that name lives here."

"Who lives here then?" Klym asked, then took a step forward and placed his foot on the threshold between the door and the door jamb. "Listen, girlie, I've got no time for idle chatter. Run and fetch Ignat Yartsev. Tell him Mr. Kniazev bows to him through Mr. Danovich."

Moving forward a little more, the girl also looked from side to side, and then lightly tapped Klym on the chest with her fingertips.

"Stay there. Not a step closer. He'll come out."

She disappeared inside, closing the door behind her. He didn't have long to wait – the door opened, this time wider. Before him stood a snub-nosed young man with long blond locks, brushing the hair back from his forehead.

Of average height, strongly built, broad-shouldered, he had shifty eyes. His jacket smelled of that familiar, cheap tobacco smoke. The fingers of his right hand were twirling and fingering a button. The jacket was unbuttoned, his gaze calm. The lad himself looked very ordinary, such people went unnoticed in the streets, no one remembered them. They stared calmly in front of them, nothing could be read in their eyes. Looking Klym up and down, he licked his cracked lips for some unknown reason and droned:

"Well?"

"You Yartsev?"

"Well?"

"Lost for words?" Koshovy looked about once more, making an excessive display of anxiety, no longer afraid that he might be overdoing it. "Can you prove you're Yartsev?"

"Who to?"

Klym had not expected this. Justifying his behavior, he pulled his head into his shoulders, lowered his voice, grew wide-eyed.

"Are we going to remain standing here? Maybe you can let me inside. Someone could be watching."

"Who?"

Yartsev continued standing, as if he was rooted to the floor. His appearance was deceptive – this snub-nosed fellow appeared to be quite strong. The sensation of danger returned.

"I don't know," Klym sputtered. "When Mr. Danovich sent me here, he warned me that I might be followed. First, he wrote a note for you. Then he changed his mind and tore it up. And burnt the pieces in my presence. God forbid they should pick you up and find this note. Better just tell him."

"What?"

Ignat had no intention of moving from his spot. His left hand grabbed firmer hold of the door. The fingers of his right hand continued to play with the button. Any moment and he might rip it off…

"A real talkative one. How do women put up with you…?"

"None of your ruddy business. Pass on the message and skedaddle."

"And you're impolite to boot…"

"Then find yourself a maître d'. They click their heels and bow. Listen, tell me why you're here."

"Out here?"

"I can hear very well from here. Well?"

"You're impossible!" Koshovy snapped back. "I have a small part to play here… Mr. Danovich has learned that the police will soon be here. He paid me to come and warn you. There's an address. It's safe there for the moment. Then he'll find another safe house, more reliable. That's all, Yartsev – if you are Yartsev."

"And if I'm not?"

"Then let Yartsev know!" he was no longer acting; his patience really was wearing thin. "Only I don't intend waiting! I'm supposed to take you there! There's no joy, see, to put up with such a thickhead!"

Turning around, either to give someone a sign, or simply to see what was happening there, the snub-nosed fellow left the house, diligently closing the door behind him. The whole time his right hand continued to tug at the button. Moving forward, he forced Klym to back off.

"I'm Yartsev," he nodded, again brushing his hair with his hand. "Take me where you need to. You can tell me the rest along the way."

"I don't know anything else! There's people already waiting there, they're in the know. I'm merely…"

"Where we going?" Ignat interrupted him.

"You should have started with that. We'll go on foot toward the railway line. There's a carriage waiting there on the other side of the line. I don't know the exact address. The coachman knows all that, he's one of ours. Mr. Danovich is being conspiratorial. He doesn't give all the information to one person, doesn't trust them."

"Rightly so," Yartsev readily agreed. "You can't trust anyone. Lead the way, though. Because I get lost here wherever I go."

"First time in Lviv?"

"Yep. I thought we'd get things done and head back straight away. But see, I got held up. Why are we standing about?"

Koshovy glanced over Ignat's shoulder.

"Are you going as you are? Don't you need to grab some things?"

"What things… I've got everything I need. You yourself said we need to hotfoot it. Hurry up, don't hang around. What's your name, by the way?"

"Klym," there was no point in inventing a name.

"It's all the same to me… Let it be Klym…"

"Then why ask?"

"Because you know my name. Come on, let's go."

They came out into the street.

At first they moved in silence, Yartsev was slightly behind him. They had gone barely two hundred steps when Ignat grabbed Koshovy by the shoulder, nodding toward the nearest laneway.

"That way."

"Why?"

"Cut corners. You yourself said someone might be tailing us."

"You want to take a short cut? But you said you get lost…"

"But you don't, as I can see," Yartsev licked his lips once more. You're the local, so lead the way. You can always cut corners when you take side streets, right?"

It was dangerous to argue. It was easy to blow his cover. An agent dressed as a coachman really was waiting for them near the railway line. But Klym had come here by a direct route, without taking side streets. As they turned into the laneway, he figured that he knew the general direction they needed to move in. It wasn't a forest, he would find his way. The suburb didn't seem too confusing and he would work it out as they went.

The side street came to a dead-end. However, Klym noticed the only turn here, and headed toward it: now he would certainly not lose his way. They would come out somewhere, the important thing was to keep moving forward.

But suddenly the unexpected happened.

Yartsev, who until now had been walking calmly and evenly, suddenly became transformed into a lightning-fast strong snake. He could think of any other comparison, after Ignatiy pounced on him, pushing him, then grabbing hold of him, attacking like a predatory reptile in the jungle – he had also read about these snakes in adventure novels. But with each passing moment, everything that was taking place with Klym, seemed less and less like an adventure story with a happy ending.

Especially the gun barrel now pointed at him.

Yartsev pulled out the weapon, after finally letting go of the button and throwing open the flap of his jacket with a quick jerk of his right hand. It flew open easily, and Koshovy recalled accounts of lead weights being sewn onto or into the bottom of the flap – which made it easier to pull a gun from under a belt, requiring only a single well-practiced movement.

"A Colt."

Klym thought he had not spoken out loud.

"Aha, a Colt," Yartsev agreed, repositioning his fingers and grabbing better hold of the handle. "An American cannon. It'll make heaps of holes, turn you into a sieve."

Ignat pushed his captive behind the nearest tree, which stood not far from the corner of a rather tall brick building. It was hard to notice them from the wide street, unless one looked closely. His eye twitched ever so badly, like it hadn't done for some time now. Inside he froze, catching his breath. He wanted to say something, instead his suddenly dry throat managed only a hoarse:

"A Colt…"

"And now I'll introduce you. Klym or whoever you are… it doesn't matter," the barrel struck Koshovy hard in the face, splitting his lip, and a salty liquid immediately began to flow. "Stop, listen. I don't care whether you answer or not. You're a blockhead! The fuzz who've set you onto me are dolts as well. You're not even a dog, just a mere pup. A blubbery pup, is that clear?"

"I…"

"You," one more blow, and now his left eyebrow was cut open. "I might have believed that Danovich sent you. But it's been four days since Kniazev left Lviv! There's no need to pass on bows from Kniazev, and for urgent communications there are passwords. Dreamed up by Danovich himself, you dumbo!"

The third blow with the handle was to his forehead, but Koshovy managed to remain standing by pressing his back against the corner of the building.

"Tell me, who's after me! You'll die sooner! Although," Yartsev looked about, "You'll die anyway. You don't have to say anything! Since you've come here, means they're onto me. I need to make moves out of here. I'm sick of the sight of all of you!"

Koshovy could find nothing to say. He did not know, did not understand, if he could save his skin, but finding the strength, he began to speak:

"Die, you pig."

Taking a step back, Yartsev raised his gun.

The muzzle was aimed at Klym's chest.

His thumb cocked the hammer.

"MISKO!"

The sharp female voice made both of them jump. The hand with the Colt dropped, hanging by Yartsev's side. Klym could feel the treacherous sweat streaming down his face, on top of the blood from his injuries. He was shaking and now no longer resembled any of the heroes from his favorite novels.

"Misko, may lightning strike you down!"

A fat disheveled woman appeared from around the corner and made straight for them. The sleeves of her simple embroidered linen shirt were drawn above the elbows. The hem of her long skirt kicked up dust. In the front she had an apron – although not a very clean one.

"Boys, did you see my Misko here?" she asked, without slowing down. "The bastard came running in here, because he knew I'd have his bull's arse by the balls! To teach him a lesson to stop drinking! The number of times that scoundrel's been warned to stay off the drink! Nah, people tell me – Hantsia, your Misko's blind drunk again, hiding all over Bohdanivka! Thinks I won't find him, the sonofabitch! D'you see him lads?"

She needed a reply. Klym continued to be lost for words, Yartsev imperceptibly slipped the gun into his right pocket, but continued to hold onto the handle.

"Maybe you were all drinking together?" the woman stopped and looked at them with suspicion. "Maybe you're hiding him somewhere here? Yeah, I can see you're his mates! Imbeciles just like him, to hell with you!"

"On your way!" Yartsev snapped back.

Which was the wrong thing to say.

"You arse with ears, telling me to piss off from my own street? I'll go walking where I bloody well please! Who the hell are you! Who are the two of you? I've never seen you before! So Misko's brought you here, you shitty little flies!"

"HANNA!"

From a nearby courtyard there emerged a rakish fellow in a shabby jacket, dusty pants, dirty shoes, and a crumpled hat. Despite this he was no less pugnacious.

"Aha! So, there you are! I can smell you all the way from here, you whoring bastard! The stench of the vodka, it's worse than a distillery! May that vodka make you shit your pants, you sonofabitch!"

Yelling, the woman remained where she stood – right opposite Klym and Yartsev. This gave Klym a faint chance to save himself, if only he could find the strength to shout. Second-guessing his intentions, Yartsev gave him a threatening look. His hand slowly pulled the handgun back.

"Why are you shouting for the whole of Bohdanivka to hear, Hanna! Aren't you ashamed in front of everyone?"

The skinny man confidently approached the woman who was creating a row, without fear of getting a taste of her wrath.

"And you, you freak, aren't you ashamed?! See, I'm meant to be ashamed! He's made me three kids, and every Saturday he spends all day in the bars!"

"The kids aren't hungry at home!"

"Pray and praise the Lord, that at least the children aren't hungry! Otherwise, I would have buried you long ago! You're not only a drunkard! You're also a whoring bastard, the likes of which are hard to find! People have told me all about you!"

By now the man had reached them, and gestured for them to be witnesses.

"Hear that? The good people told her things! What about the things I've heard about you! I'm sick and tired of hearing that you're the biggest slut in all of Bohdanivka!"

The commotion was already attracting attention. Two gentlemen, who might have wandered past, had already stopped, and watched on with interest at the unfolding events!

Slowly the first spectators began to approach, hoping for a free performance.

One of them, moving close to where Klym was standing, very much resembled a large rat.

Koshovy moved a little to the left.

The killer's hand threateningly pulled out the revolver. The barrel became exposed again.

"A-a-a-a-ah!"

Blinking hard, Koshovy lunged with all his might at Yartsev, arms stretched out before him.

Staggering back, the fellow remained standing on his feet. An experienced fighter, he was ready for anything.

The gun was already being aimed at Klym's head.

The woman screamed, probably from fright as well.

But at that moment Yartsev was attacked at once from three sides – the fellow who was called Misko, charged forward, head lowered, while two passers-by pressed in closer at the same moment, acting deftly and in unison.

Ignatiy managed to fire a shot into the air.

But he wasn't about to give up so easily. The next shot stopped Misko, who grabbed at his shoulder and fell to the ground. Quickly jumping over him, Ignat raced off toward the nearest corner to the accompaniment of the woman's shrieking. He fired another shot, this time at his pursuers.

Two more shots sounded.

Neither now nor later could Koshovy say with certainty which bullet had struck Karol Linda, the first or the second one. When the police and the rest of the undercover agents came running moments later, completely ignoring Klym, and surrounded Yartsev, he was lying face down and showed no signs of life. Linda glanced at Koshovy, wanted to say something, but then changed his mind and waved his arm, which was squeezing his 'Bulldog' revolver.

There.

The game was over.

A few shots popped nearby, sounding like the crack of a whip. The shot fellow's comrades were probably being smoked out of their hideout. The shooting died away very quickly.

They had managed then.

CHAPTER SIXTEEN
JOZEF SHATSKY'S PERSONAL HERO

"Mazel tov!"

There was liqueur in the glass which Jozef Shatsky had raised in honor of Klym Koshovy. True, the guest had tried it and found that it was rather strong, approaching a well-aged cognac. He also understood that drinking was not practiced in this house, that it wasn't the accepted thing. Because Esther looked unhappy as she placed a figured decanter made of thick glass onto the table. Klym had already discovered that Shatsky's better half was a hospitable and quite amiable hostess. But when it came to alcohol, her face looked as if she had swallowed a good gulp of vinegar rather than pineapple water. It even took on a kind of vinegary color.

Mrs. Shatska knitted her eyebrows, especially since Jozef had insisted that his feigale also take a glass and drink to their heroic guest. The well-publicized arrest of the terrorist gang in Bohdanivka, during which one of them had resisted, almost killing a police agent, and was shot dead while trying to escape, had not left the first pages of all the popular Lviv newspapers for the second day. Although Klym's name was never mentioned anywhere, Shatsky knew full well that his new friend was involved, because it couldn't have been any other way. Klym didn't deny playing a part in it, he only asked that Shatsky not broadcast the information all over Krakivsky Market. And he had agreed to come for lunch, to tell the details in an intimate family circle. Esther could not hide her natural curiosity, and, as Klym had supposed, it had overcome her negative attitude toward drinking alcohol in broad daylight in her own home.

By the way, looking through the newspapers and comparing what was written there, Koshovy noted: the incident was also mentioned in those publications which he had already learned to distinguish as having Russophile tendencies. Writing quite sparingly about the famous shootout, the authors instead focused more on the well-publicized statement of the criminal police directorate. The following morning Lviv had already learned from a brief police report that a subject of the Russian Empire, the Russian Ignat Yartsev, who had been felled by a bullet from the proficient marksman Mr. L., was also the killer of the renowned Lviv criminal Liubomyr R., nicknamed Tsipa. He had killed him prior to this and was intending to escape from the city, to avoid justice. But prior to this he had done in the lawyer Yevhen Soyka, well-known for his Russophile views. As well as his methods, not always acceptable from the ethical point of view, which, unfortunately, did not contradict the letter of the law and allowed him in most cases to justify the actions of various criminals.

The declaration was viewed by leaders of the Russophile community as an attempt to discredit their movement, their ideas, and political and world view principles.

In a free society, they wrote, the very intention to attribute every mortal sin to people who are Russian by descent should be considered an unworthy provocation. Yes, the man from whom the Russophile community hastened to distance itself, really did belong to the underworld. But this did not give the authorities the right to draw parallels between an individual and a whole group of people, whose crime, according to the ruling ideologues, is determined by their very origins. And their attraction to the fundamental ideals of the unification of dismembered Russian lands into one single territory. The Russian man, who was also a subject of His Majesty the Russian Emperor – was therefore a killer and a monster.

If this is not the case, one such fiery article concluded, then why aren't the perpetrators of unsolved murders assigned by way of drawing lots among all those who have recently been buried according to the Orthodox rite. This, the author was convinced, would be fairer.

Under different circumstances, Koshovy would have paid no attention to this or other similar nonsense. However, it was not the first day that a thought kept eating away at him, which just now, as Shatsky raised a toast in his honor, was finally transforming into a conviction. So that Klym didn't feel in the mood to brag about his heroism, which he didn't feel reflected his true actions.

Shatsky either did not notice this, or pretended not to.

No sooner had they sat down around the table, than he called over his children, asking the three of them to line up in front of the guest according to ascending height, and delivered a long speech.

The essence of which was this.

A prominent person had come to visit them, smarter than all the criminal police put together. Such a worthy man would never come to Lapidus. And his children needed to pride themselves on this friendship, telling everyone around them about the respectable people who visited the home of Jozef Shatsky. Mr. Koshovy should become an example for each of them, even for Daniel, who was only one year old and was now asleep. But when he grew up, he too would understand, that to study and work on oneself was especially important. Every well-educated child was the hope not only of their parents, may they be blessed with good health, but of the entire Jewish people. Acquiring knowledge and reading books was very important, allowing ordinary people to become wiser than some dim-witted policeman. Whose only virtue was that he was empowered with authority, which he used to put innocent people behind bars and oppress others.

The Jews, Jozef became carried away, in all times, throughout the whole history of their people, no matter how tough times were, maintained their position in society under all governments precisely because of their erudition, wisdom and talents. Those in power needed Jews because they always knew how to look after themselves.

"It makes sense, Jozef, why no one in power has any need of you," Esther poured cold water on her husband, then turned to Klym. "Don't listen to him, Mr. Koshovy. If you let my Shatsky swallow a little more liqueur, he'll tell you about every single day of those forty years that Moses led the Jews through the desert."

"Can I join Danny?" Riva piped up. "I think he's woken up."

"You only put him to bed an hour ago!" Shatsky raised his voice at his older daughter. "There's enough time to listen to what adults and wise people have to say!"

"Dad, are books written by wise adults?" inquired Shmuel.

"Vey, where did you see a book written by a child!"

"In that case I'll be off to acquire some wisdom from my books."

Swinging around, brimming with dignity and self-esteem, Shmuel marched off into his father's office. Meanwhile Riva quickly slipped away to join her baby brother, although when he was here last time Koshovy did not remember the girl possessing a burning desire to spend time with her baby brother. Left on her own, Ida looked questioningly at her mother; receiving a slight positive nod, she pattered off after her sister. Esther gave Shatsky a victorious look, although Klym failed to understand the essence of her victory.

Meanwhile Jozef, who was so masterfully silenced, decisively grabbed the carafe, filled his own and the guest's glass, and now demonstratively, arranging a show meant primarily for his wife, once more welcomed Klym and toasted him.

Shatsky had not learned to drink the way laborers or batiars were wont to do, who were quite accustomed to such practices. He began to choke straight away, turned red, and began to cough. Pursing her lips and maintaining a victorious expression on her face, Esther got up and slapped her husband on the back. While the fellow caught his breath, she no less demonstratively removed the liqueur from the table and, smiling broadly at Klym, invited him sincerely:

"Please help yourself to the food, Mr. Koshovy. Take no notice of my Shatsky. He hasn't slept for several nights. And I can't handle it when someone next to me keeps turning round and round."

"Maybe something was troubling him, respected Esther?" Klym inquired in order not to remain silent.

"He wasn't sure how to ask my forgiveness for that night spent at the police station. Plus, he was suffering because he didn't know anything about your adventures firsthand. My Shatsky finds it very painful, when he doesn't know about things that have happened in the city."

Mrs. Shatska had mentioned the night, when Jozef had been with him in Klepariv. Koshovy had already found out – back then the dentist had taken the simplest way out, dreaming up another spot of trouble with the police, having gotten out of the strife by paying a hefty sum of money. After which he was forced to apply his mental capacities to maximum, to explain to his feigale how he had come by the aforementioned hefty sum of money and why she hadn't heard about it up till then. How he had extricated himself from this misfortune, Jozef did not explain, and Koshovy decided not to insist – it seemed a way out was found, and that was that. But Shatsky really didn't know everyone and everything in Lviv, no matter that he knew many people and many things. Without realizing it, Esther was right here: considering his recent findings, Klym would find that such knowledge would come in handy.

Which was why he did not refuse the invitation to visit Krakidaly. On the contrary – he was looking for an opportunity to have a good feed, among other things.

Klym had managed to raise Jozef's mood with his account of how the police agents had made a timely appearance, thus saving his life. He even embellished the situation a little, recreating one of the scenes, playing the different characters, and recalled how he had once in his youth taken part in an amateur theater group. Having heard him out, Shatsky called on Esther to bear witness, and summed up:

"Mr. Koshovy, I confess honestly – had I found myself in a similar situation, I would have wet my long johns, if you'll pardon me."

Mrs. Shatska only wrinkled her nose and said nothing.

Talk turned to Klym's return to Lychakiv Street toward evening of that extremely long day. That is almost twenty-four hours after leaving through the window where he was being held under house arrest. Koshovy had physically been in full view of the police and his actions had been coordinated by Commissar Wichura. In addition, events had unfolded so quickly that none of those on whom it depended, had thought of replacing the sergeant, who had been guarding the prisoner's apartment. The sergeant himself, remaining at his post, had completely forgotten about the real reason for his being there. On the contrary – he was happy that those in charge had forgotten all about him and preferred not to remind them of himself without undue need.

Engaging the janitor in conversation, the sergeant had befriended him by the end of the day. Toward evening Bulbash had gotten his hands on a bottle of insidious kontuszówka[53] and the newly made friends sat down to cards. After that, the janitor got up in the morning to perform his duties. Meanwhile the sergeant slept until noon, woke, and learned that in the meantime Mr. Koshovy had not made himself known or heard, and no one had come to visit him either. He calmed down and decided to make

....

[53]   Kontuszówka – a strong (40%) sweet Polish vodka. A favorite drink of the bumbling Czech soldier Svejk.

                    ANDRIY KOKOTIUKHA

up for his loss of the day before. Now that he was sober, he attributed his loss to the kontuszówka. So, on seeing his charge arrive with a battered face and, what's more, personally accompanied by Commissar Wichura, he was frightened to death, having every reason to expect a serious and just punishment. He was lucky, and was sent packing home, although he received a warning – Koshovy had escaped from under his nose, conclusions would definitely be drawn.

Well, Bulbash himself told Klym about the cards the next day, when he engaged the janitor in conversation and verified his supposition. Having received quite a serious sum from Mr. Silezsky, he could allow himself to offer a small bonus to the janitor for his detailed consultation.

And now, feeling that he would be unable to talk any more here, Koshovy rose to his feet, smoothed his jacket, and politely bowed:

"Thank you very much, respected Esther," the lady of the house had already let it be known that she preferred to be addressed this way, rather than using her patronymic, which was not the done thing here. "Will you allow me to invite your husband for a nice coffee somewhere in the city?"

"Ah, take him away, Mr. Koshovy," the woman waved him away. "All the same these past few days he's been of no practical use as a dentist. Today I also had to refuse several customers."

Shatsky smacked his pouting lips.

"They won't go anywhere!" he got up too, pushing his chest forward. "With their wealth their only place of recourse is Shatsky! My sincere apologies, Esther, but you haven't the slightest idea how to attract customers and grow the practice! The people whom we refused these past days, Mr. Koshovy, will return here shortly all the same. And since there will then be more of them than usual, there will be a queue to see dentist Shatsky. I maintain my practice, Mr. Koshovy, mostly this way – because there is always a queue to my surgery. It means there must be a good reason to wait, and the information is disseminated throughout the entire city!"

Esther, who had probably heard similar explanations often enough, could find nothing more to say in reply. So that Jozef, having had the final say, grabbed his hat, and left the house with a proud step.

Klym bowed goodbye and hurried after him.

No sooner had they stepped out, than the expression on Jozef's face changed immediately. Grabbing Koshovy's sleeve with two fingers, he gave it a tug, thus making Klym turn to face him. He spoke hastily, abruptly, and now this was quite a different Shatsky – one whom Klym had never seen during the short but fruitful time of their acquaintance:

"Listen to me. Don't listen to Esther. Although – listen, but take no notice. And in general – do as you will. Understand… She's afraid. She has seen too many bad things and keeps it all in her head. Much of it tragic. I'll even say it – the terrible experience of her relatives. As well as my near and dear ones. And some of my friends, not only from Krakidaly. Those who strayed from the righteous path, ending their lives in gutters outside the most disgusting and cheapest of Lviv's bars, Mr. Koshovy. That's all: you heard, I spoke. We can go now."

CHAPTER SEVENTEEN
MR. GENYK, DOCTOR JUNG AND OUROBOROS

This July day turned out to be more pleasant than the previous few.

The sun was not burning Lviv's cobblestones so mercilessly. Although the weather was not the best for sobering up quickly, Koshovy enjoyed the state he was in. On the contrary, the slight intoxication loosened his tongue, his thoughts organized themselves faster, and he felt strangely lucid.

The same could not be said of Shatsky. He continued to walk several steps ahead, loudly greeting countless friends, stopping, beginning to talk about something boisterously, thus slowing their progress. Klym was forced to excuse the gentlemen and to hurry him along. Jozef would say his good-byes, and moved on – until he came across someone new.

In the end Koshovy chose a tactic, which he should have adopted straight away. When they reached Akademichna Street, finally arriving in the very center of the city despite the odd impediment here and there, he tugged Shatsky by the elbow and asked:

"Are we going to some special place or simply going for a walk?"

"You invited me for a coffee!" Jozef said in a startled voice.

"And that's what I'm on about! Shatsky, there's heaps of places here where they pour people coffee. You're the local here, not me. So, either choose somewhere, or…"

"Here!" the dentist interrupted him, decisively making his way toward the nearest cafe under the sign 'Teatralna'[54].

Klym had never been here, so it was all the same to him. The important thing now was to sit his restless companion down at a table and ply him with

------

[54]   Theatrical (Ukr.).

some strong coffee. While he was looking around, the fidgety Shatsky had already dashed inside. As he was coming up to the entrance, he heard a voice behind him:

"Mr. Koshovy!"

Klym swung around far more quickly than was appropriate and against his personal principles. The familiar carriage was parked near the sidewalk, and Magda Bohdanovych was making a sign to him from within. The young widow did not wave to him with her hand draped in a light-colored glove – she was gesturing to him. A confident lady acted this way, knowing that her loyal trained puppy would come running at her first behest. Gladly waving its tail simply because it had been noticed.

Koshovy never intended to play such a role. It wasn't in his plans to become someone else's lapdog. Not even if that person was Magda.

With these thoughts on his mind, his feet traversed the sidewalk of their own accord. Drawing closer, he greeted her, politely raising his hat. In reply Magda stretched out her hand:

"Don't just stand there. Help me down, please, be a bit of a gentleman."

Stopping himself from bowing his head a second time, for it would have been too much, Klym took her palm in his right hand. The female hand, which turned out to be not that tender and *porcelain-like*, as he had imagined, barely squeezed his hand. It was merely a display of politeness and good manners – Magda could have alighted from the carriage without his assistance.

"I spotted you quite by accident, Mr. Koshovy. Forgive me if you have important business to attend to. I've been looking for an opportunity to meet with you. I was even thinking who might assist me in this regard."

"Am I really that important and unavailable, Mrs. Magda?"

"Oh!" she rolled her eyes theatrically. "These days and in the near future here in Lviv, there most likely won't be a person more important than you. Unless something should suddenly happen and we are graced with the visit of His Holiness, Pope Pius X. Or the most illustrious Emperor Franz Joseph," her lips formed into a slight smile. "Have you forgotten? I can find out everything which takes place in our city, even more, as well as in our police department."

Only now did Klym notice that before him stood a different Magda to the one he was used to seeing.

Now she was dressed in white.

More precisely – in light-colored clothing: a jacket the color of coffee generously diluted with milk, which favorably matched her milky-white dress, embroidered with a thin thread of tiny black beads. Her light, almost weightless gloves, which clung to her hands and reached up to the elbows, gave her a somewhat provocative look.

Her hat turned out to be unusually small, and sooner adorned her head rather than covered it, becoming a small extension of her coiffure. Some particularly important occasion must have presented itself for Magda to change her style – he never thought he would see her other than in strict, although no less elegant dark clothing.

"There's no need to exaggerate, Mrs. Magda. I am merely an apprentice lawyer, who has yet to confirm his qualifications, with no prospect of obtaining a residency permit anytime soon and living in an apartment where a murder has been committed. Because it's cheaper that way. The landlord knows that he can't find any tenants at the market price."

"You speak like an orphan or a poor relative," she smiled once more. "This is how people talk when they want someone to take pity on them. Or when they beg for financial assistance."

Of course, viewed through the eyes of someone else it always looked that way…

"It's the reality of my life, Mrs. Magda."

"But it was you, Mr. Koshovy, having such realities behind you, who managed to do what Commissar Wichura would not have managed anytime soon. Although I respect him, as I've mentioned once before. But it was you, not him, who unraveled the mystery of Soyka's murder. Now we can say that he was an unworthy person, this man whom you had expected would help you out and with whom you connected your future in Lviv."

"Well, that did not happen."

"Fortunately for you, Mr. Koshovy, fortunately for you. My apologies, if I've upset you, for you knew Mr. Genyk well…"

"That's alright. I've already heard plenty about his disgraceful activities. Maybe he was always like that, and I simply hadn't noticed this earlier, when I was working for him. Or maybe he changed under the pressure of certain circumstances. Who knows, no one will ever be able to explain that."

"Agreed. It is unlikely we will ever learn the deep-seated reasons for some people's actions. However, you can't take away from Mr. Genyk, that he was a skilful lawyer, and no less skilful at the art of making enemies. It is significant that Soyka's mortal life was cut short by someone from that same milieu, whose interests he had represented."

"Why do you think it significant?"

"Have you heard about the Ouroboros, Mr. Koshovy?"

"A serpent, which eats its own tail. From memory, a symbol of the infinity of being. From Greek mythology, if I'm not mistaken. What has Soyka's murder to do with it, wherein lies the symbolism? I don't quite understand, Mrs. Magda…"

"You are perhaps not familiar with the latest theories," now her tone of voice sounded didactic. "Adas… sorry, *Mister* Wiszniewski recently acquainted me with the theories of the Swiss man, Dr. Jung. Have you heard of him?"

"Of course."

The surname meant nothing to Klym.

"He… Mr. Wiszniewski mentioned them precisely because of the fact that Soyka was killed by one of those whom Mr. Genyk had supported and defended. The fellow… what's his name…"

"Yartsev."

"It makes no difference… Day by day Soyka honed his skills by defending such do-gooders, rather – evil-doers. But, having to deal mostly with evil in all its manifestations, he was at the same time destroying himself. The self-destruction was set into motion. These are Dr. Jung's conclusions based on fresh interpretations of the symbol of Ouroboros. By proceeding along such a path, Mr. Genyk began to move toward his own violent death."

It was Sunday. A motley crowd of people slowly flowed past them in both directions. Koshovy felt that they were attracting people's attention, or at the very least that they were obstructing the passers-by. He sensed that they had been standing in the middle of the street talking for too long. But he wasn't thinking about how to wind up the conversation: instead, he suddenly felt a strong desire to move to another, more comfortable place, where there would be not so many random people staring at them. Although he understood perfectly the impossibility of achieving such desires, as well as their very nature.

"That was very nicely put, Mrs. Magda."

"Oh, please don't attribute other people's virtues to me. I'm only quoting."

"Mr. Wiszniewski?"

"Yes…" she maintained a short pause. "We've become engrossed in our conversation. Or rather, I have. Actually, I was simply looking for an opportunity to thank you one more time."

"For what?"

"Thanks to you, and please don't argue, the person who killed Soyka was found. Just between us, until the name of this incidental person was revealed, lots of my acquaintances, among them close friends and patrons, were afraid to discuss this event. They even refused to look each other in the eye. As you have managed to ascertain, I am surrounded only by worthy people. None of them wanted any of the others to suspect them of the murder."

"All the same, I don't quite understand, Mrs. Magda."

"Am I confusing you? My apologies, that is from a desire to say too much, having said nothing. It happens," her cheeks assumed a faint blush. "To make it completely clear, a lot of people bore a grudge against Mr. Genyk. There were people who could have settled accounts with him for whom, under different circumstances, such thoughts wouldn't have even entered their heads. So, when Soyka was found dead, everyone was relieved. When thanks in part to you, it turned out that this was not suicide, it gave rise to much unnecessary talk. Various assumptions were proffered, each more fantastic than the next, about the involvement of this or that person in the crime. It only seems on the surface that everyone who sincerely wanted Soyka dead because of his abominable actions, would publicly excuse the killer, if he turned out to be from a respectable background and was a conscientious citizen."

"In that case is it not possible… let's put it this way… to avoid a trial? In the Russian Empire this is practiced quite often."

"There is a different attitude to the law here, as you may have already noticed. The court would probably hand down a lenient sentence – but the killer would be tried all the same. Which would put an end to any future career. No one wants to ruin their prospects thanks to Mr. Genyk. And so, when the killer turned out to be whom he really was meant to be, Lviv sighed with relief. The scoundrel Soyka received his just deserts – and none of the worthy citizens were implicated. Which is why I was personally interested in not having the case closed due to an apparent suicide, and that an investigation take place. And that the real killer be found and punished as soon as possible. As you can see," she smiled once more, "in this instance evil has again devoured itself. The person who fired the bullet, died by the bullet."

"Are you thanking me, Mrs. Magda, on behalf of the entire city?"

"Mr. Koshovy!"

The exclamation made both of them turn around. Shatsky had emerged from Teatralna Cafe, and Klym did not hold back, slapping himself on the forehead. Really, he had completely forgotten where he was off to, with whom and why.

Though, in the light of his deductions, this conversation seemed superfluous.

But then it had largely confirmed them.

"Pardon me, Shatsky, I'm coming!"

Noticing whom Klym was taking to, Jozef touched the brim of his hat. Magda replied with a restrained nod.

"I've reserved a table!"

Suddenly Klym regretted that he needed to join Shatsky. Trust him to become involved with the fellow…

"I'm coming!"

People began to take notice of them.

"Please forgive me, Mr. Koshovy!" the gloved hand lightly touched his arm. "In order to end this: among others, through your selfless and decisive actions you have brought pleasure to someone very dear to me people. Believe me, it's like doing something for me personally. You can always turn to me; I am always available to assist you. Can you give me a hand."

Leaning on his arm, Magda Bohdanovych returned to her carriage. Making herself comfortable, she gave the order to leave.

Under different circumstances Klym would have liked to prolong the conversation as much as possible, but within the limits of decency. Or to have held her hand in his for a few seconds longer than was appropriate.

But he had done everything mechanically.

His thoughts were elsewhere.

Watching the carriage proceed down the street, he tried to understand, if it was possible for something to take place which would make things fall into place.

And the feeling, that he could have solved the problem much earlier, bored painfully into the back of his head.

His eyelid twitched rather strongly.

"Mr. Koshovy!"

"Coming!"

Inside the café they also had billiard tables which occupied the central part of the floor area, with small round tables set out along the walls. There were already quite a few people present, and Klym highly appreciated Jozef's efforts: by some miracle the dentist had managed to grab the quietest spot.

"I reserved it! It was quite difficult!" he babbled, trying to elevate his worth in Klym's eyes, although Koshovy had not requested this at all, and Shatsky definitely had no need of it. "As you can see, it's an extremely popular place! Just to let you know, this is where our city's mathematicians congregate!"

"What have mathematicians to do with it?" Klym shrugged his shoulders, thinking his own thoughts. "Although… Let it be, symbolically."

"Why symbolically? Can you explain, wherein lies the symbolism?"

"Now, let us solve a small problem, Shatsky. Have you already ordered?"

"I only reserved the table! I didn't know what…"

"Two coffees. Strong ones. The strongest they can make here."

"Please, explain to the waiter! Or – wait, I'll do it myself! You won't be able to order what we need."

The waiter rolled up and then left, after assiduously recording Jozef's words. Koshovy moved closer to the edge of the table and moved around so that Shatsky was sitting right beside him.

"Can I trust you with a secret, Shatsky?"

"You can trust me completely, Mr. Koshovy. Haven't you understood that already?"

"It's not even a secret… Just mere conjecture… But I'm more than certain…"

Klym stopped talking.

Something inside him was stopping him from voicing his conclusions.

"Stop dragging this out, Mr. Koshovy! Seeing as we've already started!"

His eye twitched.

He mechanically pressed the tip of his index finger against his eyelid.

"No one will accept this, because it's all over. I'm talking about Soyka's murder."

"No one will accept *what*?"

"Ignatiy Yartsev did not kill him."

There, he'd said it.

But it didn't make him feel any better.

CHAPTER EIGHTEEN
THE ART OF HAVING ENEMIES

The billiard player was covered in sweat.

Koshovy's chair was turned, so that he could see the billiard table in the depths of the spacious hall. And watch the battle between two pool sharks, as if he had bought tickets to the spectacle. The previous frame had been won by the opponent, a fat mustached fellow, who kept touching the edge of the table with his belly, even barely leaning over it. Preparing for a return game proposed by the young fellow, the fat man calmly rubbed the end of his cue with chalk. The rather young fellow, unnerved by what was obviously not his first loss since the start of the match, had earlier removed his fashionably cut tailcoat. He was left wearing his vest, which failed to cover his wide suspenders, and his rather short top hat. Now he removed that too, wiping his damp forehead with a large white handkerchief, and then, for certainty, with his cupped hand.

Shatsky cleared his throat.

"Excuse me, but…"

"What?"

"Who did Yartsev kill then?"

"The thief Tsipa, in Klepariv. The one whose body you and I found."

"No need to remind me, Mr. Koshovy. But… hm… it wasn't us who found it. Thankfully, I didn't see the corpse. The newspapers didn't write the full story, thank heavens. They made mention that his body was mutilated before he died, after which everyone could give free rein to their imagination…"

"Shatsky, can you please cut the bullshit, so we can get down to business?"

"Do we have business to discuss?" Shatsky's eyes grew round.

Their coffee arrived.

Waiting until the waiter had left, Koshovy grabbed the small cup and took a sip.

Very strong and fragrant.

It was unusually bitter and he thought of adding some sugar. Jozef had already added three spoonfuls and was now stirring his cup so assiduously, that the coffee splashed over the edges onto his saucer.

"Listen, Shatsky," Klym put his cup down and pushed it away. "It so happens that you are not merely the only person in all of Lviv whom I am ready to trust. You know more than the average reader of newspapers. I don't need to explain things to you, to go into details. You are also a walking source of the most varied gossip, only please don't take offense."

"I wouldn't refer to everything that I am aware of as gossip."

The rotund billiard player took careful aim, as he prepared for the break shot: the balls were racked in a triangle on the table.

"Call it what you like. Either way you have more opportunity to find something out in this city than I have. Agreed?"

"I wouldn't argue with that," Jozef took a slurp of his coffee, maintaining a dignified look. "But why are you sharing your thoughts with me, instead of the police?"

"Because the police have the killer," now Koshovy had dismissed any final doubts he might have had about being right, he only needed to repeat everything once more to himself and to consolidate his thoughts. "I myself handed him over to the commissar. To begin back-peddling now and calling on them to start everything from scratch, will look at the very least unethical. Even, I'm not afraid to use the word, suspicious. Besides, Ignatiy Yartsev really *did* kill Liubchyk Tsipa. Having first tortured him, stabbing and cutting him with his knife."

"Vey, there's no need to be so graphic."

Koshovy continued to maintain his harsh manner.

"But that's what happened, Shatsky. He literally carved a confession out of him, finding out where the money stolen from Soyka was hidden. The police located the ill-fated travel bag on those Russian bombers detained in Bohdanivka. They have their statements. Mr. Wichura later told me a little more, seeing as I am supposedly a person of interest in the case. The whole lot of them are a militant unit of the radical Russophile political wing, as they call them here. The money was passed on from Saint Petersburg. Which is why the police directorate received a good earbashing from the highest imperial authorities for disrupting an operation which had been carefully planned for ages by the local counterintelligence network…”

“But you’re supposedly from there, Mr. Koshovy.”

“From where? Petersburg? I was born and bred in Kyiv, Shatsky. And anyway, what has my former place of residence to do with anything?”

“I don’t understand much about political movements. Maybe, because of this, the local Jews have problems with political self-determination. But how could the gentlemen focused on unity with greater Russia have anything to do with those who are making home-made bombs? Those, forgive me, are supposedly revolutionaries. Away with the Tsar and all that stuff. How can those, who are against the Tsar, deal with those inhabitants of our regal city who love the Russian Tsar?”

Click!

A short enthusiastic exclamation – with a skilful shot the fat man had potted two balls at once, with a doublet.

“Shatsky, we can discuss this at length, in detail and on a separate occasion. Trust me, I know what I’m talking about. For the moment, suffice to say that not every militant organization formed here under the guise of being composed of revolutionaries who have escaped from the Russian regime, actually consists of such people. Leaders are recruited by the tsarist secret police. The rank and file, akin to Yartsev, often don’t know who they are working for.”

“You sure of that?”

“There’s no other way that I can explain the close ties between the supporters of the Tsar and the militants.”

The young man in the vest again wiped his forehead, crumpled up his handkerchief and shoved it into his pocket, then asked for a glass of rum. The fat man calmly rubbed the tip of his cue with chalk.

“Just you wait there, Mr. Koshovy! All this needs to be digested. These are state secrets, no?”

“There are no secrets here. The newspapers are already writing about this in passing, without providing specific details. I, by the way, don’t know the details either. I’m simply telling you everything I’ve heard from the annoyed commissar, no less. Obviously, no one wants to get in trouble. All the more since the criminal police really have strayed outside their jurisdiction. The chain has been broken, and now the political police will have to start everything from scratch. And imagine, after all this, here comes this disgusting stranger Koshovy, who also happens to be the subject of a country engaged in subversive activities here, and declares: gentlemen, you must look for another killer. Yartsev doesn't fit the bill."

Shatsky took another sip. Klym could see by his eyes that he was still intoxicated. He would need to order some more coffee.

"Amazing," nodded Jozef. "But I don't expect anything special from our police. So, who killed Mr. Genyk then? Do you know?"

Koshovy was in no hurry to answer. At first he repeated it a few times to himself. And then replied:

"I know, but I'm not entirely sure. Which is why I've started this conversation with you. Will you help me?"

Shatsky sat up straight, squared his shoulders, and seemed to grow a head taller.

"Jozef Shatsky can help in such a case?"

"If there was someone else – I would have turned to them."

"Thank you for your candor," the dentist was not at all offended. "Then let's go back to the very start. Why have you decided that Ignatiy Yartsev did not kill Mr. Soyka?"

The young billiard player received his rum. He gulped it down, ordered a coffee, gripped his cue decisively, and prepared to have his shot.

"Most likely, only I could have reached such a conclusion," Koshovy began, and continued calmly, for he had long been preparing the explanation in his head, and was now merely voicing it: "Or a person much like me. Someone, who for the first time in their life has found themselves not just in a new city, but right here in Lviv. Having lived here a few weeks, walked the streets every day and looked around – I still keep getting lost. You probably need to be born here, to navigate the streets painlessly, effortlessly, with closed eyes and in the darkness. Like you, for instance, Shatsky. Or that Mr. Tyma, with whom you and I wove our way through Lviv's nooks and crannies. Maybe – I'm guessing here – but just maybe, the ins and outs of the backstreets can be learned. But I put Yartsev, a person from Saint Petersburg, who was accustomed to a completely different arrangement of city streets, in my shoes. It is possible to get the hang of the streets here in a few weeks. Especially for someone like Ignat – a professional terrorist. These people study the streets and alleys very carefully, believe me. I'll tell you, some day, how I know all this. And I must remind you of things that are no secret even to the police."

Shatsky finished his coffee in a single gulp.

"What did they miss, Mr. Koshovy?"

Klym was prepared for a long explanation.

What had crystallized in his head, seemingly of its own accord, needed to be consolidated and recited first of all to himself. Now he wasn't so much sharing his conclusions with his friend and grateful listener, as he was thinking aloud. He spoke, as if he was standing in front of a mirror, rather than Jozef Shatsky's pricked-up ears:

"That's the very fact of the matter – they missed nothing," he began, carefully choosing his words. "The messengers visited Yevhen Soyka the day before he was killed. It is unlikely that Yartsev and his comrade Kniazev, whom my janitor Bulbash described as being an older man, arrived with their mission and hung around Lviv for a few days, before coming to see Yevhen Pavlovych. On the contrary, they needed to hand over the money to the intermediary as soon as possible. My mentor," Klym smiled bitterly, "turned out to be the middle link in a spy chain. My guess is everything happened in the following order. The couriers brought Soyka the travel bag stuffed full of money. Yartsev stayed behind to guard the package, but for some reason the lawyer sent him packing, assuming responsibility for the money. Then, as I thought previously, Ignat must have secretly returned to the apartment. He had an indulgence from Soyka, so no one would suspect him if the travel bag were to disappear. He had already gotten rid of the lawyer, as I had assumed. This would have all been correct, had Yartsev known his way about Lviv and its backways at least a little. He had told me himself, when he was leading me into a trap, so that he could kill me, that he had never been here before. Understand, Shatsky? How can a person, who has been in Lviv at most two days at the time of the killing, easily navigate the courtyards of Lychakiv Street?! So easily, that he is able to enter the apartment unseen. Avoiding the trained eye of our janitor! A mouse wouldn't be able to sneak past that fellow. Unless it knew every nook and cranny. So, the conclusion I've reached is this: to enter the apartment, kill Soyka and leave, remaining unnoticed, would only be possible if the person knew Lychakiv and the surrounding streets really well, together with Lviv as a whole."

Exclamations again, this time of disappointment – the ball hit by the young billiard player stopped at the edge of the pocket, refusing to roll any further. The fat man, suffering no pangs of conscience, corrected the situation with a single hit. The outcome of the game no longer seemed to interest him; he was preoccupied with the process.

"So, the killer is a local. Do you know who it is?"

"I'm ninety percent certain. At first, when Yartsev blurted out that he had never been in Lviv before, I took no notice of his words. Agree with me, there wasn't the time for that. But later, when I lay in bed and revisited the sequence of events, I couldn't understand what was troubling me, giving me no peace. Recalling our nocturnal jaunt and Yartsev's involuntary confessions, I understood: he couldn't have killed Soyka. He wouldn't have risked it."

"You think so?"

"Of course. Having learned from the newspapers the following morning what had happened, he was given the task of retrieving the money by his superior, Kniazev. Or at least to find out if the police had seized it. Yartsev acted through local helpers – apparently there are enough agents here. They didn't find the travel bag in Soyka's apartment. Otherwise the janitor, at the very least, would have known about it, let alone the building's owner, Mr. Singer. So, after Ignat had left with the note, the sequence of events probably went something like this," Koshovy finished his coffee. "The person who set themselves the goal of killing the lawyer, entered the apartment through the window. And they knew how to reach the building via the back way. From the time that Soyka saw Yartsev off, no one had come asking for him until my appearance the next morning."

"No one?"

"No one – apart from some batiar. He wanted to see the lawyer. The janitor, having received his instructions, told the lout that the lawyer was not in. The batiar, as it later turned out, was Zdenek Novotny. I questioned Bulbash about everything in detail, recreating the sequence of events almost to the minute. The thieves entered the apartment after Soyka had been killed, that much is certain. They found and took the travel bag with them, that much is true as well. When the batiar's arrest became widely known throughout the city, including from the newspapers, Yartsev realized who might have the money. He probably engaged the services of the appropriate people and sniffed out where Tsipa was hiding – and the rest you know. But Shatsky, the money remained in place!"

"What do you mean, in place?"

"In the apartment!" Klym explained patiently. "When I entered there, I didn't see any traces of a search. So, the killer had not looked for the money. He had come to settle some important personal account with Mr. Soyka, who is adept at the art of making enemies. And this had nothing to do, well, alright, should have had nothing to do with his unsavory activities."

With a few skilful hits, obviously mastered long ago, the fat billiard player finished the frame. The young man ordered another rum.

"Coffee?" Klym inquired.

"Forget the coffee… Mr. Koshovy, this is brilliant!"

"Don't exaggerate. It's merely a set of coincidences and a desire to make sense of them. Well, and a result of inactivity. One needs to occupy oneself with something so as not to go crazy when one is sitting around. We only need to work out who actually killed Soyka. And why. Although, as I already mentioned, I have seen a side to my senior colleague here, which is utterly unpleasant. So, there is a critical number of people who didn't simply wish him dead but might have personally fulfilled their desires. Mrs. Magda convinced me of this once again not more than half an hour ago."

"Bohdanovych? Our respected widow? How does she figure in all this?"

"She let it be known, firstly, that I was right. Many respected people nursed some serious grievances against Soyka. And secondly," his eyelid twitched, "she unwittingly narrowed the circle of suspects. Previously it had narrowed of its own accord. But I realized this only now."

"Meaning?"

"The day of Yevhen Soyka's funeral. Remember, Shatsky, not too many people came. Given his rather dubious reputation, one needn't have expected a large assemblage of grieving souls. But three did come, each of whom, or all of them together, badly needed to warn me off against further active participation in the investigation into the circumstances of Mr Genyk's death. You saw them all, Shatsky. You must know each of them."

Jozef knitted his brows.

"Editor Popeliak. Engineer Adam Wiszniewski. Councilor Morawski. And Mrs. Bohdanovych…"

"Mrs. Magda doesn't consider any of the people you've named as having anything at all to do with the murder. Although until that first suspect appeared, the inattentive and careless batiar Zdenek, she very much feared that one of them, or, I'll repeat myself, all of them together, might sooner or later find themselves on the list of suspects. Every one of them is dear to her in his own way. At some point, men cease to be mere guardians of those like her. Tell me now, Shatsky – are you really up to helping me?"

Before he had finished speaking, Jozef was already nodding his head:

"I'm up to it! You can count on me, Mr. Koshovy! Will this be life threatening?"

"And if it will?"

He did not think for too long.

"I'm still ready. Know, why? At times these things are more interesting, than peering into strangers' mouths, poking about in there and drilling into decayed teeth."

A strong argument, he had no objections. Klym stretched out his hand across the table toward Shatsky, palm up.

"Agreed. Then let's agree on a time for the rendezvous."

Tossed onto the velvet surface of the billiard table, the banknotes spread out in a fan. The young player walked off without turning around. He forgot about his tailcoat, only picking up his top hat. One of the spectators hurried after him, handing him the forgotten piece of clothing.

The conspirators leaned across the table toward one another, their foreheads almost touching.

Klym Koshovy presented his plan to Jozef Shatsky.

It was very simple.

The only risk might be that none of the persons would bite, that no one would come, no one would expose themselves.

But *he* turned up.

CHAPTER NINETEEN
AT NIGHT WITH BARE HANDS

The tall man wasn't dressed in black so that he could merge into the stifling July darkness.

He simply liked to dress in dark monotone clothing. He felt confident only when he was dressed this way. True, until recently he had had a rather colorful wardrobe. It had contained suits sewn from fabric of various colors, ranging from pale blue to coffee with a generous helping of milk. And in the light of the tragic events, which had in one moment changed not only his views, but also his attitude to life, the tall man, in a fit of altruism uncharacteristic of him, donated his suits to the nearest refuge for the poor. Later, in Market Square, he was gladdened to see beggars wearing what were once his clothes, realizing just how comical, even infirm a person could appear to the world in such a motley array of colors. They didn't suit everyone. And the brazen beggars, who resembled elegant scarecrows, eloquently confirmed his conclusion.

At least it seemed that way to him.

When the tall man had *dared* to do this the first time, it turned out that dark clothes also disguised a person. One needn't specially rack one's brains, selecting clothes necessary for the risky escapade. Be yourself, everywhere and always. Wear what you always get about in and you won't attract needless attention. And there was no point wasting time or, even worse, carrying what you needed with you. That evening he had taken his leave of Magda earlier than usual, alluding to important matters he had to attend to, and she hadn't even shown an inkling of suspicion. Assuming that the criminal police would work on the case more seriously, than he expected, and the circle of suspects would be as wide as it should have been, the tall man had the advantage even here. For without a second thought, without even a drop of suspicion in her heart, Magda would clearly have declared that on the evening in question the person of interest was with her. When had he left? Excuse me, gentlemen, that is none of your business.

Setting off at night for the familiar address, the man dressed in dark clothes had no clear idea of his ultimate goal. What would he return with? Would he offer this Kyiv upstart money? No, it would be better to offer a helping hand, to arrange his immediate future here in Lviv. Magda would appreciate such a gesture, especially since she also considered herself indirectly indebted to Koshovy. However, the fellow appeared to be a principled romantic. If he was unable to reach an agreement with him, then he would need to take extreme measures. Moreover, now that the fugitive lawyer from Kyiv, a hero of various newspaper publications, was seen as being in some way involved in exposing the dangerous bombers, it might appear that these same revolutionaries, or rather, their comrades, had settled accounts with him.

Such an interpretation of events would satisfy the criminal police.

Especially, if Magda inadvertently insisted on this. After their recent serious and much desired intimate conversation, the tall man had every reason to believe that he was becoming one of the few, or to be absolutely accurate – the only one, with whom the proud and impregnable Mrs. Bohdanovych would reckon with and whose opinion she would value.

If he was unable to reach an amicable agreement with Koshovy, then he would behave as he had with Soyka. That time he had settled an old account. This time he would be taking care of his future.

With Magda Bohdanovych.

She would soon be bearing another surname.

And as for Koshovy…

People would forget about him.

Not that quickly, but all the same they would not remember him for too long.

With such thoughts on his mind the tall man reached Market Square, where he let the coachman go and continued on foot to the start of Lychakiv Street. Last time he had done the same. The nightlife was raging all around him, and people here took no notice of one another. Having reached the place, the man ducked into the nearest archway, so that he could move through the courtyards, just like the previous time. Easily finding his way in these narrow labyrinths, he finally emerged in the required spot. His eyes searched for the window.

The lights were out.

It wasn't too late, but hardly was Koshovy in the habit of carousing. When people had nothing to do, they began to eat a lot more or went to bed early. With the hope that the new day would be better than the previous one. It turned out to be more complicated with Soyka, for he had been working in his office, the light had been on. But the closed bedroom door had been helpful. The lawyer, engrossed in his work, had failed to hear the extraneous sounds. He was very surprised to see the dark unbidden guest. But he showed no fear – and it was this which had enraged the tall man the most. He had looked at the intruder, as something interesting, absolutely new, capable of enlivening his disgusting everyday life.

He hadn't planned to negotiate with Mr. Genyk. He hit him straight away, realizing in the depths of his soul that if he allowed himself to be drawn into a conversation, his intentions would gradually weaken, grow pale, and become extinguished. He attacked, so as not to allow for such a turn of events. Only later, after he had fired the shot, did his nerves get the better of him – after all up until that time he had never killed anyone, even if the lawyer from Lychakiv Street happened to be a heinous scoundrel. Which is why he left everything as it was, dropping the weapon near the dead body. Slipping out of the apartment, he left by way of the network of courtyards once more. Then he remembered that he needed to decorate the murder scene at least a little, to throw the police off his trail. He recalled how he hadn't dared return at first. But when he finally did – he believed, as never before, that there was a God and higher powers. For he saw the figures of some burglars deftly clambering in through the window.

Although he was no match to their dexterity, he did have certain skills.

Which he put into practice now. Nothing restrained his movements.

A short run up.

One sweeping movement – and his foot was on the edge of a big wide board leaning against the wall, his other leg bent, pressed against the board; as he lunged up, his hands grabbed hold of the windowsill. He strained his muscles, pulled himself up, and hoisted his body inside. Now the tall man was not afraid of rousing the sleeping occupant. He intended to wake him anyway, to start a serious conversation, and give the smart alec a chance to avoid his own death. Besides, he was itching to know, how Koshovy had worked out it was him, and what had given him away. It was unlikely he would be killing anyone in the future – but it was good to learn to be careful in general and useful to learn from one's mistakes.

Stepping up to the edge of the bed, on which the victim lay completely covered with a blanket, breathing evenly with a whistle, the man in black was in no hurry to begin. He stood still, interlacing his fingers covered by thin leather gloves, which he had put on along the way, when he was in the courtyards. After standing there awhile, he released his fingers…

"Did you really come like that, bare-handed?"

The voice came from behind, suddenly, causing the man to flinch. Surprised, he must have become lost for words, not turning around straight away and not understanding, whether he would be spoken to or hit over the head with something heavy.

"Do you have a gun in your pocket, or have you come to kill me with your bare hands?"

The light went on.

After the darkness of the night it had seemed that way to the man.

In fact, only the night light had been turned on, moved into the corner and placed on a bench, which had been set up near the common door specially for this. There was enough light for the nocturnal visitor to see Klym, who was standing there in the corner, and for Koshovy to see him.

The blanket moved and slipped down.

From underneath it appeared Jozef Shatsky's disheveled head. He was at the same time frightened and curious. He even sat up in bed, pulling the blanket up over his body, as if it would have protected him in case of anything.

"Will you remain standing there like that? Do you want me to continue talking to your back?"

Slowly the man turned around but remained silent.

"Listen, you can leave now, just as you came in. The fact that you took the bait regarding my intention to tell Mrs. Magda everything and came here, is quite enough for me. There's no need to explain yourself," Klym tried to speak in a calm voice, although he realized that it was not going too well, his agitation could be sensed. "Or you can try to kill me. There are two of us here… My apologies, Shatsky, I don't consider you a serious rival. Our guest is physically stronger. After tonight I might even start taking lessons in wrestling and resume boxing. But all the same, I won't let myself be killed. So, there'll be a fight. Noise, shouts. That's when Mr. Shatsky will come onstage. He's capable of creating such a commotion, that no less than half of Lychakiv will come running here. The landlord will call the police. You can escape the way you came, through the window. But Shatsky and I won't be telling the police that we fought one another."

"Making a fool of me?" the man in black finally forced the words out.

"Not at all. Just painting a picture of your prospects. If you've evaluated them realistically and have changed your mind to kill me, let's simply talk. Let's sort out the relations which have developed between us of late."

"What is there to talk about, Mr. Koshovy?"

Klym moved away from the wall, taking a few steps forward, and stood opposite his nocturnal visitor.

"Well this, for example – I don't feel at all sorry for Yevhen Pavlovych Soyka. I know that's not Christian-like, I should be more merciful, more compassionate. He once gave me a job and taught me a thing or two. Soyka, or as I've now grown used to calling him in the local manner, Mr. Genyk, was a virtuoso lawyer. The only thing is – his knowledge, expertise, skill, and irrepressible energy were, for reasons I cannot understand, directed into a destructive stream. He cynically saved villains from imprisonment. And of late the word 'scoundrel' began to be equated with the accepted designation in Lviv of 'Russophile.'"

"Not only in Lviv," the man in black corrected him. "Throughout the entire kingdom. As well as beyond its borders to the west."

"That's not important. There are lots of wretches in this world, and they can't always be discerned by the views they espouse. I've known people whose deviousness was not all based on their convictions. But in our case, everything has come together. In short, I am convinced you had good reason to take Soyka's life…" Koshovy suddenly choked on his own words, cleared his throat, and hastened to correct himself: "Significant for you. You wanted to kill him, sought justification for your actions and, as we can see, you found it. However… no one has the right to take the life of another person. A court of law would need to rule on this, which your humble servant has countless reasons not to trust completely. The judgment of the

Lord appeals to me more. Agreed, it's often a long wait, sometimes it comes after our time. But this is much better, than someone playing God. I am not justifying your actions. And I won't demand that you voluntarily surrender to the police after our conversation."

"Your demands are pointless under any circumstances, Mr. Koshovy."

"I understand. Just like your reluctance to attract publicity. Let's assume that it falls to me to deliver you up to Commissar Wichura. So, you will be pardoned. That's the way I see it. Or – you will receive a light sentence. However, you yourself are least of all interested in a trial taking place. You don't need the publicity. You will be released as a killer, whichever way you look at it. And if you have finally changed your mind and decided to strangle me, please satisfy the curiosity of myself and *Mister* Shatsky. I'd like to know why you did it. Because how – I can already begin to imagine."

The ensuing seconds of silence were broken only by the ticking of a massive clock standing against the opposite wall. Shatsky kept snorting, with all his might straining to stem his desire to join in the conversation.

"If you have no one to talk to and nothing to discuss at night – be my guest, I'll explain everything," the man in black finally said. "But before that I would still like to hear you out, Mr. Koshovy. Your question is – 'why?'. My question is 'how?'. Because it was me you were expecting, am I not right?"

"Yes, you," Klym replied. "The exercise appears to be a difficult one to solve. I was able to arrive at the answer more quickly because I am not a local. I know little about your connections with one another. So I have no special sentiments or prejudices toward anyone. After I had worked out that the Russian revolutionary couldn't have killed Soyka, the question immediately arose: 'Who then?' Do you know where you unwittingly supplied me with the answer, without even realizing it? In the offices of the criminal police!"

"Really?"

"Yes. Yartsev had not yet been shot dead, we were sitting in the commissar's office, waiting to be summoned to the secret meeting. Among other things, Wichura had mentioned: it's very good, he said, Mr. Koshovy, that there is a murderer and that he is not one of us. Because, he said, councilor Morawski had complained that people might well think it was him. You can't shut people up; they are fond of sensations. Watch out, if it becomes public knowledge that he, Mr. Kazimierz, lost a case because of Mr. Genyk's efforts a year ago. Some admirer of the Tsar wanted to have premises for his editorial office in the center of the city. The councilor, see, used his powers to make sure that he was refused. He cast the deciding vote. And the refused man found how to take Morawski to court. And he not only won the case – Mr. Kazimierz was also forced to pay the fellow's court costs. The councilor had paid for his own defeat, you understand? What an insult, people still laugh at him in the town hall from time to time. And he'd aspired to be elected to the sejm. But how could he now with such baggage?"

"And you decided, Mr. Koshovy, that people kill because of this?"

"No. It was you who decided that."

"Me? Personally?"

"All of you. The three of you. Kazimierz Morawski, Adam Wiszniewski, Janusz Popeliak. Or one of you. The one who *truly* felt that he was in danger if people began to dig about in this direction. Seeking those who had motives. And the commissar made mention of the existence of such fears, I'll remind you. Why did the three of you come to the cemetery to see off Soyka?"

"There were others there too."

"Not many. And they tried not to look into each other's eyes. As if they had come not to say goodbye to a good friend, but to be certain that he had been indeed interred. I'm not counting those you call Russophiles here. Very few of them appeared as well. But they had no need of Soyka's death. On the contrary, the lawyer was their judicial, so to speak, legal weapon. If you'll pardon the pun."

"That's fine. So, you reached your conclusions based solely on the number of people present at the cemetery?"

"I wouldn't have reached them, had no one taken any interest in a little-known stranger, apart from your small group. And you had decided earlier to invite me to a similar conversation. A memorial lunch is such a great excuse. It appeared that all of you together or one of you individually was aware of the danger. Talking with me was insurance and at the same time a direct warning: don't poke your nose where it doesn't belong. Remember, I took note of this back then. Because I shared my thoughts with Mrs. Magda. She must have let you know. You being a close person. You know, it just occurred to me… You calmed down then, didn't you? Deciding that the vagrant from Kyiv understood where his place was and had made the decision to keep his nose out of everything. Thank God, you thought, things didn't go to plan for him, and without house or home, without money or engagements, he will gather up his things and leave. Back East. Or forward, to the West. There was that hope, agreed?"

"You stayed."

"Because at that time I really had nowhere to go. But now I don't want to leave. But let's come back to you – the three of you. Each of you had good reason to settle accounts with Soyka. Janusz Popeliak allowed himself, guns blazing, to attack the radical wing of the Russophiles. They bided their time, and then hit back in reply. More than likely they bribed someone. The money for this would have flowed from Petersburg in a continuous stream, as we now see. Otherwise it's impossible to explain why Soyka, as a representative of the plaintiff, simply didn't demand a public apology from the editor, but went on to recover significant damages in court. I had a bit of a chat with Mr. Singer, the local landlord. He told me that Popeliak had needed to mortgage his private real estate. It's not public knowledge, but the editor lost that battle. People kill over such things, don't you think?"

"In our time people kill over far less."

"I'm well aware of that. Popeliak, possibly sincerely, although by no means in a Christian-like way, rejoiced when Soyka received his just deserts. However, he wasn't the perpetrator. Know why? The editor would be unable to crawl into a first-floor window. Because he's short and fat. I rejected him straight away, that left two of you. Morawski, as I've mentioned, thanks to the efforts of Soyka, received a good wallop. His defeat was more a moral one than material. For a certain category of dignified people this can be far more painful. Don't you agree?"

"With what exactly?"

"That Kazimierz Morawski didn't kill the lawyer Soyka. Not because he had no interest in sport, but because, unlike you, he wasn't as fit. Do I need to prove your guilt to you here and now, Mr. Wiszniewski, or will you admit to it yourself?"

CHAPTER TWENTY
A VERY DEAR PERSON

The clock ticked away.

Shatsky's eyes shone with excessive, unrestrained curiosity. The remains of his fear had decidedly evaporated, and now Jozef, seated more comfortably on the bed, didn't even think of getting up off it. He resembled a person who had occupied the best seat in the house.

Engineer Adam Wiszniewski, looking exactly the way he had during their first meeting – a well-built gentleman in a black suit, a round hat with slightly upturned brims, an elegantly cut small beard, and a narrow strip of a mustache, slowly began to remove the thin black glove from his right hand.

"We are not before a court, Mr. Koshovy. You yourself said – no one is fit to judge another, except for the Almighty Himself. Moreover, we are not before God's court. And you're not the prosecutor."

"True, Mr. Adam. I'm a lawyer. Although in this case I'm not sure who I'm representing and who I'm defending."

"Meaning, I don't need to admit to my guilt before witnesses?"

"Quite. However, by matter of circumstance I now live in this apartment. So, no matter how good or bad it is, it's my little fortress. A roof over my head. A place where I can feel safe. You entered here by stealth, without being invited. You climbed in through the window. And now since I… *we*, that is my friend and I, have exposed you, I would like you to recount your intentions. Why did you come here at this time and in this way? People with good intentions, respectable people, don't crawl into each other's places through windows."

Having removed his right glove, Adam began to remove the left one. For a while he even looked away from Klym, becoming engrossed in the process. Koshovy waited patiently. Finally having finished, Wiszniewski neatly folded the gloves and carefully placed them into his pants pocket. He spoke as if he had just completed an extremely important job:

"You won't believe me, Klymentiy."

"Why is that? Try me."

"I wanted to talk to you first."

"Really? And then?"

"I would have reached a decision, depending on the outcome of the conversation. A messenger brought me a letter. Neat handwriting, a few short sentences. Signed by a well-wisher whom I do not know, but someone who wishes me well. He warns me that the lawyer Koshovy, whom I am aware of, has learned of my involvement in what happened to Soyka. And that he is ready to share his thoughts with Mrs. Magda Bohdanovych. I decided to stop you. At any cost."

"So you immediately believed some anonymous note?"

"Klymentiy, you yourself have demonstrated how good you are! Chasing a batiar across the entire city, and someone who only looked like the one who had robbed you. A zealous search for his accomplice with the subsequent discovery of a second body. Finally, you don't create the impression of a physically strong person. However, your adventurous streak prevailed – and you rushed off to the criminals' den. Of your own free will."

"Magda told you all this? No, don't answer. It was her; it couldn't have been anyone else. You two have a very trusting relationship. It can't be otherwise, when a gentleman discusses the teachings of Professor Jung with his lady friend, and she, having no idea about such things, listens enthusiastically and tells others about them. The police directorate has no secrets from the widow Bohdanovych, so she listened with interest to the details of all the adventures in which I humbly participated."

"No need for false modesty."

"Really, I never intended to become a hero. It sometimes happens: you think how to save yourself, and in the process, you save practically the entire world."

"Now that's an exaggeration."

"Let that be. We're not talking about me here though, Mr. Adam. You read the anonymous letter, set the parameters of the exercise, and decided that it was irrelevant who was warning you, but that I was capable of such a thing. That is, that I had found out something, which was not worth telling Mrs. Magda. Which is why you are here."

"Which is why I am here," nodded Wiszniewski, glancing at the silent Shatsky, and repeated: "Yes, that's why I'm here."

Klym took a deep breath, preparing to say perhaps the most important thing for both of them, and continued:

"Magda knows that you have a valid reason to kill the lawyer Soyka. You're not alone, so she didn't seriously suspect you. She took an interest in this incident straight away. The police widow determined at once: those who see an advantage will always search. And so she decided to unobtrusively assume covert control of the investigation. In Lviv's police department they are no longer amazed at such things, so no one will suspect a thing. The rest, Mr. Adam, are only my assumptions. Hopefully, you will allow me?"

"Please do."

His eyelid twitched, but not as strongly this time.

"In general, the investigator was happy enough with the version of suicide," Koshovy, continued, gradually warming to the subject. "Had Mrs. Bohdanovych not been secretly present during my conversation with investigator Olshansky, she wouldn't have heard my devastating arguments," one corner of his lips twisted into a brief smile, "benefiting, if it can be put that way, the idea of intentional homicide. Which is why Magda came on stage. Another ploy – letting everything take place under her watchful eye and influence. After which, I assume, without any suspicion, she simply related everything to you."

"I underestimated you."

"Really? Hah, Mr. Adas? Good, don't interrupt, otherwise I will lose my train of thought."

"Hardly…"

"Thank you," Klym bowed buffoonishly. "So, she told you everything. Most probably, the idea to tactfully and at the same time sternly warn me against getting involved, was yours rather than hers. And Magda willingly supported you. Because at that time neither the police, nor Mrs. Bohdanovych, nor myself knew about the stolen money. In fact – no one had any idea that the killers might have taken the money. I learned by chance that the Breguet had disappeared. Well, and then, after that events raced quickly forward, the killer and the motive were finally determined. Everything suited everyone. Everyone was pleased with everything. Magda sighed with relief. For even any ephemeral suspicion regarding you, not hers, but of the police, could thus be discounted. But suddenly we have something new, born in the head of some Koshovy. Are you afraid of a trial, Mr. Wiszniewski?"

"I have no need of it. No one is interested in going to court, especially because of the murder of such a corrupt bastard as Soyka."

"That's a separate conversation. I'm talking about something else, far more important. You would have survived the trial, Mr. Adam. Or at least your dealings with the investigator, the interrogation and the acquittal. But more than the suspicion, the investigation, the arrest, the trial, and the sentence, you were afraid of losing Magda. She is a person who is no less dear to you than you are to her. Which is why, Mr. Adam, she was afraid, that at least in the long run you might become a suspect. If everything was confirmed, Magda was ready to understand you," Klym again paused for a short while, looking Wiszniewski straight in the eye. "Ready to understand you, Mr. Adam. But..."

"What?"

"Not ready to forgive you. For her, the widow of a policeman, a servant of the law who was respected even by hardened criminals, to continue to maintain a warm relationship with a killer would not be possible. Which is why you are here. Had you not appeared – I would have admitted my mistake, my defeat, and would have forever wiped Soyka's murder from my mind. It would make no difference to him, whether his real killer was found or not. I never intended to reveal anything to Mrs. Magda. I really need to concentrate on my own future, not Soyka, whom no decent person here misses. You did not know my true intentions. You came after my soul. And resolved to take on another sin. Have you changed your mind?"

Adam Wiszniewski looked at Shatsky once more. Sizing him up with an indifferent look, he slowly turned around and stepped up to the window. He clenched his fists and leaned against the edge of the windowsill.

"Thank you. But why did you not change your mind about killing Soyka?"

The nocturnal visitor froze, looking ahead, as if trying to see something in the darkness of the night. Without turning around, he said:

"I had a younger sister, Jadwiga. That is," he hesitated for a moment, "she's still alive. But consider that she's no longer with us. She's now being treated in Kulparkiv[55]. From time to time I take Jadzia from there, rent a house outside the city and hire the services of a woman who looks after her. Then, when her health deteriorates, I again return her into the hands of the doctors. Everyone had high hopes. But in late June I was told that there was no point in expecting any changes for the better. To at least keep her in the state she's in, Jadzia needs to be kept in strict isolation from men. She shouldn't even see them. Otherwise she will have another attack, requiring more intensive treatment."

"Is this at all relevant…"

"It is!"

Wiszniewski turned sharply to face Klym. His fists remained clenched. His exclamation was acrid, making Shatsky shudder involuntarily.

"It is! Last autumn Jadwiga decided to go for a walk in Striysky Park. She loved October, always wrote poetry during this season. Not just any old stuff, it was good enough to be read in the salons. Two fellows attacked her in the twilight. They took her to the outskirts of the city, had their way with her, and believe me: this was that rare case when physical violence, physical abuse seems a lesser evil and, accordingly, causes less grief. Need I explain that Magda played an active part in speeding up the search for these scumbags. They turned out to be young members of the Russian National Party. These two had just been solemnly accepted into the party's ranks. Their leader, Mr. Markov, had personally shaken hands with each of them. My sister was unlucky enough to have caught their eye, when both were thinking, how to better celebrate this solemn occasion, to make it memorable for the rest of their lives."

"Let me guess. They were defended by Yevhen Soyka, right?"

"He defended them and got both of them off the hook. Cynically taking advantage of Jadwiga's state of mind. She recognized her attackers. But later reacted just as painfully to other men shown to her. Including Soyka himself. Here Mr. Genyk shone, showing himself in all his glory! And meanwhile the Russophile rags began to write about the political persecu-

....

55   Kulparkiv – place in Lviv, most often mentioned in connection with a psychiatric hospital located there. Built in 1875 by a decision of the Galician Regional Sejm. Patients from across the crown lands were sent there. Medical care for the mentally ill during this period was mainly limited to simply keeping the patients there.

tion of dissidents, provocations by the authorities, they even organized a procession with church gonfalons. The police failed to gather any solid evidence; they were in too much of a hurry. Apart from poor Jadzia, the only other witness was easily bribed. And what's more – they were let out soon after the resonant murder of Count Potocki. Our authorities are much more worried by the upsurge in your Ruthenian protest movement, than the actions of the Russian National Party and similar organizations. Do you know why?"

"No."

"Because Russophiles aren't considered to be controlled and are not taken too seriously. Our government plays on the contradictions which have plagued these two forces. So, it will more willingly grease the palms of the pro-Russian communities – so that they will put additional pressure on those who want to find and build that Greater Ukraine of yours. See, politics has intervened here, as always. Only that doesn't make it any easier. I have no sympathy for either of the sides, but it was I who suffered in the end. What they did to my sister, was also done to me. That's my story. I have nothing more to add."

The clock ticked away.

But now it sounded a lot louder. Each sound reverberated like a bell tolling in his ears.

"Me too," Koshovy announced hollowly.

"Please?"

"I have nothing to say in reply too, Mr. Adam. Apart from what I've already said. You were able to explain your actions to yourself. And to me too, to be honest. The father of four present here, Jozef Shatsky, will also live peacefully with this knowledge. Even the courts would have been lenient with you. Although you entered Soyka's apartment at night by stealth, which in itself indicates criminal intent. Premeditated murder. Your state of mind would have been taken into account, but all the same it was intentional, premeditated murder. Magda would not accept that."

"I know. Which is why I came."

"To shut me up?"

"I told you…"

"No, there's no need!" Koshovy raised his voice. "There's no need to seek justification! You intended to kill me! Just like you killed the lawyer Soyka who, after what I have just heard, has unequivocally died in my mind! But you equated him with me! That happens, Mr. Wiszniewski! That often happens: at first you kill someone in a fit of passion, seeking revenge, and then you choose your next victim to conceal your previous crime! That's all I am guilty of in your case! Do you want me to forgive and forget someone who has been honing a knife to kill me? I'm sick and tired of continually watching my back, Mr. Wiszniewski! That's not why I moved here! You know, I expected that you would come through the door. Shatsky here, he's my witness – really expected that too! You could have knocked and entered as a guest. We could have sat down at the desk in the office. And, if you'll pardon the pun, you could have placed all your cards before me on the table. Believe me, in those circumstances, this conversation of ours would have been quite different! But now…"

Wiszniewski unclenched his fists.

"I declared my love to Magda," he said hollowly.

The ardor suddenly disappeared from his voice. Klym could not understand, why he suddenly felt a hollow emptiness inside, and on the outside – an uncomfortable coolness.

"Meaning?"

"You're no small child, Klymentiy! Do I need to explain what it means when a man declares his love for a woman! It took me a long time to reach this point! You've seen her, surely! At first glance – an impregnable fortress, the approaches to which are paved with ice. But I've managed to melt that ice! If only you knew, oh, if only you knew, what it cost me!"

"I can imagine…"

"Hold your tongue! He can imagine! You can't even start to imagine, laddie!"

"I saw Magda several days ago," Klym tried to stay calm. "She really did look different. She was glowing. Did she say 'yes'?"

"She didn't say 'no'. At this late stage that too is an achievement."

Koshovy finally took control of his feelings.

"All the more reason."

"What do you mean – all the more reason?"

"You have just explained, why you intended to kill me. I am a threat to your future with Magda."

"Don't exaggerate your importance."

"Not at all. While someone like me knows your secret, you won't be at peace with yourself, Mr. Adam. Anyone, who someone wants to kill, has the right to protection. Agreed?"

"Whole-heartedly. The simplest solution is to beat them to it. Are you intending to take my life, Mr. Koshovy? Having read me my sentence?"

Klym sighed.

"I'm no judge. Less so an executioner – we've discussed that. You need to decide for yourself how to proceed from here."

"Do you propose I shoot or hang myself, or should I quaff some coffee laced with poison?"

"No," Koshovy said, amazed at how quickly the right decision had come. "Hell no. I don't want to bear such a sin. After all, you respect Mrs. Magda Bohdanovych, yes?"

"What is this in aid of? The question is devoid of meaning, it makes no sense."

"All the same I would like you to answer. Mr. Shatsky needs to hear too."

"Alright, if you haven't quite understood yet. Magda… *Mrs.* Magda is very dear to me."

"Thank you for your sincerity. Then are you agreed that she does not deserve to know about your crime? It's a crime, Mr. Wiszniewski, no matter what motivated its commitment. So?"

"Well, if you like… Of course, Mrs. Magda needn't know about this."

"Because she won't be able to accept a killer?"

"Yes. Because she is not ready to accept a killer."

"That is, she doesn't deserve to spend her life with a killer?"

"Exactly."

Koshovy clapped several times, calling on Shatsky to be his witness:

"All present here have heard you. Magda Bohdanovych does not deserve to tie the knot with you, Mr. Adam Wiszniewski. You yourself have just named the only acceptable way out for all concerned from a rather delicate situation. Sins must be atoned for."

The engineer froze. At first, he wasn't sure, what had happened. Then he shuddered, shook his head, as if banishing a nightmare. Klym continued to clap his hands, trying at the same time not to clap too loudly.

"You… you want…"

"I don't want anything. Today I managed to save my life, and I intend to adapt to life in Lviv. I'm not sure how it will turn out. And it's always better to start things with a clean slate, without needing to look over one's shoulder all the time. You can guarantee me non-aggression. All the same your standing in this present society is sufficient for you to wipe your feet on me, sooner or later. If you respect Mrs. Magda as much, as you have just admitted, you will have the strength and intelligence to arrive at exactly the right decision. In which case you will be forced one day to start everything from scratch with this woman – on the condition that she herself wants to resume relations with you. Your separation, Mr. Wiszniewski, is a guarantee of my safety. Unless one day in the future you decide to settle accounts with me, as you did with Soyka, finally putting us on an even playing field. However, either at first, or later you will have to make a decision what to do with Mr. Shatsky here. Is it possible that you, someone who has in fact lost his sister, will be capable of one day taking the life of a father of four? So, the conclusion is as follows. Either you condemn Mrs. Magda to an unworthy life with a killer – or you and I give each other guarantees of non-aggression. Of course, in this way you may possibly lose a person who is doubtlessly dear to you. However, forgive me my unwarranted pathos, you will save yourself."

"Meaning?"

"You won't be killing any more people, Mr. Adam. For a person of your character this is particularly important."

Klym had finally run out of things to say and grew silent, waiting for a reply.

As expected, Wiszniewski said nothing. He clenched and unclenched his fists several times. He glanced several times at Shatsky, then at Koshovy, and again at Jozef.

"I need to think things over," he said in the end.

"You are free to make any decision you want. You're not doing it for my sake. Decide for yourself, Mr. Adam. It's your decision. I have nothing more to add. Unless you yourself suggest a subject for discussion."

Instead of answering, engineer Adam Wiszniewski stepped decisively toward him.

But then suddenly stopped.

And just as resolutely turned around.

Without saying another word, he came up to the open window, sat down on the windowsill, swung around, and turned over onto his stomach.

Another moment – and he slipped out of sight.

He landed on the ground almost without a sound. Unable to restrain himself, Klym ran up to the window and looked out into the night. He couldn't see anyone; the nocturnal visitor had dissolved into the darkness.

There was coughing behind his back.

Turning around, Koshovy sighed wearily, and nodded to the dentist:

"We managed. I thought it would be worse. What do you say, Shatsky? You said nothing the whole time, quite unlike you…"

From the bed came the familiar smacking of lips.

"Pity I can't tell my Esther what a genius you are, Mr. Koshovy."

"You and I will have enough things to tell her," Klym placated him. "Even if we tell her how I invited you over to my place and you had so much liqueur, that I was forced to tuck you into bed here. You yourself suggested the alibi, because you know your wife better."

"We'll need to make some adjustments," there was a note of despondency in Shatsky's voice.

"What do you mean?"

"For the sake of maintaining our common secrets, Mr. Koshovy, we'll need to make an even greater sacrifice."

"What do you mean?"

"Vey, something even more shameful," Jozef said, snuffling like a small child, which Klym hadn't noticed him doing ever since they had met. "When that black giant climbed in through the window and stood over me, I was overcome with fear. I wet my long johns. Such things are difficult to explain, even to my feigale."

Koshovy understood that it was inappropriate to behave like this.

He understood – and yet he was unable to restrain himself.

He burst out laughing, no matter how offended Shatsky might be by his action.

1908, LVIV, LYCHAKIV STREET

They met for the first time in two weeks.

Klym had not sought to meet her. However, had the opportunity arisen, he wouldn't have tried to avoid it. He and Magda Bohdanovych frequented quite different circles for them to bump into one another other than by accident. Especially since these past few days Koshovy, frankly, had other things on his mind.

Almost every day he had to visit the police department – Olshansky filled out a whole stack of documents relating to the completion of the investigation. Klym was one of the principal witnesses in the murder of Yevhen Soyka, so it was clear why his testimony was important. He had agreed not to press charges against Zdenek Novotny. And since the long-haired batiar had begun to spill the beans after Liubchyk Cipa's murder, Olshansky was more than satisfied with his confession: the fellow had said that Cipa had practically forced him to come along, threatening and intimidating him, and then handed him the gold pocket watch as part of his take, ordering him to keep mum. Who then took over his defense and how they managed to do it, who paid for the expensive lawyer – that no longer concerned Klym.

Novotny was soon released, and for his part in the burglary the batiar would unlikely be severely punished. Especially since far more important people figured in the case.

After their nocturnal adventure, Shatsky also disappeared for a long time. Klym considered visiting the dentist, but after thinking it over he changed his mind. Before this, Jozef must have given his Esther good reason on many an occasion to give him a solid earbashing, but now he was probably busy with his business of fixing people's teeth. Idle moments needed to be compensated with hard work and, hand on heart, Koshovy agreed with such an approach. So, he accepted as his due the solitude and monotony he was experiencing after the earlier furious whirlwind of events.

He needed to rest and finally gather his thoughts. Because sooner or later the investigator would leave him in peace, and he would have to start looking for ways to make a living. The money received from the mysterious and almighty Gustav Silezsky would not last forever, it would run out sooner or later.

With such thoughts playing on his mind, Klym went out one afternoon to the Dobrovolsky Cafe. He had grown to like the place, for despite the fact that there were often no free tables, it was almost always quiet, people came here from across the city center to read the day's newspapers, and they went outside into the fresh air to discuss the news, moving to the Hetmanski Valy. At times he would join in the street debates, although for the most part he was just an avid listener. He had decided to venture out for a walk on this day, when he heard the familiar, although long since heard voice:

"Mr. Koshovy!"

Magda called out, sticking her head out of the carriage as it drove past Klym. She gestured to the coachman to stop. Obviously, she had no intention of joining him in the street. So that Koshovy unhurriedly, maintaining his dignity, made his way toward the carriage, stopped, and raised his hat, greeting her:

"Mrs. Magda! I haven't seen you in ages!"

"It hasn't been all that long."

She was once more wearing a dress in restrained colors – dark blue with green stitching, and for the first time he could remember her small hat was not emphasizing anything, nor accentuating it, nor setting it off. Not well versed in female habits and manners, Koshovy was not about to assume if it could be possible that the lady had not put on a hat but had simply attached something for appearances' sake. Without caring whether it was fashionable, in season, suited the clothes she was wearing or whether it was even appropriate. Magda didn't look too attentive, and it appeared that the thoughts of the young widow Bohdanovych were somewhere far away, and that she had called out to Koshovy more out of politeness, having spied a familiar figure on the sidewalk.

"Headed home? Can I give you a lift?"

"Thank you, Mrs. Magda," he again raised his hat. "I'll walk, there's no need for you to change your plans because of our chance meeting."

"At the moment I have no plans. At least not any, which can't be changed or delayed for half an hour or so. Hop in, please. Besides, I need to speak with you."

Shrugging his shoulders, Klym hopped into the carriage.

He was immersed in the delicate scent of perfume. Magda moved to the far end of the bench which was upholstered in velor. Had she noticed how he had somewhat indecently inhaled the perfumed air with his nostrils, or had she decided at the outset to keep her distance.

The carriage set off.

"I have long been meaning to ask you, where did you learn to speak Polish so well?"

"If this was all that you were interested to find out all this time – then please. My dear mother's older brother, my uncle, was married to an impoverished Polish aristocrat. When he died prematurely, Auntie Teresa moved in with us. I was brought up by a Polish woman, so it's not surprising."

"Understood."

For a while they rode in silence.

"So how are things progressing then, in general?" Magda asked, although Koshovy sensed that she showed no special interest in his persona.

"Depending on which ones you mean. I have a lot of things on my plate now. But addressing them will in no way affect my future here in Lviv."

"And how do you imagine it to be?"

"Nothing has fundamentally changed since our last conversation. I'm a lawyer. I had hoped to find work in my field, relying on the support of Mr. Soyka. An infamous man, it turned out. I've found out since that I first need to obtain a residence permit. Then – to confirm my qualifications, which means almost starting from scratch. All this requires time, time, and more time, which is unlikely to bring in any money soon. So I'll need to tighten my belt and subsist on bread and kvas[56], as they say in Kyiv."

"I see you are determined."

"There's no other way."

....

[56]   A traditional fizzy fermented beverage made from toasted rye bread.

"Ready for anything. Strange, you are living in a large city, but pretend as if you are living on a desert island."

"Oh, don't exaggerate, Mrs. Magda. Although I won't argue, you are quite observant. It's alright, things will change. I will accept, I'll become accepted."

"I'm happy to hear you have such an attitude, Mr. Koshovy. Will you allow me to help you a little? After the events of the previous weeks of which we spoke, I wanted in some way to play a part in your destiny. So that you don't think that all around you there are only strangers and that everything is inhospitable."

"I have never thought such things. But given my situation there's no point in thumbing my nose at people, being arrogant. I would be grateful."

The horse's hoofs clopped evenly on the cobblestones.

"Mr. Koshovy, let us agree once and for all…"

"Let's! What about?"

Magda screwed up her small nose. Only now did Klym notice the ever-present fan in her right hand, with which the woman played mechanically, without any special interest.

"Well, first of all, that I don't like being interrupted."

"My apologies."

"Secondly, it annoys me when people continually apologize and thank me, and kowtow to boot. Verbally or otherwise, it makes no difference. You owe me nothing, and I'm not indebted to you. Even if it should be the case some day, there's still no need to be adulatory and to kowtow to me. I have managed to form rather a high opinion of you, Mr. Koshovy. And let those others kiss people's feet, who can't otherwise endear themselves to people. I'm not talking solely about myself here, but I have myself in mind. Agreed?"

The fan swung to the left. Koshovy nodded wordlessly, expecting that after such a statement Magda would offer her right hand to shake on it. People did this to seal an agreement. Instead she merely transferred her fan from one hand to the other.

"Thank you for your understanding. Next. Remember Mr. Kazik? My apologies, Kazimierz Morawski? You met him there in Virmenska Street…"

"Ah, yes-yes," Klym diligently remembered the meeting. "As I recall, a councilor in the city council?"

Magda nodded.

"An opportunity presented itself here recently. We somehow thought of you, and Mr. Morawski agreed to help with your residency permit. I don't quite understand what it involves. Find the time and visit the town hall, you can find him there. He will be glad to see you and will tell you how best to act. If need be, he can write a cover note. Popeliak, the editor, was with us then too."

"The rotund fellow?"

"Yes. Make a point of seeing him as well. Mr. Janusz is bedecked with acquaintances, like an old coquette with necklaces. Among those strings of beads there will probably be one or more, which will prove useful to you. We're talking about practicing lawyers and notaries, to whom you can turn on his recommendation for practical advice. Popeliak won't refuse you."

"The Lord himself has sent you to me today."

"Leave the Almighty in peace," Magda waved her fan and said nothing. "Tell me, do you remember the engineer Wiszniewski?"

Klym grew tense, hoping the woman would not notice.

"Mr. Adas, if I'm not mistaken?"

"*Adam*," Magda corrected him dryly. "A strange and unfortunate history. He left Lviv. Said it was only for a while. But I think he will be away a long time. If not forever."

"Are you saddened on account of this?"

"Not because of him," Magda corrected herself far too hastily, although it might have only seemed so to Klym. "Of course, I will miss a good friend. But it's not just to do with him. He has been forced to move away from Lviv, to Truskavets. They say the town is being actively developed now, they're building a resort there and everything associated with it. Mr. Wiszniewski has to look after his younger sister. Poor Jadzia, she's only twenty-three…"

"Sick?"

"Different. It's not my misfortune, although it affected me directly at the time. I helped the gentleman as much as I could. Actually, he required moral support, first and foremost, the material side was not so important… But now the young girl is in a rather bad state. The doctors say the process is irreversible. Only complete peace and quiet can save her. He was unable to find anything better than Truskavets. He can't allow Jadzia to be looked after by a stranger, while he steps aside and merely pays for the services. Very noble on his part. Although, I repeat, I will miss him."

Touching his eyelid out of habit, Koshovy asked, looking past Magda: "What is she suffering from?"

"Nerves," Magda replied laconically. "These are not easy times, the new century has begun rather tumultuously. God willing, things will calm down in time. Well, here is your Lychakiv Street.

In conversation with her he had not even noticed that they had reached his building.

"You forbade me to thank you, but allow me one small transgression here," Klym smiled, and got up, preparing to leave.

"Sit down."

It sounded sharp, like an order.

Klym acquiesced. Magda was no longer playing with her fan, resting it on her knees.

"I have certain connections."

"You have amazing connections in Lviv, Mrs. Magda."

"They're not limitless. But some things, yes. For example, I can organize to get a background check done through the appropriate authorities."

"You've learned something terrible or indecent about me?"

"Koshovy Klymentiy, son of a well-known Kyiv lawyer. Studied at the University of St. Volodymyr. In early June this year arrested by the security department on suspicion of anti-government activities. The reason – defending the organizers of an illegal printing shop, where banned literature was being printed. In particular, books and newspapers, which promoted the Ukrainian national movement and called on people to fight against the oppression of Ukrainians on national grounds."

His throat became completely dry.

"It was educational literature, actually. Books and newspapers of an educational nature."

"The printing house also stored various printing fonts and firearms."

"The gun and two home-made bombs were planted on the lads by a provocateur."

Magda pretended not to hear his words.

"You spent a week in prison. Through the efforts of your father, you were released on the undertaking that you would leave Kyiv within a clearly defined period of time. As I understand it, Mr. Koshovy, you decided to completely leave the territory of the Russian Empire. And become an emigrant, yes?"

"Not a political one. At present I want to keep as far away as I can from politics. Of any kind."

"I warn you, you shouldn't swear such things, especially in our times. I also don't like politics. But today it still has meaning for each of us."

"We'll see. Why did you decide to tell me what you know about me now?"

"No special reason, Mr. Klymentiy Koshovy."

"Klym."

"Magda."

"So why did you tell me what you know about me, *Magda*?"

"Because you never told me anything about yourself, *Klym*. I think you will one of these days. It is unlikely that this is our last meeting."

Koshovy got out.

He stood on the sidewalk, watching the carriage continue up Lychakiv Street.

And afterward he racked his brain for a long time, trying to understand what this had been: a demonstration of power, an attack – or a badly-concealed insinuation.

I know everything about you, I have you on the palm of my hand.

But I won't tell anyone.

Or – you're all mine…

And everything is only just beginning.

Forefathers' Eve

by Adam Mickiewicz

Forefathers' Eve [*Dziady*] is a four-part dramatic work begun circa 1820 and completed in 1832 – with Part I published only after the poet's death, in 1860. The drama's title refers to *Dziady*, an ancient Slavic and Lithuanian feast commemorating the dead. This is the grand work of Polish literature, and it is one that elevates Mickiewicz to a position among the "great Europeans" such as Dante and Goethe.

With its Christian background of the Communion of the Saints, revenant spirits, and the interpenetration of the worlds of time and eternity, *Forefathers' Eve* speaks to men and women of all times and places. While it is a truly Polish work – Polish actors covet the role of Gustaw/Konrad in the same way that Anglophone actors covet that of Hamlet – it is one of the most universal works of literature written during the nineteenth century. It has been compared to Goethe's Faust – and rightfully so...

Buy it > www.glagoslav.com

The Fantastic Worlds of Yuri Vynnychuk

by Yuri Vynnychuk

Yuri Vynnychuk is a master storyteller and satirist, who emerged from the Western Ukrainian underground in Soviet times to become one of Ukraine's most prolific and most prominent writers of today. He is a chameleon who can adapt his narrative voice in a variety of ways and whose style at times is reminiscent of Borges. A master of the short story, he exhibits a great range from exquisite lyrical-philosophical works such as his masterpiece "An Embroidered World," written in the mode of magical realism; to intense psychological studies; to contemplative science fiction and horror tales; and to wicked black humor and satire such as his "Max and Me." Excerpts are also presented in this volume of his longer prose works, including his highly acclaimed novel of wartime Lviv *Tango of Death*, which received the 2012 BBC Ukrainian Book of the Year Award. The translations offered here allow the English-language reader to become acquainted with the many fantastic worlds and lyrical imagination of an extraordinarily versatile writer.

Buy it > www.glagoslav.com

Hardly Ever Otherwise

by Maria Matios

Everything eventually reaches its appointed place in time and space. Maria Matios's dramatic family saga, *Hardly Ever Otherwise*, narrates the story of several western Ukrainian families during the last decades of the Austro-Hungarian Empire, and expands upon the idea that "it isn't time that is important, but the human condition in time."

From the first page, Matios engages her reader with an impeccable style, which she employs to create a rich tapestry of cause and effect, at times depicting a logic that is both bitter and enigmatic. But nothing is ever fully revealed—it is only in the final pages of the novel that the events in the beginning are understood as a necessary part of a larger whole, and the section entitled Seasicknesspresents a compelling argument for why events almost always have to follow a particular course.

The Frontier

28 Contemporary Ukrainian Poets - An Anthology

This anthology reflects a search of the Ukrainian nation for its identity, the roots of which lie deep inside Ukrainian-language poetry. Some of the included poets are well-known locally and internationally; among them are Serhiy Zhadan, Halyna Kruk, Ostap Slyvynsky, Marianna Kijanowska, Oleh Kotsarev, Anna Bagriana and, of course, the living legend of Ukrainian poetry, Vasyl Holoborodko. The next Ukrainian poetic generation also features prominently in the collection. Such poets as Les Beley, Olena Herasymyuk, Myroslav Laiuk, Hanna Malihon, Taras Malkovych, Julia Musakovska, Julia Stahivska and Lyuba Yakimchuk are the ones Ukrainians like to read today, and each of them already has an excellent reputation abroad due to festival appearances and translations to European languages. The work collected here documents poetry in Ukraine responding to challenges of the time by forging a radical new poetic, reconsidering writing techniques and language itself.

Edited and translated from the Ukrainian by Anatoly Kudryavitsky.

A Bilingual Edition.

Buy it > www.glagoslav.com

Dear Reader,

Thank you for purchasing this book.

We at Glagoslav Publications are glad to welcome you, and hope that you find our books to be a source of knowledge and inspiration.

We want to show the beauty and depth of the Slavic region to everyone looking to expand their horizon and learn something new about different cultures, different people, and we believe that with this book we have managed to do just that.

Now that you've got to know us, we want to get to know you. We value communication with our readers and want to hear from you! We offer several options:

— Join our Book Club on Goodreads, Library Thing and Shelfari, and receive special offers and information about our giveaways;

— Share your opinion about our books on Amazon, Barnes & Noble, Waterstones and other bookstores;

— Join us on Facebook and Twitter for updates on our publications and news about our authors;

— Visit our site www.glagoslav.com to check out our Catalogue and subscribe to our Newsletter.

Glagoslav Publications is getting ready to release a new collection and planning some interesting surprises — stay with us to find out!

Glagoslav Publications
Email: contact@glagoslav.com

Glagoslav Publications Catalogue

- *The Time of Women* by Elena Chizhova
- *Andrei Tarkovsky: The Collector of Dreams* by Layla Alexander-Garrett
- *Andrei Tarkovsky - A Life on the Cross* by Lyudmila Boyadzhieva
- *Sin* by Zakhar Prilepin
- *Hardly Ever Otherwise* by Maria Matios
- *Khatyn* by Ales Adamovich
- *The Lost Button* by Irene Rozdobudko
- *Christened with Crosses* by Eduard Kochergin
- *The Vital Needs of the Dead* by Igor Sakhnovsky
- *The Sarabande of Sara's Band* by Larysa Denysenko
- *A Poet and Bin Laden* by Hamid Ismailov
- *Watching The Russians (Dutch Edition)* by Maria Konyukova
- *Kobzar* by Taras Shevchenko
- *The Stone Bridge* by Alexander Terekhov
- *Moryak* by Lee Mandel
- *King Stakh's Wild Hunt* by Uladzimir Karatkevich
- *The Hawks of Peace* by Dmitry Rogozin
- *Harlequin's Costume* by Leonid Yuzefovich
- *Depeche Mode* by Serhii Zhadan
- *The Grand Slam and other stories (Dutch Edition)*
  by Leonid Andreev
- *METRO 2033 (Dutch Edition)* by Dmitry Glukhovsky
- *METRO 2034 (Dutch Edition)* by Dmitry Glukhovsky
- *A Russian Story* by Eugenia Kononenko
- *Herstories, An Anthology of New Ukrainian Women Prose Writers*
- *The Battle of the Sexes Russian Style* by Nadezhda Ptushkina
- *A Book Without Photographs* by Sergey Shargunov
- *Down Among The Fishes* by Natalka Babina
- *disUNITY* by Anatoly Kudryavitsky
- *Sankya* by Zakhar Prilepin
- *Wolf Messing* by Tatiana Lungin
- *Good Stalin* by Victor Erofeyev
- *Solar Plexus* by Rustam Ibragimbekov

- *Don't Call me a Victim!* by Dina Yafasova
- *Poetin (Dutch Edition)* by Chris Hutchins and Alexander Korobko
- *A History of Belarus* by Lubov Bazan
- *Children's Fashion of the Russian Empire* by Alexander Vasiliev
- *Empire of Corruption - The Russian National Pastime* by Vladimir Soloviev
- *Heroes of the 90s: People and Money. The Modern History of Russian Capitalism*
- *Fifty Highlights from the Russian Literature (Dutch Edition)* by Maarten Tengbergen
- *Bajesvolk (Dutch Edition)* by Mikhail Khodorkovsky
- *Tsarina Alexandra's Diary (Dutch Edition)*
- *Myths about Russia* by Vladimir Medinskiy
- *Boris Yeltsin: The Decade that Shook the World* by Boris Minaev
- *A Man Of Change: A study of the political life of Boris Yeltsin*
- *Sberbank: The Rebirth of Russia's Financial Giant* by Evgeny Karasyuk
- *To Get Ukraine* by Oleksandr Shyshko
- *Asystole* by Oleg Pavlov
- *Gnedich* by Maria Rybakova
- *Marina Tsvetaeva: The Essential Poetry*
- *Multiple Personalities* by Tatyana Shcherbina
- *The Investigator* by Margarita Khemlin
- *The Exile* by Zinaida Tulub
- *Leo Tolstoy: Flight from paradise* by Pavel Basinsky
- *Moscow in the 1930* by Natalia Gromova
- *Laurus (Dutch edition)* by Evgenij Vodolazkin
- *Prisoner* by Anna Nemzer
- *The Crime of Chernobyl: The Nuclear Goulag* by Wladimir Tchertkoff
- *Alpine Ballad* by Vasil Bykau
- *The Complete Correspondence of Hryhory Skovoroda*
- *The Tale of Aypi* by Ak Welsapar
- *Selected Poems* by Lydia Grigorieva
- *The Fantastic Worlds of Yuri Vynnychuk*

- *The Garden of Divine Songs and Collected Poetry of Hryhory Skovoroda*
- *Adventures in the Slavic Kitchen: A Book of Essays with Recipes*
- *Seven Signs of the Lion* by Michael M. Naydan
- *Forefathers' Eve* by Adam Mickiewicz
- *One-Two* by Igor Eliseev
- *Girls, be Good* by Bojan Babić
- *Time of the Octopus* by Anatoly Kucherena
- *The Grand Harmony* by Bohdan Ihor Antonych
- *The Selected Lyric Poetry Of Maksym Rylsky*
- *The Shining Light* by Galymkair Mutanov
- *The Frontier: 28 Contemporary Ukrainian Poets - An Anthology*
- *Acropolis: The Wawel Plays* by Stanisław Wyspiański
- *Contours of the City* by Attyla Mohylny
- *Conversations Before Silence: The Selected Poetry of Oles Ilchenko*
- *The Secret History of my Sojourn in Russia* by Jaroslav Hašek
- *Mirror Sand: An Anthology of Russian Short Poems*
- *Maybe We're Leaving* by Jan Balaban
- *Death of the Snake Catcher* by Ak Welsapar
- *A Brown Man in Russia* by Vijay Menon
- *Hard Times* by Ostap Vyshnia
- *The Flying Dutchman* by Anatoly Kudryavitsky
- *Nikolai Gumilev's Africa* by Nikolai Gumilev
- *Combustions* by Srđan Srdić
- *The Sonnets* by Adam Mickiewicz
- *Dramatic Works* by Zygmunt Krasiński
- *Four Plays* by Juliusz Słowacki
- *Little Zinnobers* by Elena Chizhova
- *We Are Building Capitalism! Moscow in Transition 1992-1997*
- *The Nuremberg Trials* by Alexander Zvyagintsev
- *The Hemingway Game* by Evgeni Grishkovets
- *A Flame Out at Sea* by Dmitry Novikov
- *Jesus' Cat* by Grig
- *Want a Baby and Other Plays* by Sergei Tretyakov
- *I Mikhail Bulgakov: The Life and Times* by Marietta Chudakova
- *Leonardo's Handwriting* by Dina Rubina

- *A Burglar of the Better Sort* by Tytus Czyżewski
- *The Mouseiad and other Mock Epics* by Ignacy Krasicki
- *Ravens before Noah* by Susanna Harutyunyan
- *Duel* by Borys Antonenko-Davydovych
- *An English Queen and Stalingrad* by Natalia Kulishenko
- *Point Zero* by Narek Malian
- *Absolute Zero* by Artem Chekh
- *Olanda* by Rafał Wojasiński
- *Robinsons* by Aram Pachyan
- *The Monastery* by Zakhar Prilepin
- *The Selected Poetry of Bohdan Rubchak:
  Songs of Love, Songs of Death, Songs of the Moon*
- *Mebet* by Alexander Grigorenko
- *Everyday Stories* by Mima Mihajlović
- *The Orchestra* by Vladimir Gonik

More coming soon...